"THEY SAY
I KILLED
THAT GIRL?"

★ ★ ★

Laura nodded.

"I never killed her."

"They have enough to fry you fifty times, John. And there isn't a person in the world who'll lift a finger to help you except me."

"You think you're special, huh?"

"No. I'm your lawyer, that's all. You've got one chance to live your life and one chance only. You cut the crap, be straight with me, and let me work my magic. If you do, maybe I can save you from the chair. If you don't, there's absolutely no question you'll die very young."

Also by Harrison Arnston

ACT OF PASSION

Available from HarperPaperbacks

TRADE-OFF

HARRISON ARNSTON

HarperPaperbacks
A Division of HarperCollinsPublishers

This is a work of fiction. The characters, incidents, and dialogues are products of the author's imagination and are not to be construed as real. Any resemblance to actual events or persons, living or dead, is entirely coincidental.

HarperPaperbacks *A Division of* HarperCollins*Publishers*
10 East 53rd Street, New York, N.Y. 10022

Cover photograph by Herman Estevez

First printing: March 1992

Printed in the United States of America

HarperPaperbacks and colophon are trademarks of HarperCollins*Publishers*

10 9 8 7 6 5 4 3 2 1

For my brother Frank, who made his own distinctive trade-off.

Special thanks to attorneys Linda Renate Hughes and Arthur D. Deckelman, for their technical contributions. As always, their counsel is much appreciated. To my wife Theresa, for her countless hours of proofreading and unflagging support. Thanks also to my agent Susan Lipson and to my editor Carolyn Marino. Their contributions were invaluable.

Extreme law is often extreme injustice.

—*Terence* (Publius Terentius Afer)

CHAPTER

1

THE NIGHT WANDA BROOKS WAS MURDERED, BILLY Haines became a hero. Billy was not the hero type. Slovenly, insolent, terminally lazy, and chronically unemployed, he'd managed to survive to this point in his young life by the desultory pursuit of several illegal activities, the most prominent being the sale of small amounts of homegrown marijuana and alligator hides taken from freshly killed reptiles.

Unlike those of his contemporaries, Billy's enterprises were sporadic. He worked only when the need for money overcame his inbred lethargy, an apathy that surmounted greed. Most of the time, he lay in a hammock strung up between two trees, smoked his weed, and dreamed of being important.

Billy considered both marijuana growing and alligator killing to be public services. Not that Billy was civic-minded. If someone were to ask him to name the governor of Florida, he'd probably give them a blank stare, but he did have certain principles. As far as Billy was concerned, the only difference between marijuana and liquor was the fact that marijuana was easier to carry in one's pocket. He considered its illegality as proof that laws were made only to protect the interests of big business, like the liquor manufacturers. Since almost anyone could grow the stuff and the effects were more exciting than those produced by the ingestion of booze, the legality of growing and using marijuana would put the liquor people out of business. That's how Billy saw it.

As for the alligators, the prehistoric monsters had been a threatened species not too long ago, and laws had been passed to protect them. Now they flourished and could be found almost everywhere in the state of Florida. Billy saw the ugly creatures as hazards to little children and slow-moving animals. Killing them was a matter of simple common sense.

Such were Billy's rationalizations for breaking the law. In this, at least, he was sincere, or as sincere as someone like Billy can be.

He possessed a prodigious temper. The only time Billy was charged with a felony, his attorney tried to explain to him that haranguing a judge was counterproductive, but Billy couldn't see it. To him, it was a matter of honor to speak one's mind. Besides, Billy's attorney was a woman and Billy didn't think women knew much about anything, especially matters involving male honor. During his third outburst, he called the judge an old fool and subsequently spent a month in jail for contempt, though his lawyer did manage to beat the felony rap. He never profited from the experience.

At the age of twenty-four, Billy was pretty well set in his ways. He grew his marijuana in a small plot out in the woods about ten miles south of the city of Seminole Springs, just north of the county line. The soil conditions weren't the best and many plants died off, but the place was reasonably secure from prying eyes. Those plants that did manage to survive produced a rather tepid weed, despite the fact that the seeds were supposed to have come from California's Humboldt County, where they supposedly grew the best grass in the world. Billy sold a little to his friends and used the rest to create his personal dream world, and that, for him, was enough.

Billy had but one customer for the alligators, a Korean he had met at a bar one night, who paid a hundred fifty dollars per hide. Although the man would gladly have bought more, Billy limited his volume to one a month. It was the Korean who hired attorney Laura Scott to defend Billy the only time he was arrested. Laura demanded and received her fee in advance. The Korean agreed and paid her in cash.

If a Gypsy fortune-teller could peer into the innards of a crystal ball and discern Billy's future, she'd probably see nothing more than roiling black clouds. She'd be wrong. Because tonight, Billy Haines was about to become a hero.

*   *   *

It was a steaming Friday night in August, close to ten o'clock. Billy had pulled his battered ten-year-old Ford van off the access road that cuts through the southeast corner of the woods. He was parked about a hundred feet in (which was as far as he could go) at a spot he knew well, a half mile from his current marijuana stand. He was in the company of Mary Ellen Coosman—plain-faced, fifty pounds overweight, and not very bright—one of three young ladies in the city who found Billy desirable in an odd sort of way.

With his long, stringy, unkempt hair, his acne-scarred skin, and his tall, bony frame, Billy was not what one would think of as prime material. To Mary Ellen, he was dirty, both figuratively and literally, but that was probably part of the fascination. She'd been reared by devout Baptists and taught the evils of sin, but she was a lonely young woman who craved affection, attention, and, most of all, escape from the mind-numbing boredom that was her life. Billy was the only man she knew willing to provide escape, if only occasionally. Billy's laziness went right to the bone.

They were sitting in the back of the van, on a worn mattress Billy had rescued from the county landfill, the only illumination coming from the small dome light affixed to the roof. Billy lit a hand-rolled cigarette, inhaled deeply, then passed it to Mary Ellen. She took it from him, inhaled deeply herself, then passed it back.

The interior of the van was stifling, even with the front windows open. Odors long-entombed within the old mattress broke free, permeating the air with the sickening sweetness of rot. The sun had set well over an hour before, but the air outside was still. Mangroves and tall pines formed a natural three-sided wall around the van, hiding it from all but the closest observer. Tonight, the trees seemed to radiate retained heat. The sandy soil beneath the thick carpet of brown pine needles blanketing the ground threw off more unneeded warmth.

In central Florida, when the sun goes down, the relative humidity rises, and at this moment it was a pore-popping ninety percent. Billy, sitting with his shirt off, was covered in a thin layer of perspiration. Mary Ellen, still wearing the cotton blouse and skirt she'd worn to her job as a clerk in a flower shop, was also perspiring profusely and soaked half through.

"You wanna go outside?" Billy asked, rubbing a hand across his chest and flicking off the sweat. "I got a blanket."

Mary Ellen shook her head violently, remembering. The stench within the van was almost overpowering, but there were worse things. "No way," she said. "The last time we did it outside, the ants and mosquitoes about ate me alive. The heat don't bother me." She stared at the boom box lying on the floor. "Your radio still busted?"

"Uh-huh."

"I thought you was gonna get it fixed."

"I did," he said. "Went down to Kenny's and he put some new parts in it. Lasted for a day is all. He says it needs another part. Hadda order it." He passed the cigarette back to her.

Mary Ellen sighed. The van's air conditioner had broken down over a month ago and Billy had claimed *that* was waiting for a part, too. It seemed

Billy was always waiting for something. "You shudda told me," she said. "I coulda brought mine. You know I like music when we do it."

"We'll make our own music," Billy said, grinning as he remembered a line from some movie he'd seen.

He reached to unbutton her blouse, but Mary Ellen slapped his hands away. "I'll do it," she said. "Your hands are all dirty. It's bad enough I'm all wet. I don't want my father askin' questions about how I got dirt all over my clothes."

Billy shrugged and took off his alligator boots, a gift from the Korean, then started undoing his Levi's 501's, the ones with the button fly. Mary Ellen, moving quickly, because she was expected home in about another thirty minutes, was down to her panties when all hell broke loose.

It was a scream like nothing either of them had ever heard, except in the movies or on TV. A high-pitched shriek that seemed to die at its peak. The sound of a woman, and not that far away. For a moment the two lovers looked at each other. Then, Billy became galvanized. A woman was in trouble, his mind flashed. Bad trouble, by the sound of it. And close, too. Like most men, he'd always had this fantasy about saving a woman in trouble, becoming a real hero, like Stallone or Bruce Willis or Mel Gibson. Now was his chance.

"You stay here," he said as he struggled back into his jeans. Billy didn't believe in underwear, or socks either. Less to worry about on his monthly trip to the laundromat.

"You're not goin' out there," Mary Ellen whispered, concern thick in her voice.

"I gotta see what happened," Billy said as he pulled on his alligator boots. "Somebody's gettin hurt out there. Can't just let it be."

"You're not leavin' me alone!" she wailed, her voice rising.

Billy clapped a hand on her mouth. "Don't be such a sissy," he chided. "Just close the windows and lock the doors after I'm gone. And be quiet about it."

She was about to grab his arm but didn't. One thing she knew about Billy. When he had his mind made up about something, there was no point to arguing. When he pulled his hand away, she went about the business of getting dressed as Billy unlatched the power lantern strapped to the floor, the one he used for alligator hunting. He scrambled into the front of the van, unlocked the glove box, and removed the .357 Magnum he kept there.

Billy looked back at Mary Ellen, held a finger to his lips, then quietly slipped out of the van. The lantern in his hand still unlit, he cocked his head, listening, letting his eyes adjust to the dimness and his ears to the sounds of the woods. For a moment he heard nothing except the mouth harp whine of tree frogs and the chattering of insomniac birds. Above him, a partially obscured half-moon cast a yellow pallor upon the slowly drifting clouds. The few shards of soft light that filtered through the trees shimmered on the carpet of pine needles.

Billy, his hearing tuned, caught a sound. Not a scream, but the sound of someone mumbling, almost under his breath, about thirty or forty feet away. Billy knew how to walk these woods without making a sound. Carefully, a step at a time, he moved forward, toward the continuing babble—a strange incantation, a chant of some kind. His vision blocked by the thickness of the heavy forest, he couldn't see much until he was almost on top of it. Then he could see it all.

A small clearing, the moonlight bright through a hole in the partial overcast. On the ground, a naked woman, her body covered in splotches of dark wetness. On his knees, leaning over the woman, a long knife in his hand, a man wearing only a tattered tank top, rocking back and forth as he chanted words with no meaning.

Billy felt his stomach tighten and his throat constrict. He knew that feeling well. In a few seconds, he would throw up. He had to move now. He pointed the lantern with his left hand and the gun with his right. With his thumb, he flicked the lantern's switch.

For less than two seconds, Billy's brain recorded the image now clearly visible. The blotches covering the woman's body were dark red. Blood. The startled man with the knife in his hand was staring wide-eyed at the source of the light like an animal caught in headlights, his body taut, all motion and sound having ceased. And then, the man lunged at Billy. Low, in a crouch, like a football linebacker, the knife held out in front of him. Instinctively, Billy pulled the trigger of the big gun in his hand.

At the sound of the gun, Mary Ellen burst from the back of the van and started running for her life.

CHAPTER

2

THE NIGHT WANDA BROOKS WAS MURDERED, DAN AND Laura Scott were attending a party at the home of Brad and Mary Cain. The party was a casual affair, a cookout and general get-together with six couples who'd become socially involved and took turns hosting this monthly ritual. Tonight, it was the Cains' turn, an eagerly awaited event, for the Cains lived in one of the nicest houses in town, a rambling, California-style stucco situated on the banks of the Holasutola River.

Other than Mary, Brad's two passions were electronics and food. The house was crammed with every electronic gadget known to man, a menagerie that always included the latest creations dreamed up by inventive Oriental minds.

The plethora of electronic toys combined with Brad's adventurous edibles made each visit a gustatory and scientific adventure. In addition, because the house was situated at the crest of the only hill in town, it afforded the best view of often spectacular sunsets created when superheated storm clouds finally dissipated and allowed the sun to peek through. Tonight had been a perfect example.

Now that it was dark and dinner was over, they'd all come inside to the welcome coolness and assumed their usual positions—the men off on one side of the family room swapping tall stories, the six wives huddled in the adjacent living room, exchanging gossip and commiserating with one another on a variety of traditionally female complaints. The Cain children had retired to the electronics room, replete with its extensive library of video games that could be mastered only by those under the age of ten.

It was an even mix of native Floridians and non-Floridians. The Cains, the Wilsons, and the Picketts were natives. Laura and Dan were from Montana, the Smiths were from Pennsylvania, and the Braddocks were from, of all places, London, England.

This evening, Laura Scott found her mind wandering, a common occurrence lately. She'd tuned out of the conversation when she'd noticed Dan in the family room, sagging against the wall, a glass of Jack Daniel's in his hand, his eyes hooded, his mouth fixed in that silly grin he wore when he was half-drunk. When he was fully drunk, the smile faded and he became sullen and hostile. Laura, anticipating the worst, could feel the tension building within her.

She wasn't a party person at the best of times, preferring instead the intimacy of one-on-one conversations with trusted friends. The inane, forced conviviality at most parties bored her, as did the drinking. Sometimes, a friend would drink too much and say too much and feel so stupid the next day. Or worse, one of them would choose a party as the perfect place to unlock a vault of repressed feelings, unleashing a stream of verbal venom toward spouse or friend—words that could never be forgotten, if forgiven. Twice, Dan had verbally cut her to ribbons at one of these gatherings. Since they'd been picking at each other all week, she sensed it was about to happen again.

She excused herself from the group, slipped through the sliding glass door at the rear of the house, walked down the hill to the water's edge, and sat on a bench placed there by the thoughtful Cains. The lulling sound of the fast-moving river failed to calm her as it normally did. She looked at the moon, half-full but very bright, hanging in the sky like, in the words of Noyes, a "ghostly galleon." In the distance, she heard the soft thunder of an F-16 taking off from nearby Tasker Air Force Base, where Dan worked as a civilian electrical engineer. Suddenly, her feelings of despair deepened and tears flooded her face.

She heard a sound behind her and cursed the fact that she'd left her handbag behind.

"Laura?"

It was Gerry Wilson. "You okay?" she asked softly.

"Yes." A pause. "No."

Gerry sat beside her, an arm on her shoulder. "What's the matter?" She handed Laura some tissues.

"You always know, don't you, Gerry?"

"Well, you looked a bit down in there."

Laura wiped her eyes, blew her nose, and leaned back on the bench. "If I had any guts," she said, "I'd give up. I'd get a divorce. Did you see Dan leaning against the wall like some wino?"

Gerry nodded. "He's really getting bad, Laura. Rick was talking to him last week, asking him to come in for a physical, just routine, and Dan reacted very badly. Rick's always bugging his friends to come in for a checkup, but Dan thought it was because of the drinking. He got very defensive. Rick says Dan's starting to show some signs of paranoia, that when alcoholics get to that point they're pretty far gone. He needs some serious help, Laura."

"I know. I've tried at least a hundred times to get him into a clinic, but he just won't go."

"Well, maybe the threat of divorce would scare some sense into him. Surely, he must know how you feel."

"It doesn't matter how I feel," Laura said. "You know how alcoholics are. They wear their denial like a badge of courage. I've tried to get Dan past that point for years, without success. He insists he's a social drinker, period, but gets drunk every night now." She sighed. "At least I don't clean up after him anymore. I told him the mess could sit there until he cleaned it up himself." She put a hand to her face. "God! I'm so tired of it."

"Then why not put the pressure on? You know you have to do something. You can't just let it go on like this."

"I know," Laura said, "but Dan doesn't respond to pressure. Threats won't work. If I ever decide to get a divorce, it'll go all the way. It can't be an idle threat, and I guess that's what stops me."

"So you're just going to carry on like this?"

"I have to, I guess. Divorcing him isn't the answer right now. Ted and Dan are really close. If I lose Dan, I also lose Ted."

Gerry looked at her wide-eyed. "You can't be serious. Surely, under the circumstances, you'd be awarded custody. You're his mother."

"It's not that simple," Laura said. "Proving Dan's a drunk isn't enough. Ted adores his father. No judge would deny joint custody under those circumstances, and Ted would never forgive me." A note of desperation crept into her voice. "He and Dan are more than close. They're best friends. Ted sees his father as a hero of sorts."

"Well, you have to do something," Gerry insisted. "He won't see anyone?"

"No one."

"Didn't you take that intervention course the hospital sponsored?"

"Yes, but I know that won't work with Dan either. Not until he hits bottom. Until he gets past the denial stage, there really isn't much anyone can do. He's never lost a day's work, never had an auto accident, and never been arrested. He sees his drinking as perfectly normal and not interfering with his life."

"Well," Gerry said, "you have to make a decision, Laura. You can spend the rest of your life in misery, or you can act. If you've really tried everything, that decision should be easy."

"If it was just me," Laura said, "I'd leave him in a heartbeat. I have to think of Ted. Maybe in a couple of years..." She squeezed Gerry's hand.

They'd grown close since the first day they'd met, when Gerry had squired Dan and Laura around as the two newcomers looked for a place to live. Gerry was the most successful real estate agent in town and Rick was a well-respected and much-liked surgeon at Memorial, an anachronism in these days of the specialist, performing everything from gall bladder surgery to hip replacements. Their marriage seemed as fresh as the day they exchanged their vows, a shining tower of unity undulled by the normal frictions of life. Laura envied them, yet liked them both, and considered herself fortunate to count them as friends.

Gerry said, "Laura, I wish I could help, but you know you're the only one who can change your life."

"I know it. Perhaps someday, I'll find the answer to the puzzle." She squeezed Gerry's hand a second time. "I guess we better get back."

"I wish I could be more help, Laura, but I can't. I hope you understand that."

"You are a help. More than you realize."

It was close to eleven when the party began to break up. True to form, the Smiths were the first to leave, followed by the Braddocks. Normally, Dan and Laura would be the last, and only after some heavy prodding by the hosts. Once Dan arrived at a party, he didn't like to go until close to unconsciousness.

Jim Pickett, discreetly slipping into his cop's persona, was quietly assessing the condition of each of the drivers. He stood beside Laura and whispered, "You driving?"

"Don't I always?" she answered.

Jim gave her a friendly pat on the shoulder.

Right then, a beeper sounded. Rick and Jim looked at each other, then at their belts. "It's mine," Jim said, and headed for the kitchen and the phone. Rick watched him leave, then murmured, "Thank God for small favors."

Laura thought it was probably an accident. Friday night was a bad time for accidents, with many of the air force boys off for the weekend. Since most of the real action had moved to Coopers Corners, a small village on the other side of the air base, Jim was rarely involved in serious crime problems. Coopers Corners was patrolled by the state troopers.

While Jim was on the phone, the group stood around and talked, their natural curiosity aroused. No one wanted to leave until they knew what had happened. When Jim got off the phone a few minutes later and walked back into the living room, they all looked at him as though waiting for some official announcement. They got more than they'd bargained for. Jim looked so stricken everyone stopped talking and just stared at him. He pointed a finger at Rick, saying, "We're gonna need you, Rick."

Rick didn't question it, just picked up his jacket. If it was an accident, Jim was taking it very hard. Did that mean it was someone they all knew?

"We just had a killing," Jim said, answering the

unspoken question in all their eyes. "Some bastard stabbed a girl to death out in the woods south of Coopers Corners," he said. "I gotta go out there."

They were all speechless, all except Ethel. "That's county land," she said. "The troopers should look after that."

Jim had a hand to his head, as though trying to understand it himself. "The troopers are there," he said. "That was them on the phone. They say Billy Haines was involved somehow. Put a slug in the son of a bitch. The troopers are bringing Billy in now. An ambulance has the suspect." He looked at Rick. "The bastard's still alive."

Rick nodded. "I'll go directly to the hospital," he said.

Jim grunted something and started to follow Rick out the door. Then he stopped, turned, and looked at Brad. "The reason I gotta go is . . . Billy saw the victim. He says the girl is Wanda Brooks."

It stunned everyone. Brad and Mary were perhaps the most shocked. Wanda Brooks was not only their daughter's best friend, she'd clerked all summer at their hardware store.

On the drive home, Laura felt morose. Everyone in town knew Wanda Brooks, a seventeen-year-old youngster with a cheerful personality and bright smile. Straight A's in school and on her way to college in two days. She'd said she wanted to be a doctor. Everyone was sure she'd make it. Laura thought about Harold and Grace, her parents. Fine people. Long-time residents of Seminole Springs, folks who'd encouraged their daughter in every way. The Brookses wore their pride in their daughter like a Santa Claus suit. It was hard to miss.

How devastating, Laura thought. What must they be feeling? she wondered. Bitterly, her thoughts turned inward. What was worse, having a child die in a matter of minutes, or having one die over a period of years?

Dan, sitting in the passenger seat, his head resting on the window, muttered, "It's not fair." For a moment Laura thought he was reading her mind.

"You're right," she said. "It isn't fair. She had everything to live for. God! To have a life snuffed out at so young an age, with a future so bright . . . "

"That isn't what I mean," he said, his voice thick and slurred. "Wanda Brooks was a sweet girl with everything going for her, sure. She had brains, looks, personality . . . everything. Now she's dead. Okay, that's tough, and I'm real sorry. But then there's Victoria, who can't see, can't hear, and has no future, and she's alive, draining us of every nickel we have and more. What's the sense of that? At least Wanda died quick. That's what I mean about fair."

Laura felt the rage well up in her like magma, but held her tongue. She'd expressed her feelings to her husband at least a hundred times before, and it had never made an impression on him.

"I'm going up to see her in the morning," she said, fighting to keep her voice even. "Would you please come this time?"

"What for?" he said, lighting a cigarette and blowing the smoke at the windshield. "She doesn't even know who I am, or you either. It's a waste, Laura. What's the goddamn point?"

"She's your daughter. You can't possibly know

what's going on in her head. Maybe she hears us and maybe she doesn't. If you never visit and she never hears your voice, how can you assume to know what she thinks? Isn't it possible she feels you've abandoned her? What's so damn difficult about spending a few moments with your own child?"

"I don't like it," he said. "I don't like seeing her like that. You know that."

"You don't like it? You think I do? It's a responsibility, Dan. Like or not like isn't important. We're her parents, dammit."

"We *were* her parents," he said. "Far as I'm concerned, she's already dead. What in God's name is the matter with you, Laura? What's the point of keeping Victoria in a private hospital when she doesn't even know *where* she is? What goddamn right do you have to mortgage our future like that? I count too, dammit, but I get no say in this. You're the goddamn big shot. You're the goddamn lawyer. I'm nothing, right? I don't count."

"Dan . . . "

He was not to be deterred. As she'd feared, the expected explosion was happening. At least this time, they were alone. "You wanna know something?" he continued. "I'll be happy when she finally dies. I really will. Maybe then you'll get back to being a wife instead of a fucking drudge. All you do is work, eat, and sleep. Then you take all the money and piss it away on a fucking vegetable."

Laura was so instantly enraged that—almost involuntarily—one of her hands left the steering wheel, flew through the air, and slapped him across the face. The cigarette fell from his lips and started burning a hole in his trousers. He picked the cigarette up, put it in the ashtray, and stared out the window. In a voice filled with menace, he said, "That's the third time you've done that, slapping me like that. One of these days, I'm going to forget you're a woman and slap you back. I guarantee you won't like it."

"You called your daughter a vegetable," she cried. "I won't stand for it."

"Well, that's what she is," he bellowed. "If you can't accept it, that's your goddamn problem. Fact is, Laura, you live in a goddamn dream world where Victoria's concerned. You have this crazy idea that the money we're spending is gonna buy her a new brain. Well, it isn't. The one she's got is all done and all the money in the world isn't gonna change that.

"You always bitch about my drinking and my attitude. You're always shooting off your mouth about the two of us seeing a shrink. Well, maybe you need to see a shrink. Maybe it's time you took a good look at yourself instead of running up and down my goddamn back all the time."

For the second time that night, Laura's eyes filled with tears. She could hardly see, three blocks from home. Her husband drunk and abusive. But worse, she'd lost her temper. She never lost her temper.

I mustn't let him have the keys, she thought. Fighting the tears, she tried to make them stop. No luck. She pulled the car over to the side of the road, got out, and took the keys with her, leaving him sitting there in the car.

She was sitting on the bed when she heard him come noisily through the front door, heard him clamber up the stairs. Then, he was standing in front of her, pure venom in his eyes. Without a word, he stripped off his clothes and threw them on the floor.

Standing naked in front of her, his hands on his hips, a curl on his lips. "Doesn't do a goddamn thing for you anymore, does it?"

"You're drunk," she said, turning her head to avoid his stare.

"So what? There used to be a time when you could look at me without puking. You used to grab hold of me and have a great old time. You called it your favorite toy. Now, you can't stand to look at it anymore. Who's fault is that, Laura? Mine?"

"You're being disgusting, Dan."

He laughed. "Disgusting? You never used to feel that way. Take it in your hand, Laura. It won't hurt. You know how long it's been since you touched me?"

She was on her feet. "Don't lay a guilt trip on me, Dan. You know how I feel about that. I've told you enough times that when I make love to my husband, I want to taste him on my lips, not Jack Daniel's."

He sneered. "You love to put me down, don't you? Makes you feel so damn superior. You're just like your fucking father. All that religious talk, all those rules and regulations. You got 'em too, Laura. You may not go to the same church your parents did, but you're still just like your old man. You don't drink or smoke and you figure that makes you holy or something. With you, sex is a weapon. Stop drinking and we'll screw, you say. Just another power play."

"It's not that at all," she cried. "I'm not interested in power. I just want to make love to a husband who's sober. Is that too much to ask?"

"It is with me," he said, his face expressing pure loathing. "I'll tell you something, my sanctimonious, perfect wife. The only time you appeal to me anymore is when I'm drunk."

They stood there and stared at each other. Then, Dan, tired of the fight and giving in to the effects of the liquor, fell into bed. In seconds, he was snoring.

Laura walked down the hall and peeked into Ted's room. He was sound asleep, the sheets on the floor, his tall, fourteen-year-old body spread-eagled on the bed, one leg almost hanging to the floor. As usual, the room was a disaster, the dresser drawers open, clothes strewn on the floor, the desk, the chair—everywhere but where they should be. His father's son.

A pair of Walkman earphones were still stuck in his ears. She switched off the small radio and started to remove the earphones. Ted woke up.

"Hi, Mom." A voice surprisingly deep. It had begun to change six months ago. Laura still couldn't get used to it.

"Hi yourself," she said.

"Did I fall asleep?"

"I think you did."

"What time is it?"

"A little after eleven."

"Oh. That's early, isn't it?"

"A little," she said.

"Your eyes are all red. You and Dad fight again?"

"I'm afraid so."

"You on him again about drinking?"

"No. It was something else."

"I won't ask," he said.His eyes closed.

She brushed some errant strands of blond hair away from his eyes, kissed him on the forehead, then looked at him for a while as his breathing deepened. Her son. A man already. Tall and trim, his long hair making him seem older, his allegiance to various and sundry rock groups displayed by garish posters that covered much of the wall space. Not too long ago, they'd been posters of another kind; a quartet of singing turtles with old-world names.

He'd been such a joy to her. Unexpected, but loved very much. He'd had a smile on his face the day he was born. A smile that grew larger as he learned to walk and talk. He seemed to find exhilaration in the slightest achievement. When he'd assembled his first Tinkertoy at age two, he'd rushed to show her his triumph, a stick with two wooden circles, one at each end. A teenager now, most of what interested him was discussed with his father instead of Laura. She was losing him, day by day, and she knew it.

He was like his father in so many ways, as though he'd personally chosen Dan's genes over hers. They did everything together—father and son— fishing, hunting, going to movies. Her obsession with Victoria and her work had brought Dan and Ted together, forging an impenetrable bond that excluded her, leaving her an outsider in her own home. She could see it now, much too late.

Dan's heavy drinking didn't seem to faze Ted in the least. Although he'd never expressed it, Laura was sure Ted thought his father had a valid excuse.

Her. She had deserted both of them. She knew that's what Dan thought, and she was sure Dan had successfully implanted the idea in Ted's mind.

She resolved to change that. She'd just have to be more of a mother to her son. Soon, he'd be all she had left.

Suddenly she felt cold. She showered, put on her cotton pajamas, and went into the bedroom. The honks emanating from Dan's mouth and nose were enough to wake the dead. She grabbed her pillow and took it with her to the spare bedroom.

As she lay there in the darkness, her thoughts turned to Harold and Grace Brooks and the awful pain they must be feeling. To have a daughter die of natural causes was one thing, but to have a daughter murdered—so young. Jim had said she'd been stabbed to death by some drifter. Stabbed . . . and what else? Her imagination was working overtime and the images floating through her mind were horrible.

It was hours before she fell asleep.

CHAPTER

3

DAN AND TED WERE STILL SLEEPING WHEN LAURA LEFT THE house the next morning. The drive to the hospital took its usual forty minutes. Even on a Saturday, the highway was crowded with locals and tourists headed for the many theme parks located southwest of the fast-growing city of Orlando, some thirty-five miles northeast of Seminole Springs. It was only nine in the morning, but already, the heat and humidity were building quickly to their summer infernolike heights. She had to keep the windows of the car closed and the air conditioner running.

In most parts of the country, the last Saturday in August heralds the coming of fall. In central Florida, it signals another six to ten weeks of intense heat and dangerous thunderstorms. Laura's mind flashed back to her hometown of Havre, Montana. By this time of year, summer was practically moribund.

She switched on the radio. Usually, she listened to music from an Orlando station that played good classical fourteen hours a day. This morning, she turned the dial to Seminole Springs's single offering, an A.M. station that on Saturdays featured the town's resident curmudgeon, Tom Ferris, owner-editor of the city's weekly newspaper. Laura assumed he'd have an update on the Wanda Brooks murder.

He did, of sorts. He was in mid-interview with Billy Haines.

"So, then what did you do?"

"Well," Billy said breathlessly, still on a high from the excitement of last night, "I seen this guy on the ground leanin' over poor Wanda's body. I didn't know it was Wanda then, 'cause, well, you know, it was kinda dark. Like, I could see okay, 'cause I got eyes like a hawk, but not real good enough that I could tell it was her right then, you know? But I knew it was a guy, like I said, and I could see it was a woman naked on the ground, lyin' face up with blood all over her. I didn't know it was blood until I turned on the lantern. God! It was a sight, you know?"

"What did he look like?" Ferris asked, the impatience in his voice clear and strong.

Billy thought for a moment, then said, "He was crazy-lookin', you know? I could tell right off that he was some nut. He wasn't wearin' no pants, just a tank top, and his . . . family jewels was hanging out like . . . "

"Okay. What else?"

"He was makin' all kinds of crazy sounds, like some kinda chant or somethin', with his eyes spinnin' around, like he was off his head fer sure. He wasn't that old, about my age, I guess, but he was sure crazy."

"So then what happened?" Ferris asked.

"Well, he had the knife in his hand and I tol' him to drop it. He jus' stared at me. I tol' him again to drop the knife but he didn't. Then he made a run for me, screamin' at the top of his lungs. I couldn't do nuthin' but drop him right there. The troopers said I definitely done the right thing. I mean, he was about to kill me only he didn't know I had the gun, it bein' dark and all. Good thing I did, you know? I had no choice. I hadn't a shot him I'd be lyin' out there myself."

Ferris cut in, as he usually did with his guests, wanting to get his point across. Guests were little more than launching platforms for a barrage of Tom Ferris pontifications, most of which Laura considered unrecycled garbage.

"If you've just joined us," he said in his unique, clipped speech, an affectation designed to reflect some sort of perverse wisdom, "we're talking to Seminole Springs's own Billy Haines, the man responsible for the capture of the man *suspected*— I must watch what I say here—of stabbing Wanda Brooks to death. Billy shot the man as he was about to stick a knife in Billy's heart after Billy found him standing over the dead, mutilated, naked body of our own Wanda Brooks.

"This is just another example, ladies and gentlemen, of the wisdom exhibited by those charged with the responsibility of protecting the rights of the good citizens of the state of Florida. In some less-enlightened states, it would be illegal for Billy Haines to carry a handgun in his vehicle. Had this incident occurred in one of those states, I have no doubt that Billy Haines would not be with us today. He'd be dead, and his killer would be walking the streets. But this is Florida, folks, where people *are* allowed to exercise their rights under the Constitution. Thank God for that.

"As we speak, the alleged killer of Wanda Brooks lies in a coma after an all-night operation performed by Dr. Rick Taylor. The hospital has refused to list his condition, but we have it on good authority that he may not live out the day. We can only pray it's true. By dying, this animal will save all of us a lot of money . . . "

Ferris was still wailing about the inadequacies of the criminal justice system when Laura switched to the Orlando station. The car filled with the sounds of Bach. She'd learned all she needed to know—that Wanda's killer probably would not live to stand trial for her murder.

She turned off the interstate two miles from the city and headed north to the hospital, all brick and glass, shiny and new, with carefully manicured sweeps of lawn and meticulously tailored flower beds nestled amid a stand of tall pines. The entire landscape looked serene and pleasant.

The receptionist greeted her with a smile, as always. "Good morning, Mrs. Scott. How've you been?"

"Just fine, Mizz Crain. Yourself?"

"Never better. You can go right on up. Victoria's waiting for you."

"Thanks."

It was a charade, this talk of Victoria waiting for her. In truth, Victoria's brain was incapable of knowledge of any sort, but the people who worked at this hospital played a little game with her—with Laura a willing participant—as if in the playing the pain was lessened.

"Oh," the receptionist said, "I heard on the news this morning about that murder you had down in Seminole Springs. It's just awful. The town must be in an uproar."

"It's a terrible thing," Laura said.

"Did you know the poor girl?"

"Yes. Everyone in town knows . . . knew her. She was a treasure. She'll be missed."

"Oh, one more thing. Mr. Collins asked me to tell you—if you came in today—he'd like to see you for just a minute."

Laura's body sagged. "I'll stop by his office," she said.

"Thanks, Mrs. Scott."

Victoria's room was on the fourth floor, a floor occupied by patients ranging in age from four to ninety, all with one thing in common, the need for almost constant medical attention. The day nurse most often caring for Victoria was in the room when Laura entered.

"Hello, Mrs. Scott," she said.

"Hi, Ruth. How's my girl?"

Victoria was sitting upright, the nurse holding her so she wouldn't fall over. "She looks pretty good today, I think. How're things with you?"

"Fine."

Laura took her daughter's hand and held it tightly as she kissed her on the cheek. Ruth had taken the trouble to braid Victoria's freshly shampooed hair and apply a whisper of lipstick and rouge, giving some color to her frightfully pale face. Ruth meant well, but it always upset Laura to see her daughter like that. Victoria was now thirteen years old, but the last fragment of conversation between them had taken place when the child was nine. In many ways, Laura still thought of Victoria as that age, and the application of makeup on a nine-year-old seemed bizarre. It reminded her of an undertaker applying makeup to a corpse.

She pushed the thought from her mind, understanding Ruth's motives. Laura had but one daughter in this hospital, one source of unceasing pain, but to Ruth, all the patients in this ward were her children no matter their age.

There was no response from Victoria to her mother's kiss. The blankly staring, dead eyes looked straight ahead, devoid of expression. Some spittle had collected at the corner of her mouth. Ruth quickly wiped it away with a tissue.

Victoria. Fine, golden hair like her brother's, once an innocent sweetness in the now-dead eyes, once vitality in the legs and arms, now withered. Once a giggle on the lips, now thin and drawn and distorted. Bluish, lifeless lips hanging slack, like the rest of her. On the bed, an old, worn teddy bear lying on the pillow, probably the last thing she saw before her sight faded forever. Now, it looked as wan and lifeless as she.

Victoria had been seven years old when she was stricken with subacute sclerosing panencephalitis. SSPE for short. A delayed-action viral infection that hits a few children afflicted with normal childhood diseases. In Victoria's case, it was measles. Six months after the measles had cleared up, the SSPE struck. At first, the doctors didn't know what they were dealing with. Victoria was languid at times, active at other times, sometimes forgetful and often unable to sleep. One doctor did some tests proving nothing, which often happens with viruses. Then, a few weeks later, Victoria started having sudden outbursts of temper coupled with hallucinations.

Laura had her admitted to the hospital for observation where she was treated for a variety of illnesses. Then, the seizures started, violent spasms that would leave her unconscious. By the time the diagnosis was finally made, it was too late, not that it mattered. There is little that can be done for people afflicted with SSPE, other than control the seizures. They usually die within a year or two.

Victoria didn't die. Not then. She lost her sight first, then her hearing, her ability to communicate, and finally her ability to move at all. By the time Laura had her placed in a private hospital, she had stopped responding to tests designed to provoke involuntary reactions. A pin stuck in her leg and not so much as a blink.

Dan and Laura were given a grim prognosis; further deterioration of the brain to the point where death is certain. A year, two at the most, they were told. Strangely, one doctor told them, there had been spontaneous remissions in a small number of cases, allowing the child to regain health and most, if not all, of their lost faculties. For reasons not understood, previously unused brain cells picked up the tasks abandoned by the nonfunctioning ones, new nerves grew to replace those long since dead, the brain began to perform again, and the patient had a partial remission. Rare, yes, he explained, but it did happen. There was no known treatment to secure such a remission, but some specialists thought strong emotional support could be a positive contributing factor.

Laura made the decision to place Victoria in a private hospital instead of a public one. The private hospital provided additional attention that Laura thought might make the difference. Even though the odds were a hundred thousand to one, she thought it was worth a try. Dan didn't. He'd already given up.

Dan and Laura reacted to the tragedy in discordantly different ways. Dan started drinking and Laura became obsessed with her work and her sick child. The seeds for eventual marital destruction had been firmly planted.

The sun streamed in the window, warming the room and casting a dark shadow—Ruth's outline—against the far wall. For just a moment, the shadow reminded Laura of the angel of death. She shuddered, then said, "Hello, sweetheart. It's your mom come to visit. You feeling okay today?"

Laura took Victoria by the arm and let her frail body lie back on the bed. Ruth smiled, then left them alone. The ritual began. It was a one-sided conversation, with Laura bringing Victoria up-to-date on the week's activities and Vicki just slumped there, immobile, incapable of expressing a thought. The child's face was still pretty, despite the distortion caused by the lack of facial muscle control. Every time Laura saw her, it took something out of her, but she couldn't stay away.

She went to the foot of the bed, picked up the aluminum-clad chart, and opened it. Quickly she scanned the records. Despite the large amounts of anticonvulsive drugs being fed into Vicki, she'd had a very bad seizure during the night. She'd also dropped another eight ounces in weight, Laura noted. Down to sixty-four pounds even.

Laura felt a tightness in her chest. It was just as they had all predicted. The deterioration was inexorable. Another year, perhaps, and then she'd be gone. Two at the most. Miracles are rare events.

After an hour, it was time to go. Laura rang for Ruth and, when she entered the room, asked, "Is Dr. Carter in this morning?"

"Yes, he is. In fact, he wants to see you. He told me to mention it. He should be on the third floor somewhere."

Laura leaned over the bed and kissed her daughter good-bye. "See you next week," she said. "You too, Ruth."

"You have a good week, Mrs. Scott."

"I'll try."

She found Dr. Carter near the nurse's station on the third floor. They shook hands, talked about the weather for a moment, and then Laura said, "You wanted to see me?"

He touched her elbow and escorted her to the doctor's lounge. There, he put some coins in the machine and brought her a cup of coffee. He sat on a chair across from her, looking grim, and said, "If you hadn't come in this morning, I would have called you."

Laura felt her heart begin to pound. "I noticed she's lost some more weight," she said.

He nodded. "That's not the worst of it, Laura. Victoria had a seizure last night, a bad one."

"I know," she said. "I looked at the chart."

His eyes scanned her face for a moment, then locked on. "I don't think we have much time," he said softly.

Laura felt the tightness in her chest returning, stronger this time. She was fighting reality, engaged in her own denial process, and she knew it. "You mean less than a year?"

His lips tightened. "Her ECG is becoming erratic, Laura. I think the brain damage is exacerbating. The part of the brain that controls involuntary actions is now affected. Her heartbeat is showing some irregularity. The other organs are acting erratically as well. I think we're looking at weeks, perhaps days." He paused. "I'm very sorry."

Laura was stunned. "That soon?" she gasped.

"Once the vital signs start to fluctuate regularly, it's usually a signal. You've already made it clear that you don't want heroic measures implemented. There are some things we can do if you change your mind, though . . . "

Laura shook her head violently, her soul suddenly filled with a disturbing bitterness. "No. That would only prolong the inevitable." She sighed, then said, "I guess I've been a fool after all."

She felt his hand strong on her shoulder. "You mustn't say that, or think it either. I know how you feel, but your decision was made for valid reasons. I'm convinced your attention and caring has been responsible for her living these precious extra years."

"Precious?" Laura almost choked on the word. "Precious what? She's been a . . . vegetable . . . for four years. That's what Dan called her last night. I got angry and screamed at him, but he was right. She has been a vegetable. What's so goddamn precious about that?"

The doctor was not offended by her outburst. "Do you know what's going on in her head?" he asked.

"Of course not."

"Then who's to know that your regular visits, your constant displays of affection, haven't made the last few years more pleasant for her. Just because she's unable to express her feelings doesn't mean they don't exist. There've been a number of studies to indicate that . . . "

Laura stood up and emptied her coffee cup into the sink. "I've been telling myself that for years. I've also been telling my husband the very same thing. His answer has always been, 'She doesn't know what goddamn day it is.' Can you assure me he hasn't been right all along?"

Dr. Carter looked at her for a moment, then wrote something on a piece of paper. "This is the name of a friend of mine. He's a doctor who specializes in working with parents who've lost a child. It's probably the most difficult thing a human being can endure. I think it would be very worthwhile for you and your husband to talk to him."

"You really think a shrink can help us?" she asked, the bitterness spilling out.

"I think you need to discuss your pain with a professional," he said calmly. "One who fully understands the magnitude of losing a child. Dr. Gable lost two of his own to cystic fibrosis. He knows what he's talking about. He's helped many of my patients and I'm sure he can help you."

He turned and started to leave the room. Laura grabbed his arm. "I'm sorry, Doctor. I didn't mean to take it out on you. I know how hard you've tried. I really do."

"No apology necessary, Laura. No one condemns you for feeling very angry. I'd be more concerned if you weren't angry." He turned and left the room, but not before Laura detected the tears forming in the corners of his eyes.

Back on the main floor, Laura walked slowly to the office of George Collins, the hospital's administrator. He greeted her with a hearty handshake, and after a few more pleasantries got to the point. "Your account is seriously overdue, Mrs. Scott. If it were up to me, there wouldn't be a concern, because I know this bill will eventually be paid, but unfortunately, I have a board of directors I must answer to. They've asked that I talk to you about it."

Laura knew it was nonsense. Boards of directors have much more important matters to be concerned with than slow-paying accounts. "I understand," she said. And she did. Deadbeats usually receive short shrift, but when the deadbeat is a lawyer, an overdue account is handled with a high level of obsequious discretion, and not a little backside protection. Collins was just being careful.

"Look," she explained, "it's no secret that property values have taken a tumble the last couple of years. We had to make a principal payment to reduce the second mortgage on the house or risk losing it. Now that we've taken care of that, my payments to you should be much larger. In fact, I've brought a check with me today."

She handed the check to him. He looked it over, smiled, then asked, "Would it be possible to set up a regular schedule of payments? I realize how difficult this is, but they . . . well, they're insisting, Mrs. Scott. I really am sorry."

She took a deep breath. "What exactly do they want?"

"The suggestion"—he lingered over the word—"is two hundred a week. Just until the account is less than ninety days overdue. Of course, the regular monthly charges will have to be maintained as well. I'm aware that this is a rather large burden, but . . . "

She waved a hand at him. "It's all right, Mr. Collins. I understand your position. There's no need to apologize."

"Have you considered . . . "

She didn't let him finish. "I suggest you talk to Dr. Carter," she said. "Victoria will be out of here soon."

"Oh," he said, sounding relieved. "You've decided to move her?"

"Something like that," she said, the bitterness giving her voice a sharp edge.

C H A P T E R

4

THE HOUSE WAS EMPTY WHEN LAURA RETURNED HOME. Dan had left a note stuck to the fridge saying they'd decided to do some back-to-school clothes shopping in Orlando. That stung. We could have gone together, she thought. All of us. Dan and Ted could have done their shopping while she saw Victoria. Dan hadn't mentioned a thing about it last night, and she knew why. It was his way of punishing her.

She looked at the note again. There was a P.S. Judge Walter Fry had called. Two telephone numbers on the note. Laura recognized one of them as the direct line to the judge's chambers. The other she assumed to be his home. Mildly puzzled, she called the first one. Judge Fry answered immediately. "Thanks for returning my call," he said.

"What can I do for you?" she asked.

"Are you busy at the moment?"

"Not really," she said. "What'd you have in mind?"

"I wonder if you could come by for a few minutes."

"Is this in reference to the Gilbert case?" she asked. The Gilbert case was a civil suit she'd been working on for over two years. *Voir dire*, the picking of a jury, was scheduled to begin Monday before Judge Fry.

"No," he said. "Another matter entirely. I'll see you in about fifteen minutes, then?" He seemed eager to get off the line.

"Fine," Laura said, her curiosity piqued.

Walter Fry was new to the circuit court bench, having been appointed just six months ago to finish out the term of a judge who'd died suddenly of a heart attack. Prior to being appointed to circuit court, he'd spent three years handling nickel-and-dime traffic cases. Before that, he'd been an assistant state prosecutor. At forty-one, he was the second youngest of three judges on the circuit court bench.

Laura drove to the civic center, a bland, sprawling, concrete-walled building that housed both the city and county police stations, the fire hall, as well as both circuit and county courtrooms—one of each. The courtrooms, chambers, and other judicial offices were located on the top floor of a three-story building. The floors below contained offices assigned to city, county, state, and federal business—vehicle licenses, building permits, county records, post office, and a combined county-city jail. Though Holasutola County was the smallest county in Florida, the building had been obsolete the moment it opened, a testament to the incredible bureaucracy found at all levels of government.

It had been constructed to save money, but the savings, if any, were minimal. People doing business there sometimes had to park as far away as a block, and the city fathers had been forced to pass a city ordinance requiring those vehicles with sirens and trumpets not to use them until at least a thousand yards away from the building. Until the ordinance was passed, many a court case had been interrupted by the sound of an ambulance, fire truck, or police car.

Judge Fry, not a fastidious man, greeted Laura at the door to his chambers and wedged her among the briefs and boxes of files. "Thank you for coming," he said.

"No problem." She smiled at this short, thin dynamo. A bachelor, his work was his life. He was a decidedly unattractive man, with beady eyes and angular features exaggerated by his gauntness. The skin on his face seemed to rest directly on bone, with no flesh beneath. Some had questioned his health, but his appearance was hereditary, not due to illness. A polite and gentle man, he was well liked by those who worked with him, as well as those who knew him only socially. His chambers were small and cramped, located adjacent to the courtroom.

"When I talked to Dan this morning, he said you'd gone to see your daughter," he said.

"Yes."

"Any improvement?"

Laura shook her head. The strange tightness in her chest returned. Had it been any other day, she probably would have been sharper with some clue to what he wanted. But today, after hearing the news that Victoria's hopeless struggle was near its end, Laura's mind was a morass of melancholy thoughts. "I'm afraid not," she said.

He pulled a magazine from his desk and opened it to a previously marked page. "I was reading an article yesterday. The writer, some doctor in New York, claims that an experimental therapy he's testing has shown some promising results in cases that have some similarity to your daughter's." He handed the magazine to Laura. "I thought you might like to read it."

She was moved by his consideration and caring. "Is that the one by a doctor named Stein?" she asked.

"Yes, it is," he said, sounding surprised. "You've already read it?"

"Yes, I have," she said. "His treatment is effective only while the virus is active. In about twenty-five percent of the cases, it inhibits replication of the virus. That's a real breakthrough, but unfortunately, in Victoria's case, it's much too late for the treatment. But you're very kind to have thought of us. I appreciate it very much."

He was impressed. "You certainly do your homework," he said, putting the magazine on top of a pile on his desk.

"I've learned a lot about this thing since it hit my daughter," Laura told him. "I'm on the mailing list of a couple of medical clipping services. They send me all the relevant data when it gets published."

"Well, obviously, that isn't why I wanted to talk to you." Suddenly, he seemed pained. "I understand you've heard about the murder of Wanda Brooks?"

Laura had a terrible sinking feeling in her stomach. "Yes," she said. "It's awful."

"The man alleged to have been responsible may not make it. Dr. Taylor had him on the operating table for over five hours. I understand the bullet struck some vital organs, but missed the heart. Nevertheless, there are numerous complications. Dr. Taylor is quite concerned."

"It would be better if he did die," Laura said.

The judge ignored her intemperate comment. "He woke up this morning for a few minutes and the first words out of his mouth were 'I want a lawyer.'"

"I understood he was in a coma. Near death, in fact."

Judge Fry frowned. "The troopers exaggerated his condition deliberately to give the hotheads time to cool down. He's awake, and his chances of recovery are rated at fifty-fifty."

"Have they identified him yet?"

"Not yet."

She could almost hear the next words before they were spoken. As if to fend them off before they were uttered, she said, "Surely, you're not asking me to take this?"

"Yes, I am," he said. "Laura, you're well aware that we live in the smallest county in Florida in both population and area. Neither of our two public defenders has any capital case experience, and that means bringing someone in from Orange or appointing someone local. I've talked to PDs in

Orange this morning and they're completely tied up. It seems Orlando is having a murderous summer this year. If I shop around, I may get someone suitable, but having given it some additional thought, I'd rather have you."

"Isn't this all a bit premature?"

"No. Not once this man asked for a lawyer. Even if he dies, I want his rights protected."

"Well," she said, "the public defenders have to get their feet wet sometime. If what I hear is true, this case would be the perfect opportunity for that. It doesn't seem very complicated. Open and shut, I'd say. Whether he dies or not, what better time to break in a public defender?"

Leaning forward, Judge Fry said, "I gave that due consideration, Laura, and I've decided I want experience on this." He pursed his lips for a moment, then added, "I realize how financially strapped you are. Fifty dollars an hour is terribly inadequate, but at least they've lifted the cap on capital cases." He paused. "You'd be doing me a personal favor."

"A personal favor? I don't understand," she said.

"I'll explain," he said, pressing his fingers together as if praying. "As you know, I'm new to this bench. This will be my first murder case. Chris Marshall will be prosecuting. He's an excellent attorney and very straightforward. You're the same, but more than that, you've had experience with capital cases."

"Just one in Florida," she said.

"And three in Omaha," he added quickly. "That's more than everyone else in town except Frank Tilley, and we both know he's not up to it at this time." That was true. Frank Tilley, once a legend in town, was becoming old and feeble.

Laura held her hands in the air. "Please, Judge. I have a full plate myself. Monday morning, we pick a jury for the Gilbert thing. I expect that case to last a week. I've got two other cases coming to trial within the next few months. I'm in no position to take this on right now."

Laura had good reason to protest. In Florida, court-appointed attorneys' fees were strictly limited. Even a modest defense was a money loser and every criminal lawyer knew it. Most took them for the publicity value. But Laura, a maverick in many ways, hated publicity.

"At the moment, there isn't that much to be done," Judge Fry said, "but I want this man's interests protected right from the get-go. I don't have to remind you of the debacle that occurred in Jacksonville on a similar case."

He didn't. Laura was familiar with the case. A man had been shot by police in the act of robbing a gas station. Two bodies were found on the floor of the station. While the suspect was in the hospital, he was questioned and confessed before being given access to a lawyer. The appellate court had thrown the entire case out because the man had been denied his rights. A month after his release, he killed another gas station attendant.

"Once this man recovers," Judge Fry said, "I'll give you all the time you need to prepare, and if the allotted fees prove inadequate, I'll see what I can do about getting more."

The look in his eyes was riveting. "I need you on this, Laura. I feel I can trust both you and Chris to work with me and help me overcome my inexperience. If a conviction is returned on this, the last thing in the world I want is to be overturned on appeal on my first capital case."

Still, she hesitated.

"There's something else," he said, pushing harder. "Since I've been appointed to fill out the term of another man, I'll be running for election next year. I want to ensure that everyone feels I've handled this competently."

Finally, the real reason for his concern had surfaced. Politics. Laura was one of those who thought judges should be above the pettiness of politics. The alternative to the elective process was a political appointment not subject to public scrutiny, a system vulnerable to another kind of politics. But most voters had no way of determining the qualifications of a judge, and often a judgeship went to the best-looking or the richest, and that wasn't justice either.

Laura shook her head. "With all due respect, Judge, I don't think you'll end up trying this case at all. Wanda Brooks was known by everyone in town. Whoever defends this man will probably request a change of venue, which takes it completely away from you. I can't see any defense lawyer allowing this case to be tried here. I certainly wouldn't."

"You may be right," he said, "but I want you to be the one to argue for it. If the motion is granted and you want out then, you won't get any argument from me, providing, of course, that you have a legitimate reason." She thought she detected a wink. "But for the moment," he continued, "I'd feel much more comfortable with you handling the defense, at least to the point where a ruling is made on the change of venue. And as I said, you'd be doing me a favor. You know as well as I do it doesn't hurt to have a judge owe you one. Besides, it might help your practice. These cases sometimes generate a lot of publicity."

"It might destroy it," she countered. "You know how people are about this kind of thing. They often link the attorney with the accused. I can just imagine what Tom Ferris will say about this. It didn't take him long to get his hands on Billy Haines. Did you hear him this morning?"

"I never listen to Tom Ferris, and I only read his rag when forced to. He's an ignorant redneck asshole," he thundered. Powerful words from a man who rarely expressed strong opinions. "People pay him heed because he's controversial and shocking, but don't think for one minute that he represents the views of the majority who live in this town. I have tremendous faith in the people of Seminole Springs. They may surprise you."

She threw him a very small smile. "If they don't tar and feather me, I *will* be surprised."

"Look, someone has to do it," he said, still pushing. "I don't want someone who'll just give this a walk-through, which is what some will expect, and I don't want to bring in someone from the outside. I want someone I know and trust, a lawyer who'll play it by the book. You're my choice."

"Is there no way I can dissuade you?" she asked, almost pleading.

He grinned at her. "Don't make it sound worse than it is, Laura. This is a simple case. A man whose name and background we don't yet know has been accused of the vicious, brutal rape, torture, and murder of one of our most popular citizens." The grin faded quickly. "I apologize. I shouldn't make light of it. We are all asked to do the impossible, Laura. We're supposed to be dispassionate, removed from the reality of a horrible crime. We're required to act as though the victim is . . . did you know her?"

"Yes," she said. "I did some work for her father once. Wills, a trust, stuff like that. I saw her a couple of times when I'd be over there discussing things. I'd see her at the hardware store from time to time. She was a pretty girl and charming. I can only imagine the pain Harold and Grace must be feeling. She was their only child. I heard she'd been stabbed to death, but the other . . . I had no idea."

He sighed deeply. "I'll let Jim fill you in on the details. You'll do it?"

"Judge, I simply can't afford it. As much as I appreciate your problem, this case will drain me financially. You know as well as I do that to defend someone charged with first degree murder is . . . "

He held a hand in the air to stop her. "All right. Let's look at the facts. I know I can have three thousand dollars released immediately. I'm confident I can have another seven released in the near future. I think the guy is going to die. If he does, you'll file some papers and that will be that. You'll probably be able to keep most of the first three thousand. If he lives and you exhaust the second allotment, you come to me and I'll see that you either get more or another attorney is assigned. You'll have just cause. This will not be a financial burden, Laura. I won't allow it."

Laura found his insistence unnerving. She was flattered by his confidence in her, but the timing was all wrong. What with Dan, and Ted, and Vicki . . . Yet, here was a judge practically begging her for help. It was folly to anger a judge.

"All right," she said, finally. Had she not needed the money so desperately, she probably would have said no, favor or not.

Judge Fry beamed and stuck out his hand. "Thanks, Laura. I really do appreciate it. We'll have first appearance tomorrow morning . . . say ten? I'll have to do it myself as John has the weekend off."

"Could you make it nine?" she asked.

"No problem, Laura. No problem at all."

Laura left the courthouse with a deep sense of foreboding. Her daughter was in the last days of life, and she'd just accepted the responsibility of defending a man accused of murdering another young child. There seemed to Laura to be a connection, some bizarre betrayal of Vicki. What kind of woman betrays her dying daughter? she wondered.

CHAPTER

5

IT WAS A SHORT WALK TO JIM PICKETT'S OFFICE. Heather, his secretary, waved Laura through, telling her she was expected. Laura took a seat in front of Jim's institutional green metal desk, which looked as tired as he did. The police chief's crew-cut hair was lying flat on his skull, as if the wax he used to keep it standing straight up had suddenly melted. His black tie was loosened, a rarity for him, and there were patches of wetness under his arms and on the chest of his khaki shirt. Laura assumed he'd been outside in the heat until just recently, for cold air was pumping from the vent in the ceiling and the two additional window air conditioners. The room was as cold as a meat locker.

"You look a little tired," she said.

"More angry than tired," he replied, throwing the pen he was using onto the desk, leaning back in his chair and locking his fingers behind his head. "I've done it so much I'm used to working on two hours sleep, but God help me, I swear I'll never get used to mindless, brutal . . ." He gave her a wan smile. "Don't tell anyone I said that, though. Bad for my image."

He unhooked his fingers and placed his hands palm down on the desk. "We're supposed to take everything in stride, right? Cool, unemotional, detached, that's the ticket. Scrape the drunks off the highway, talk to husbands who've just beaten the living hell out of their wives . . . Jesus! I've lived in this town all my life. Sure, we're small, but we're every bit as bad as the big cities. We have less of it, but we have it all, and it makes me wanna puke. How the hell do you stop it from getting to you, Laura?"

"You do the best you can," she said. "And don't worry about your image. Your image is secure, but I think mine's about to take a very big nosedive."

For a moment he seemed puzzled. When she'd called from the judge's office, she'd refrained from telling him why she wanted to see him. "Judge Fry just assigned me to defend the guy they arrested for Wanda Brooks's murder," she said.

Jim's eyes widened. "And you accepted? Are you nuts?"

"I hope not. Judge Fry asked me and I need the money, truth to tell. This has been a banner year for expenses."

"Jesus Christ, Laura. There ain't much money in this one. Even if the guys lives, you'll get paid peanuts."

"Judge Fry is just being prudent," she told him. "What's the difference? This will get moved to some other city before we go to trial. Once that happens, I'm out of it."

"Maybe," he said, "but in the meantime, you're in it, my friend." He jerked a thumb at the phone. "My phone's been ringing off the hook all day. Most want to know by what authority I allowed this guy to be treated at Memorial. They say they're worried about AIDS contaminating the place."

"The man has AIDS?"

"No. Rick checked that out real fast. What they're really saying is that we should have sent him to Orlando, thinking, of course, that he'd of bled to death on the way. They're pissed at the troopers for moving 'too fast' as they put it, so they take it out on me. Wait'll the word gets out about you."

"They're angry and hurt, Jim. People do and say terrible things when they feel like that. I know I'll get some heat, but it can't be helped."

He shook his head. "If there's one good thing about this, it's that the son of a bitch was white. If he'd been black, we'd be looking at serious trouble." He let out a deep sigh. "When I was up in Tallahassee training, we had a black guy rape and murder a white girl. It was a very brutal thing, like this one. Took three days to calm things down. It was rough. Very rough. There's a lot of hate simmering beneath everyone's skin."

"Well," Laura said, "we don't have that problem."

He picked up the pen and played with it a moment. "As this guy's lawyer, you're in for months of abuse, my friend. Months. You could be messing up your whole practice by taking this on, you think of that?"

"I thought of it," she said, "but it doesn't matter. I told the judge I'd do it and that's what I'll do. The troopers ID the guy yet?"

"Nope."

"So what have they got?"

He picked up a manila file folder and opened it. "Not much at the moment. Most of this is based on the statement they took from Billy Haines. This is their deal, you know. The only reason they called me in was that both Wanda and Billy were citizens of Seminole Springs. That and professional courtesy."

"No ID at all?"

"Just a phony Social Security card. No driver's license, no credit cards, three bucks, some speed, some camping gear, a roll of duct tape, a Bible, some beggar cards, the knife, and . . . oh, yes, an army surplus shovel."

"A shovel? Beggar cards?"

"The shovel was one of those collapsible jobs. I guess he was planning on burying Wanda out there." He leaned forward and rubbed his chin. "Guy had this in mind from the start, Laura."

"And the beggar cards?"

"You know. The kind panhandlers use. Cards saying they're blind or deaf or raising money to get an operation for their kid. These ones were for some phony church."

He put his head back, stared at the ceiling for a moment, then said, "He's about twenty-four or-five, near as I can tell. Had open sores all over his legs, arms, and back. Came through the operation okay. Musta been the speed kept him going. It can do that."

"Did you get a copy of the report on Wanda?" she asked.

He hesitated for a moment, then nodded. "Prelim. She was raped, sodomized, and tortured. They found traces of semen in both her vagina and her rectum. Indications are that the whole time this was happening, she had her arms and mouth taped up with duct tape. Billy says he heard only one scream, so the guy musta took the tape off at some point. Can you figure that?"

"No," she said.

Jim scowled. "He cut her lightly at first. Just enough to hurt real bad. Burned her, too. Her chest, neck, stomach, and . . . " His voice trailed off to nothing. He took a moment to collect himself, then said, "When he finally got bored, he stabbed her real hard. Maybe twenty, thirty times. Some of the wounds are so large, he may have hit her more than once in the same spot. From what Billy says, the guy was in some kind of killing frenzy."

"Unless there was someone else," Laura said. "Maybe there were two of them and the other one got away. It was dark. Who knows?"

"That's not what the prelim says. Rick had the lab workin overtime. The blood type is a match on both semen samples. Same guy. The troopers are gonna do a DNA comparison. That should really clinch it. And he was covered in Wanda's blood, the bastard. There might have been another guy like you say, but we've got the one who did the killing, that's for sure." He slammed his hand on the desk. "Bastard! He took a .357 slug in the stomach and lived, can you believe it? Rick says an inch in any direction and he would have bled to death in minutes. Took out his spleen is all. Gave him six units of whole blood, sewed him up, and the asshole lives. Jesus! Billy Haines was on Ferris's radio show this morning, shooting his mouth off. You hear him?"

"Some."

"I'd like to kick his ass for being such a lousy shot. I really would. Ferris is making him out to be a hero. There's talk of giving him some kinda citation." He snorted. "Jesus! Billy Haines a hero? Give me a break."

"Well, Ferris is right about one thing. Had Billy not been there, we might never know what happened."

Jim grinned. "He's a client of yours, right?"

"Was."

He nodded. "Billy, the marijuana king. You beat the rap."

Laura laughed. "Not exactly. Billy was prosecuted by a raw rookie. The case against Billy was poorly prepared. Can I have a copy of those reports?"

"What I got, sure, but like I said, the troopers are handling this since it happened outside town. You'll have to deal with them and the state attorney's office for all the official stuff."

Most Florida counties had their own sheriff's departments, but Holasutola County was an exception. It was much too small to afford such an expense, so county law enforcement was provided by the state, for which the county received a monthly bill.

"Any witnesses besides Billy?" she asked.

"Not so far. The Coosman girl was out there with Billy, but she never saw anything."

Laura looked surprised. "Mary Ellen was there with Billy?"

"Yeah, but she never saw anything. We're trying to keep her name out of it. If her parents ever find out . . ."

"I understand," Laura said.

"We know Wanda was on her way home from the supermarket, but that's about it. That's the last anybody saw of her. Less than a half mile from home. Troopers figure she picked up this guy wandering down the road. He was probably hitching and like a fool she stopped."

"Did you talk to Grace and Harold yet?"

He gave Laura a funny look. He wasn't the kind of man who'd allow a stranger to tell two people their daughter had just been murdered. "They're still in shock. I don't think Grace has stopped crying yet, and Harold can't even talk. He just sits there and stares at the wall in the waiting room."

"The waiting room?"

"He's still at the hospital. He refuses to leave until the body is released. He says he doesn't want strangers taking his daughter unless he's with her. He's gonna go with her to the mortuary and then take her home. He says he won't let her out of his sight until she's in the ground. What does that tell you?"

"It tells me he thinks it's his fault," Laura replied.

"Exactly. He's the one who asked her to go to the supermarket and pick up some milk. He figures if he'd done it himself, Wanda'd be alive today. Grace let Rick give her a sedative, but Harold refuses to take a thing. He won't listen to a soul. I'm a little worried about him, tell the truth. This might have unhinged him. I tell ya, if it had been my kid, it would sure as hell unhinge me."

"When did she go to the supermarket?"

"Just before nine. When she didn't come back, Harold called the office. That was at nine twenty-eight. Officer Collins started lookin for her car, but didn't see it. He figured maybe she'd met a boyfriend or somebody and was parked somewhere. Then, we got the call from the troopers."

"Who called them?"

"Nobody. A trooper saw the Coosman girl walking down the highway and stopped to check it out. She got hysterical and told him that she'd heard a gun. They went back to the woods and found Billy trying to get his van started. The battery'd gone dead. Billy told them what happened. The trooper checked the body, then called in. Troopers called me at the party." He looked away.

Laura stood up. "Can you give me those copies?"

"Sure." He summoned Heather on the intercom and gave her the file. "Give a copy of everything in here to Mrs. Scott."

Heather left and Jim faced Laura. "You gonna talk to your client now?" There was some acid in the word "client." Jim knew the system, but even with that experience and their friendship, he was transferring some anger to Laura. Human nature.

"First, I'll talk to the troopers," she said. "I don't think my client is going anywhere soon. I just wanted you to do me a favor and call them, let them know I've got the case. We best keep this official, I guess."

Jim nodded. "First words out of his mouth, 'I want a lawyer.' The sonofabitch has a record somewhere. Knows the system. They should have his ID soon."

"I'm sure they will. Maybe I can get him to tell us."

"I hope."

She stuck out her hand. "Thanks, Jim."

He shook it, stood up, and said, "I won't wish you good luck, my friend. And I hope you have the good sense to walk this through. By the way, you know Chris Marshall's been assigned the case?"

"Yes. Judge Fry told me."

"You oughta find that a mighty interesting experience."

"I've worked with him before," Laura said. "He's a very competent attorney."

"And a whole lot more," Jim said, grinning.

The troopers had nothing to add to what Jim had given Laura. They made note of the fact she was representing the suspect and told her they'd give her information as it was processed. She left their small office on the second floor of the civic center and drove to the hospital. It was almost three in the afternoon by the time she arrived.

Her client, listed as John Doe, was in a room at the end of a hall. There were no prison facilities in the hospital, and since the patient was a suspected killer, he'd been given a private room instead of being kept in intensive care, the room farthest away from normal hospital routine.

A young trooper was assigned to guard the door. As Laura approached, he put his hand on the butt of his service revolver the way those armored car guards do when they take the money in or out of a bank.

"This is Mrs. Scott," the orderly accompanying her stated. "She's been assigned to represent the suspect."

The cop looked her over, asked for ID, checked it, then handed it back. Without a word, he waved at the door. He was young, probably fresh from the academy, she thought. He'd learn.

Inside the room, Rick was on one side of the bed, a nurse on the other. The nurse was changing a dressing while he got a second look at his handiwork of the previous night. Rick's eyes were red-rimmed with exhaustion.

"Don't tell me," he said, grimacing.

"I'm afraid so," she said.

Rick gritted his teeth, then looked at his patient. "Your lawyer is here. We'll let you two be alone for a while."

There was a grunt from the man in the bed.

The nurse picked up the dressing tray and moved quickly out of the room. Rick pulled off his rubber gloves, put them into a plastic bag, then washed his hands in the sink on the wall. "I don't think you'll get much out of him for a couple of days," he said, his voice barely above a whisper. "He's still pretty doped up and still in serious trouble. Don't take more than a minute or two and when you're done, come see me. I'll be in my office."

"I will," she said.

Laura was alone with her new client.

He was a pathetic-looking creature. His body was thin and emaciated. His long, tangled hair covered much of the pillow. His waxy-white face was thin and angular, much like Judge Fry's, with small rat eyes close together. A heavy layer of scar tissue like that of boxers who've stayed in the game too long marred the eyebrows. His nose was broad and flat, and looked as if it had been broken countless times. His lips were puffy, and there were small lumps all over his chin and cheeks. Thin, light scars were evident on his face, chest, and arms, the only areas of his body not covered by the sheet.

An IV tube was attached to one arm, which was shackled to the bed, as was one ankle. An oxygen tube had been placed in his nose, and another tube ran from his stomach to a collecting bottle beneath the bed. Probes from an electrocardiogram machine were attached to various places on his chest, neck, and arm.

Laura had known other murderers and was intensely curious about all of them in a perverse sort of way. How, she wondered, could a human being deliberately take the life of another? What mechanism had failed within the brain to retard rational thought and allow such terminal violence to be released? She'd read volumes on the subject. There were almost as many theories as there were murders. Some made sense, while others seemed couched in some indecipherable psychobabble, but there were some nuggets that had stayed firmly etched in her mind.

She'd learned that some people capable of murder exhibit behavior patterns that are often signals, red flags waving in the wind, announcements to the world that here was a person who could kill. With them, the pattern of violence was often progressive. Others killed on the spur of the moment, an action born of sudden, uncontrolled rage. Still others, the true psychopaths, could plan and carry out a murder down to the smallest element, with no remorse or pangs of conscience whatsoever. Laura wondered what manner of murderer her client was.

She had helped defend three murderers while in Omaha. Two had acted passionately, with little but emotion driving them. Fury, in one case fueled by drugs, in another stoked by alcohol, had caused a temporary loss of control. One angry person had lashed out at another with fatal consequences. She'd lost both those cases, but won another; a fired employee of a convenience store returned with a gun tucked in his waistband as he entered the store. The clerk behind the counter leveled a shotgun at the man before a single word was spoken, and fired it. Incredibly, he missed. Her client, thinking his life was almost over, fired back before the clerk could pump another shell into the chamber.

Her client had claimed he'd come back to apologize for the events that had gotten him fired and had brought the gun with him because he knew the manager was a hothead. Laura had won the case because a witness who'd seen everything stuck to her story in court.

Her only murder case in Florida had been that of a man who'd lived in mortal fear that his ex-wife was going to kill him while he slept. He'd taken to keeping a gun under his pillow. He'd claimed she'd threatened him on several occasions in front of witnesses. It turned out to be true. One night, he awoke to find her standing above him in the semi-darkness of early morning, a knife raised above her head. He shot and killed her instantly.

At the trial, the prosecution contended that it was all a sham. The man was still the beneficiary of his ex-wife's life insurance, a substantial sum. They claimed he'd set up an elaborate scheme to foreshadow the reasons for her death. The evidence did not support that view and the man was acquitted. Nevertheless, the insurance company refused to pay. Three days after his acquittal, Laura's client killed himself. He left a note saying he could no longer live with the knowledge that the woman he'd once loved had wanted him dead. Most assumed his suicide was linked to the actions of the insurance company. Laura was not among them.

In all four cases, she'd been dealing with defendants who knew their victims. This case was going to be different, and as she sat in the chair beside the bed and looked at her client, she felt a chill in the air. She felt she was in the presence of pure evil.

"My name's Laura Scott," she said. "I've been assigned to be your lawyer."

A grunt.

"You want to tell me about it?"

"No bitch," he rasped, the sound barely audible. His eyes were closed.

"Will you tell me your name?"

Nothing.

"Do you want to say anything at all?"

A grunt.

"You asked to see a lawyer," she said. "Well, I'm here. If you don't want to talk to me, why did you ask for a lawyer?"

Silence.

Laura stood up, "I'll wait until you've recovered enough to talk about this. Tell the doctor when you feel up to it."

"Hey!" Surprising strength in the voice.

"Yes?"

"I meant what I said," he rasped. "I don't want no bitch. I want a real lawyer." The voice was stronger this time.

"You don't get to pick," Laura said. "You get a lawyer, that's all. If you don't like it that I'm a woman, that's too bad. This is Florida, where we do things differently."

His eyes were open now, staring at her vacantly. "What's your name?" she repeated.

"Fuck you," he said.

Laura placed her card on the bedside table. "At least you know you have a lawyer."

She told the trooper at the door that no one other than medical staff was to see her client without her permission. The trooper gave her a dirty look and said, "He's under arrest. There'll be people wanting to talk to him as soon as he's able. We can't be chasing you all over the place."

"I've been appointed this man's lawyer," she said, "which means I'm an officer of the court. I've given you notice and I'll give the same to the doctor. The Supreme Court has ruled that once a suspect requests the services of an attorney, that attorney must be present whenever the suspect is being questioned. Now, I don't expect you to know every facet of the law, but I've just told you what applies in this situation. If I find you've let someone talk to him without my permission, you'll be in serious trouble. If you haven't learned it yet, you'll come to realize that it's unwise to interfere with officers of the court."

The trooper's face turned beet red.

"Understand?" Laura asked, pushing harder than normal.

"I heard you, lady."

"Good."

Laura left the floor and went directly to Rick's office, sitting wearily on a couch. "You're sure he's going to live?" she asked. "He looks pretty bad."

Rick said, "There are no guarantees in this business. He lost a lot of blood, but his heart is amazingly strong. Who can figure? Youth, I guess. The guy's a drug addict, anemic, and covered with infected boils. Probably hasn't had a shower in a month. The slug he took would've killed most people, but he made it through." He sighed. "Amazing."

"You're a good doctor," she said. "He was lucky to have you available. What's the prognosis?"

"I can't say. Because of the anemia, we had to give him coagulating agents. He still has some internal bleeding, but I can't risk another operation for a couple of days. He could throw a clot any second. The infected boils are also a problem. I've given him broad-spectrum antibiotics, but the boils could be what eventually kill him." He shook his head. "Ironic, isn't it? He takes a slug in the stomach and lives, but something too small to be seen in a microscope might bring him down."

"It might be a blessing," Laura said.

Rick frowned at the comment, then said, "If he lives, it'll take a week or so just to get him stabilized. I figure his chances are fifty-fifty at this point.

Did you two talk?"

"Some."

"By any chance, did he give you his name? I'd like to get my hands on any medical records he might have."

"No," she said. "All he said was he wanted a male lawyer. I told him I was all there was."

"I hope you haven't made a mistake," Rick said. "I really do. You have to defend someone like him? You have no choice?"

"Not really. This is the judge's decision. It's not considered wise to refuse to accept a judge's appointment. Can we talk about that another time?"

Rick shrugged. "Sure."

"He looks like he's a boxer," she said, bringing the subject back to her client. "All that scar tissue and those lumps all over his face."

"I don't think so. His muscle tone is terrible. It's never been developed. I doubt very much he's ever been involved in athletics of any kind."

"So where did all the lumps and scars come from?"

For a moment Rick didn't answer. He seemed to be mulling things over in his mind. Then he stood up. "I'll show you," he said. "Come on."

They went to a small room where the X-ray films were kept. Rick pulled out a file, removed a large black sheet of film, and slapped it into the viewer. "I had these taken before the operation," he said. "Standard procedure. Just the midsection." He pointed to several thin white lines on the rib cage. "Those are fractures, and all of them were inflicted when this guy was a kid. Here, here, and here." He pointed to several points. "Before this guy was in long pants, almost every rib had been broken at least once. This one here has three old fractures. The sternum, too. His nose has been broken so many times I can't count, and his jaw. If I were a gambling man, I'd bet the farm that a full set of X rays would reveal old bone breaks all over his body from—the time he was a baby, I'd say."

He flicked off the light, turned and looked at Laura. "I'm a doctor, not a lawyer. I'm telling you this because the man is a patient, but don't expect me to help you defend him. I'm a surgeon, not an apologist. Maybe you can afford to have everyone in this town angry with you, but I can't. Understand?"

"I understand," she said.

If Rick Taylor had an obsession, child abuse was it. He was a regular speaker at various functions like meetings of the Kiwanis, Lions, and PTA groups. His topic was always the same. Children had to be protected from abusing parents. As distressed as he was about the death of Wanda Brooks, he still considered his patient a patient first, a suspect second. Nevertheless, he was a realist and wanted Laura to know from the start that he wasn't about to become involved in the defense of her client. What he didn't understand was he didn't have a choice in the matter.

CHAPTER

6

WHEN LAURA ARRIVED HOME, DAN WAS WAITING FOR her, standing in the center of the kitchen, his hands on his hips, his jaw thrust forward, fire in his eyes.

Laura sat wearily in a chair. "What's the problem?" she asked softly.

"What's the problem? Oh, nothing much. Just total humiliation, that's all."

"Are you going to tell me or not?" she snapped.

He opened his billfold, extracted a credit card, and threw it at her. It hit her neck and fell to the floor. "I tried to use this at K mart. It was refused! You neglected to tell me our credit is no good. Thanks a lot. When the hell did this happen?"

Laura was the one who handled the family

finances. She was also the one who did the dishes, the laundry, the cleaning, and just about everything else. Ted mowed the lawn, but that was about all the help she got from her two men. Another area of conflict that had never been resolved. When Laura would ask either of them to do something, they would either refuse or forget. When Laura would attempt to discipline Ted, Dan would intervene.

"I told you about this two days ago," she said, "but you weren't listening. You were smashed at the time, like you are every night. No matter. Nothing I say to you registers, drunk or sober, so don't yell at me. If you'd mentioned to me that you were going shopping this morning, I would have reminded you not to take the credit cards. Why didn't you?"

"Because I didn't intend to go shopping, that's why. Now, thanks to you, Ted will look like a fugitive from Coopers Corners when he goes to school."

"He'll look fine," she said. "I've already sent them a check. Our credit will be back on-line in a couple of days."

Dan turned his back to her and opened the refrigerator door, removing a can of beer. On weekends, he drank beer until five, then he'd switch to the hard stuff, claiming it was proof he wasn't an alcoholic. Such delusions. As he snapped open the beer can, Laura said, "Before you get blotto again, there are two things you need to know."

Dan put the can to his lips and drank.

"Number one," she said, "if you think you were humiliated today, you haven't seen anything. Judge

Fry has just appointed me defense counsel for the guy who is supposed to have killed Wanda Brooks. You can expect some serious hostility from the people in this town for the next few weeks. Of course, you're used to hostility. You thrive on it. I think it's what keeps you going."

He gave her a hateful look. "That's why you took it, isn't it? It's because of me. You want everyone in this town to hate me, don't you?"

"I know this will come as a terrible shock, but you were nowhere in my thoughts when I made the decision to accept the case."

"That figures."

"There's something else."

"And what might that be?" he asked, sneering.

"I talked to Victoria's doctor today."

"Really? You talk to that quack every day. What now? He's found a new brain? Yours for only one hundred thousand dollars. Frankenstein lives!"

She felt that terrible tightness in her chest again. She was about to tell her husband that their daughter was very close to death, but she didn't want to tell him in the midst of an argument, another senseless quarrel. She wanted to tell him while his arms were around her, holding her close, sharing the pain. She stood up, moved toward him, and reached out to draw him to her. He pulled away as one might recoil from a snake.

Her hands dropped to her side. It would have to wait, she decided. She turned away.

"Well?" he yelled at her back.

"Nothing," she answered.

She needed to get out of the house, now. She was about to cry and she didn't want him to see her cry. Whenever she cried, Dan took it as a sign of victory.

Outside, Ted was throwing a basketball at a hoop and backboard nailed to the garage. Laura stood there for a moment and just watched as she fought back the tears. Ted was a week away from entering high school, and with his height and skill had a strong chance to make the freshman basketball team, a goal every bit as strong as Laura's teenage aspirations to become a lawyer. He was the picture of fluid grace as he dribbled the ball past a line drawn in chalk on the concrete, then whirled and, one-handed, arched the ball toward the net. It fell through with a snapping sound, having never touched the rim. Laura clapped her hands, an appreciative audience of one. "Nice shot," she said.

Ted picked up the basketball, tucked it under his arm, and stood in front of his mother. "Thanks."

"You're welcome," she said. "Are you looking forward to next week?"

"What do you mean?"

"Well, they start basketball practice right away, don't they? I know how much you want to make the team. I'm no sports expert, but I think you've got what it takes and I know you've been practicing hard. I think you've got a good chance."

He looked away.

"What's the matter?" she asked

"Nothing."

She took his face in her hands and forced him to look at her. "What is it?" she asked. "Are you upset about the credit card? Don't worry. It'll all be straightened out next week, then you can get what you need."

Ted just stared at her. She could see the torment in his eyes. "What is it, Ted?" she probed. "Did you and Shirley have a fight?"

"No. We're going to the movies tonight."

"What, then?"

He seemed very embarrassed about something. Suddenly, Laura's heart sank. "You haven't . . . you and Shirley haven't been . . ."

He looked up at the sky. "No, Mom! Jeez. Even if I wanted to, Shirley would never. I've never even touched her boobs. She's got boobs now, you know."

"I know," she said, smiling. "She's a very pretty girl. Of course, you're a very handsome guy."

"Oh, Mom."

"Okay. Look, you're upset about something. What is it?"

He reached up and pulled her hands away. "I can't say," he said solemnly.

"What do you mean, you can't say? Say what?"

He shook his head. "I promised Dad."

"Promised Dad what?"

No answer. "Ted. Tell me what's troubling you. Please?"

He took a deep breath and said, "You'll have to talk to Dad." Before she could say another word, he turned and started running down the street, dribbling the basketball as he loped away from her.

Reluctantly, she went back inside. Dan was in the living room watching television. She took a seat beside him on the sofa and asked, "Would you please explain to me what Ted is so upset about?"

"How would I know?" he said, his gaze never leaving the TV.

"Ted says you do know."

He turned and looked at her, then picked up the remote control and switched off the set. He stood up and walked to the center of the room, facing her, his hands on his hips again. "I guess this is as good a time as any," he said.

Laura waited.

"The company has made me an offer," he said. "They want to transfer me out west. Edwards Air Force Base in California. I have to let them know Monday."

"When did this come about?"

"Last week."

"And you told Ted but not me?"

"I discussed it with Ted for a reason," he said. "A damn good reason. He's all excited about getting on the basketball team, and he's got this big love affair going with Shirley Taylor. Well, if I move, it'll be real soon, and he can forget about both the team and his girlfriend. I just didn't want him getting his hopes up."

"If *you* move?"

For a moment he just glared at her, his eyes filled with hate. Then he hitched his pants, hooked his thumbs under his belt, and said, "Yes . . . me. Me and Ted."

Laura was hardly able to speak. "And just what does that mean, exactly?"

"I wasn't sure I wanted you to come."

She stood up so fast she felt slightly dizzy. "What are you saying?"

He was swaying gently, a sneer on his face. "I'm saying I've made two decisions all by myself. I've decided to take the job and I've decided I don't want you coming with me."

"*You've* decided?"

"Yeah. Me. It's all over between us, Laura. I've had it. I've had it with your holier-than-thou attitude, your goddamn superior bullshit, and your fucking nagging. I've been offered a transfer to California and I'm going to take it, and I'm taking Ted with me."

"The hell you are."

He held a hand in the air. "Oh, I know. You're the lawyer, right? You think you know everything. Well, you don't know shit. I've already asked Ted whether he wants to stay with you or come with me. You know what he said? He said he wants to come with me." He pointed a finger at her. "You want to go to court and have the judge ask him? Be my guest. I have just as much right to Ted as you do. Being a mother doesn't cut as much ice as it used to."

He seemed very sure of himself. "You've already talked to a lawyer?" she asked.

"I have."

"So what you're really saying is you want a divorce?"

He grinned malevolently. "You're finally catching on."

"And you told all this to Ted?"

"Not that part. All I said was I might be transferred to California and you might not want to come. I asked him if he wanted to stay with you or come with me. He said he wants to come with me. He's no fool. He knows what's going on in this house."

"You manipulative bastard!" she howled. "How *dare* you!" She felt the air go out of her lungs. She sat back on the sofa and tried to collect her thoughts.

"The lawyer says it would be best if we work out the settlement details ourselves," Dan continued. "Far as I'm concerned, you can have the house and most of the stuff in it. All I want is my clothes, my fishing gear, my baseball card collection, my car, and some other small stuff. I won't ask you for any support, though I could, and I won't expect you to be making demands on me. You can come out and see Ted whenever you want."

Her mind was reeling. "What about Victoria?" she said weakly.

"What about her?"

She looked into his eyes. "She's dying, Dan. It could happen very soon. Maybe within days."

He laughed. "Sure she is. She's been dying for years."

"You think I'm lying?"

"Probably."

"I would never lie about something like that. I've never lied to you."

"So you say." He was being insufferable. The thought of divorce was not her fear. Her fear lay elsewhere. "Dan, listen to me," she said. "I'm telling you the truth. Victoria is dying."

His face hardened even more. "Victoria died a long time ago, Laura. You could never get that through your thick head. It's one of the reasons you've become such a giant pain in the ass."

She took a deep breath and asked, "When exactly do you have to let them know?"

"I told you. Monday."

"Don't they give you some time to make arrangements?"

"A little. Once I say okay, I have to report in two

weeks. I'll have to drive it, thanks to you. I can't afford to fly. That means I'll be leaving in a week."

"But," she said, "if Victoria dies while you're on the road, how will I get in touch with you?"

He leaned forward. "I'm all done putting my life on hold while you wait for Victoria to go. You'll have to bury her without us, that's all."

She felt tears forming at the corners of her eyes. She fought them back. "You can't possibly be this heartless," she said. "I can accept that you've come to hate me, but this is beyond hate."

"It's nothing of the sort," he said. "It's just being practical. I already told you that as far as I'm concerned, Victoria is dead. I've already buried her. Which brings me to another point. Don't be asking me to pay any more of her hospital costs. That's your responsibility now. I've paid too damn much for too damn long."

They just stared at each other for a moment. "So," he said, breaking the silence, "you gonna make a big fight out of this or are you gonna be reasonable?"

"I don't know," she said. "This has all come a little too quickly."

"Well, you'd better make up your mind fast. We need to decide if you want to draw up the papers or if my lawyer does it. Now that I've made up my mind, I'm not wasting time. I'm going to be outta here in a week." His face softened slightly as he said, "I'm sorry about this, Laura, but let's face it. This marriage went south a long time ago. We're both forty years old. There's still time for us to find some kind of happiness with someone else."

A strange coldness was making her shiver. "You

never gave us much of a chance, Dan. I don't know how often I've asked you to come to . . ."

He cut her off with a wave of his hand. "I don't need a goddamn shrink to tell me what's wrong with this deal. I've had it figured out for years. You happen to be a woman who wishes she were a man. That's our entire problem. You were never much of a mother. You were always more interested in your goddamn career than me or anybody, and there's no way you'll ever change. Well, you can have your precious career now. I'll find a woman who wants to be a real woman. Maybe you should too."

All he wanted to do now was hurt her. He was reveling in his newfound strength, fueled by alcohol, anger, and bitterness, and the last statement was too stupid to draw anger. "I'll think it over," Laura said quietly. "I can tell you one thing, though. I don't know who you talked to, but there's no way on God's earth you're taking Ted with you."

Dan stuck out his chin. "Ted comes with me."

"No he doesn't," she insisted. "He's too young to make that kind of decision, and his feelings notwithstanding, no court will allow him to stay with you on a permanent basis. Being an alcoholic doesn't cut it either."

He had a strange smile on his lips. "We'll see about that, Laura. We'll just see."

CHAPTER

7

IT WAS THE NEXT MORNING, SUNDAY, AND JUDGE FRY WAS peering over half glasses at Chris Marshall. "Chris?" he said, his voice echoing in the almost-empty courtroom.

"Your Honor," Chris answered, "the State requests pretrial detention at this time. The suspect has yet to be identified or questioned, but there is sufficient probable cause. The State requests that the arraignment date be left open at this time."

Judge Fry looked at Laura Scott. "Laura?"

"I have no objection at this time, Your Honor. My client is recovering from a severe gunshot wound. I haven't had a chance to talk to him myself. I request that a bond hearing be held at such time as I've had the chance to talk to him."

"So ordered," the judge said.

"Your Honor," she continued, "the suspect has indicated a desire for counsel to be present whenever he is questioned. I request that an official order to that effect be issued."

Judge Fry looked at Chris who simply shrugged. Then the judge turned his attention back to Laura. "I think everyone is aware of the law, Laura. Unless there's been some violation of the suspect's rights, I don't see the need for a special order. Do you have some specific complaint?"

"Yes, Your Honor. It appears the troopers guarding my client in the hospital are not aware of the law. I just want it on the record."

"Well," the judge said, "I think you can bring the troopers up to speed, Chris."

"I'll take care of it," Chris said.

"That it?"

Laura and Chris nodded. The legal necessities had been attended to in a matter of seconds with just nine people in the courtroom. Chris Marshall, Laura, the judge, another assistant state prosecutor, another lawyer and his client who was picked up the previous evening after robbing a convenience store at gunpoint, a bailiff, a clerk—and Tom Ferris, owner and editor of the *Seminole Springs Clarion*, the weekly newspaper.

As Chris and Laura left the courtroom, the rotund, bearded Ferris fell in step with them. "So, you still don't know who this guy is, eh?"

Chris fended him off. "Tom, you don't go to press until Friday. Why don't we talk about this later in the week? We don't really have anything to say now."

"Come on, Chris. I got two out-of-town dailies want me as a stringer on this. Besides, I think we'll publish an extra edition this week. Probably Wednesday. We'd already gone to press when this hit Friday night. Damn! There are times I wish I had a daily."

Chris stopped and faced him. "Did you get a copy of the police report?"

"Uh-huh."

"Then you know as much as I do. I haven't even talked to the man yet. Neither has Laura."

"Yes, she has," Tom said, jerking a thumb in Laura's direction. "I heard you were at the hospital yesterday."

"I was," she answered, "but my client was semi-conscious. All he said was he wanted a lawyer. He's still in pretty bad shape. He might not make it."

"I'll drink to that," Ferris said. "At least you can tell me what he looks like."

Laura smiled at him. "I'm sure you've already talked to the nurses about that. Give it a rest for a couple of days, okay?"

Ferris made a face. "What am I supposed to write about if you two won't talk?"

"Did you interview Billy Haines?" Chris asked.

Laura laughed. "Obviously, you weren't listening to Tom's radio show yesterday."

"You heard the interview?" Tom asked, smiling.

"Part of it," Laura answered.

"What'd you think?"

"About what?"

"The interview. I thought it went well."

"You made it appear as though Billy Haines was some sort of hero. From what I understand, he was in the wrong place at the wrong time. It doesn't take much courage to pull the trigger of a handgun."

Ferris grinned. "That's where you're wrong, Laura. You're a woman, so you wouldn't know what it's like to be in combat. When I was in Vietnam we had lots of guys who didn't have courage enough to pull the trigger. Most of them are dead, just like Billy would have been. This guy was coming at Billy with a knife. Billy could just as easily have frozen, but he didn't. That makes him a hero in my book." He scowled. "Besides, if Billy hadn't shot that bastard, we might never have known who killed poor Wanda. You should be thankful for that alone."

Laura didn't answer. Tom turned to Chris. "Come on, Chris. I need something fresh. Give."

"It's Sunday, Tom. Talk to me tomorrow," Chris said, picking up the step again. Tom threw them both a sour look, then shuffled off.

"Got time for a quick coffee?" Chris asked.

Laura glanced at her watch. "Sure."

They walked the block to Carrie's, a small restaurant, the only one open Sunday morning, and took a booth in the back. After coffee was served, Chris said, "I guess I got nervous for nothing. I thought there'd be more interest than this."

He didn't look very nervous. "This is your first murder case, isn't it?" Laura asked.

"Uh-huh. Not you, though. I remember you working that wife-killing case. Very interesting. And I understand you handled some in Omaha. True?"

He was no fool, this assistant state prosecutor. Chris Marshall was a hometown boy, forty-two, tall, his carefully combed black hair slightly gray at the temples. His brown eyes were penetrating and his soft voice was disarming. Behind the pleasant face was a brain that ticked like a fine watch. Laura had seen him in action before. His aw shucks, just-off-the-farm manner of speaking might lead some to think a jury would be lulled to sleep, but they'd be wrong. Chris had a way of emphasizing the key word in a sentence so that no one missed the import of what he was saying. Now, she realized he was trying to draw her measure.

"Yes," she said. "I handled three murder cases in Omaha. I was officially second chair, but ended up doing most of the cross. I was working for a big firm then, and they used me because they thought the jury would be more impressed with a woman than a man, being as the juries were almost all women."

"And were they impressed?"

"I don't think so," she said, smiling. "We lost two of the cases."

"But you won one," he said. "And you won the case you tried here. That gives you a fifty percent batting average. Pretty far above the norm."

"I guess," she said, "but it's not a true reflection. I should be grateful though, considering that most capital crime juries are usually hanging juries. There are lots of older people with fixed values on juries. They aren't the most liberal people in the world. As for the interest in this one, I think the town is still in shock. It's only Sunday. Give it a couple of days and you'll see some interest. Maybe too much. Unless he dies."

"You think he will?"

"Rick says the chances are fifty-fifty."

She could feel his eyes appraising her candidly. His gaze went from her face to the ample swell of her breasts beneath the blouse, then back. Normally, she would have been put off by such directness, but the way Chris did it was more a compliment than demeaning.

The word around town was that Chris, long divorced, had never made a play for many of the women in town—available or not. He'd dated many, some more than once, but apparently had always been the perfect gentleman. To some, that had been a big disappointment.

He was dressed in a dark blue suit that failed to hide a strong, muscular figure. A white shirt and blue tie, no jewelry other than a college ring on his left hand and a flat, gold watch on his left wrist.

"I guess it's too early to talk about this," he said.

"There's plenty of time," she said. "First, we have to see if the man lives."

"Did you read the police report?

"Yes, but that's about it. I haven't talked to Billy Haines yet, and I haven't read any of the other reports. How about you?"

"I talked to Billy last night," he said. "I'll send a copy of his statement over to you in the morning. Would you like me to tell you what he said?"

"No. It'll keep."

"So, you're just going to wait?"

"Yes," she said. "I've got plenty to keep me occupied. I've got a product liability trial starting in the morning. I don't want to clutter up my mind with thoughts of anything but that."

"Is that the Gilbert thing?"

"Yes."

"I don't know how you do it," he said. "You do it all, civil, criminal, family. Do you really love it that much?"

She smiled. "Off the record?"

"Sure," he said.

"Promise?"

"Cross my heart."

"The truth is I hate it," she told him. "I used to love it, but now I hate it all. It's a game, Chris, a game involving people's lives. I guess there's justice occasionally, but most times not. You know as well as I do that the poor get the short end of the legal stick. They always have and always will, be it a civil or criminal matter. It takes money to win any important case.

"Take this one," she continued. "We've got a man in the hospital who may never face trial, but if he does, the evidence I've seen so far is so compelling, there's no way on God's earth I'll ever stop him from being executed, and that bothers me very much."

He seemed surprised. "Why? You hate to lose that much?"

"It has nothing to do with losing. I have a personal aversion to capital punishment."

"Why?"

"Nothing too original. I think it reduces us to the same level as the person we're executing. I don't see legalized murder as that far removed from just plain murder. We give it our imprimatur, and that's supposed to make it all right, but I see capital punishment as nothing but rationalized vengeance."

"That's not a particularly unique position," he said.

"I didn't say it was," she said, "but it's still a valid one. We both know that innocent people have been executed. Mistakes can and are made. That alone should be reason enough to stop it, but that's all beside the point. What bothers me is the role money plays in the criminal justice system."

"Every system," he corrected.

"Let me finish," she said. "We were talking about the justice system."

"Go on."

"Let's suppose, just for the sake of discussion, that the suspect in this case, the Wanda Brooks case, was very wealthy. Let us further suppose that he hired F. Lee Bailey as his lawyer. Besides being dazzled by Mr. Bailey's celebrity, the jury would be exposed to any number of experts, all of whom work for a fee. They'd also be subjected to weeks of testimony covering every facet of the case. In the end, the jury might well convict, but they'd be sufficiently confused to refuse to recommend the death penalty, and so would the judge. You and I both know that money *can* buy a jury in some very subtle ways."

Chris just smiled. Laura was a little wound up, so she kept on with it. "Take the Gilbert case, for another example. She was walking down the street two years ago at Christmas time. As she passed in front of Holly's Card Shop, a young kid who was putting up some decorations in the store window slipped and fell off the ladder he was using, and came crashing through the window. Mrs. Gilbert's face was slashed to ribbons. Amazingly, the kid came out of it with nothing but a small cut on his arm.

"Anyhow, Mrs. Gilbert was taken to the hospital

and stitched up, but it was clear she'd need extensive plastic surgery. Her insurance company would only cover part of the cost, so she called me.

"I discovered that Holly's liability insurance coverage was canceled three months before the accident because she didn't pay the premiums. Holly was hoping the Christmas season would see her over the hump but it didn't. She had neither money nor insurance. There wasn't much I could do about that, so I did some digging. I found that the people who manufactured the window had made a very big boo-boo. Their brochures contain certain claims for their windows, claims that can be misinterpreted. Because their insurance coverage is in the millions, I decided to go after them.

"The window was made twenty-four years ago. It wasn't designed to withstand a kid falling off a ladder, but what the hell. I've got a woman with a scarred face, potential financial and emotional disaster, to whom I have an obligation. I've also got a company with lots of insurance coverage, so that's who we sue. It stinks, but Mrs. Gilbert deserves some compensation, don't you think?"

Chris frowned. "Of course she does," he said. "I don't understand your problem. If the glass company's insurance people pay a few hundred thousand dollars, why should you feel bad about that?"

"Why? Because the accident was not the fault of people who made the window. Not really. It was mostly the kid's fault, but we know he doesn't have any legal responsibility. The real responsibility is Holly's because she owned the store, hired the kid, and didn't keep up her liability policy. Naturally, we've sued her as well, though we're aware she doesn't have a dime. Thanks to the 'deep pockets' law, all I have to do is prove that the glass manufacturer's responsibility was a minimum of one percent, and they'll be forced to pay the entire judgment, should one be awarded. That's what stinks."

Chris shook his head. "I see it differently, Laura. If there was no deep pockets law, your client wouldn't have a hope of collecting *any* actual or compensatory damage money. Then where would you be? Nowhere. You should be happy there is such a law. If you win, and I'm sure you will, the money will still be paid by the insurance industry. What's the difference whether it's Holly's company or the glass manufacturer's? I don't see the distinction."

"It's the way we assess responsibility," she said. "The people of this country are not being held responsible for their actions anymore. It's always somebody else's fault, or nobody's fault. What kind of example is that to set? Is it any wonder we have problems with our kids these days?"

Chris fiddled with his spoon for a moment, then said, "You're complaining about a societal problem, not a legal one. Is your disillusionment with your profession specific or just part of a generalized disenchantment with life?"

Laura smiled. He was being overly clever, digging into her psyche, looking for weaknesses that could be used later should they face each other in court. Smooth, and she was letting him get away with it. "Let's just say that I'm not alone in my feelings," she said.

He didn't want to let it go. "If you hate the practice of law so much, why do you do it?"

She sipped her coffee for a moment, then said,

"That's a very good question."

"Were you always this cynical?" he asked, the tone of his voice non-threatening. He wasn't being nasty, just curious.

"No," she said. "When I started, I was filled with excitement, charged with energy, thrilled that I was going to be a *lawyer*. It was always my dream. I started by trying to keep the banks off the backs of the farmers in Montana. What a crock that was."

"In what way?"

"Well, the bankers would come out to the farms and tell the farmers they had this money to lend, money backed by a government supposedly interested in helping farmers. No interest loans with a big balloon due in five years. Don't worry, they said, when the balloon comes due, we'll just refinance. So the farmers borrowed and when the five years was up, the bankers were there with their hands out. No refinance. Pay now or we foreclose.

"As it turned out, some very big businesses had a vested interest in getting their hands on those farms and their dirty fingerprints were all over those loan applications. Later, they became more brazen and actually bought the banks, but in those days, they were more covert. Anyhow, when I went after the banks, I was facing a stacked deck, a deck where every card was an experienced litigator from New York or Philadelphia. I lost, and so did the farmers. It was a very quick and dirty education in reality."

"But you kept at it," Chris said.

"Not exactly. I left the practice of law when the kids were born. When they started school, I was bored to death, so I got involved again, but this time I made sure I had nothing to do with farmers.

For a while I was filled with the same enthusiasm I'd had initially, since I was dealing with a very interesting client base, but my enthusiasm didn't last. I see the system for what it is, driven by personal egos and biases that too often determine the result." She sighed. "I guess it's like anything else. The older you get, the more you see things from a different perspective—the way they are instead of the way they should be."

He grinned. "I'm surprised you haven't mentioned your real beef—that women are still the lesser of equals in this or any business."

She laughed. "Do you really think so, or are you just saying that to make me feel good?"

"I really mean it," he said. "The legal profession is still a male bastion, notwithstanding the strides made by women in recent years. Nevertheless, I don't think that's reason enough to hate it. Nothing's perfect, Laura, but I look upon our problems as a challenge. Change from within, that's the ticket."

"It'll never happen, Chris."

"Maybe. Maybe not. I think you're just the kind of person to make a difference. If you channel that anger of yours properly, you might find your work more fulfilling. Of course, it's also possible you could become even more frustrated."

"Why do I have this feeling you're teasing me?"

His face got very serious. "I'm not. I don't mean to, at least. I think it takes guts to be a female lawyer in the South. You happen to be a very good one, better than most of the guys in this town. You may not realize it, but there's much respect for Laura Scott around here."

"And much resentment," she added.

"Some," he said. "Only because some people are intimidated by intelligent and aggressive women. There are those who find that hard to take, but if a lawyer is to be successful, he or she had better be aggressive. Sure, there are those who resent you, but it's not as personal as you might think. They can't separate the professional persona from the real person. You can't stop people from being stupid, Laura."

Again, she laughed. "True. Have you always been this liberated?"

"No," he said. "Until my divorce, I was as macho as the next guy. Then I realized I'd blown a perfectly good marriage for no reason at all. She was a wonderful woman and I cheated on her. It was a stupid, thoughtless thing to do. It's a lesson I've never forgotten."

It was a story she'd never heard before. "You're amazing," she said, genuinely in awe. "Most men never learn that lesson, or if they do, they never admit it."

"They're the poorer for it. Facts are facts, Laura. I screwed up and I've had the courage to own up to it. If we bullshit ourselves, we're indulging in fantasy. I have no time for fantasy anymore."

"It's none of my business," she said, "but you've never remarried. Any special reason?"

"I guess I'm still a romantic. Can a pragmatic realist be a romantic, or is that some sort of oxymoron? Whatever the case, I'm waiting for the sparks to fly and the bells to ring. Chemistry. It just hasn't happened yet."

"And you'll settle for nothing less?"

"Not at this point. Give me a few years and I may settle for a lot less."

She smiled at him. "I don't think so."

"I'll tell you something," he said. "You're the most feminine woman I've ever known, and that is *not* a pass."

"Thank you," she said, somewhat shocked by his outburst.

"I admire your skills," he said. "I also admire your fortitude in handling some very difficult situations, both professionally and personally. I'm not stroking you, Laura, I mean it."

"Do you always butter up opposing counsel like this?"

"Always," he said, grinning. "Try to get 'em off guard right from the start. Such is not the case today, however. If I don't win this one, I should become a bag boy at Publix.

"That's what it all boils down to, right?"

"Winning? I guess so. Why else are we here?"

She looked at her watch. "I have to go. I'll call you in a few days and we'll talk again . . . if he lives, that is." She stood up, threw a dollar on the table, and grabbed her attaché case. Then, she felt his hand on hers. "How's your daughter?" he asked.

She shuddered. It was as though he could read her mind, see through her bluster. His intense gaze seemed to penetrate her brain, transmitting a message. He knew. There was no use pretending.

"She's fading pretty fast," she said.

"I'm so sorry," he said in a soft voice edged with bitterness. Laura saw sincerity in his eyes and heard it in his voice. Not just platitudes, but a genuine sharing of pain, a quiet scream at the unfairness of life, despite his earlier blasé comments. She felt goose bumps rising to the surface of her skin.

"Thank you," she said.

"I thought it must be something like that," he said.

"What?"

"I'm sorry. I just noticed you looked a little preoccupied this morning. I assumed it had something to do with your daughter. You're used to your husband, so it couldn't have been that."

His insight was unnerving.

CHAPTER

8

AT EIGHT THAT NIGHT, LAURA RECEIVED A TELEPHONE call. She recognized the voice immediately. It was Philip Holmes, the attorney representing the company that had made the window in Holly's store. He was the stereotypical big-city corporate lawyer, all pinstripes and confidence. They'd met at least a dozen times during two years of depositions taken from experts in everything from glass to plastic surgery to psychological damages caused by traumatic shock.

Laura had spent eighty thousand dollars of Mrs. Gilbert's money and expended one hundred and fifty non-billable hours pursuing this case. Before doing so, she'd given her client as clear a picture of their chances as possible. Since juries were notorious in their unpredictability, the chances were roughly four-to-one against, Laura had explained.

Mrs. Gilbert had made the final decision to proceed. Laura's fee would be a percentage of the settlement, if any, or a percentage of the award, if any. Should the case be lost, Laura would not be compensated for her time, just her out-of-pocket expenses.

Few clients could afford to spend the money Laura had spent on this case. If Mrs. Gilbert had been poor, the suit would never have gone forward.

Holmes was from Cincinnati—the home base for the glass company—and was licensed to practice law in six states where the company had large distribution centers. He'd visited Seminole Springs several times, had deposed Mrs. Gilbert, Holly, and the poor kid whose clumsiness had brought this on, and had decided to handle the defense of his client personally, rather than hire a local man. In Laura's opinion, that was usually a mistake and she was delighted that Holmes was blessed with a prodigious ego. It improved the odds.

He'd initially tried to have the case moved to Jacksonville where the company maintained its distribution center, claiming that it would be difficult to find an unbiased jury in Seminole Springs. Laura had argued in court that her client was emotionally devastated by this continuing ordeal and presented an affidavit from a psychiatrist to back up the claim. Mrs. Gilbert would suffer undue emotional stress if she was forced to expose her hacked-up face in another city, Laura had claimed. Besides, she argued, the incident had received little press and the people of Seminole Springs would not be biased in any way. There was no need to move the case. Since the accident had occurred in town, the trial should take place locally. Judge Fry had ruled in Laura's favor.

Still, Holmes didn't get the message. Laura had the feeling that his legal experience was limited to paperwork, which wasn't that unusual. Nevertheless, she prepared for the case as though he was Clarence Darrow reincarnated. Now, he was calling her at home, requesting a meeting prior to trial.

"Am I to assume you wish to discuss a settlement?" she asked sweetly.

He did a couple of hurrumps, then said, "Yes. We can meet at your office or my hotel. Whichever you prefer."

"Let's do it at your hotel," she said. She'd spent most of the day at the office preparing her *voir dire* charts and was not eager to return. Normally, she preferred to have these kinds of discussions on home turf, but in this case, she didn't think it was going to matter much. "I'll be there shortly," she told him.

"I have to go out for a while," she called into the family room to Dan and Ted, both engrossed in television. Dan gave her a baleful stare. She left the house.

She didn't expect Holmes to be alone and he wasn't. He was accompanied by Walter Garibaldi, the president of the glass company, and John Springer, a representative from the insurance company, both of whom Laura had met previously.

Obviously, they planned to gang up on her. Everyone shook hands in amiable fashion, then took seats around a conference table that had been installed in the suite. It was time to get down to business.

"Mrs. Scott," Holmes began, wrapping his fingers around his suspenders, "I'm sure you realize that your case is totally without merit. You may have successfully persuaded a local judge that you had a cause for action, but that's a shallow victory. I can, and will, present seventeen precedents whereby similar cases have been thrown out of court."

His eyebrows arched as he said, "To be perfectly candid, there's been a question in my mind since this began, a question relating to your motives for pursuing this matter."

He was leaning back in his chair, now grinning like a man who'd caught an employee with a hand in the till. His thin, wispy hair was combed sideways, left to right, in a futile effort to disguise his baldness. Suddenly the smile vanished. "You're an unethical attorney," he said, "and I'm going to expose this little game of yours for the sham it really is. I've had you investigated, Mrs. Scott, and I *know* what you're about." His jowly face quivered as he spoke, like Nixon's near the end. His voice was harsh, accusatory, threatening.

"Really?" Laura said. "You've had me investigated?"

"We have indeed."

"And what did you find?"

Holmes glanced at the other two men in the room, then continued. "I found that you are a woman desperately in need of money. You have a very sick daughter who's been ensconced in private hospitals for six years. Her care is costing you thirty thousand dollars a year. Your husband is an unemployed alcoholic."

Despite her best efforts to remain unresponsive, Laura could feel her eyes widening in shock. "My husband is an electrical engineer," she said. "He's worked at Tasker Air Force Base for the last three years."

"Past tense," Holmes crowed. "He was fired last week."

Laura's mind was racing. Things were suddenly coming into focus. Holmes seized the moment. "Please don't pretend you didn't know. I'm sure you're well aware of the fact that his employers have given him several ultimatums, all of which he has rejected. You must have known it was only a matter of time. I understand he was a drunk even before you moved to Florida."

Laura found her voice. "This is reprehensible!"

Quickly Holmes jumped to his feet. "Save the outrage, Mrs. Scott. You and your husband have no equity in your home and you're in debt up to your ears. In truth, you're on the verge of bankruptcy." He stuck out his chest. "I think you took this case for personal gain, Mrs. Scott. I think you pursued your client and persuaded her to be a party to this unconscionable action. I think an official inquiry could get you disbarred."

Laura stood up red-faced. "I'll see you in court, Mr. Holmes."

"Yes, you will," he said, his own face reddening. "The inquiry can scarcely begin before trial, but if your tin-pot judge allows that jury of idiots to award damages to your client, we'll appeal. We'll appeal for the next ten years if we have to, and in the end, we'll win. We'd rather spend ten million dollars exposing you for what you are than give you a dime."

Laura started for the door, fighting to control her anger. She'd expected a hardball negotiating session, but not this! Not to have her personal life exposed and her ethics questioned. They'd caught her by surprise with the information on Dan, if it was true. She hated to be surprised.

"This is a sham, Mrs. Scott," Hughes screamed at her back. "My client is not responsible for what happened to Mrs. Gilbert and you well know it. We won't stand by and see justice thwarted just so you can get your personal finances in shape. Once our investigation is complete, I have a strong feeling you'll be going back to whatever it was you did before you became a sleazeball lawyer."

Laura was almost out the door before she realized what was happening. She saw it for what it was now, the opening gambit in a short, hardball negotiating session. She knew that experienced attorneys rarely threatened or insulted opposing counsel when they were really sure of themselves. She hadn't done any of what they'd suggested. Holmes was just fishing, hoping, assessing, reaching, trying to upset her.

Another surprise. She'd thought she'd adequately prepared herself for Holmes. Obviously not. She'd badly underestimated his determination, and he was too clever by far, playing his little game, and she was falling for it.

Fighting the fury within her that almost begged to be released, she turned and faced the trio with an impassive expression on her face. "To repeat," she said icily, "I'll see you in court, Mr. Holmes. You do what you think is best, and I'll do the same. That's how the system works, right?"

She started out the door.

"Mrs. Scott!"

It was Springer, a tall, courtly looking man in his sixties. A no-nonsense pro who lived in the real world. Laura turned and faced him, her hand still on the door handle. "Yes?"

He was as red-faced as Holmes, but it wasn't Laura he was upset with. "You're asking for two million," he said calmly. "That's totally out of the question. If, and I repeat if, we were to reach some sort of agreement, it would have to be somewhere in the two-hundred-thousand-dollar range."

Laura stepped back inside the room and let the door close behind her. Calmly she said, "You have the facts, gentlemen. Mrs. Gilbert is now forty-one years old. She *was* a beautiful woman. Today, even with the reconstructive surgery, she's a mess. After the accident, her husband was so repelled by her appearance that he disappeared into the night, leaving my client high and dry. The chances of her ever finding happiness or another husband are not too terrific."

Springer smiled. Softly he said, "We have evidence that the relationship was in trouble prior to the accident."

Laura smiled back at him, her emotions well in check. "Only Mr. Gilbert would say something like that, and Mr. Gilbert is not on your list of witnesses. Interesting. I'm sure the judge will find it interesting as well. Frankly, I'd be happy to have him testify.

I'm sure you'll all find the cross illuminating."

She addressed Holmes. "You've seen my witness list, and you've read the depositions. I have three people who will swear Mr. and Mrs. Gilbert were crazy about each other prior to the accident. You can't produce a single witness to support his claim."

"We have several," Holmes said.

"Then why aren't they on the witness list?"

"They came forward only this week. We haven't had time."

"Really? Then why am I here? To listen to insults? I have better things to do with my time."

"Mrs. Scott," Springer said softly, "you cannot win this case."

"I *will* win this case." She pointed a finger at Mr. Garibaldi. "Your brochures say that your plate-glass windows will withstand certain forces. In reconstructing the accident, we've been able to determine that the forces applied by the kid on the ladder were less than what you've warranted. We've proved it twice. If we have to, we'll prove it a thousand times. You're liable, pure and simple."

"Bullshit!" he snapped. Short and fat, with a little Adolf Hitler mustache perched on his thin upper lip, he looked like an escapee from some thirties vaudeville act. "That window was over twenty years old," he sputtered. "Nothing is supposed to last forever, dammit. Our reconstructive team says the force was well beyond the design limits. Your experts don't know what the hell they're talking about."

Laura stood her ground. "We'll let the jury decide," she said. "As for your appeals, I don't really care if you do appeal this case for the next ten years. The interest meter is running. I've already spent what was needed to prove my client's claim. The rest is just time, and I've got all the time in the world. Time is money to some people, but it's just time to me. If you want to play games, be my guest, but in the long run, you'll pay three times as much as you could have, and you'll look like the insensitive robots you really are when it all finally ends."

She faced Garibaldi. "I'd also be willing to bet that ten years of bad press should effectively counter the millions you spend on advertising. If we win in court and you fight us, I'll make sure Mrs. Gilbert's face is plastered over the cover of every tabloid in the country." She put her attaché case on the floor and held up her hands like a movie director framing a scene. "I can see it now. Slasher Corporation Fights Helpless Woman, or something to that effect."

She dropped her hands and leaned against the wall. "There are several sleazy TV shows that would eat this up, don't you think? They love to book freaks and Mrs. Gilbert looks as bad as the worst of them. She can bring photos, maybe even some videotape. Every operation, every slice, every scab. It should have half the country throwing up before the first commercial break. That's an area I've stayed away from, because I am not, as your attorney states, a sleazeball lawyer. But if you want to play rough, I'll play rough. I can get into the sewer with the rest of the rats when I have to. If you don't believe me, try me."

For a moment no one spoke, then Springer waved a hand in the air. A hand of surrender. The pro was taking over. The game was at an early end. "Let's cut the crap," he said. "So how much, Laura? That's the bottom line. How much? We already paid her plastic surgeon over a hundred grand. We've paid for her shrink and two other doctors. How much do you want to make this go away?"

He'd called her Laura. The brass knuckles had been put away. Now they were really getting somewhere. "Make me an offer," she said.

"Five hundred thousand."

He said it fast, like it wasn't really money.

"I'll discuss it with my client," she said.

"Will you advise her to accept it?"

"Of course not. It's much too low."

Holmes was almost beside himself. "You're the worst kind of lawyer, Scott, you know that?"

Laura picked at some imaginary lint on her best gray suit—the one she'd worn to court at nine this morning—played with the bow on her silk blouse for a moment, then looked him straight in the eye. "The fact is," she said, keeping her voice low and even, "I'm acting in the best interests of my client. That's my job. It's what I get paid for and it's what I'm expected to do. You people have made it personal, and I don't appreciate it. I don't know how they operate in Ohio, Mr. Holmes, but investigating the plaintiff's attorney and his or her spouse is a no-no in this state unless you have probable cause indicating unethical or illegal activity, which you surely don't.

"In truth, it's you who'll be facing an inquiry. No matter what happens with this case, I'm going to ask for your censure. You're a disgrace, and I'm going after your ass, mister."

Holmes was on his feet. "Why you . . ." A hard look from Springer shut him up.

Laura picked up her attaché case and said, "Mr. Springer, if you want to talk, we'll talk, but we'll talk alone. I won't be in the same room with either of these two for another second."

Without a word, Springer turned and motioned to the other two men. For a moment they remained where they were. Then they glanced at each other and, realizing that Springer was the man with the checkbook, reluctantly left the room. Springer waved a hand at the table and said, "Let's sit and talk, Laura."

Laura sat.

"Coffee?"

She nodded.

As Springer poured coffee from a silver tea service, he said, "I'm sorry about the rough stuff. That was Holmes's idea."

"I have a thick skin," Laura said, "but I'm still going to seek sanctions. His behavior was uncalled for."

Springer placed a china coffee cup in front of her. "I cannot disagree. Now, how can we resolve this?" He sat across from her, his hands flat on the table.

"I would recommend to my client," Laura said, "that she accept a settlement that nets her seven hundred and fifty thousand dollars. Plus, she'll need to be reimbursed for her out-of-pocket expenses. I can't say she'd take such a deal, but I would certainly recommend that she do so. Unstructured. You continue to pay appropriate medical expenses for the next three years. After that, she's on her own."

Springer shook his head. "That's too much, Laura. We'll go for an annuity that gives her fifty grand a year for fifteen years. That gives her the three-quarter mil. You sign off for a hundred thou. The medical stops now."

"No," Laura insisted. "No deal. You want an annuity deal, she'll have to net a hundred a year for ten years. You pay her costs and my fee immediately and you take care of her medical for two years. And that, Mr. Springer, is my final offer."

He shook his head. "Laura, that's much too high. I'm not authorized to go beyond what I've offered."

"That's too bad. I'm really doing my client a disservice by even talking to you about a settlement. When the jury gets a look at her and hears how her life has been totally destroyed, sees how terrible she looks, they may make a huge award."

Springer smiled. "And they may dismiss the case completely. How much are your costs to this point?"

"We've spent almost a hundred thousand so far in out-of-pocket expenses. Mostly experts. As you know, they don't come cheap."

He nodded. "How many hours have you put into this?"

"At least a thousand," Laura said with a straight face.

"And your regular hourly rate?"

"Normally, my fee is a hundred and fifty dollars an hour, but this is a contingency case."

"I'm aware of that," he said. "Forty percent if you go to trial?"

"Uh-huh."

He scribbled on a yellow pad. "I think a thousand hours is something of an exaggeration. Be reasonable."

"You're offending me," Laura said. "From now on, every time you offend me, it's going to cost you more. A hundred thousand per insult."

Springer laughed. "I thought you said you have a thick skin?"

"I do," she said, "but I'm still human."

"All right," he said, throwing down the pen. "Here's *our* final offer and I really mean it. Your client nets seventy-five thousand, give or take, for ten years. We pay you two hundred and fifty thousand directly. You can reimburse your client from that. The medical continues for two years. That's it."

Laura gave careful attention to his eyes. Either he was a very good poker player or this was the limit. She thought about it for a moment. "I'll talk to my client," she said.

"And?"

Laura smiled at him. "I'll recommend it."

"Then we have a deal, Mrs. Scott. We'll have the papers ready for the judge in the morning, along with the checks."

"I can't say that until I've talked to my client."

"Of course."

They shook hands. Then Laura asked, "What Holmes said about my husband. Is it true?"

Springer looked shocked. "You didn't know?"

Laura shook her head. "No, I didn't. I really didn't."

"I'm sorry," he said.

She stared into his eyes. It appeared he was telling the truth. "Thanks," she said.

*   *   *

Ruth Gilbert was getting ready for bed when Laura knocked on the door. She was dressed in a faded silk robe, her hair piled up on top of her head, heavy makeup covering the terrible scars.

"I've just had a meeting with the glass people," Laura said.

Ruth's eyes lit up. "Yes?"

"They've offered a settlement. I'd like to explain it to you."

Ruth quickly ushered Laura in to the living room and sat on the edge of a chair while Laura explained the details of the proposed settlement, including the part about the continuing medical expenses, both physical and mental. Summing up, she said, "I think it's worthwhile, Ruth. It means you'll receive approximately seventy-five thousand dollars every year for the next ten years, all tax free. If you sock about half that away every year, you'll have a tidy sum in ten years. You'll be able to live on the interest alone. They've also offered to reimburse you for the costs you've incurred."

Ruth let out a deep sigh. Then she began to cry. "I don't know how to thank you, Laura," she said, sobbing. "When you told me that Holly had no insurance, I was devastated. I was convinced it was hopeless. It's a miracle."

"Not quite."

"I'm so grateful for all you've done. My goodness. It's been over two years. I never . . . Do I still have to go to court in the morning?"

"No," Laura told her. "I have your power of attorney. The other lawyer and I will meet with the judge.

We'll take care of the paperwork. There's no need."

"How can I ever thank you?"

"You just did," she said, looking at her watch.

Laura was utterly exhausted, totally drained, but she had another task to perform. One of her expert witnesses had flown in from upstate New York and checked in to a local motel. He was still going over the evidence he'd expected to testify to in court later in the week. Now, Laura would have the pleasure of telling him he wouldn't be needed.

She headed for the motel.

CHAPTER

9

WHEN LAURA SCOTT FINALLY ARRIVED HOME, DAN WAS sitting in the kitchen, smoking, sipping his Jack Daniel's, almost completely drunk. Ted was in the living room, watching MTV. In deference to his parents' aversion to heavy metal music, he'd placed earphones on his ears.

"So? Have a nice time?" Dan said.

She sat beside him and looked at his eyes, bloodshot, the lids drooping precariously. This was not the time to be discussing serious matters, but Laura was a jumble of emotions, angry with Dan, elated over the success of the Gilbert negotiation, and extremely concerned about her children. "Why didn't you tell me about the problem at work?" she asked.

The drooping lids lifted slightly. "What the hell are you talking about?"

"They gave you an ultimatum, didn't they? Get some help or get fired."

"Where'd you get that?"

"It's not important," she said. She took a deep breath, then said, "This talk about a transfer . . . it's all baloney, isn't it? There is no transfer. You've been fired. It's written all over your face."

"That's bullshit," he said, but his heart wasn't in it. The eyelids fell again and he looked away. He seemed vulnerable, wounded, much of the fight knocked out of him.

She gently placed a hand on his hair-covered arm. Once, Dan's profusion of body hair had been a turn-on. Now, nothing about him turned Laura on. He was more to be pitied than hated. "Dan," she asked, "how often have we talked about your drinking? How often have I begged you to get some help?"

No answer.

"Don't you think this is a golden opportunity?" she said. "It won't be easy, but I know you can do it. I'll help you every way I can if only you'll try."

He pushed her hand away. "Cut it out. Number one, I haven't been fired. I don't know who you talked to but they're crazy. Number two, I don't need help. I never drink hard liquor until five and there's nothing wrong with that. You have a bug up your ass because you're such a goddamn prude. You don't smoke, you have one drink a week, and you think everyone should be just like you. Well, they aren't, lady. They never will be."

Nothing had changed. Not even being fired had forced him to face reality. "All right," she said, "but

I have this terrible feeling you're planning to run away. If you want to destroy yourself, I can't stop you, but I'll damn sure stop you from ruining Ted's future."

He just stared at her.

"Dan," she said, gripping his hand, "you need help. I'll help you. We'll get you into a hospital for treatment. After you're dry, if you still want the divorce, you won't get a fight from me, but I won't let you run away with Ted while you're still drinking like this. You have to get sober first. If you want my cooperation, you'll have to earn it. That's the deal."

"I'm not a drunk," he said.

"Yes, you are, Dan. You're a drunk, and you've lost your job because of it. Do you really think you could win a custody battle with that kind of background?" She gritted her teeth. "You wouldn't have a chance. Don't you see what's happened to you?"

"Fuck you," he said, his eyes suddenly ablaze with anger.

Laura leaned back in the chair. Arguing with a drunk was an exercise in futility.

Later that night, after Dan had finally gone to bed, Laura walked quietly into Ted's room. He was still awake, lying on his back, the ever-present earphones stuck in his ears. Gently she pulled them away and sat beside him. "We have to talk," she said.

"Yeah? What about?"

"I had a talk with your father tonight."

He looked distressed. "He finally told you, huh?"

"Well, he told me some things. I'm not sure if

what he told me is the same as what he told you. Is it okay if we compare notes?"

"I guess," he said glumly.

"I'll go first," she said. "Your father says he's been offered a job in California. He says he wants a divorce and that you want to go to California with him. Is that pretty close to what he told you?"

Ted sat up in bed, looked at her for a moment, then slowly nodded. "Mom, I know it looks like I'm taking sides. I don't mean to hurt you, but Dad needs me, you know? He's a little messed up. I'm sorry about the divorce and all, but all you guys do is fight anyway. What's the point of staying married?"

Laura took a deep breath. "We'll leave the divorce out of this for the moment. Your father is more than a little messed up, Ted. He needs help. I'm not sure he's been offered a job at all. He may have been fired. If that's true, he's going somewhere just to escape the shame of it. He wants you to come because he feels closer to you than anyone else in the world. He needs you much more than you realize."

Ted's eyes were as wide as saucers. "He was fired?"

"It appears so," she said. "He was told at work to get treatment for his drinking. He ignored the warnings and now I think he's been fired. He's in serious trouble, Ted. We have to help him."

"He said he never drank at work," Ted asserted. "Did he tell you he was fired?"

"No."

"Then how do you know it's true?"

"I don't know for sure. I was at a meeting with some people. They told me. Maybe he drank at work and maybe he didn't, but you know what he's like in the morning. It doesn't take a rocket scientist to see that he's suffering terrible hangovers."

Ted cupped his hands behind his head and leaned back on the pillow. "Jesus," he said, "he's never lied to me before. He can't have been fired."

Laura squeezed his shoulder. "I'm sorry, Ted. The truth is, when people get desperate, they start to lie. Eventually, all they ever do is lie." She chewed on her lower lip for a moment, knowing her next words would be crucial. "I know you love your father very much. It may not seem like it, but I do too. We fight a lot because there are things we can never agree on. We're both stubborn and we're both aggressive, but we are what we are, and now we all must deal with the truth of that.

"Your father needs treatment badly. If he doesn't get it, he'll either get very ill, or get himself killed behind the wheel of a car. At the very least, he'll do some things that will cause you to stop loving him. I don't want that to happen. Right now, he's about as low as I've ever seen him. I think he lied to you about the job because he was ashamed. I can understand that.

"He may never admit to you he's been fired, but that's not the point. If you leave with him, you'll be doing what I've been doing for years, refusing to force him to face himself and his addiction to alcohol. That's the worst thing in the world you could do right now. If you refuse to go with him, I don't think he'll go alone. It might be just the thing to compel him to get some help. Do you understand?"

"I think so," he said.

She ran a hand through his hair, then kissed him

on the cheek. "I want you to be happy, Ted. I'll make a deal with you. If your father gets treatment and stays sober for a couple of months and still wants the divorce, I won't stand in his way. Once he's sober, if you two want to go away somewhere together, I won't make a fuss. I promise. But until he's sober, the only thing we can do to help him is to make sure he gets treatment. If you go with him now, under these circumstances, it will be a disaster. Don't you see that?"

"I guess," he said.

"Will you help me?"

Ted stared at the ceiling for a moment. Then, his arms reached up and pulled Laura to him. She felt the wetness of his tears on her neck. His silent answer. For the first time in two days, she felt the grip of terrible tension start to release.

CHAPTER

10

IN THE MORNING, LAURA AWOKE FEELING AS IF SHE HADN'T slept at all. The emotional turmoil of the interminable weekend had almost overwhelmed her. The murder of Wanda Brooks, the news of Victoria's rapid descent toward death, the fights with Dan, the appointment to defend an irrefutable killer, learning that Dan had been fired and suspecting he was seriously considering running away taking Ted with him—all had taken a heavy toll. Laura was barely able to crawl from her bed.

The feeling of release from the previous night had been replaced by a sense of dread. The glorious settlement she'd worked out with the insurance people just hours ago seemed like a crazy hallucination created by her subconscious to disperse a thickening blanket of gloom. When the slow ascent to consciousness reaffirmed reality, her spirits were just slightly lifted in its wake.

She slowly moved to the edge of the bed and let her feet touch the floor. To avoid Dan's incessant snoring, she'd spent the night in the guest room again. She smiled ruefully. That was what she told herself, but it was just another excuse not to be near him. Other wives endured the snores of their husbands using a variety of means, but Laura sought escape from his presence rather than noise.

Now, as she slipped on a robe and shuffled back to the master bathroom, she realized Dan was gone. With pounding heart, she checked Ted's room. He was gone as well. Laura felt a sudden surge of adrenaline as she ran to the top of the stairs, then stopped as she heard the sound of quiet voices. Dan and Ted were in the kitchen, talking. She was weak with relief.

She tried to will her heart to stop pounding so hard. She was on an emotional roller coaster that was tearing her apart and knew instinctively that something had to be done soon, or she'd be the one needing professional help.

She went into the bathroom and looked in the mirror. The face that stared back at her seemed like that of a stranger. Her eyes were red and puffy and large bags had developed beneath them. She smiled to herself bitterly. Last night she'd talked about Dan's alcoholism, but this morning, it was she who looked like the drunk.

She was due in court at nine to finalize the Gilbert case. She had time, so she showered much longer than usual, letting cold water, as cold as she could stand, run on her face for three long minutes. Then, shivering, she toweled off briskly to bring some warmth back. She quickly blow-dried her hair and applied her makeup. Fifteen minutes later she looked almost human again.

After dressing, she went down to the kitchen. Dan had left and Ted was sitting at the table, looking lost.

"What's the matter?" she asked.

"Dad went to work," he said softly.

"Oh." She poured herself some coffee. "You think I might be lying to you?"

He looked away.

"Did you discuss it with him?"

He shook his head.

"He never said anything to you?"

"No. All he said was he was going to work and tell them that he was accepting the job. He said he'd be home about noon for lunch." Dan often came home at noon for lunch—or a drink.

Laura peered at him over her coffee cup. "I didn't say he *was* fired. I simply said it was a possibility, but I think we need to know for sure before this goes any further. Tell you what, why don't you call your father at work about ten?"

Ted made a face. "That's like spying," he said.

"I guess it is in a way, but we have to know, don't we?"

He shrugged.

"Ted," Laura said softly, "you're almost a man. It's time you knew the truth, if that's what it is. You can't make important decisions unless you know the truth, and I know that's what's running through your mind. If your father has lied to you, it would change some things, wouldn't it?"

"I guess," he said unenthusiastically.

Laura looked at her watch. "I have to go to court to sign some papers," she said. "Then I have to stop by the office. I should be through by eleven. Why don't we do this? As soon as I get home, I'll make the call with you at my side. Would that be better?"

"What do we do if he isn't at work?" he asked.

"Nothing," she said. "We'll wait until he comes home. We'll talk to him together. By sticking together, we just might be able to make an impression. We'll tell him how much we love him and how much we want him to be well. We'll tell him we understand how hurt he is, that losing his job is terrible, but we have to stick to our guns and explain that he'll never hold a job unless he gets some professional help. Then, we'll tell him we know he's a good man and a wonderful father and how much we want this family to be a family again."

"What if he says he won't take treatment?" Ted asked.

"Let's take it a step at a time," she said. "That's all we can do."

Ted let out a deep sigh and nodded. Laura gave him a hug and a kiss, then headed for court.

As promised, Springer had the documents ready—and the checks. Holmes was subdued as he signed. Judge Fry added his signature and Laura was out of court in less than ten minutes. She stopped off at Ruth's house, gave her copies of the documents and her check, begged off having a small celebration, then headed for her office.

When she walked in, Kim Traubell, her secretary, said, "What happened? When I came in this morning, I noticed the *voir dire* files still on your desk. I knew you'd never forget them, so I thought there must have been a last-minute postponement. Then the phone started ringing. They say you've won."

"News travels fast, doesn't it?" Laura said as she picked up the telephone pink slips and smiled at Kim. "We won, all right." She handed Kim copies of the court documents and the check. "You can deposit this check and pay some bills. While you're at it, you can write a bonus check for yourself for five hundred dollars for all the overtime you've logged on this thing."

Kim, a pert twenty-five-year-old, glowed. "Oh, thank you, Laura. It's so marvelous you won. They settled?"

"Yes. Last night. It was quite a scene. You would have loved it." Laura raised her arms and posed theatrically. "I was magnificent."

"You must have been," Kim said. Looking at the check, she let out a yelp. "Not bad! You get to keep thirty-three percent of this?"

"No. We have to write a check to Mrs. Gilbert for eighty thousand to reimburse her for her costs, but the rest is ours. I've already given Ruth the first of many checks she'll be receiving over the next ten years, plus they've agreed to continue paying her medical costs for two more years. It's all spelled out in the documents."

"Oh, Laura. I'm so happy for you. You've worked so *hard* on this. You really deserve it."

The phone rang. Kim picked it up, listened for

a moment, then slammed it down without saying a word.

"Who was that?" Laura asked, puzzled.

"Just a crank," she said. "We've had six or seven this morning. "

"Oh," she said, realizing instantly what the calls were about. "I'm sorry about that. It will probably get a lot worse before it gets better."

"I can handle it," Kim said. "When did this all happen? I knew about Wanda, but her killer . . ."

"Saturday," Laura told her. "Judge Fry asked me to take it as a personal favor. He's worried he may screw things up. It's his first murder trial and he's a little insecure."

"You've had a busy weekend," Kim said.

"I have indeed."

"Don't people realize that even the worst person in the world is allowed to have an attorney? What's the matter with them?"

"You'd be amazed how little most people understand about the law. Even the basics. They watch lawyers on television and think it's real. The few lawyers who even watch that stuff either fall on the floor laughing or throw up. The problem is, if they ever had a show that told it like it really was, nobody would watch. They'd be bored to tears."

As she started toward her office, she added, "Let's not let a few crank calls dim our happiness this morning. Speaking of our new client, I'd better call Dr. Taylor and see if he's still alive."

It took a few minutes to reach Rick. He sounded as tired as she felt. "Hello, Laura. I assume you're asking after Mr. Slocum."

"Slocum?"

"Haven't you talked to anyone this morning?"

"Not about this."

"Well, the troopers identified your client this morning," Rick said. "His name is John Slocum. Jim can give you the details."

"How's he doing?"

She heard Rick take in a deep breath, then expel the air. "We've almost lost him three times," he said wearily. "He's got a clot in his left lung that's giving us fits. Another in his left leg. We've had two codes during the night and frankly . . . I think we're swimming upstream. I had to operate to stop the internal bleeding and I'm having a hell of a time stabilizing his platelet count. I can't remember when I've worked so hard to save someone."

"Has he said anything?"

"He mumbles some, but no one can make heads or tails of it. He's totally out of it. I think we've got a handle on the infection, but this guy is hanging by a thread, believe me."

"You'll let me know what happens . . . whatever happens?"

"Of course."

Laura found Jim Pickett in his office. "I heard you identified my client," she said.

Jim gave her a strange look. "I got nothing to do with this now. You'll have to talk to Chris or the troopers."

The air conditioners were growling normally, but the chill in the air was not due to their efficiency. "What's the matter, Jim?" she asked.

"Nothing."

"It's not nothing," she insisted. "If you're angry with me, there must be a reason. We've been friends a long time. I think I deserve to know what's wrong."

He winced. "Laura, I know we're friends, and I want to keep it that way. The problem is . . . this thing with Slocum. This may be bigger than we thought. If I were you, I'd get off this case right now." She could almost feel the heaviness in his voice.

"Bigger? What are you talking about?"

Jim stood up and stuffed his hands in his pockets. "I can't tell you, Laura. If you need information, it's going to have to come from Chris or the troopers. I've been told not to discuss this case with you. It's out of my jurisdiction, as I told you earlier. You'll just have to deal with the right people."

"Okay," she said. "If that's the way it has to be, then that's the way it will be."

Jim was staring out the window as she left the room. Chris Marshall's office was in the same building, but a different floor. She saw him standing in the hallway, in deep and quiet conversation with two men who looked like troopers, though they were dressed in civilian clothes. When Chris saw her, he held a finger to his lips to end the discussion, then broke into a smile. "Good morning, Laura."

Arching his eyebrows, he said, "This is Laura Scott, gentlemen."

The two men introduced themselves and shook hands with Laura. As she'd surmised, they were troopers.

"I understand you've identified my client," she said.

One of the troopers, a lieutenant named Cox, said, "We have tentatively identified the suspect as

John Slocum, resident of Buffalo, New York. At the moment, we don't have verification, but as soon as we do, you'll be notified."

"Thank you," Laura said. "Is there something else you'd like to tell me?"

"Like what?"

"Is there more to this than the murder of Wanda Brooks?"

"What makes you ask that?"

"I just got the cold shoulder from Jim Pickett. He told me that I have to get my information from official channels. He wouldn't have done that unless this case is more than it appears to be. He suggested I talk to you people."

Cox stiffened. "He did, eh? Well, it's a little premature, Mrs. Scott. This investigation is just getting started. We have nothing official at this point, but we'll want to talk to your client as soon as possible."

"That might prove difficult," she said. "Dr. Taylor says he may not make it."

Cox looked at Chris, then back at Laura. "I certainly hope that doesn't happen. It's very important that Mr. Slocum, if that's who he is, makes it. Very important."

"Why are you being so mysterious?" Laura asked. "What's the big secret? If there's something more to this, it'll come out soon enough. I'm his attorney. Don't you think I have a right to know?"

Cox was about to respond, but Chris put a hand on the trooper's arm. "It's no big deal, Laura," he said. "As you might expect, we've been in touch with several police departments while we've been trying to identify this guy. Buffalo has responded to one query and claims the man is John Slocum.

Details are being forwarded later today. Some other police departments have become interested because of the photo we faxed and an article that appeared in the Orlando paper yesterday." He grinned. "You know how it goes. Whenever there's a brutal killing like this one, police departments with unsolved murders or missing persons cases like to stick their oars in the water. It's just routine."

Laura pressed it. "Other jurisdictions have an interest in this? What have we got here?"

"There's nothing to get exercised about at this point. I think Jim, being a small-town cop, hasn't had much exposure to this kind of thing, so he's overreacting a tad."

It was much more than routine, and Laura knew it. There was an air of anticipation in the room that was almost palpable. She resented being patronized, but understood it. Until there was some clear evidence, there was no need to be overly concerned by silly attempts to keep information under wraps. At this point, her only access to information was that relating to the identity of her client and the evidence relating to the murder of Wanda Brooks. The troopers were within their rights to withhold anything else not directly connected to the charges already made.

"We'll be in touch," Lt. Cox said, dismissing her.

"Thank you," she said, bristling. "For the record, should my client live, there'll be no interviews without my presence, clear? It doesn't matter what the interviews are about. Slocum, or whatever his name is, has requested I be present during any interview."

Cox smiled. "That's not what I hear."

"Really? What did you hear?"

"I heard that your client wants a man to represent him. Maybe you should give him a break and give him his wish."

Laura's face reddened. "Is it just me, or do you dislike all women, Lieutenant?"

"It's not a question of gender, Counselor. I don't like lawyers who assume the police don't know the law. We keep abreast of the changes and we don't need to be told what they are by you. Next time you wanna make a beef, wait until someone screws up before you try to make us look bad in front of a judge."

"Someone did screw up," she snapped. "I don't expect to be given a hard time by one of your people when I see my client. I was. It better not happen again."

His face was impassive. "Anything else?" he asked.

"No."

"Then don't let us keep you."

It was almost eleven before Laura got home. Before getting out of the car, she thought about her earlier conversation with Ted. For a moment she vacillated, wondering if it really was spying, as Ted had suggested. Perhaps it would be better if . . . No. Ted had to know the truth. She got out of the car.

When she walked into the house, a sixth sense told her something was very wrong. She called Ted's name three times as she wandered through the house looking for him. No answer. The sense of foreboding deepened, and when she finally found the note stuck to the refrigerator in Ted's handwriting, she felt the air go out of her lungs. The note read, "I'm sorry, Mom. Dad really needs me right now. He's really low and I can't just let him go all by himself. Try to understand, okay? I'll call as soon as I can."

Her heart pounding, Laura raced up the stairs and into Ted's room, flinging open the closet door looking for his suitcase. It was gone. So were some of his clothes. She ran into the master bedroom, into the large double closet. Dan's suitcase was gone, as well as some of his clothes.

Still not wanting to believe her eyes, Laura hurried to the garage. Dan and Ted's fishing gear was gone. Back in the house, she looked for the baseball card collection. Gone. Finally accepting reality, Laura sank to her knees on the thick carpet and banged her fists in frustration. Her own son had lied to her. Clearly, Dan and Ted had discussed this, possibly as late as this morning. Ted had betrayed her best intentions. She buried her face in her hands.

A half hour later Laura was back at her office, considering her options. Essentially, she had two: she could swear out a complaint and have both Dan and Ted forcibly brought back, or she could do nothing.

The first option meant that the entire family would then be in the grip of the system, with all its attendant bureaucratic—and public—machinations. How would Ted react? Laura thought she knew the answer to that question. He would turn against her with a vengeance and possibly be lost to her forever. She was about to lose one child. She didn't want to lose them both.

If she did nothing, there was a chance—slim at best—that Dan might have second thoughts. There was also a chance that Ted, being fully exposed to his father's drunkenness twenty-four hours a day, would tire of what he initially had perceived as adventure. Deprived of the comforts of home, forced to care for himself as well as his father, he might well conclude that being on the run was not as exciting as he first thought.

For almost an hour, Laura weighed both options carefully, then made her decision. She would wait it out awhile. But she needed answers to some questions. What was Dan using for money? Had he really been fired? Had he really run away, or was he simply testing her will?

First, she telephoned Dan's boss, a man named Lou Hawkins. It took some doing, but with some prodding, they finally reached him in one of the hangars. Lou had been a guest in their home several times and she liked the man. She was sure he'd be truthful with her.

"Lou," she said, "I hate to bother you, but I have to ask a couple of questions. You don't mind?"

"I'll tell you what I can," he said, sounding impatient.

Laura got right to the nub. "Was Dan fired?"

"He didn't tell you?"

"No," she said, her heart sinking. "When did this happen?"

"About . . . let me see . . . it was a week ago last Friday."

Laura was stupefied. All last week, Dan had acted like a man going off to work. A complete charade.

"That long ago?" she asked, her voice unsteady.

"There was nothing we could do, Laura. Dan knows the rules. Three times and you're out with this company."

Again, he'd taken her by surprise. "Three times?" she asked.

Their conversation was interrupted by the sound of an F-16 firing up in the background. When the fighter finally taxied away, Lou said, "The 'three times' rule, Laura. Drinking on the job. Dan's been warned before, but I guess it didn't register. One of the inspectors caught him in the men's room with a bottle for the third time. It meant automatic dismissal. There was nothing I could do. I hope you understand."

"I'm not blaming you, Lou," she said. "Has he picked up his last check yet?"

"He picked it up this morning," he said. "It took over a week to be processed. There were pension payouts and some sick time stuff. It had to come from Detroit."

"And it came this morning?"

"Actually, it came Friday, but Dan picked it up this morning."

"Can you tell me how much it was?"

"Laura, I'm in one of the hangars. I'll have to talk to someone about that."

"Lou, it's really important. Can I hang on? Please?"

"All right," he said. "I'll put you on hold. This may take a few minutes."

"I'll wait."

When Lou came back on the line, he said, "Laura . . . I don't feel right about all this. It seems to me . . ."

She cut him off, a note of desperation in her voice.

"Lou, Dan's left town and he's taken our son with him. As you know, I'm an attorney. Please don't make this any more difficult than it has to be."

That got his attention. "Okay," he said. "You understand, Dan's been with the company a long time and all. What goes on between you two is none of our affair."

"How much?" she said.

"The check was for seventeen thousand three hundred. There was some severance that we really didn't have to pay, and then there was the pension money. He's been paying into a fund. That was the big part of it. He loses the company portion, of course, because of the firing."

She thanked Lou, pressed the hang-up button, then called the bank. She reached Sherrie in customer accounts. "Was Dan in there this morning?" she asked.

"Yes, he was, Mrs. Scott," she said cheerfully. "Cashed a pretty big check, in fact. Took most of it in traveler's checks. He said the three of you were going on a vacation. Where to?"

Laura simply played along. "We haven't decided yet, Sherrie. Did he take any other money?"

"Well, yes. He wrote checks on both the checking and the money market accounts."

"Can you tell me the balances right now? I think Dan and I got our signals crossed as to who was going to the bank. I don't want to write a bad check."

"I understand," Sherrie said. "This'll just take a minute." She was back quicker than that. "There's ten dollars even in each account. You're aware that we'll have to charge you a fee now. You're supposed to maintain a balance of . . ."

Laura hung up on her. She couldn't help it. Her cheerfulness was making Laura nauseous. Dan. The bastard! He'd gutted both accounts, small sums certainly, but it was the principle of the thing. Dan had no knowledge of the Gilbert settlement, yet he'd taken almost every dime in their joint accounts and left her with nothing. The mortgage was due in less than a week, along with the power bill, the phone bill, and some others. He'd planned on leaving her with nothing.

As angry as she was, Laura allowed herself a smile. Earlier today, Kim had deposited a check for two hundred fifty thousand dollars in the office general account. They had issued a check to Mrs. Gilbert for the eighty thousand, which left one hundred and seventy thousand dollars available to Laura. Laura had access to more money than she'd had at any time in her entire life. Sweet justice.

Later that night, arriving home to an empty house, Laura felt a sense of panic. Her imagination conjured up images of Dan and Ted lying dead in a shattered car. It was too much to bear alone. She called Gerry.

Gerry was there within minutes. For almost a half hour, she listened patiently. When Laura had finished, Gerry asked, "Have you eaten tonight?"

"I'm not hungry."

"That won't help. You have to eat. Sit here and read a book or something, while I cook you some dinner. Then we'll talk this out."

"Gerry, I really don't . . ."

"No arguments."

Laura leaned back on the sofa and closed her eyes. Gerry went into the kitchen and whipped up an omelette with potatoes and onions and herbs. Then she dragged Laura into the kitchen to eat it. As Laura ate, she said, "It seems to me you have only one choice. You say you don't know where Dan's going?"

"I haven't a clue. All I know is that he has enough money to go wherever he pleases. Did you ask Shirley about Ted?"

"Yes. She says Ted never mentioned a word about this. Not a word. That really surprises me."

"And me," Laura said. "I'm sure it was Dan's idea not to tell her, part of that paranoia you were talking about at the party."

"Does Dan have a passport?"

"Yes. It's upstairs in the bedroom dresser. Mine too."

"You eat," she said. "I'll go look."

In a moment she was back, the passports in her hand. "Well, at least we know he didn't leave the country. Think, Laura. You know the man. Where would he go?"

After a moment Laura said, "Probably back to Havre."

"That makes sense. Well, I don't think you have a choice at all. You'll worry yourself sick this way. You know Dan won't stop drinking."

Laura rubbed her temples. "But what about Ted? He'll hate me if I get the police involved in this."

"He may and he may not," Gerry said. "But that's beside the point, isn't it? Which would you rather have, a son who hates you or a son who's dead?

You're taking a terrible chance, Laura."

Her blunt logic brought Laura to her senses. "I really have to do it, don't I?"

"Yes," Gerry said, "you do."

Within an hour the arrest warrant for Dan had been sworn and sent out on the wire.

CHAPTER

11

AS THE FIRST FRESH RAYS OF SUNLIGHT BEGAN TO STREAM through the bedroom window, Laura was still wide awake. Even the sleeping pill she'd taken at three in the morning had failed to work. She sat up, rubbed her eyes, and tried to focus on the day ahead. First, a cold shower, then coffee, then some ice cubes under her eyes to deflate the bags.

She dragged herself to the bathroom and stayed under the cold needle spray for as long as she could stand it. When she finally stepped out of the shower, she could hear the doorbell being rung insistently.

She threw on a robe, ran down the stairs, and flung open the door. Gerry, leaning against the wall, said, "You look really terrific."

Laura turned away. "It was a long night."

"I'll bet." Gerry swept through the doorway and headed for the kitchen. "You need some coffee. Before you ask, I already checked. No word on Dan yet."

Over coffee, Gerry looked Laura up and down. "Let me guess," she said, "you spent the night blaming yourself for everything that's happened."

"How did you know?"

"Because we always think it's our fault. Maybe if we had done this or that, things would have been different. The truth is, Laura, the problem is Dan's alcoholism and his failure to accept it. Maybe, if you were the perfect woman, you might have delayed the inevitable for a time, but it's dumb to beat yourself up for being less than perfect. And even perfection would only delay, not prevent what's happened."

Laura held her head in her hand as she sipped the coffee. "I drove him to it."

"The hell you did," Gerry snapped. She sighed. "When you turn on yourself, you show no mercy. Come on, Laura. It's time to get real."

"I'm just facing facts."

"No you're not. Dammit, Laura. I've been to countless seminars on alcoholism. You've been to one or two. Take the time to research the subject and you'll find that you've got nothing to do with it. Nothing at all."

As Laura worked at her desk, she debated the wisdom of attending Wanda Brooks's funeral. Kim had suffered through several crank calls yesterday, and Laura's answering machine at home held others. If she went to the funeral, what purpose would it serve? Her physical presence would only intensify the level of hostility directed toward her, and sending flowers would seem hypocritical.

It was just another of many things Laura hated about the legal profession. She mourned the death of Wanda Brooks as much as any casual acquaintance. But, by acting as Wanda's alleged killer's lawyer, she was perceived as taking his side, becoming his champion, preparing to present arguments designed to obfuscate the truth and deny the vengeance so deeply sought.

Perceptions were sometimes more important than the truth. What was she to do? Go to the funeral and make a speech? Announce that she knew the man was guilty but just because she was doing her job didn't mean she . . . Impossible. The funeral of such a popular girl would bring out the best and the worst in this town, not to mention reporters. Laura knew her attendance would clearly be disruptive and that was the overriding consideration. The living, Grace and Harold, would feel terrible if the lawyer representing the man accused of butchering their daughter was there. Grieving parents could not be expected to judge in other than emotional terms. To ask more was inhuman. Laura made her decision. She would not go.

Kim stuck her head in the door. "Tom Ferris is here. Says it's urgent."

Laura stood up. "I'll talk to him out there."

She walked to the outer office. Ferris had a strange gleam in his eyes. "Tom, I have nothing to say to the press. I thought I made that clear."

"You did," he said. "This is about something else."

"What?"

"Can we talk in your office?"

Laura reluctantly ushered him in. Ferris sat across from her and leaned forward, charged with energy.

"What can I do for you?" Laura asked.

"You've got it reversed," he said.

"Pardon me?"

"I have something for you," he said, his eyes shining even more brightly.

"What is it?"

"I want something in return."

"Tom," she said tiredly, "it's too early in the day for games. Either speak your piece or take a hike."

"A little testy this morning, aren't we?"

Laura stood up, the expression in her eyes giving fair warning.

"All right," he said. "Hear me out."

She slowly resumed her seat.

"It seems your client is more than just an ordinary, garden-variety killer," he said, his tone conspiratorial, as if they were pals or something. "He might even be a serial killer."

His eyes were sparkling, as if this were good news. Perhaps, to a reporter in search of a story, it was. To Laura, it was revolting, and Tom's attitude was even more so.

"Where did you get that?" she asked as her mind flashed to memories of yesterday and the aborted conversation with Chris Marshall.

"I'll be happy to give you everything I have," Tom said, looking much too cocky, "but I want a deal, like I said."

"What kind of deal?"

He was almost panting with excitement. "I've been approached by a New York publisher," he said. "They called this morning. They're offering a book deal should this turn out to be a serial killing." He spread his hands in the air expansively. "I'm willing to share the wealth. You act as my agent and negotiate with these people. You also handle whatever legal stuff comes up—copyright protection and stuff like that—at your normal fee. And . . . you give me exclusive rights to your part of the story. In return, I'll act as your bird dog and give you a share of the book deal."

She just stared at him for a moment while she fought to control her temper. Then she said, "Tom, I can't be a part of this. If you have some information relative to this case, I'd like to hear it. If you don't want to tell me now, just wait. I'll subpoena you so fast your beard will fall off. But if you want to play games, play them somewhere else. I have no interest whatsoever in participating in the exploitation of Wanda's death. Understand?"

He looked crushed. "You're missing a big opportunity, Laura."

Her patience was exhausted. She pointed to the door. "Out!"

Ferris glared at her, then stood up and shuffled out of the office. Laura followed him and told Kim, "I'm going over to talk to Jim Pickett." Kim nodded, picked up the ringing phone, listened for a moment, then slammed it down.

"They're still coming in?" Laura asked.

"I'm afraid so. I was wondering . . . do you think I should go to the funeral?"

Laura put her hand on Kim's shoulder. "I think

you should. They're mad at me, not you. I should be back in less than an hour. The funeral's at two?"

"Yes."

"Well, you go. If I have to leave the office, I'll just lock up and put the machine on. No need to return after the funeral."

"Thanks, Laura," she said, looking relieved.

Jim kept Laura waiting for fifteen minutes, then came out and waved her into his office. "I thought I told you I was out of this," he said as he took his seat behind the battered green desk. The place was freezing, as usual. Jim's hair was standing at attention, thanks to a generous application of wax.

"You did," Laura said. "You also gave me the bum's rush, but that's not why I'm here. I just had a visit from Tom Ferris."

Jim looked interested.

"He says Slocum may be a serial killer," she went on. "Where did he get that?"

Jim grinned wryly. "He's one obnoxious son of a bitch, but you have to admit, he's pretty good for a small-town newspaper guy, don't you think?"

Laura made a face. "Jim, forget the fact we're friends. On a professional level, I shouldn't be getting this from some outsider. What's going on?"

The grin faded. "You should talk to Marshall. It's his case."

"I *have* talked to Marshall," she said, looking at the goose bumps popping up on her arms. "I'm getting nothing but fluff. Look, I'm not asking for information that won't be made available to me sooner or later. I'm not asking for anything confidential.

Surely I don't have to apologize to you for defending Slocum. If you don't know the score . . ."

"All right," he said, glowering, "but you never heard it from me, understand?"

"Of course."

"Have you read the final autopsy report?"

She shook her head. "Marshall said he'd send it over, but nothing's arrived so far. I haven't been pushing it because Rick's not at all sure Slocum will live. I hate to waste my time."

"Well," he said, "I've read it. It makes me very angry, Laura. It also makes me angry that I'm being frozen out on this thing. Somebody's adopted the attitude that I'm a stupid small-town cop liable to screw up an ongoing investigation." He slammed a fist on the table. "They have very short memories. If some of my anger gets transferred to you, I can't help it."

"I forgive you," she said, smiling.

"I wish you'd get out of this," he said. "I really do. They can bring someone else in. You're making a big mistake. The way I hear it, you don't need the money anymore, so why the hell don't you tell Fry to get someone else?" There were few secrets in Seminole Springs.

"That's not how it works, Jim, and you know it. Once you're appointed, you better have a damn good reason to pull out. What am I supposed to do? Go to Judge Fry and say I can't handle this because my drunken husband just took off with my son? I could kiss my law practice good-bye."

He hung his head. "I'm sorry we haven't found him yet. I sent out a second bulletin this morning when I came in, but you know how that goes. If the troopers are reading between the lines, they've already assumed this is a domestic problem. They hate getting involved in that stuff."

"I know," she said. "Forget Dan for the moment. Is Slocum a serial killer or not?"

He leaned forward, lowering his voice to the point it was barely audible above the rumble of the air conditioners. "The troopers faxed Slocum's photo all over the country when they were trying to get an ID. They heard back from Buffalo first. Someone there recognized the picture."

"He's got a record?"

"Not officially."

"Pardon me?"

He sighed, then said, "Ten years ago, when Slocum was eleven, he killed his mother during some kind of brawl. He claimed she was trying to kill him and was just protecting himself. The police investigation collaborated his story. They determined that Slocum had been regularly abused by his mother, physically and sexually. Family court reviewed the case and chose not to press charges, taking the position that Slocum was in fear of his life when he killed his mother. Since he had no other living relatives, he was placed in a children's home and given psychiatric counseling. They don't have all the details because the records are sealed, but we know that Slocum was released on his eighteenth birthday. He hasn't been officially seen in three years."

"Three years! You mean he's only twenty-one?"

"Uh-huh. I thought he was older. Looks it, doesn't he?"

"He does indeed. What else?"

He clasped his hands together in front of him.

"On Sunday, the Orlando paper did a story about the killing here and ran a photo of Wanda Brooks. Yesterday morning, when one of the state investigators got the information package that had been sent down from Buffalo, he noticed that the picture of Slocum's mother looked a hell of a lot like Wanda. The mother was older, of course, but she had the same hairstyle, eye structure, and basic facial features. They could've been mother and daughter. On a hunch, he faxed another message to about three hundred police departments asking two things: One—did they have any unsolved missing persons who matched the description of either Wanda or the Slocum woman? Two—did they have any outstanding warrants for a man fitting the description of Slocum?"

He took a deep breath, then said, "Last night, the shit hit the fan. They heard from three different police departments. Three cases that fit the profile. Three missing girls, all of whom look a little like Wanda—and three suspect descriptions, all of which match Slocum in some ways: long hair, young, skinny. Right now, it's all conjecture, but when you consider Slocum's been out of touch for three years, it's possible. When you consider his background, it's even more possible. Naturally, there's some idea that this thing may turn out to be the biggest case this county has ever had. That's why Marshall and the state guys want me out of it. They have that right, because Wanda was killed outside town, but I think some egos are getting primed here. That's why I want you out of this, Laura. If my hunch is right, this whole thing's gonna turn into a circus. I don't think you need that right now."

Laura started to shiver, more from the coldness of the room than this new, disturbing information. "Jim," she said, "I can't take this anymore."

He beamed. "You're gonna talk to Fry?"

"That isn't what I mean," she said. "I'm talking about your office. It must be forty degrees in here. I'd like to talk some more, but if I stay in here, I'll catch pneumonia."

He grinned. "Works every time."

"Pardon me?"

"Fact is, I hate being stuck in this office and I hate long conversations. I keep it cold in here for a reason. That way, nobody stays longer than three or four minutes."

She grabbed her attaché case. "I never realized you had that cruel a streak in you. So, you think there's a chance that Slocum is involved in these other cases?"

He was standing now, looking earnest. "Laura, cops from three cities are flying down today and the fax machines are running overtime. I understand there are queries from other police departments that have come in just this morning. I've got a feeling this is Big Time. You'll be covered in shit if you stay with this. A brutal serial killer. Hell, they'll run you out of town. If you were getting paid, I could understand it, but you're doing this for peanuts. What's the goddamn attraction? You're no headline grabber. That just isn't you."

"I'm not after anything, Jim," she said. "I told you why I took the case. Judge Fry asked me to defend this guy because it's Fry's first murder case. He wants to make sure he doesn't screw up."

"On-the-job training? Is that what he wants?"

"We all have to start somewhere, Jim. The public defenders have no capital experience. If Slocum is convicted and gets a new lawyer after the trial, there's a good chance he can plead incompetent representation. If, on the other hand, Fry brings in an experienced defense lawyer from out of town, the guy might use Fry's inexperience to get away with all sorts of things. I understand what he's trying to do, and I'm going to do my best to help him."

Jim was about to respond, but a female officer stuck her head in the door. "Laura," she said, "there's a call for you. Line three."

Jim pointed to the phone. "Be my guest."

Laura rubbed her arms for a moment to get the blood moving, glared at the air conditioners, then picked up the receiver. "This is Laura Scott," she said.

"Laura, this is Dr. Carter."

Her heart stopped beating.

"You asked me to contact you directly if anything happened," he said. "Your office told me where to reach you."

"Yes?"

He got right to the point. "She's gone, Laura. About fifteen minutes ago. There was no pain, I'm sure. I'm very sorry."

She could feel that awful tightness in her chest again, more severe than ever. It took her breath away. She was almost unaware of Dr. Carter asking, "Do you want to come in and make the arrangements yourself or would you rather I looked after some of it for you?"

"I'll be in," she said. "Please don't move her until I've had a chance to see her."

"I won't," he said. "I'll wait here for you."

"Thank you, Doctor," she said as she hung up the phone.

She felt Jim's stare. "Victoria?" he asked simply.

"She's dead, Jim."

He rubbed his forehead. "Jeez. I'm real sorry, Laura. Real sorry."

Laura took a deep breath. "It's strange," she said. "I've been expecting this for a long time. Yet, now that it's finally happened, I'm still surprised. Does that make any sense?"

He didn't answer. He just moved around in front of his desk and took her in his arms. She laid her head against his chest and shook with sobs.

"I'll call Ethel," he said softly. "She can drive you."

Just over an hour later, Laura was standing by her daughter's hospital bed, staring down at her lifeless form. Victoria looked so frail lying in the bed. Laura had thought she would seem at peace, but she didn't. The loveliness she'd chosen to see when the child was alive had vanished, replaced by a gauntness Laura had refused to accept until this very moment. Just as Dan continued to delude himself about his drinking, Laura had deluded herself about Victoria's appearance. Now, in death, she looked more like a freshly unwrapped Egyptian mummy than her own flesh and blood. The reality of her death finally struck Laura with the force of a hammer blow.

She placed the back of her hand against Victoria's cheek and felt the coldness, jerking it away as if she'd suddenly touched flame. There are times when the senses become confused.

The frayed teddy bear still lay on the pillow by

Victoria's head. Laura picked it up and held it close for a moment, then leaned over and placed her head beside Victoria's on the pillow. "I'm so sorry," she whispered.

She spent about five minutes with her daughter, saying good-bye, feeling totally lost, and more angry than she'd ever felt in her life—at Victoria for dying, at Dan for leaving, and at herself for allowing herself to be talked into taking Slocum's case. She left the room and fell into the arms of a weeping Ethel, who'd been waiting in the hall. Ethel helped her find her way to Dr. Carter's office.

Laura told him where she wanted Victoria's body sent. He made a note, even though it really wasn't his job, but he was a caring man. Then, Ethel put her arm around Laura and escorted her to the parking lot.

The two women leaned against the car for a moment and listened to the distant thunder of a building storm, not saying anything, while Laura tried to get a grip on emotions. "We have to get back," she said finally.

The highway entering Seminole Springs from the north passed the cemetery, where the funeral for Wanda Brooks had already moved. Hundreds of cars were parked on either side of the road. Laura looked past the wrought-iron fence and saw a mass of humanity by the graveside. It seemed as if the entire town was there. How many people would be there for Victoria?

CHAPTER

12

GERRY AND ETHEL STAYED WITH LAURA. THE CAINS came to pay their respects, without mentioning where they'd heard the news. The Braddocks called, as did the Smiths, and two other couples from down the street dropped by. By midnight, Laura felt much better, but Gerry and Ethel insisted on staying the night. Laura had to practically push them out of the house. She gave them both a hug and told them she'd be fine. "My parents arrive tomorrow. I'll have plenty of company."

"When do they get in?" Gerry asked.

"Two in the afternoon."

"Do you want me to take you to the airport?"

"No," she said, "I can do it. Really, I'm fine."

They reluctantly said good night. Laura went

upstairs and crawled into bed. Exhausted, she was asleep in minutes.

She spent the next morning at the office, going over a stack of files that Chris Marshall had forwarded, all related to John Slocum. As Laura read through the material, there was no doubt in her mind that her client was, indeed, a serial killer. There were now a total of thirteen cases that seemed tied to him. She finally put the file aside and delved into something less distasteful, her preparation work for a pending civil suit, pertaining merely to money, not human lives. In a small corner of her soul, there was the niggling hope—a hope wrapped in a thin layer of guilt for thinking it—that John Slocum would die, and she'd never have to actually deal with this increasingly despicable case. She ate a sandwich for lunch, then steeled herself for the trip to Orlando airport to pick up her parents.

It had been four years since Laura had seen them, two people dedicated to their work, their church, and not much else. Stolid, with demeanors as cold as the harsh Havre, Montana winters, they displayed little affection to either each other or Laura, but Laura had inherited personality traits from somewhere in the family tree that set her apart. Even as a child she was aware that much was missing from her life.

It was more than just the lack of affection. Her parents read the supermarket tabloids and listened to country music on the battered radio that sat atop the mantel. No books or daily newspapers, not even a television set deterred their strange need to be isolated from the world that lay beyond the wire fences of their micro-universe. When, at the age of sixteen, Laura announced she wanted to become a lawyer, she was treated as though she'd declared her desire to be a prostitute.

Her father, unable to dissuade her, adamantly refused to help her financially, and Laura had worked her way through college and law school by taking a succession of jobs. For seven years, she'd lived on five hours of sleep or less a night, but she'd made it.

The relationship had always been an ordeal. Laura, reaching the limit of her humanitarianism, had confined her contact with her parents to letter or phone, to the point where the last two times Dan had returned to Havre to see his parents, he'd been forced to go without Laura. Laura knew she was letting him down, but her antipathy toward her parents was stronger than her need to please a husband who seldom tried to please her.

If Laura had followed the true dictates of her heart, she wouldn't have revealed to her parents that Victoria had died. She knew they would make the long trip from Havre to Seminole Springs to attend the funeral, not because of any special love for their grandchild, but because their strict moral code demanded attendance at the funerals of family members. With their presence in Laura's home would come a barrage of unanswerable questions, unless Laura put them up at a hotel, an unacceptable breach of her personal moral code.

Convention, she thought, was the engine that drove us all; different paths, different results, but the roads were traveled nonetheless.

Now, as Laura watched them make their way down the ramp leading from the airplane clinging to each other for support, she perceived for the first time her parents as old and feeble. With this came sudden pangs of guilt. They were still her parents, after all. Perhaps, she thought, it was time to heal the wounds before it was too late.

Her mother had lost considerable weight, and the gauntness was almost frightening. Her father, on the other hand, had gained some. Both his hands, now badly afflicted with arthritis, were grotesquely mis-shapen and he walked with a severe limp, a legacy from a seemingly minor hip injury suffered years ago. Laura impulsively ran forward and embraced them both, telling them how glad she was to see them. Her parents who abhorred displays of affec-tion—public or private—seemed embarrassed.

They were gathering the bags at the carousel when her father first mentioned Dan, wondering aloud why he hadn't come to the airport.

"He's at work," Laura said.

"Too busy, I guess."

"He's been very busy," Laura agreed.

Not a word had been spoken about Victoria; not a single expression of sympathy or bereavement. It was as if they'd decided to take a Florida vacation on the spur of the moment, a ludicrous thought. Nor did they mention the child's death on the drive to Seminole Springs, choosing instead to bring Laura up-to-date on the lives of people she no longer remembered or cared about.

Once home, Laura made them comfortable in the living room, prepared coffee, and told them every-thing that had happened. The bare, unvarnished truth. She watched their eyes widen in shock as she piled fact upon fact, and when she finally ran out of things to say, they could do little but sit and stare at her. Finally, her father stood up, removed the jacket from the Sunday suit he'd worn on the plane, and laid it carefully on back of the sofa. Then he loosened his tie, took it off, and placed it on top of his jacket. He slowly rolled up his sleeves and resumed his seat. Beyond him, through the window, the sun disappeared behind quickly gathering clouds. Laura saw it as an omen.

Her father shook his head. "I just don't understand it," he said. "You sit there and you tell me that Dan is some no-good, when you know very well he ain't nothin' of the sort."

She had expected nothing less. "You think I'm lying to you?" she asked.

"I don't remember you bein' much of a liar, Laura. I'll say that for you. But when a man and a woman split up, it's for a reason, and that reason ain't that one or the other is always to blame. It's usually that both people are to blame. Naturally, since you're the only one we've had the chance to talk to, we're hearing your side of things. I ain't about to make a comment until I hear Dan's side of it."

"That's very honorable of you," she said. "Perhaps you have a way of finding him. Then you can hear his side."

Her father dug into his jacket pocket and removed his pipe and tobacco. He filled the pipe, lit a match to it, and leaned forward. "You really called the police in on this?"

She sighed in exasperation and frustration. Thoughts of reconciling with her parents were turning into almost invisible wisps. Four decades of bitter, barely repressed resentment were taking charge of her emotions. "I called them before Victoria died. What else was I supposed to do? It would be irresponsible of me to sit and do nothing."

"You coulda waited until he called you," her father said. "You know Dan ain't gonna stay away long. By callin' in the police, you've shamed everyone, includin' yourself. This whole town knows your business, and that ain't too smart. I'da thought you'd have more sense than that."

"It's even more important that he be reached, now that Victoria's dead," Laura said. "I think Dan and Ted should be here for the funeral. Don't you?"

"Of course they should. If you hadn't pushed him so much, he'd be here now. Truth is, if Dan saw fit to leave you like that, you probably gave him cause. Dan was always a responsible type of person, and this talk about him being liquored up all the time just don't sit well with me."

"So, you think I'm lying?"

"I didn't say that."

She was close to the edge. "Yes, you did," she said. "You forget what it was like the last time we visited Havre together. I poured Dan into bed early every night. He could hardly walk, and that was four years ago. He's just gotten worse."

Her father looked at his pipe for a moment, then stuck it back in his mouth. "I remember very well. He didn't seem drunk to me. He was tired, that's all."

"Tired?"

"Yes, tired. I think you make too much of things, Laura. You were always strong-willed. You like to have things your way. You make it hard on a man to breathe."

"Why are you here?" she asked.

Her father stared at her. "What?"

"Why are you here?"

"That's a stupid question."

"No, it isn't. I called you yesterday and told you my daughter, your only granddaughter, had just died. You said you'd fly in for the funeral. I'm asking you why you decided to do that."

"It's only fittin' and proper," he said, seemingly bewildered by such a stupid question.

"Really? Fittin' and proper? But it's okay to tell me I'm responsible for everything that's happened. Don't you think it's fittin' and proper to show some respect for a daughter who has just suffered the death of her child?" She held up a hand, "No, strike that. Respect is the wrong word. Let's try compassion." Again, she held up a hand. "Strike that as well. Let me put this another way. I don't want your criticism, understand?"

"I'm not criticizing you," he said.

"No? It's been scarcely an hour since you arrived, and already you've blamed me for Dan's leaving, called me a liar, and said I don't know what I'm talking about. Well, I had to live with your blind ignorance when I was a child, but I don't have to live with it now." She stood up quickly, her emotions a curious mixture of hot and cold; her stomach churning like an old-fashioned ice cream maker, the blood in her veins running hot, like liquid fire. "I'm forty years old," she said. "I've lost a daughter, a husband, and a son, all in a matter of hours. I might as well make it a clean sweep and cut the umbilical cord that still seems to tie me to you. You either show me some respect or haul yourself back to Havre this very minute. Understand?"

She pointed a trembling finger at her stunned father. "You haven't expressed a scintilla of sorrow over Victoria's death. You're a heartless, stubborn, insensitive man. I understand why you like Dan so much. You're two peas in a pod. Well, you hear this. Dan's a drunk. An unemployed drunk. Our marriage is over, and it *isn't* my fault. You're free to believe what you want, but you won't tear me up in my house again. Ever again."

He was slack-jawed, his eyes wide, his expression one of complete shock.

And then the phone rang. Laura briefly considered letting the machine take the call while she finished what she had to say to her parents. With a grunt, she whirled, walked into the kitchen, and answered the phone. It was Chris.

"Laura," he said, "I realize this is a terrible time. I'm so sorry about Victoria. My deepest condolences."

"Thanks, Chris," she said. "You're very kind."

"Not so kind," he said. "I know this is a bad time, but I can't do anything else."

"What are you talking about?"

He hesitated for a moment. "Rick Taylor says your client is well enough to be interviewed. I just got off the phone with him. If it was just me, I'd let it go for a couple of days, but we have some visitors who want to talk to him as well, and they just aren't in the mood to wait. I know it's rough, but it has to be today."

"It doesn't have to be done at all," she said. "No one has the right to interview my client once he's been charged. You know that."

She heard him sigh. "I realize that, Laura. Look,

this isn't your normal dog and pony show. I was hoping you'd help us out a bit. You'll be there, of course, and I know you'll tell your client not to say anything incriminating. Hell, these people just want a look at the guy, really."

"They can look at pictures," she said.

Another sigh. "Laura, give me a break. There are missing girls involved here. This guy may be some sort of monster. As far as the Wanda Brooks matter is concerned, I've got everything I need or ever will need. All I'm asking is that you bend a little. In the long view, it's not going to make much difference to your client, but it could sure make a difference in the lives of some very innocent people."

"Unless he talks," she said, "and I won't allow that."

For a moment Chris was silent. Laura mulled things over. Normally, a criminal defense attorney wouldn't expose her client to possible self-incrimination. Too risky. But this *was* a different case, as Chris had pointed out. There was little question Slocum was guilty of killing Wanda. Accepting that was no breach of trust. Slocum had the right to be protected by his attorney, but as long as his rights were protected, what was the harm in allowing him to be interviewed by other jurisdictions? If he started to talk, she could end the interview immediately. As a rule, it was often wise for a criminal attorney to cooperate with law enforcement authorities whenever such cooperation did no harm to a client. That was how relationships were developed, deals made, and justice done—in the real world.

"I want to see him first," she said, finally.

"Certainly."

"How many visitors?"

A pause. "Fourteen."

She felt her heart begin to pound. That was one more than just this morning.

"I think there'll be more," he said as though reading her mind, "but right now, we've got fourteen that look real positive, and another twenty that I think are just shots in the dark. I'll have someone bring over copies of the latest one."

"We can't have fourteen people interviewing Slocum today," she said. "He's barely off the critical list."

"I know," he said. "We'll do what we can, take it a day at a time."

"I'll go over to the hospital now," she said. "After I've talked to him, you and your people can start to have at him, provided he's still able to talk and I'm there."

"That'll be fine, Laura. You call the shots."

She looked at her watch. "It's three-thirty now. I'll be there in five minutes. You can see him at five, if Rick allows it."

"That's fine," he said. "Again, I'm sorry to have to do this to you, Laura, but . . ."

"It's okay, Chris. The world doesn't stop for anyone. I know that."

She went back in the living room and faced her still shocked parents. "I have some things to do," she said. "Your room is the one with the fresh towels on top of the bed. I'm sorry I have to rush out, but the police want to talk to that man I told you about and I must be there. I should be home in a few hours. Why don't you rest for a while?"

They just stared at her.

* * *

Fifteen minutes later Laura Scott had her second look at John Slocum, and her first real colloquy. He was recovering, albeit slowly, with considerable pain in his chest and leg from the clots, more pain in his stomach from the operation and the other internal damage, but his chances for survival had improved from fifty-fifty to eighty-twenty. Rick had said the clot in the lung had dissolved and the healing process begun, but three more in the leg were worrisome, stubbornly remaining in place. There was a chance circulation in the leg could be completely blocked, which would mean the leg would have to come off. There was also a chance one of the clots, or a part of it, would break loose, travel to the brain, and cause a severe stroke that would either kill or completely incapacitate Slocum. In view of Slocum's condition, Rick had limited visitors. All interviews were to be concluded by six P.M.

Slocum was sitting up. The drainage tubes were still in place, as was the IV, but the oxygen tube in his nose had been taken away. One of his arms and the good leg were still shackled to the bed. The other leg was heavily wrapped, elevated, and looked to be twice normal size. His hair had been washed and tied back in a ponytail with a rubber band. Parts of his face had been shaved, and the boils marring the rest had scabbed over. He looked frail and sick, but there was more color in his face than she'd seen the first time.

As she neared the bed, his gaze washed over her like a sudden spray of ice-cold water. Though she was a stranger to him, she saw hatred in his eyes.

Her other senses told her she was in the presence of pure, almost palpable-evil.

"I'm Laura Scott," she said, sitting on the chair beside the bed. "You probably don't remember, but I was here before. I'm your lawyer."

His small, ratlike eyes held her. "I don't remember," he said.

"You were a little under the weather," she said.

He looked down at his wrist, then raised his arm a few inches. "They got me tied up like an animal. What for?"

"You don't know?"

"No, I don't." His voice was still hoarse from the abrasions caused by a variety of tubes shoved down his throat during treatment. "You sent here by the law?"

She nodded.

"I don't want no bitch as my lawyer."

"Why not?"

"I want a man," he said. "Don't want no bitch."

"Is that what women are . . . bitches?"

He looked at her impassively for a moment, then said, "Fuck you."

"John," she said, "don't waste your breath trying to insult me. It can't be done."

While he tried to determine the strength of that pronouncement, Laura let her gaze wander over the room. Blue-white pristine, and unlike other rooms in this hospital, there was no television or radio to be seen. The brackets were still on the wall, but the television set had been removed. She wondered who'd done that.

"You're under arrest for the murder of a very sweet girl," she said. "You can scream, yell, curse, do whatever you want, but you won't get loose of those shackles and you won't get another lawyer. I'm it. If you don't like it, that's too bad. No one really cares much what you like. You're lucky to be alive—maybe. To be frank, I think it would have been better if you hadn't made it, but you have, and now we all have to deal with that fact.

"A very good doctor has been busting his tail to save your life. Now, a very good lawyer is going to bust hers to prevent you from being executed. You probably don't appreciate it and you probably never will, but it doesn't matter. You're just part of the system now, just like you were until three years ago. It probably failed you then and it probably will fail you now, but nobody really gives a damn, except me.

"If you cooperate with me," she continued, "it'll make things easier. If you don't, I'm still going to be your lawyer. I'm still going to defend you. So, do you want to talk about what happened or not?"

His eyes glazed over. "What'd you mean when you said about three years ago?"

"I know something about you," she said. "I know that you were abused by your mother almost from the day you were born. I know that when you were eleven, you killed her in self-defense. You were sent to a children's home in Buffalo where you remained until the age of eighteen. Upon your eighteenth birthday, you were released and nobody's seen you since. Well, almost nobody.

"There are fifteen police officers in town eager to speak with you, fourteen of whom are from other parts of the country. They say they have witnesses who *have* seen you. So far, I've managed to keep them away from you, but in about an hour, some of them will be allowed to start questioning you. I want you to know that you don't have to say anything to them, and you're allowed to have me there when they talk to you. You can insist on that, and if I'm not available, you can make them wait until I am."

"What the hell they want with me?"

She ignored the question. "Right now," she said, "I want to talk about what happened the night you were shot."

He grunted. "They sayin' I killed that girl?"

"Uh-huh."

"That's bullshit. I never killed her."

"No?"

"No. All I remember was I was takin' a crap in the woods and I seen this girl lying on the ground. There was a knife stuck in her chest. I was takin' a look to see what happened when somebody shot me. That's all I know." The lies rolled from his tongue like melted butter.

Laura knew that a true psychopath is the greatest of all liars. Just as a dead person is no longer capable of feeling physical pain, a psychopath, unburdened by the twin weights of conscience and remorse, is incapable of experiencing psychological distress. It was one reason lie detector tests are rarely admitted as evidence in a courtroom. A psychopath will beat a lie detector every time. The stories they tell can be real or imagined. To them, there is simply no difference.

"Really?" she said. "That's it?"

"That's it."

She stood up, walked over to the window, and listened to the fat drops of rain beating a tattoo on the glass. Trees swayed as moderate to heavy gusts of wind swept through the area. Flashes of lightning seared the gray clouds, followed by heavy, rolling thunderclaps. One, two seconds apart. The storm was close now, almost directly overhead. She turned and leaned against the wall, facing Slocum. "Let me fill you in on what they have, John. Okay?"

He didn't respond.

"When they brought you in," she said, "you were almost dead. They took some blood samples and had them analyzed. They took some seminal fluid found in the body of the victim and had it analyzed as well. Just to be sure, they did a DNA test on the seminal fluids. Do you know what a DNA test is?"

"No."

"Well, I won't bore you with the technical aspects, but it's a test that's more accurate than a simple blood test. More like fingerprints. The chances of them being wrong are about one in a billion. It goes over very big with juries.

"I'll tell you something else that goes over big with juries. When they put a doctor on the stand and he shows them pictures of the dead girl, and describes everything you did to her—the burns, the cuts, the bruises—before you killed her, they won't listen to another word I say. They'll tune me out, John. No matter what I say, they won't believe a word of it. Did I tell you that the DNA fingerprints match?"

He never batted an eye.

"So, what they have is this," she continued, "your sperm in her vagina and her rectum, her blood all over you. They have a knife with your prints and her blood on it, and a witness who swears he saw you by the body with a knife in your hand." She sighed. "They have enough to fry you fifty times, John."

She walked toward the bed. "Now, I'm a very good lawyer, but as good as I am, there's a very strong chance you'll be convicted and sentenced to death in the electric chair. Two thousand volts of high-amp electricity will cook you like a chicken in a microwave oven. Your hair will burst into flames and your fingernails will turn black. You'll die, John Slocum, unless you cooperate with me.

"You've got one chance to live out your life and one chance only. You cut the crap, be straight with me, and let me work my magic. If you do, maybe I can save you from the chair. If you don't cooperate with me, there's absolutely no question you'll die very young. If you think you'll have a better chance with some other lawyer, think again. I'm the best there is in this town and the judge will refuse to kick me off the case no matter what you think or say, so you're stuck with me. You'd better get used to it."

"I know my rights."

"You don't know shit," she said. "You're a stone killer without a soul and we both know that. I know why but it doesn't matter. I've got a job to do and that's what I'm about."

It was the first time she saw any expression in his eyes. "You think you're tough, huh?"

"No. I'm not tough. Not the way you think of tough anyway. Why don't you tell me what happened?"

"You're so fuckin' smart, you tell me."

She sat beside the bed again. "Okay. You were hitchhiking along the highway around eight o'clock

a week ago last Friday. A girl named Wanda Brooks
. . . Did you know her name, John?"

No answer. No expression. He simply stared at
her.

"Well, Wanda stopped and picked you up. God
only knows why. You got in the car and drew a
knife. You told her to take you somewhere south of
the city. She did. When you saw the woods and the
access road leading to it, you told her to turn in.
She did. Once you were out of sight of the highway,
you both got out of the car and walked into the
woods. Once you found a clearing, you told her to
take her clothes off. She did. You took some duct
tape and taped her mouth and her wrists. Then
you raped her. That wasn't enough. You took some
time to torture her with the lighted end of a
cigarette. Then you slapped her around a bit. After
about half an hour, you raped her again, only this
time you used the back door. Then you tortured
her some more, by using the knife to make small
cuts all over her body. Pretty soon, she was so covered in blood you could hardly see her skin.

"Finally bored with it all, you took the duct tape
off her mouth so you could hear her scream once,
just before you stabbed her real hard that first
time. Before you killed her, you needed to hear her
scream. Curious. How am I doin', John?"

His gaze left her. He stared impassively at the
ceiling. Then, as if in slow motion, he broke into a
grin and chortled.

"You ain't very fuckin' smart at all. None of that
happened."

"You think it's funny?" she asked.

"You're what's funny," he said.

"Why?"

"You're so fuckin' prim and proper. 'Back door,' you called it, like it was a house or somethin'. You ever had it up your ass, lady?" He laughed again. "I'll bet not."

He kept on with it, the insults, the personal remarks, the specific references to her various body parts. He used the foulest of language and the most graphic descriptions, but Laura wasn't listening. In Omaha, she'd learned to let them talk until they tired of it. To respond was to encourage them.

Funny, she thought. She could switch off her brain with criminals, but not her kin. For some reason, she always rose to the bait when it was someone she cared about. Why was that? she wondered.

She stood up and went to the window again, mentally blocking out the nasal sound of his monotonic voice, looking outside where the world was being cleansed by nature's gigantic washing machine.

John Slocum was another of nature's machines, a killing machine, suffering from a disease for which no cure existed. Yet, she had some small compassion for him, feeling he was a product of his environment, badly used, his mind forever twisted by forces beyond his control. Just as the disaffection of her parents had formed Laura, giving her the strong desire to rise above her lot, so had the unhealthy drives of John's mother molded him, in far less beneficial ways.

The room was quiet. Slocum had finally run out of steam. Laura turned and faced him. "I'm your lawyer," she said. "Do you know what that means? It means I can't reveal anything you don't want me to reveal. Everything you tell me is our secret.

That's the law. If I break it, I'm in deep trouble, you understand?"

"I know about that stuff," he said.

"Good. It's not important for me to believe that you didn't kill that girl. Fact is, you did, and there's no way on this earth we can pretend that you didn't. The evidence is there for everyone to see. They found a shovel in your backpack. Do you always bury them, John?"

No answer.

"If you think that by sticking to some stupid story, it's going to make it go away, think again. All you're doing is limiting your chances. I'll defend you no matter what you tell me, but by confiding in me, you give me a chance to save you from the chair. Do you want me to save you from the chair or not?"

He continued to stare at the ceiling.

"Tell me about your mother," she said.

A giggle. A silly little giggle. "My mother?" Another giggle. Then silence.

"Your mother," she repeated. "She beat you and sexually abused you. You finally killed her to make it stop. That's what you're doing now, isn't it? Killing her all over again." She removed a photograph from her attaché case and stuck it in front of his face. "Is that your mother?"

He spit at it.

Laura took it away and placed a photo of Wanda Brooks in front of him. "This is the girl you murdered," she said. "She'd never lifted a finger to harm you, but you killed her anyway. You notice something about this girl?"

No answer.

"She looks a bit like your mother, John. Don't you see what's happening here?"

"I didn't kill anyone," he said. "I was in the woods takin' a crap is all. I saw this girl and I went over to see . . ."

Laura took the photo away. "Okay. Enough. Where've you been the last three years?"

"Around."

"Where around?"

"All over."

"How about Birmingham? Have you been there?"

He gave her a blank stare. "Never."

She looked at the notes she'd made earlier in the day. "Fourteen places, John. Fourteen towns and cities you were spotted in. Fourteen girls who went missing just about the time you were spotted wandering around the same city. They have witnesses. The dates and places are like a road map, John. One after the other, like a giant milk route. You went from place to place and you met girl after girl and you killed them all. And every time you did, it was like killing your mother all over again, wasn't it?"

"I never killed nobody," he said.

She sighed. "Why do you carry a shovel, John?"

"Fuck you."

"So where've you been the last three years?"

"Why should I talk to you?" he said. "You're supposed to be my lawyer, but you talk like a cop. You keep sayin' I killed that girl and I keep tellin' you I had nothin' to do with it and you ain't listening to me. Why the fuck should I tell you anything? How do I know you're really a lawyer anyway? You might be playin' a trick on me. Maybe you got a tape recorder stuck between your tits. How am I supposed to know? Why don't you take off your clothes and show me you ain't got a tape recorder stuck between your tits?"

"No, John."

He remained silent for a moment, then said, "I don't know nobody in this town. I told you. I was just passing through on my way to Miami. I heard there was some work down there. There ain't nobody in this town I can trust."

"All right," she said, putting various papers and photos back in her attaché case. "In about five minutes, the assistant state prosecutor is going to come in here and ask you a bunch of questions. I'll be here, and I'll tell you if there are questions you don't need to answer, but since you don't want to talk to your lawyer, I'm not too worried what you'll say to the prosecutor.

"During the next few days, there will be others who will be talking to you. Just one thing. If I can't be here, tell them you won't say anything until I am."

Slocum stared at the ceiling.

She stood up and started toward the door. Then she turned and asked, "When you were in the children's home, you were treated by a psychiatrist. Do you remember his name?"

He shook his head. "I never saw no shrink. You think I'm crazy, huh? Is that your idea of savin' me from the chair? So I can be locked up with all them crazy people? I ain't crazy. I'm as sane as anybody. I ain't tellin' you nothin', you miserable bitch cocksucker."

She threw him a smile. "Yes you will, John. You'll talk to me, but when you decide to, about fifteen minutes before they strap you in to the chair, it'll

be too late. The people in this state like to fry people. Sometimes they hold parties outside the prison
when a particularly nasty one goes up in smoke. I
expect that's how it'll be with you. A party. Beer
and hot dogs and all that stuff. Balloons, the works.
You'll talk, John. Too damn late, but you'll talk."

He turned his head toward her and grinned. "No,
I won't."

Laura opened the door. Chris was leaning against
the wall with two other men.

"Okay, gentlemen," she said.

CHAPTER

13

LAURA ARRIVED HOME AT SIX-THIRTY, MENTALLY AND physically exhausted. Her mother was in the kitchen cooking, and her father was sitting by himself in the living room, staring off into space and puffing on his pipe. He ignored Laura's entrance into the room.

Laura went into the kitchen, glanced at her mother, checked the answering machine, poured some white wine into a glass, and sat down wearily at the kitchen table. "How is he?" she asked finally, her voice more tentative than she would have liked.

Her mother kept her attention glued to a pot on the stove. She used a wooden spoon to stir the beef stew, one of three dishes that comprised the bulk of the Lawsen family diet. "You were a bit hard on your father, Laura."

"You don't think he was hard on me?"

"You're his daughter," she said. "He has a right."

"A right?" The anger was building again. "What right is that?" she asked.

"I told you," her mother said. "He's your father."

Laura let out an exasperated sigh. "And that's enough, I suppose."

"You're all grown up now," her mother said, still avoiding the glaring eyes of her daughter, "but that don't change the fact that you're still his only child. No matter how old you get, your father will always have the right to speak his mind, even if you don't agree with what he says. That's something that never goes away, and you should respect that."

"Respect is a two-way street, Mother."

"You're wrong, Laura," she said. "Your father has earned his place by working to provide for you and me. You owe everything you have to him, just like me. The difference between me and you is I understand that and you never did and still don't."

Laura choked back some angry words. Instead, she asked, "Do you have the slightest understanding of *my* feelings?"

"I think I do," her mother said.

"And?"

She stopped stirring for a moment, thought it out, then looked at Laura with an expression near disgust. "You were always headstrong, Laura. You know that. I don't think you ever liked being a girl, even when you were a child. I think that's what gets you in so much trouble, like with Dan and all. You're still a tomboy in many ways, still trying to be the boss. You don't understand about men much. They don't like it when the women wear the pants. It's not right, Laura."

"And you think that's what I do? Wear the pants?"

"It sure seems that way," she said. "When you were sixteen, the farm wasn't good enough for you, and you wanted to be a lawyer, you said. That was bad enough, because you knew, even then, how your father felt about lawyers. It was a slap in the face to him, and coming from his only child, it hurt him a lot."

Laura sipped her wine. "So, because I refused to obey my father and stay on the farm, I am to be despised."

"He don't despise you at all," she said. "He's just disappointed is all. He'd hoped for something . . ."

"What? Something better? To have a son, perhaps?"

"No."

"What, then?"

"It's hard to explain," her mother said, turning her attention back to the stew.

"Mother," Laura said, "if every child was to follow in the footsteps of their parents, we'd all still be wandering around the countryside with nothing but spears in our hands."

"You talk foolishness," her mother said. "When you got married and started having children, your father put aside that you'd left the farm for him to worry about, even though he had to hire strangers. It isn't the same with strangers, Laura. And now that he can't do it himself anymore, he has to think about selling the place."

"What about Aunt Jessie? I thought he was going to give the farm to her?"

"Jessie don't want it, so your father has to sell it. A farm that's been in the family for two generations. All gone to strangers."

"But you say he forgave me for that."

"He did," she said. "And when you went back to being a lawyer when your kids were hardly out of diapers, he forgave you for that, too. Your father has been good to you, Laura. You just can't see it, 'cause you never liked him much."

"I never liked him much? I've always loved you both, Mother. You're just not very good at love, you know?"

Her mother finally stopped stirring and sat at the table. "You should talk," she said. "How do you expect your father to feel? You're always yelling at him about everything like he's a stupid old man. He's not. Your father has worked hard all his life. He's provided well for me and you, too. You don't appreciate it. You've never appreciated it. You just took it all for granted."

"I guess that's true," Laura said bitterly. "I did take it for granted, like when I was a baby and you fed me. I guess I should be grateful for that. Most kids get thrown out on the ground when they need things, right?"

"That isn't what I mean."

"No? What was this wonderful thing that you two provided? Food, clothes, values? My God! I was nothing but a hired hand. From the time I was four years old, I did nothing but work the farm. All through elementary and high school, it was work and nothing but. I never got paid a nickel, but that was all right. A simple recognition of my contribution would have been enough, but I never received it. Not ever. Neither of you gave me emotional support or compassion or affection. You never have and you never will. I *worked* my way through college without a penny's help from you. Even now, at a moment in my life when I need . . ."

Closing her eyes, she took her mother's hand and squeezed.

There were two Laura Scotts, she knew. The intellectual Laura, the woman who'd overcome seemingly insurmountable obstacles to achieve her goals, a woman keenly aware of the intransigence of her poorly educated, unsophisticated parents. They were products of *their* harsh environment, their sensitivity and sagacity stunted by circumstances beyond their control. They'd never change, and part of Laura accepted that fact.

Then there was the other Laura Scott—the child within, still seeking approval and—more importantly—love. It never came and never would, yet each rejection turned Laura into a woman feeling sorry for herself. Each time Laura allowed her emotions to defeat her intelligence, tiny needles of self-loathing pricked her soul.

"I guess I'd better have a talk with him," she said softly.

Her mother smiled for the first time since they'd arrived. "That would be a good thing, Laura."

As though on cue, the phone rang. This time, Laura left it for the machine until she heard the words of Jim Pickett.

"We found them," she heard him say.

Her heart was pounding as she grabbed the receiver. "They're okay," he said quickly. "They were holed up in a motel someplace in Oklahoma.

I've got the telephone number for the police there. You wanna call?"

"Yes," she said.

"Okay. Trooper's name is Hesketh. Lt. Hesketh." He gave Laura the number.

"Laura?"

"Yes?"

"The Oklahoma troopers have made arrangements to fly them back in the morning. I'll be meeting the plane. Dan's waived extradition already. They told him about Victoria and he said he'd come back without a hassle. I guess he's a little shook up. You want to come to the airport?"

"Yes," she said.

"Okay. I'll be leaving here about ten. You want to come with me or take your own car?"

"I'll take my car."

"Okay. Chris wants you to call him. I guess he wants some direction from you on how you want to handle this."

"I'll take care of it," she said.

Laura hung up and dialed the Oklahoma number. In seconds, she was connected with Lt. Hesketh. They talked for a few minutes and then he put Ted on the phone.

"Are you all right?" she asked.

"Yeah," he said. She could tell from his voice he was fighting back the tears. "I'm sorry about Vicki, Mom. I mean . . . I'm really sorry."

"I know you are, Ted. How's your father?"

"Pretty bad," he said. "We got here two days ago. We were supposed to just stay the night and then Dad got drinking real bad. He's still drunk, I think. I was gonna call you, Mom. I really was, but I was afraid Dad would hear me, and I didn't want to leave him alone while I went to a pay phone. He's been pretty upset."

"That's all right," she told him. "I understand. Have you eaten?"

"Not yet. The police said they'd take me out to Burger King in about half an hour. Mom?"

"Yes?"

"They say that Dad's charged with kidnapping. That's real serious. They got him locked up right now, but . . ."

Laura interrupted him. "Don't worry about that," she said. "It was the only way I could arrange to find you two. I'll talk to the prosecutors before you get back. But, Ted," she added, "something has to be done. Maybe not jail, but your father is going to have to accept treatment. It's for his own good. Do you understand?"

"Yeah," he said. "I never saw him this bad before. It's kinda scary."

"I know," she said. "I'll see you tomorrow, okay?"

She could hear him crying. "Okay," he said.

"Let me talk to the officer again."

Lt. Hesketh got back on the phone. "Where will my son be spending the night?" Laura asked.

"Well, normally on a deal like this we'd have to place him in juvie hall for the night, since his father's gonna be locked up until we get him on the plane."

"Is there an alternative?" she asked.

He hesitated for a moment, then said, "I understand you're an attorney."

"That's right."

"Your son ever give you any trouble other than the regular stuff?"

"No," she said. "He's a great kid. He just loves his father very much. Too much. He was worried about him, that's all. He would never have done this on his own."

Lt. Hesketh grunted something, then said, "Well, I got a son about his age. If you want to fax me an authorization and take full responsibility, I'll let him bunk in with my boy for the night. How'd that be?"

"Lieutenant," she said, "if I could, I'd kiss you."

"Good thing you can't," he said. "My wife's the jealous kind."

"You said you were flying them back?"

"Uh-huh."

"What do I do about the car?"

"Well, you can call one of them drive-away outfits that move cars from place to place. I can give you a couple of phone numbers if you like."

He gave Laura the fax number, the phone numbers for the car outfits, and they said good night. Laura then called Chris. "Can you meet me at my office in about half an hour?"

He said he would.

She'd typed out the letter for Lt. Hesketh, arranged by phone to have the car driven back to Florida, faxed messages to both parties, and started preparing a pot of coffee when Chris arrived. He ambled to a chair, sat down, and crossed his legs. "Long day," he said.

"They all seem long," she said. "Too long."

Chris chewed on his lower lip for a moment, then said, "Goddamn, you've had a tough run."

She took her seat behind the desk, leaned back, and

stared at the ceiling. "I guess things run in cycles," she said. "Maybe it's my biorhythms or something, but I've been on a low for much too long."

"I guess you talked to Oklahoma already?"

"Uh-huh."

"How are they?"

"Dan's in the tank," she said, "and Ted's pretty scared. I think it's the best thing that could have happened, to tell you the truth. A good dose of reality is just what they both need. Maybe we can move forward."

"How do you want this handled?" he asked.

"I want Dan in a treatment program," she said. "It's his only chance."

"You want me to drop the kidnapping charges?"

"Yes."

"I have to charge him with something," he said. "Jim'll have to justify what he's done somehow. I can't just let Dan walk. We managed to keep this local, but we can't just drop it altogether."

"I know that," she said. "What about reckless endangerment of a minor child? You could recommend probation provided he get treatment, and if he's clean after two years, you could have the record expunged."

Chris gave her a sharp look. "Getting records expunged is not the easiest thing in the world, Laura."

"I know that," she said, "but there's a judge in town who owes me a favor. Maybe I can call in the marker after the Slocum trial is over."

Chris grinned. "Maybe you can at that, though I wouldn't put it quite that way to Judge Fry."

"I don't intend to," she said.

They both listened to the coffee maker gasping for air as the last of the water filtered through.

"You can't very well handle Dan's deal yourself," he said. "You were the one who swore out the complaint. You're already much in the public eye. I'd distance myself from this as much as possible. Officially, at least."

"I agree," she said. "I'll talk to Sam Johnson in the morning. He can represent Dan."

The coffee was ready. Laura poured cups for both of them. Chris sipped his for a moment, then said, "This Slocum thing. What with everything that's going on, do you think maybe you should talk to Fry about . . ."

Laura held up a hand. "No. Right now, I need this, Chris. Not for the marker, but for other reasons. When I talked with Slocum today, I realized that as bad as things are for me right now, they could always be worse. Slocum is the personification of evil, a mind ravaged by circumstances, most of which were beyond his control. He's insane, Chris. Defending him gives me a chance to focus on something other than myself."

Chris remained silent.

"I realize how selfish that sounds," she said, "but I can't help it."

"It's not selfish," he said. "The bastard is lucky to have you. It's more than he deserves."

"Maybe."

"Is that your angle, then? Plead him insane?"

"I don't know yet," she said. "I have a lot of people to talk to first."

"What time does Dan arrive tomorrow?" he asked.

"Eleven."

"Are you going to the airport?"

"Yes."

"Rick has limited Slocum's interview time for from two to five. That's all we get. You'll be there as well?"

"Yes."

He stood up. "All right. You call Sam first thing in the morning. Have him call me, and we'll work out this thing with Dan. Far as I'm concerned, I can drop this down to a misdemeanor if you want."

She shook her head. "No, Chris. Dan needs to understand the seriousness of what he's done. I want to scare the hell out of him, make him understand that he has to make the treatment work. A misdemeanor won't get it done."

He looked at her for a moment, then said, "Okay. We'll play it your way."

"Thanks, Chris. I really appreciate your help."

"What happens now? With you and Dan, I mean?"

"I don't know," she said. "It depends."

"Don't you think you're entitled to a little happiness?"

"Of course I do, but leaving Dan in this situation won't give it to me. Maybe once he's sober, I can start thinking about my own life."

"Mind if I ask you a personal question?"

"You've already asked several," she said, smiling.

"Do you love him?"

She didn't answer right away. She was trying to read his mind, interpret the signal he was projecting. And then, to her utter surprise, she said, "No. I care for him, but I don't love him."

Chris gave her a strange look, then said, "I'll be talking to you."

* * *

The beef stew was hot and tasty, but the atmosphere surrounding the dinner table was dreadfully chilly. Laura's mother and father sat stone-faced, slowly eating their food, with not a word to each other or to Laura. It had been that way ever since she'd returned from her meeting with Chris. She put down her fork, sipped some wine, took a deep breath, and said, "Dan and Ted will be here tomorrow."

They ignored her.

"The prosecutor has decided not to press the kidnapping charges," she said.

"And well he shouldn't," her father said, still avoiding her gaze. "There was no good reason to do such a thing in the first place."

Laura got up from the table, went into the kitchen, searched through her handbag, and removed a note with Lou Hawkins's telephone number on it. Returning to the dinner table, she placed the note in front of her father. "That's the phone number of Dan's former boss," she said. "I'd really appreciate it if you called him in the morning."

"What for?"

"He'll tell you why Dan was fired. Maybe if you hear it from a stranger, you'll believe it."

Her father put down his fork. "You just don't get it, Laura. I'm not sayin' Dan wasn't fired. I'm not even sayin' he don't drink a little more than he should."

Laura leaned back in my chair, her appetite ruined. "So what *are* you saying?"

Her father shook his head and waved a thick,

contorted hand in the air. "I don't think the dinner table is any place to be talkin' about suchlikes."

"But it's okay to sit there and say nothing? You two are treating me like a leper in my own home."

Her father sighed, pushed his plate away, and put his elbows on the table. "You just can't let it go, can you, Laura? You always have to wheedle, pickin' away 'til there's nuthin' left. You're like a dog with a bone."

"Perhaps," she said. "Maybe it's just that I'd like some support from my parents at a very difficult time in my life. I guess I'm just depressed. Forgive me."

Her father snorted. "You aren't any different than you ever were."

"I guess I'm not," she said, "but that's not really what's at issue here. You both feel that I'm the reason Dan is an alcoholic. You think I drove him to drink. The truth is, neither of you knows the first thing about alcoholics because neither of you have ever taken the time to research the subject. But I have.

"I can't change the way you feel about me and I'm not going to try. God knows, your attitudes have existed for long enough that nothing on this earth will change them. Okay, I can live with that. I'm not asking you to accept what I say as the gospel. I'm not even asking that you express some sort of love for me. All I'm asking is that you treat me with a measure of respect, not because I'm your daughter, but simply because I'm another human being. Do you think you can do that?"

Her father pulled out his pipe and began to fill it. "That cuts both ways, Laura," he said.

"I agree. If I've displayed disrespect, I apologize. I'll do my very best to show respect if you'll do the same."

He stuck the pipe in his mouth and stood up. "We'll see," he said.

CHAPTER

14

AGAIN, LAURA SCOTT WAS CONFRONTED WITH UNWANTED, almost unbearable reality. Her husband was standing before her in a small room within the bowels of sprawling Orlando airport, his wrists handcuffed as if he were a criminal. His hair and clothes were disheveled and his bloodshot eyes seemed to scream in pain. He looked at her once, then hung his head like a defeated warrior. The anger that had been roiling within Laura for days gave way to strong compassion.

"Could I have a few moments with him?" she said, her misty eyes struggling to focus on Chris.

"Of course," he said, motioning to Jim, who immediately removed the cuffs. Moments later Laura and Dan were seated across a small table from each other in this windowless security room, the familiar sounds of the airport beyond the door barely audible.

"I want you to know some things," she began.

He looked at her for a moment, then hung his head without a word.

"I'm very sorry I had to do what I did," Laura said, "but you really didn't give me much choice. I know you're scared right now, but you won't be charged with kidnapping, so don't let that worry you. You'll be charged with a felony, but that's not as bad as it sounds."

He raised his head and this time kept it up. "That's real comforting, Laura."

"Look," she said, "I've made some arrangements. You'll have an attorney representing you, one who's already cut a deal for you. There's a hospital in Orlando that specializes in drug and alcohol abuse. If you agree to accept treatment, you'll be placed on probation. No jail time, other than tonight. I can't do anything about that until you've made your first court appearance tomorrow morning. Immediately after that, there'll be an emergency hearing, at which time the charges against you will be reduced. A lot of people are sticking their necks out to help you, Dan."

"I'll bet."

She ignored his sarcasm. "If you cooperate, you'll be released. Sam Johnson will represent you, and as soon as we're done here, he'll come in and talk to you about everything. You're getting a break, Dan."

He sneered at her. "I guess you're pretty happy, huh? You finally got to put the boots to me."

"Do I look happy?" she asked.

He didn't answer.

"Dan," she said, "there's something else you should know. I'll see you through this, all the way. I'll be there for you when you leave the hospital, and I'll be there for you as long as you want me to be. After you've undergone treatment, if you want to explore the possibility of counseling to put our marriage on the right track, I'll be there for that as well. On the other hand, if you want a divorce, I won't make it difficult for you. If that's what you really want, it's fine with me. Our future is in your hands now."

She waited for some response. There wasn't one.

"The funeral for Victoria is tomorrow," she said. "It's going to be private. Just you and me and Ted, my folks, and a few close friends. Did you call your folks?"

He shook his head.

"I didn't call them," she said, "because I thought you'd want to do that yourself. If you want, I can postpone the funeral until they get here."

"No need," he said. "They wrote Victoria off years ago. There's no point in them wasting money coming down here."

Laura felt an icy hand grip her heart. "She's their granddaughter, too."

He laughed. "You're worried about their feelings? Is that why you refused to come back with me the last two times?"

She blushed. "You know why I didn't go back. I could hardly see your folks and not mine."

"So you said. Doesn't matter. My folks aren't much interested in you or Victoria. They've got no reason to come."

"Well, that's up to you," Laura said. "After the

funeral, if everything goes the way it should, you'll have to check into the hospital. I know this is blackmail, but at the hearing tomorrow if you don't agree to go to the hospital, you'll probably go to jail. I don't think you want to take the chance."

He held up both hands, like a man surrendering. "You got it all figured out, Laura. Just point me in the direction I'm supposed to go, tell me whose ass I'm supposed to kiss, and I'll do it. I know when I'm licked."

"I'm not trying to win," she exclaimed. "I'm trying to help you."

"Right," he said. "Some help. I'm sleeping, minding my own business, and two cops come in and arrest me. They shove me in jail for the night and take my son away. Then I get put on a plane in handcuffs, in full sight of my son, and hauled back to Florida like some sleazeball drug dealer. Now, I get to sit here and listen to your goddamn preaching and I know I have to take it, because you're the one holding all the cards. You're the lawyer, with all your lawyer friends. I'm just a working stiff, Laura. I don't have connections like you do."

"Don't you understand what you've done?" she asked, pleading with him.

"Sure," he said. "I decided to leave you. I took money I'd rightfully earned and a son who loves me, and I set out to go home for some peace and quiet. And for that, I'm a criminal." He shook his head. "I always knew this country was really screwed up, but I never knew how bad until now. Your old man was right, from the very first day he started bitching about lawyers. You bastards make the laws and rue the poor sonofabitch tries to exercise his right to be free in this country. We're all prisoners and slaves, Laura, just like the niggers used to be. The lawyers make all kinds of laws to protect the niggers and the rest of us get shit on. A real turnaround, I'd say."

He was talking such nonsense, Laura realized that her words were being wasted, but she tried once more. "You lost your job because of your drinking. You took your son and exposed him to dangers because you were driving while drunk. Then you holed up in a motel and stayed drunk for two days and nights. For that, at least, I'm grateful. If you'd kept on going, you both might have been killed."

"So you say."

She gave it up. "Dan," she said, "I didn't come here to fight with you. I came to help you. I know you don't see it, but it's true."

"Sure."

She stood up, almost in tears from the frustration of it. "Well," she said, "I've done what I can. I told you I'd stand by you and I will. The rest is up to you."

"You gonna leave now?" he asked. "Good. If you help me much more, I'll probably be dead by nightfall."

Laura turned and rapped on the door. Chris, Jim, and Sam Johnson came in. Laura glanced at a still-sullen Dan one last time, then left.

Ted was being held in another room. Laura threw an arm around him, drew him close, kissed him on the forehead, and said, "Let's go home."

"What's going to happen to Dad?" he asked.

"He'll be fine," she said, explaining what lay ahead as they made their way to the parking lot.

CHAPTER

15

AT TWO O'CLOCK, CHRIS ARRIVED AT THE HOSPITAL WITH the first of four visiting policemen who would interview John Slocum that afternoon. This one's name was Petrillo, a detective sergeant who looked anything but a cop. With his carefully groomed light brown hair parted in the middle, his old-fashioned, rimless glasses, and his plain blue bow tie, he looked more like a refugee from another era than a police officer. He was of average build and walked with a limp. With a tight smile fixed on his lips, he showed Laura his credentials, nodded, then looked at her client. "How's it goin', John?"

Slocum just glared at him.

"Okay if I ask him some questions?" Petrillo asked.

"That's what you're here for, isn't it?"

"I guess so." He pulled a chair to the side of the bed, propped an attaché case on his knees, then placed his elbows on the case. "They treatin' you okay, John?"

Slocum ignored him.

"How's the food?"

Finally a response. "Fuck you," Slocum said.

Petrillo laughed. "Don't like cops, eh? Can't blame you for that, John. I'm not too crazy about 'em myself, 'cept I'm stuck with 'em, you know? I'm too old to get another job now, so I gotta play this one out."

Slocum turned away and faced the window.

"I'm from Baltimore, John. Born and raised. You see the movie *Avalon*? It was all about Baltimore in the old days. My old man saw that movie. Cried the whole time. Said it made him remember how it was when he was growin' up. My old man's sentimental like that, you know? Only cop I ever liked. 'Course, he's retired now. Goes down to Atlantic City twice a month and pisses his pension away on keno games. Most he ever won was forty bucks, but he figures someday he's gonna strike it rich. Crazy old fool. You ever been to Atlantic City, John?"

Chris looked at Laura, then rolled his eyes toward the ceiling. Petrillo opened his attaché case, pulled out a photo, then placed the photo facedown on the case. Without looking at Laura, he asked, "Is your client aware that he doesn't have to answer my questions?"

Laura almost laughed out loud. Then, she realized what Petrillo was doing. It was an old technique that sometimes worked; he was portraying himself as Slocum's ally, attempting to forge a bond through some strange kind of chemistry, even though Laura would be standing there and advising her client not to answer any questions that could possibly be damaging. "He knows," she said simply.

"Good," Petrillo said. "I don't want Mr. Slocum's rights to be trampled on in any way."

He took the photo and placed it in front of Slocum's face. "This girl here, her name is Melanie Roberts. Pretty name, don't you think?"

Slocum refused to look at the photo.

"Would you take a peek for me?" Petrillo asked. "Just a peek?"

Reluctantly, Slocum looked at the photo. He turned his head away for a second, then took another look. "I never seen her in my life," he said.

"You sure?"

"I'm positive. Besides, I never been in Baltimore."

Petrillo took the picture and put it back in his attaché case. "I got another one here." He took another photo from his case and showed it to Slocum. "How 'bout this one. Ever see her?"

Slocum looked at it for a moment, then said, "Never. I told you, I never been in Baltimore."

Petrillo chuckled, then put the photo back. "I know. You said that. You're probably tellin' me the truth, John, but I got this asshole boss who says I gotta come all the way down here and show you pictures of every woman who ever went missing in Baltimore over the last fifty years. I know it's a pain in the ass, but I'm just doin' my job."

He pulled out a folder and placed it on his case.

"In here, I got thirty-six pictures. I showed you the first two already, and I gotta show you the rest. You help me out and I think we can get this over in a hurry. Okay?"

Slocum looked at Laura. "Do I hafta put up with this shit?"

"You have the right to refuse to answer any questions," she said, "but he has the right to question you."

"Give me the pictures," Slocum said, reaching for the folder. Petrillo quickly snatched it away, clucking his tongue. "Not too fast, John. I don't want to get 'em all mixed up. Let me show 'em to you one at a time. It won't take long."

As Laura watched Petrillo show photo after photo, she observed that the cop from Baltimore never so much as blinked. Every fiber of his being was locked in total concentration on Slocum's eyes. The parade of photos continued. After each, Petrillo would make some innocuous comment, chuckle like a fool, then move to the next one, as if the whole thing was one big joke. By now, she too was watching Slocum's eyes, trying to see what Petrillo was seeing, if anything. "How 'bout this one?" Petrillo said as he placed what must have been the twenty-fifth photo in front of Slocum.

It wasn't much of a reaction, but it was something. A slight flutter of eyelids by Slocum, then quickly a vacant stare. "Never seen her in my life," Slocum said.

"You sure?"

A groan. "Jesus! I keep tellin' you I never been in Baltimore."

"This one's name is Betty Lou Krache," Petrillo said. "She disappeared about a year ago after talkin' to some guy in a coffee shop on Biddle Street. Two people in the restaurant gave us a description of the guy. He looks a hell of a lot like you, John. Matter of fact, when I showed them a picture of you, they swore it *was* you she was talkin' to. Whaddaya say about that?"

"I never seen her before in my life, I told you, and I never been in Baltimore. How many times I gotta say it?"

"You think those people are wrong? That what you're saying?"

"It wasn't me they saw."

Petrillo finally blinked. He put the photo back in his case and leaned back in his chair. "I ain't sayin' you killed her, John. I ain't even sayin' you had anything to do with her disappearance. All I'm sayin' is you were the last guy to see her before she disappeared. Maybe you saw something. Maybe you saw her leave with some other guy. That what happened?"

"I never been in Baltimore," Slocum repeated, his voice dry as dust, his gaze directed at the far wall.

Petrillo took out a handkerchief, removed his glasses, and wiped his eyes. "I'm real glad to hear that, John. I really am."

He put the handkerchief away, then looked at Laura. "When John had his operation, did they test him for AIDS?"

That took Laura totally by surprise. "Of course," she said. "Those things are automatic now."

"Some places," Petrillo said. "Fact is, some of those tests aren't all that reliable." He shrugged, still staring at Slocum. "I think maybe you should do another test. Betty Lou Krache was a drug abuser. She tested positive for AIDS about three months before she disappeared. I was just thinkin' that maybe John here, if he got lucky with her, well . . . maybe he didn't get so lucky, you know?"

If there was a reaction from Slocum, Laura didn't catch it, but Laura had to object to the approach. "Mr. Petrillo, that will be enough."

Petrillo stood up. "I think I've got what I need for now," he said, sticking out a hand that Slocum ignored. "I know there's lots of others waitin' to see you. I'll be talking to you later."

"Just a minute," Laura said. "I'd like to discuss something with you before you leave."

He grinned. "I thought you might." He turned to Slocum. "You take it easy, John. If you think of anything that might help me, you let your lawyer know, okay? I'd sure like to get my asshole boss off my case."

Slocum didn't answer.

Laura went with Petrillo to the lounge area. While he put some money in the coffee machine and lit up a cigarette, she asked, "What was all that crap about AIDS? You know very well my client was tested."

"You worried, Counselor?"

"No," she said. "This hospital does a very comprehensive HIV test on every incoming patient. Slocum does not have the virus. At least if he does, it hasn't shown up in any test as yet. My understanding is that the virus can stay hidden for months."

"That's true," Petrillo said. "Has he been told that he was tested?"

"Not that I know of," she said. "There'd be no need. Maybe, if the results had been positive, he'd have been told."

Petrillo smiled. "Good. You notice anything when I dropped that on him?"

She shook her head. "All I noticed was his eyelids fluttering when you showed him the picture of Betty Lou Krache."

Petrillo grinned. "You caught that, eh? Very good."

"So, what's the story? Who were all those other people?"

The grin turned into a broad smile. "It was a setup, Counselor. I showed him photos I picked up from a Baltimore model agency. Women who all look a bit alike, you know? I knew he'd never laid eyes on one of them, but I wanted him to get comfortable, a little off guard. Then, when I showed him the photo of Betty Lou, he couldn't help himself. He wasn't ready for the real thing, like a photo of one of his actual victims. That little bit of relaxation brought his guard down and his eyelids moved before he had time to think."

He pulled the coffee from the machine, sipped it, then said, "Not bad for an old cop, eh?"

There was a twinkle in the eyes behind the rimless glasses, and a different tone to his voice. When he'd talked to Slocum, he'd sounded like a street person, but talking to Laura, it was different. She realized that the other voice had been an affectation.

"You're quite cunning, Sergeant Petrillo, but what you did isn't exactly kosher. This getup of yours. I assume it's just a ploy."

Petrillo removed a comb from his pocket and ran it through his hair, combing it straight back. "Very observant, Mrs. Scott." He removed the glasses and replaced them with a more modern pair. "I dress the fool, hoping these people will take me for one. Many times, they get feeling superior. The ego starts to bubble and they make mistakes." He sighed. "A waste in this case."

"Why?"

He looked crestfallen. "John Slocum killed Betty Lou as sure as God made little green apples, but he'll never appear in a Baltimore court, and that makes me sad. You can only kill a guy once, Mrs. Scott, and Florida has first dibs on Slocum."

"You never answered my question," Laura said.

"About what?"

"About the AIDS thing."

He smiled. "A small lie," he said. "Betty Lou never had AIDS." His eyes began to mist. "She wasn't a druggie either. She was . . ." He shook his head as though trying to rid himself of an unpleasant memory. "I just wanted to find out if this guy was afraid to die. Some of them aren't, you know. They really don't care."

"That's what you were trying to find out?"

"Exactly. You can learn a lot about a man when you throw some unexpected monkey wrench into his thoughts. He didn't react much, but I'm sure he's thinking about it. If he asks you about an AIDS test, you'll know for sure he wants to live. Frankly, I don't think he will. He's too smart for that. He's probably figured out he'd be told if he had the virus."

Laura liked this man, with his offbeat approach.

He was also one of the very few who didn't associate her with her client. She thought his refreshing smile to be genuine, despite the created persona he'd developed for interrogation purposes. "It's also possible he isn't responsible for what happened to your missing woman," she said. "An eyelid flutter isn't much to go on."

Petrillo gave her that warm smile again. "Oh, he's the one all right. I wasn't lying about those witnesses. At least now I know who did it. That's something that's been bugging me for over a year. Now all I gotta do is find out where he buried her, the bastard. That's the hard part."

"You're that convinced?" she asked. "On the basis of an eyelid flutter?"

He nodded. "It's more than that, actually. He fits the profile, we know he killed a woman here, and I have two people who are willing to swear they saw Slocum in a restaurant just hours before Betty Lou disappeared. They saw them leave the restaurant together. Slocum has to be the man. No question in my mind."

"I'm glad you're not judge and jury," Laura said.

Petrillo took no offense. "So am I. I understand this isn't your first murder case."

"No, it's not."

"But you've never had one like this, have you?"

"I think you already know the answer to that."

He laughed. "Guess I do at that." Then the smile left his face. "Tell you what, Mrs. Scott. I've been at this game a long time. I took a couple of extension courses on serial killers at the university when Betty Lou disappeared and I've studied similar investigations. I've learned a few things."

"I'm sure you have."

"These people usually fall into two catagories," he said. "Organized and unorganized. Slocum is in the first group, but he's the most organized killer I've ever heard of. Matter of fact, if it wasn't for the fact that Billy Haines just happened to be in the woods that night, John Slocum would have buried his latest victim, moved on to the next town, and we'd still be looking for him. We all got a break there, Mrs. Scott."

She held up my hand. "Sergeant Petrillo, I don't think I should . . ."

"I know," he said quickly. "I'll get out of your hair in a moment. I just want you to be aware of something."

"Which is?"

"Now that Slocum's been caught, you can expect a few things."

"Like?"

"For one, he's gonna spill his guts to you sooner or later. Probably sooner, if I have it figured right. He's gonna tell you everything. So much so, that you'll have a hard time keeping down your lunch. Then, he's gonna keep telling you and keep telling you until you're good and sick of hearing about it."

She let out a sigh. "I'm not so sure."

"Well, I am," he said. "These guys follow a pattern, the organized ones. They think they're smarter than everybody else. I'll bet Slocum's got details locked in his mind on every single woman he killed, and he *has* to tell somebody, else there's no reason to do it in the first place. That's why they do it, you know, to prove they're smarter than everybody else."

"I don't think that applies in this case, assuming

of course that he did it, which I'm not saying . . ."

He cut her off with a laugh. "Don't worry, I'm not trying to trap you. The way I hear it, Slocum was physically abused as a child. Child abusers don't just beat their kids, they abuse them mentally as well. Your guy was probably told he was an idiot a hundred times a day. That stopped when he killed his mother."

He looked around, then leaned forward, so close she could smell his cologne. "I was in Buffalo last week," he said, "and managed to have a look at those sealed records. Sometimes, when you know the right people, you can get a peek at almost anything. I've read them all. That story about Slocum's mother being killed by accident is not the way it happened. He murdered her, and got away with it simply because some cops felt he was justified in killing a woman who was abusing him on a daily basis. Which goes to prove that cops shouldn't be making those kinds of judgments, like you said."

"What makes you think the police felt sorry for him?"

He shrugged. "I'll let you decide for yourself when you have the records unsealed. The point is this—Slocum feels he got away with something when he was just a kid. He thinks he can outwit us all, and up to this point, he has, except now he knows he's in serious trouble. Since you're his lawyer, you're the only one he can brag to, because you have to keep his secrets. The temptation will be too strong for him to resist."

"I don't think he'll do that," she said.

Petrillo gave her a big grin. "We'll see. In the

meantime, I'll give you a list of books to read. You study up, and you'll be better prepared, but I say again, he'll tell you soon enough, and it's important that he does."

"Why?"

"Because that's all you've got to deal with. You got twenty or thirty cops trying to close cases here. You got all those parents wondering what the hell happened to their kids. That's pressure."

"Not to Slocum."

"I wasn't talking about your client. Unlike some other states, Florida has very narrow guidelines for insanity defenses, and I doubt Slocum fits the single slot that's left. Florida also has the death penalty and the people who vote will want this guy to pay the price. Your only chance to save Slocum from the chair is to make a deal, a deal so good they can't refuse. The only kind of deal that qualifies is one where your boy tells everybody where all the bodies are buried. If he fails to do that, he'll die. I think he already knows that. So, if it turns out he's not anxious to die, you have an edge. When he starts shooting off his mouth, you've got something to deal with, you know? It's important you open him up."

He opened his attaché case, took out a yellow legal pad, and scribbled the names of four books on the top page. He looked at what he'd written for a moment, then crumpled the paper and threw it in the wastebasket. "I have a better idea. I'll lend you my copies. If you read these books you'll have a better idea what you're looking for, but I have one word of warning."

"What's that?"

"After he talks, if you want to make a deal, you'll need to go over Marshall's head."

Her eyes widened. "Chris? What makes you say that?"

"I'm a student of human nature, Mrs. Scott. Chris Marshall is not about to make any kind of deal. No way. He's looking to fry this guy, because if he doesn't, he figures his career is over. You'll have to get past him."

"Why are you telling me all this?"

"Simple," he said. "I've got a missing girl. Slocum killed her sure as hell. She's buried somewhere and Slocum's the only one who can tell us where. I need that information real bad."

"So you can close the case?"

"Just partly," he said. Suddenly the warmth left his face, replaced by a look of pure malevolence. "I've got a sister, Mrs. Scott. Terrific woman. Salt-of-the-earth type, you know? Give the shirt off her back to anyone. Good church person, great mother, terrific wife, the whole nine yards. For the past year, she's been having a very rough time. You see, she married a fireman named Joe Krache twenty-four years ago. Four kids, and a wonderful life until this happened. Betty Lou is her kid . . . and my niece."

Laura felt a rush of anger. "You have no business being on this case," she snapped. "And I don't like being manipulated."

Petrillo blushed. "I'm sorry," he said. "That was uncalled for."

"You bet it was."

"I'm sorry, Mrs. Scott. I guess I've lost some of my own humanity this past year. This case is probably tough enough on you. I have no right to make it tougher."

"I've had easier cases," she said. Then, expelling a breath of air, she added, "I repeat. You shouldn't be involved in this case. You have a personal interest."

"You're right," he said, "but we live in an imperfect world, Counselor. I happen to be the only one in the division qualified to work this case. The chief thought about it long and hard. In the end, he decided it was more important to find out what happened than to stick to policy."

She felt the sudden burst of anger recede. "Explain something to me," she said.

"Sure."

"If this man killed your niece, why would you be satisfied with life in prison instead of the electric chair?"

"It's a matter of priorities. Sure, I'd like to see him dead, but if finding my niece's body means he has to live, I can accept that. So can my sister. Slocum's death won't bring anybody back from the grave. Best we get what we can out of him. If it all works out, my sister can get her life back. That's a hell of a lot more important than vengeance, at least to her—and me."

"You're an unusual man, Sergeant Petrillo," Laura said.

He grinned. "Call me Vince."

"I'll stick with Sergeant if it's all the same."

He nodded. "Look, I'm really sorry. Will you let me make it up to you? Maybe dinner somewhere."

Laura shook her head. "I think not, Sergeant."

He looked pained. "I meant dinner, that's all."

"I believe you," she said. "I appreciate the invitation, but I just can't. I have some personal reasons and there's the perception of impropriety to be considered. There are a lot of visiting policemen wandering around this town. If I was seen having dinner with you . . ."

"I understand, Mrs. Scott. Again, I'm sorry."

"So am I, Sergeant."

CHAPTER

16

LAURA SLEPT VERY LITTLE THAT NIGHT. TO HER GREAT relief, Ted was back in his room, the ever-present earphones plugged into his ears, giving the house some semblance of normality.

As Laura lay awake, she reviewed this afternoon's session with Sergeant Petrillo and the other people who'd talked to her client. Slocum had treated them all in the same manner he'd treated Laura, clinging to denials, and offered nothing else. Another session was scheduled for tomorrow afternoon with yet another group of law enforcement officials. Laura wasn't looking forward to it, and yet she was intensely curious.

Each of the men who'd questioned Slocum today had been an expert in the field of suspect interrogation. One had used techniques similar to Petrillo's and another had come on like King Kong, but none had been as skilled as the man from Baltimore, a man Laura was having difficulty pushing from her mind.

After she'd come home she'd spent an hour explaining to her parents and Ted her motives for having Dan arrested. She'd also outlined what she expected to happen at the hearing in the morning. Ted, having been exposed to his father's true character, sided with his mother throughout most of the discussion, but Laura's parents were unmoved, even after Ted described some of his terror.

Ted's support had lifted Laura's spirits immeasurably, and afterward, she'd spent a quiet half hour in his room, telling him how much she loved him, how she wanted the three of them to have a good life, and what she was prepared to do to make it happen. At long last, Laura and her son, motivated by mutual need, were drawing close together.

After a fitful few hours of sleep, Laura arose before dawn, slipped on a robe, and went downstairs. As the coffee brewed, she stepped outside and picked up the *Clarion* from the front step, the special extra edition that Ferris had promised.

Almost the entire newspaper was devoted to details surrounding the murder of Wanda Brooks. Slocum was pegged as a serial killer and Billy Haines as Superman. Pictures of all the major players were splashed throughout.

There was a short report on the present condition of John Slocum, with a comment that he was expected to live. Rick had refused to be interviewed and that was noted.

Page seven held photographs of ten young women, all missing from various parts of the country. Under each photograph was a story dealing with the disappearance of the girl, as well as a bio of each police officer now in Seminole Springs trying to determine if his particular missing girl was a victim of John Slocum's.

Laura looked carefully at the photos of the missing girls. There was a disturbing similarity in age, hair color and style, even some of their facial features. She felt a chill run down her spine.

And then, on the editorial page, she saw something that disturbed her even more. Tom Ferris, obviously enraged by her refusal to cooperate in his book deal, had lowered the boom on Laura Scott.

It seems odd that a woman who has suffered the loss of a beloved daughter (private burial today) would take it upon herself to defend John Slocum. Wouldn't a mother who'd just suffered a terrible loss be repelled by the thought?

Yesterday, Dan Scott, Laura's husband, was brought back from Muskogee, Oklahoma, in handcuffs after being arrested there on a charge of kidnapping the couple's son Ted. Clearly, a domestic dispute of major proportions rages within the Scott household.

Sources tell us that the charges against Dan Scott will be reduced at a court appearance scheduled for this morning, but Dan Scott may still eventually wind up in jail. The charges of kidnapping, it should be noted, were pressed by Laura Scott herself.

The *Clarion* suggests that Laura Scott, for both

personal and public reasons, remove herself from the Slocum case, and allow those who are paid by the county to do this kind of work to carry on. We have no doubt that John Slocum will be well represented, and at considerably less expense to the taxpayers of this county. Nor do we doubt that the Scott family will be better served as well. We hate to see a family destroyed by the distorted ego of one of its members.

It was a disgusting, vengeful piece of writing, with no other purpose than to humiliate Laura. Since much of what was written was true, there was nothing she could do, and she knew that Tom Ferris was well aware of that fact.

Laura remembered the words of William Congreve, who once wrote that there's no fury like that of a woman scorned; of Nietzsche, who wrote that in revenge, a woman is more barbarous than man; of Aristophanes, who wrote that no wildcat was as ruthless as a woman. Three men with a similar view. In Laura's view, all of them were wrong. Tom Ferris had just proved it.

Laura didn't attend Dan's hearing. Instead, she and Ted spent the morning saying their private good-byes to Victoria. At ten, Dan arrived at the funeral home, accompanied by Laura's parents.

The ceremony lasted a brief ten minutes. About twenty of Laura's friends were there, including Chris Marshall. At the graveside, they huddled together as some final words were said, and then Victoria was lowered into the ground. Laura felt numb. Later, Chris took her aside and told her what had happened at the hearing. Dan had agreed to enter the clinic immediately. Judge Fry had accepted a plea of guilty to reckless endangerment of a child, had placed Dan on probation for two years, and had directed monthly blood tests. If Dan was discovered consuming alcohol during his probation period, he'd be jailed for a minimum of one year.

"And the record?" she asked.

"It'll be expunged if he stays sober," Chris said.

She clutched his arm. "Thanks, Chris."

"No problem," he said.

Laura and Ted walked over to Jim's car. Dan was seated in the back. "We'll come and visit as soon as they say it's okay," she said.

"Don't bother," he said without looking at either of them.

Jim got behind the wheel and drove off. Laura glanced at her parents. They were staring at her as if she were a piece of excrement. Tears stung her eyes. And then she felt a hand, strong and dry, grab hers.

She looked into the concerned eyes of her son. "You okay, Mom?" he asked.

She put an arm around him and drew him close. "As long as I have you, I'll be fine."

He started crying. "Where are they taking Dad?"

Laura explained what had happened at the hearing.

"He'll be home in a month?" Ted asked.

"Yes," she said. "Then, we'll see if we can't put this family back together again."

Three hours later Laura took her parents to the airport. As the three sat in the gate area waiting for the flight to be called, the wall of antipathy remained, blocking conversation, even small talk.

Laura remembered, as though it had been yesterday, sitting at the kitchen table in the old house in Havre, filling out college application forms.

A bitterly cold night. In the basement, the oil-fired furnace growled as it fought to counter the thirty-five below zero air trying to seep through every crack and crevice in the frame house. As in many farmhouses, the kitchen was the biggest room, and that's where the family spent most of its time.

"So your mind's made up?" her father said as he looked over her shoulder.

She nodded and returned to her forms. Her father took a seat at the table, puffing on an old, battered pipe, peering at his only child over rimless glasses, his hands folded over the overalls he constantly wore, except Sundays. "A waste of time," he said.

"What makes you say that?" she asked.

"Nothing, if you was a man," he said. He had a way of talking with the pipe in his mouth, perfected over the years, where neither the pipe nor his lips moved, but she could still understand every word spoken. She often thought he would have made a great ventriloquist.

"I know these days there's women goin' to college," he said, "but that still don't make it right. It's a waste of time and money, far as I'm concerned. Four years of college won't do you no good. You'll come back and get married and have kids and then what? You want to learn something useful, you can go to agricultural school, but that's a waste too. You already know all you need to run this farm."

Laura said nothing, just stared at the papers in front of her.

"I suppose you figure that after you graduate from college, you'll go to law school?"

"That's my plan," she said, not looking up.

They stared at each other with undisguised enmity. At long last, the battle was truly joined.

"Who's supposed to run this farm, girl?" her father said.

"What if I don't want to run this farm?"

"Why wouldn't you?"

"Because I want to be a lawyer."

His round face flushed with sudden anger. "That's just plain stupid," he said. "Lawyers are nothin' more than thieves in fancy suits. I didn't raise my only child to be no thief. There's never been a thief in the Lawsen family and we ain't about to start now."

"Oh, Daddy," she said, "you know very well that there are crooks in every kind of job. Lawyers aren't any more dishonest than any other profession."

He pulled the pipe from his mouth again. "Profession? You call bein' a lawyer a profession? You want a profession? Farming ain't good enough for you?"

"It's not that."

"What, then? You want a profession, you can be a doctor. At least doctors try to help people, not destroy 'em. I don't hold much with women being doctors, but I could live with that if need be. Not lawyering. All lawyers do is destroy people's lives."

"That's not true," she said, stiffening in her chair.

He scowled, something he did often. He was uneducated and unsophisticated and insecure, the insecurity breeding a harshness that approached cruelty. He didn't like arguments. In his home, as in his father's before him, a father's word was law. There was not supposed to be any discussion. Long ago, Laura's mother had decided to play the role assigned to her, but, at the age of eighteen, Laura didn't intend to.

He waved an arm in the air. "Half the farms in this county have already been stole by lawyers at one time or another. That what you really want to do? Steal farms from hard-workin' people for the banks?"

"I have no intention of being a thief," she said, fighting to keep her voice level. "I want to help people."

"Help people? How you gonna do that?"

"You talk about farmers having their land taken away by lawyers. Suppose I was a lawyer and I was able to stop that from happening? Wouldn't you feel that was worthwhile?"

"You may be smart, Laura, but you ain't that smart."

"You can say that now," she said, "but after I've been trained, things might be different." She looked into his eyes. "Daddy . . . I'm your daughter. I love you and Mom very much. You must know that. But I know what I want to do with my life. I've thought about little else for three years. If you loved me, you'd support my decision. I'm not talking about something awful. I'm talking about going to college and becoming a lawyer. You should be proud of me."

The anger expressed in her father's face increased. He took the pipe, now cold, out of his mouth, stared at it venomously, put it back in his mouth, and struck a match. As clouds of smoke rose in the air, he said, "It's not a woman's place to be no lawyer. It's a woman's place to be a mother and a wife and make a good home. Your mind is all mixed up. If I have to disown you to make you see what's right, then that's what I'll do."

She looked at him in awe. Through the years, she'd come to accept her father's ways, but the intensity of his rejection of her hopes and dreams was beyond anything she'd experienced.

"You got a boyfriend who seems real nice," her father continued. "Make a good husband." His voice softened. "I agree with you on one thing. It's a little soon, but supposin' Dan wants to marry you someday? You'll be away at school for . . . how long's it take?"

"Seven years," she said.

He clapped his hands together. "Seven years. You think Dan's gonna sit on his hands for that long?"

"I don't know," she said.

"You don't know?" He glared at her. "He's a good-lookin' boy, Laura, and steady, too. I'm sure there's lots of girls in this town got their eye on him. With you away at school, you may's well kiss him good-bye right now."

"If it happens, it happens," she said.

They both fell quiet. The only sounds in the room were the hum of the electric clock on the wall, the whine of the icebox motor, and the growl of the furnace beneath them.

He had exhausted his patience. "You're strong-headed like your mother," he snapped, banging a fist on the table. "That's the Irish in you. Stubborn." He stood up, signaling the end of the discussion. "You're eighteen now, all grown up. You can do as you please. You want to go to college, you do it on your own. I ain't payin' a dime of it. You want to go to agriculture school, that's a different story."

Laura stood up and planted her feet firmly on the floor, her chest almost touching his. They were eye to eye, chin to chin, father and daughter. "That's up to you," she said coolly. "If you don't want to help me, that's fine. I'll do it on my own."

"We'll see," he said, turning away from her and stomping out of the room.

Now, twenty-two years later, sitting in an airport lounge, things were no better than they'd been back then. She'd committed the unforgivable sin of going against her parents' wishes. Every move she'd made since to win back their love had failed. Too late, she'd realized that she'd married Dan only to please them. It hadn't worked. Nothing had worked.

There was every likelihood she'd never see them again. And as their flight was called and they awkwardly said their good-byes, she knew that they felt the same.

It was something she'd have to learn to live with.

CHAPTER

17

THE DAY AFTER LABOR DAY, WITH TED IN SCHOOL, DAN in the clinic, and her parents back in Havre, Laura was free of visible distractions, but the emotional residue of unrelenting and arduous confrontations had taken its toll.

Tom Ferris's editorial had increased the number of crank calls coming to Laura's house, and some of the towns bolder citizens had gotten physical, throwing eggs at the house from passing cars. Her friends, like the Cains and the Smiths, and especially Gerry and Ethel, had been unwavering in their support. Ethel had even started a telephone campaign, something like a chain letter, to counter the negative effects of the editorial. But even with the support of her friends to bolster her, Laura looked haggard.

Kim noticed immediately. "Are you okay?" she asked as Laura fiddled with the coffee maker for the third time. Twice, she'd put twelve spoons of fresh grounds in the basket when the normal requirement was five.

"I guess I'm a little preoccupied," she said.

Kim came to her side. "I know we have this rule around here where the boss makes the coffee," she said, "but why don't you let me do it this once? I'm already convinced you're the best boss I'll ever have. You have nothing left to prove to me."

Laura managed a weak smile. "Thanks, Kim."

"Dr. Taylor called," she said, handing Laura a sheaf of pink slips. "He's the only important one in the pile. And Mr. Marshall sent over a fresh stack of reports. They're on your desk."

"Anything else?"

Kim made a face.

"Are we still getting crank calls?"

She nodded. "Nothing to worry about. I can handle the cranks. It's the newspaper and TV people who drive me crazy. They just won't take no for an answer. I told them what you asked me to tell them, but I still think you should hire a security guard to keep them away. They're sure to be up here again today."

"I passed a couple in the parking lot," Laura said. "If they come up here, just tell them to leave. If they refuse, call Jim. This is a private building. They have no right."

"I'll do my best."

Laura went into her office, sat behind the desk, and fought off the thick cloud of melancholy that threatened to overwhelm her. For five minutes she closed her eyes and focused on the positive aspects of her life. It worked. The cloud was already lifting as Kim brought in the coffee, put it in front of her, smiled, then said, "Do you want me to get Dr. Taylor on the phone?"

A gentle prod, the mark of an excellent secretary. "Yes," she said.

"I've placed your client off-limits again," he told her. "No visitors until further notice."

"What's the problem?"

"The clot in the leg. I'm afraid the leg's going to have to come off, Laura. The infection is starting to spread. We just can't seem to clear the blockage."

"When will you know?"

"Probably another twenty-four hours. In the meantime, I don't want you or anyone else seeing him. I want him calmed down before we go in."

"Have you discussed this with him?"

Rick grunted. "Yes. He's asked for another doctor. He says I'm deliberately dismembering him, one limb at a time."

"So he's refused permission?"

"Yes, but that's no problem. I've got three specialists coming down to see him today."

"Three?"

"Yes," he said. "It wasn't hard to get volunteers. Can you imagine? They just want to have a close look at this guy. I guess doctors can have as much morbid curiosity as laymen. I'm not bothered by that, though. I want all the backup on this I can get. I have a feeling I'd better cover my butt."

"I think we all do," she said. "You'll let me know?"

"Certainly. Unless there's an unexpected change, we'll operate in the morning. I want him isolated for two days after that, so you can plan accordingly."

"Is there any chance this could be life-threatening?" Laura asked.

"There's always a chance, Laura. In this case, not much of one, but every operation carries an element of risk. I think he'll come through it all right physically. As for his mental state, that's another matter. As far as I'm concerned, he's already a maniac, so anything is possible."

"Can I quote you on that?"

He laughed. "Sure. Won't do you any good, though."

"I know," she said.

Laura hung up the phone, then turned her attention to the pile of reports that Chris had sent over. Another set of missing persons reports, another list of young women who had suddenly disappeared from locations all over the country, never to be seen again. There were now a total of twenty-five cases where witnesses had claimed that a man answering the description of John Slocum had been seen in the vicinity at a time when one of the women disappeared.

There was an additional batch of reports, but in these, there were no witnesses. However, the description of the missing woman approximated the description of Wanda Brooks; not enough for law enforcement officials to actively pursue the issue, but enough for them to be curious, which was the reason the various police departments had forwarded the reports to Chris.

The more Laura read, the more convinced she

was that they had good reason to be curious. It was only a matter of time before they too would be here in person. There would be others. Already, the press was all over the story of John Slocum and his many suspected victims. In police departments throughout the country, officers would be pulling out unsolved case files, dusting them off, and trying to tie them to Slocum. Most would have no reasonable cause, but with pressure strong to close *any* case, Laura knew Seminole Springs would soon be inundated with cops.

She sighed, leaned back in her chair, and finished the last of her third coffee. There was no question in her mind. Her client was responsible for the deaths of most of the missing women, the ones with witnesses at least. There was no knowing the true immensity of his crimes. She was representing a man who could arguably be considered as one of the worst monsters in American criminal history, a man who would probably live to be defended by her in court.

She shuddered at the thought, then picked up the phone and called Chris. "I've been reading the reports you sent over," she said.

"Great stuff, isn't it?" he said sardonically.

"It's horrible," she said. "I was talking to Rick earlier. He says Slocum is off-limits for a few days. The leg may have to come off."

"I know. He called me as well."

"Well, since Slocum can't be interviewed for a while, I think this would be an ideal time for me to go to Buffalo and talk to some people."

"I had a feeling you might want to do that," he said. "You still thinking of the insanity plea?"

"Yes," she said.

A pause, and then, "Have you had lunch yet?"

Laura looked at her watch. It was half past noon. The thought of food had never entered her mind. "I'm not hungry," she said.

"In that case, how about you have a coffee while I eat? I'll meet you at the club, okay?"

"All right," she said.

He was there before her, waiting at the maître d's post. John, the maître d', usually a most affable man, guided them swiftly to a table by the window overlooking the eighteenth green, handed them menus, and hustled off without uttering a word. As Laura pulled her chair closer to the table, she glanced around the room and noticed several hostile stares aimed in her direction. Chris noticed it too. "You better get used to it," he said. "Ferris's piece has had an effect."

Laura looked out the window at a quartet of golfers as they lined up putts. She recognized three of them, all men in their sixties, attired in outrageously loud pants and shirts. For a moment she wondered what it was about the game of golf that inspired men to wear clothes they wouldn't be caught dead in anywhere else.

"I can see that," she said, turning her attention back to Chris. "Although I don't think it's all due to him. It was sweet of him to mention Dan, though."

"You must have turned him down."

"Pardon me?"

Chris grinned. "The book deal. He was after me on that."

"What did you tell him?"

"To get lost. I expect I'll be pilloried in this week's issue. That should even things up."

Laura laughed. "After what I've been through the past few days, I'm getting used to hostility."

Chris opened his menu and said, "Dan's still in the denial phase. Once the doctors get him past that, he may start to understand that you're trying to help him."

"I wasn't thinking about Dan," she said, "but I hope you're right."

"Do you really?" he asked, a strange look in his eyes.

"Yes."

He leaned forward. "You said you didn't love him anymore."

"I don't," she said. "But I don't hate him. I still want him to do well, and I don't want him to spend the rest of his life hating me."

Chris pondered her words for a moment. "Still not hungry?"

"I think I can manage a sandwich. A club."

He ordered for them. Lowering his voice, he said, "Laura, I think you should seriously reconsider this insanity thing. It's clear to me that Slocum meets the requirements of the M'Naugten test, and anything else won't fly. You know that. Bringing it up is going to expose you to even more hostility. I don't think it's worth it."

She'd been wondering when he'd make his pitch. It had come earlier than expected. They were months away from a trial, but Chris was not one to waste time. "It's not a question of it being worth it, Chris."

"No? Look, off the record, you know damn well

that your client killed Wanda Brooks. The evidence is overwhelming and irrefutable. I'm sure Slocum's responsible for many other murders as well. As human beings, we both have a responsibility to stop this man from killing anyone else. Forget the legal aspects for a minute and think of the man himself. Is he a reasonable candidate for rehabilitation? Is he ever to be a useful member of society? You know the answers to those questions as well as I do."

"My defense strategy with regard to Slocum has nothing to do with the man himself," she said, smiling.

"Oh. It's capital punishment you want to fight."

"Partly. I would have expected you to embrace the idea of an insanity plea."

His eyebrows arched. "What makes you say that?"

"If I explore every possible defense, and Slocum is convicted, the chances of the conviction being overturned on appeal are lessened. That makes it better for you, for Judge Fry, and for society as a whole. If, on the other hand, I ignore the insanity angle, I leave the conviction subject to appeal on the basis of having provided a less-than-competent defense. I don't think either one of us wants this case to drag on any longer than is necessary."

Chris shook his head. "You should be selling some kitchen gadget on TV. You know, one of those deals that makes roses out of radishes for only $69.95? You'd be good at that."

She sipped her water and fluttered her eyelashes at him. "You think I'm giving you a bill of goods? Little ol' me? I'm just a farm girl from Montana. I can't compete with you city slickers."

"Right."

"Seriously, Chris, and we're still off the record here, it seems to me there are several possibilities. There is evidence that Slocum was emotionally, physically, and sexually abused as a child. There's no question that he's psychologically damaged, and I'm well aware of the legal limits on that, but there's a chance he's brain-damaged as well, and that's something else again. There's also the irresistible impulse defense. I know that Florida doesn't recognize these defenses, but I have an ethical responsibility to attempt to extend the law."

"This is the wrong case for that, Laura."

"This is exactly the *right* case for this," she insisted. "To fail to explore every defense would not only be a disservice to my client, but could lay the foundation for an appeal."

"You keep talking about an appeal," he said. "An appeal by whom?"

"Come on, Chris. If Slocum is half the monster he appears to be, this case will be headline material for months. Whenever you have a media circus, you get the ax-grinders. Any number of organizations will latch on to this, some because of their fierce loyalty to a principle and some just to further their interests. No matter how the case is resolved, organizations with a vested interest will be going over every page of transcript with a fine-tooth comb, looking for a way to make political hay.

"I can guarantee you that I won't be the only lawyer defending this man over the next ten years, no matter what happens. If I fail to give him the best possible defense, there will certainly be a series of appeals over and above the automatic ones. Remember how long it took with Bundy?"

"I remember," he said.

"Well?"

"Bundy was the exception. Some people were charmed by that clever bastard. They just couldn't believe he was a monster, and besides, the evidence was more circumstantial. Here, we've got Slocum dead to rights and Slocum is certainly no charmer. He even looks like everyone's worst nightmare. I doubt there will be too many groups rushing to associate themselves with him. He's more likely to be ignored."

The food arrived. As they ate, they continued the discussion. "Let's consider the possibility that John Slocum has killed at least twenty-six women," Laura said. "The very acts are irrational to us, yet they make sense to John Slocum. He fits the FBI profile almost to a T—that of an organized lust murderer who is cunning, mobile, and sexually driven. Most criminal psychologists will tell you that people like that are insane by any yardstick. Okay, so where's the clear intent? If this man is not in control of his emotions, how can he be held responsible?"

Chris grimaced. "Laura, you're trying to reinvent the wheel. The state of Florida does not accept irresistible impulse as a legitimate defense. To bring it up is redundant. Forget the legalities for a moment and look at the facts. The victims are still dead and someone has to pay. Since we can't prosecute some ethereal theory, we'll take Slocum, damaged or not. Someone *must* be responsible, Laura. Insanity is nothing but a cop-out. All killers are crazy. Murder, in and of itself, is an irrational act. If we follow

California's lead, we'll soon be building nothing but mental institutions in this state."

Laura persisted. "The fact that the state refuses to recognize irresistible impulse is a reflection on us, not Slocum. Why is it so difficult to understand that mental illness is just as real as physical illness? We accept the reality of a diseased organ like a lung or a kidney, but we can't seem to understand that a diseased brain can cause people to act in unacceptable ways. That's almost as barbaric as murder itself.

"It doesn't take a shrink to understand what Slocum's been doing. Did you look at the photos of those women? He's reliving the experience of killing his mother, the woman who probably made his life hell on earth. Killing her was probably the only moment of joy he's ever had in his life. He wants to feel that joy again, just as a drug abuser wants to feel that high time after time."

"I suppose," Chris said, "that you intend to bring in some expert who will testify to that?"

"If I'm right, yes."

"I'll fight it coming in," he said.

"I expect you to," she said.

He sighed. "Let's assume, for the sake of discussion, that you're right. What difference does it make? Okay, so Slocum is not at fault because he's crazy, be it brain damage or whatever. The fact remains he's a killer and will never change. We both have a responsibility to protect society from the Slocums of the world. Executing him serves that responsibility best."

"I don't think so," she said.

Chris slowly put his fork on the table. "Laura," he

said, "you've been in this business long enough to
know what's going to happen. You can spin your
wheels for however long you like, but in the end, a
jury of twelve people is going to find John Slocum
guilty of murder, and a judge is going to sentence
him to death. After four to ten years of legal bullshit, Slocum will be executed. All you'll accomplish
by mounting an insanity defense is waste money
that could be better spent elsewhere. If you're truly
the liberal you purport to be, your concerns should
be directed to those in need, not some sick animal
who can no longer be considered a human being.
There's only so much money available. Every dime
you piss away on this piece of slime is a dime that
can't be spent on someone worthwhile."

She grinned. "Would you like to examine that
statement a little more closely?"

"What do you mean?"

"The money. If you're really concerned about
saving money, consider this. If Slocum is convicted
and sentenced to life, and if he lives to age eighty,
the cost of keeping him locked up until the day he
dies is about a million dollars. If he's sentenced to
death, the cost of finally executing him will be
twice that because of the cost of countless automatic appeals. That's not even considering special
appeals. Economically, execution makes no sense
at all. The only reason we do it is because of plain,
old-fashioned vengeance."

"Not true," Chris said. "We live in an age of dou-
blespeak, where a life sentence means something
less in most cases. There's always the chance that
a man like Slocum could eventually be released.
Both Charles Manson and Sirhan Sirhan have been

given any number of parole hearings. While neither has been released to date, you can bet that both will be someday. Thousands of convicted killers *have* been released over the years, some after serving as little as three or four years in prison, and many of them have killed again. That, in my opinion, is irresponsible.

"To take it a step further, consider this—no one can predict the attitudes of courts or parole boards twenty or thirty years from now. If you look at the history of criminal punishment, it isn't far-fetched to assume that the courts may someday rule that life imprisonment is cruel and unusual punishment. They may rule that killers are just misunderstood. Who the hell knows? There are no guarantees except one. If Slocum is executed, we know damn well *he'll* never kill again. What's more important? His life, or the life of another innocent girl?"

"That isn't the issue," Laura said.

"It *is* the issue," he insisted. "If Slocum's released in forty years, he'll kill again. I know it and you know it. That's not fair, and it's not justice."

"So you've abandoned your economic argument?"

"I've placed it aside for the moment," he said, smiling. "Seriously, don't you agree that Slocum is dangerous?"

"Of course."

"Then how can you champion the possibility that he'll walk the streets again?"

"I'm not."

"Sure you are. If, by some magic, you convince a judge and jury that John Slocum is not responsible for his acts, you leave open the possibility that he may someday be set free by well-meaning but ill-advised people who are looking back at something that happened twenty, thirty, or forty years ago."

"Chris, you know I have no other choice. None."

He leaned back in his chair, stared at her for a moment, then grinned. "I know," he said. "When are you going to Buffalo?"

"As soon as I've made arrangements for Ted."

"I want to come with you," he said.

"I'm just asking questions. It's too soon for depos."

"I know. I just want to hear what they have to say. Neither of us can see Slocum for a while. As you said yourself, it's an ideal opportunity. Have you applied to have his old record released?"

"Not yet."

He picked up his coffee cup. "I'll save you the trouble. I'll do it."

Over dinner, Laura told Ted of her plans. "I talked to Gerry and she said she'd be delighted to have you stay with them until I get back."

His face brightened. "Neato!"

She smiled at him. "I thought you might like that."

He blushed.

"You realize, of course, that Gerry is saying something important by doing this."

"I don't know what you mean."

"I'll explain. You and Shirley. Gerry is saying she trusts you both very much. So do I."

The blush deepened. "You don't have to worry

about that, Mom. If Shirley and I were gonna fool around, we sure wouldn't do it in her house."

Laura's eyebrows rose. "So, you've discussed it?"

"Yeah, we've discussed it. Do you know almost half the kids in school have had sex already? Everybody talks about it all the time, but Shirley and I made a deal."

"A deal?"

"Yeah. We figure that everybody at school thinks we're doing it, so in about a year, we're gonna tell them we did, but we're not, if you know what I mean."

"I think so."

"Then, maybe they'll get off our backs."

"It might make it worse," Laura said. "What's so terrible about telling the truth? Just saying that you don't believe in having sex until you're an adult?"

He made a face. "Mom, we have to get along, you know? If we start acting like we're some kinda nerds, we won't have any friends."

Laura sighed. "Speaking of school, how are things going?"

His face fell.

"What's the matter?" she asked.

"Nothing."

"You don't look like it's nothing."

He wrestled with his thoughts for a moment, then said, "It was just some stupid smart-asses, that's all. We've got a few guys at school who think they know it all. They don't know anything. They just think they do."

Laura's mind flashed to the editorial that had appeared in the *Clarion*. Of course. Children could be cruel beyond words.

"I'm sorry, Ted. It was about us, wasn't it? That thing in the paper?"

His gaze was fixed on his plate. "I guess. I don't let them get to me, though. I think they're on my back 'cause I'm into athletics and they're into other kinds of sports. You know what I mean? I've never let them bother me before and I'm not going to start now. I don't listen to them."

She squeezed his arm. "Ted, I can imagine how tough this is for you. How awful it must be."

"It's no big deal."

"Yes, it is. I know it. The only thing I can say is that we'll get through it. All of us. It's unfair that everyone in town knows our business, but we can't help what others do. All we can do is accept the truth. Your father is a good man. Alcoholism is a disease as much as cancer is a disease. Not everyone feels that way, but there's nothing we can do about that, either. We've talked a lot about that."

"I know," he said. "There's nothing we can do about Dad until he wants to make it happen. I understand that. But there is something else you could do."

"What?"

"You could get someone else to defend the guy who killed Wanda."

Laura leaned back in her chair. "Have you got a half hour to spare?"

"Sure."

"I think we'd better talk this out," she said.

They'd never seriously discussed the law. Ted had picked up some of the jargon through osmosis and he was aware whenever Laura's name had been mentioned in the newspaper, but he'd never asked a serious question before. This was something new, and required a full and detailed explanation.

They talked for over an hour, during which time Laura pulled out books and read complete paragraphs, not just on the law, but on life itself. When they finished, Laura wasn't sure he fully understood why she was defending John Slocum.

"Ted," she said, "we can't allow our lives to be dictated by the prejudices of others. I know what it's like to be an outsider, to be considered different. When I was your age, I faced it too, though I'll admit I've never had to face anything as tough as the stuff being thrown at you. It's no fun. It can be brutal, in fact, but we can't run away from the truth. We can try and explain, but we can never run. It just doesn't do any good. This will probably get a lot worse before it gets better. We won't go to trial for months. Do you think you can handle it?"

"I'll do my best," he said.

"That's all anyone can ask."

"What if I can't? What if the whole school turns against me? What if I don't have a single friend? What will you do then, Mom?"

She put her arm around him while she considered her answer. "You try as hard as you can," she said. "If it reaches the point where you honestly feel you can't take it, I'll get off the case."

He turned his head and looked into her eyes. "You mean it?"

"I mean it."

"It would cost you though, right? I mean, you'd be in trouble with the judge?"

"That's not important," she told him. "You're the most important person in my life, Ted. But you've got to try your best. Okay?"

"Okay," he said.

"If you want, I'll cancel the trip."

"Naw, you don't need to. I'll be okay." He grinned. "You just said we can't have other people running our lives. You can't very well come to school and hold my hand, can you? I'll just have to tough it out, Mom."

There was a husky manliness in his voice that made her want to burst with pride. "You're sure," she asked.

"I'm sure."

She held him very close.

CHAPTER 18

LAURA SCOTT AND CHRIS MARSHALL FLEW TO BUFFALO the next morning. Thanks to Chris's prior arrangements, they were hardly airborne when an Erie County assistant district attorney appeared in a Buffalo court on behalf of Chris, presenting a writ asking that the sealed records concerning John Slocum be released. An attorney representing the Department of Social Services appeared to argue against the release, claiming breach of public trust. The judge ruled in favor of the assistant DA, and the records were waiting at the hotel when Chris and Laura checked in. Laura was suitably impressed.

"This assistant DA is obviously a very good friend of yours," she said.

He grinned. "His name's Donnelly. We went to law school together. Kept in touch over the years. You never know."

"Do you always think ahead in your relationships?"

He frowned. "Are you asking if I use people?"

"No," she said. "That isn't what I meant. I'm sorry. The remark was uncalled for."

"Forget it."

For the next two hours, they sat in Chris's room and went over the records. When they were finished, Chris said, "Why don't you relax while I make some telephone calls."

"Who'd you have in mind?"

"The cop, the social worker, and the shrink, I think. At least to start. Do you want to talk to some of the doctors as well?"

"Yes," she said, leafing quickly through the pages. "There's one here named Conners, a pediatrician. He treated a skull fracture early on."

Chris smiled. "I thought he'd be the one. I'll try and set it up."

Laura went to her room, six doors away from Chris's, stripped off her clothes, and took a shower. She'd showered this morning, but reading the reports had made her skin crawl. She needed to be clean again.

Three hours later Chris phoned, told her all the appointments had been arranged with the exception of the social worker, and suggested dinner.

"What about the social worker?" she asked.

"She's no longer with the agency. She works in a dress shop. I think it would be better if we just dropped in. According to her former boss, she burned out years ago. Burnouts don't usually like to talk about their cases."

"Isn't that a bit unfair?" Laura asked.

"Yes," he said, "but so is killing innocent women. You'd rather leave her out of it?"

Laura thought about it for a moment, then said, "No."

They ate dinner in the hotel, talking about everything except the case, then said good night. Laura called Ted on the telephone and talked for almost a half hour. He reported that things at school had calmed down a little, primarily because he wasn't rising to the bait, choosing instead to ignore the taunts. He sounded proud of himself. Laura felt even prouder.

In the morning Chris and Laura started with the cop who'd investigated the death of John Slocum's mother. Lieutenant Roger Trickle had the look of a war-weary soldier. A big man in his mid-forties, with deeply hooded, red-rimmed, bloodshot eyes and a puffy, blotched round face, he wheezed as he talked, probably from the cigarettes he smoked incessantly.

"So you two are on the Slocum deal," he said as he showed Laura and Chris to a pair of wooden chairs fronting his battered walnut desk. They were in the squad room, a big, noisy room half-filled with police officers making reports, even at this early hour. People in various stages of distress were either complaining about a crime committed against them or wailing about the fact they'd been arrested for some crime they didn't commit. The cacophony of sound reverberated off the green-painted walls, assailing the ears with every kind of voice and every kind of emotion. The smell of urine fought disinfectant for attention.

"Is there somewhere else we could talk?" Laura asked.

He shook his head. "I don't have an office, Counselor, and I'm ten reports behind. You two asked for this meeting. You got questions, ask."

The place was so noisy, it was almost impossible to think. "You were the investigating officer at the time John Slocum killed his mother," Laura began. "I've read the report, but I wanted to talk to you personally."

Trickle looked at Chris. "And you?"

"I'm just along for the ride," he said. "This is Mrs. Scott's deal."

"Yeah, right." Trickle fixed his watery eyes on Laura. "You read the report. What else is there?"

"The report, like every police report I've ever read, is a condensation," she said. "There has to be more."

Trickle lit another cigarette, inhaled, and blew the smoke in her face. "That was ten years ago, lady. I can hardly remember what happened last month. If the report says I was the investigating officer, then I guess I was. You want more, you talk to the social workers."

"I intend to," she said. "Surely, you must remember something."

He frowned. "I've probably investigated three hundred killings since then. They all blend together, you know?"

"Surely you'd remember an eleven-year-old boy killing his mother," she insisted.

He leaned back in his chair. "How'd you get into this deal?"

"I was appointed."

He picked up a copy of the local newspaper. "The way I hear it, your client was caught with the god-damn knife still in his hand. Open and shut. He may have killed as many as fifty women according to what I read in the papers. So, what's the deal with you?"

"I'm just doing my job."

"Seems more than that to me," he said. "Seems to me you're trying to complicate something real simple. Maybe you're one of those people who likes to get their name in the paper. You looking to this case as a career-builder, Counselor, or are you one of those fanatics who sees every killer as a poor, misunderstood *shlemiel* just reaching out for a little understanding from a cruel, insensitive society?"

Chris was about to respond, but Laura cut him off with a glance. "I'm in it for the glory, Lieutenant," she said. "There's a certain comfort in being treated like a piece of garbage for defending this man. I guess I'm a masochist at heart. I realize that our society would be far better off if we simply let the police make the arrest, determine guilt or innocence, then carry out whatever sentences you great thinkers feel are appropriate. This antiquated system of ours is expensive, illogical, and often unjust, but for reasons I don't understand, it endures. I sincerely apologize for being part of it. I really do. But I'm stuck with it, you know? I've got some idiot judge back home who feels John Slocum should be defended. What can I do?"

Trickle's eyes turned even colder. "Up your ass, lady."

Chris could take no more. "Lieutenant Trickle,"

he said, his voice sure and even, "we're here on a legitimate inquiry, and we don't have a lot of time to waste." He dropped a copy of Trickle's original report on his desk. "This is the report you prepared at the time Slocum killed his mother ten years ago. Take a few moments to review it, then tell us what you remember. This isn't pleasant for either Mrs. Scott or myself, so let's not make things any more difficult than necessary."

A man being held in a temporary cell against the far wall started yelling obscenities at no one in particular, then began banging his head against the bars. A police officer got up from his desk, walked over to the cell, opened it, went inside, grabbed the screaming man's arm and twisted it behind his back. He placed handcuffs on the man's wrists, then chained him to a steel bench away from the bars. Once the police officer had returned to his desk, the still-screaming man continued to utter obscenities, blood streaming down his face, then began banging the back of his head against the wall. This time, no one moved.

Trickle pulled his attention back to Laura. "He's doing the same thing I'm doing, banging his head against a brick wall. He'll eventually knock himself out. I should be so lucky."

"About Slocum," Chris said.

Trickle gave him a hard stare, then picked up the report. He glanced at each page, then dropped the report back on his desk. "This is my report, all right, but I don't remember a thing about the case." He smiled. "You're prosecuting this guy?"

"Yes."

"Then go prosecute. I got things to do."

"Not so fast," Laura said. "The report states that Slocum killed his mother during a struggle in which she fell down on top of the knife. Your report called it self-defense. You were sure?"

Trickle stood up and pointed to the door. "Out."

"Lieutenant Trickle!" Laura protested.

"You want information from me, you get a court order," he snapped. "Now, get the hell out of my face."

According to the records, Constance Brown was a woman in her early forties, but she looked ten years older. She worked in a small dress shop a block from Delaware Avenue in suburban Kenmore, less than a half mile from the children's home where John Slocum had spent one third of his young life. Her gray hair was carefully styled and she wore appropriate makeup, but she looked as worn and weary as Lieutenant Trickle. She gave Laura and Chris a smile salespeople give all potential customers, but when they introduced themselves and told her why they were there, the smile quickly faded. "I have nothing to say to you," she said in a tight-lipped whisper.

"Mizz Brown," Laura said, "I realize this is difficult, but this investigation of John Slocum's background is very important. We wouldn't bother you if it wasn't so. Perhaps we could discuss this over coffee."

She shook her head. "There are only two of us on today. Business isn't all that good, but I still can't afford to take the time."

"What about this evening?" Laura suggested.

"Perhaps we could get together at my hotel. It shouldn't take long."

"No," she said quickly. "I have plans for this evening."

"Mizz Brown," Laura insisted, "we really must talk to you. We've both traveled all the way from Florida to see you. We wouldn't have done that if it wasn't important."

"I'm sure it is," she said, "but I really have nothing to say. What happened with Johnnie happened a long time ago. I haven't been involved in social work for eight years. I don't really remember much about him. I'm sorry you've wasted your time." She'd called him Johnnie, giving Laura an insight as to her true feelings.

"How long were you involved in social work?" Laura asked softly.

Constance Brown grimaced. "Seven years," she said. "Seven terrible years."

"Then you know," Laura said, lying with a straight face, "that I have a right to subpoena you and require you to appear in court and testify if need be. If you cooperate with me now, I don't think it will be necessary, but if you refuse, I'll have to play it by the book. I'm required to give my client the best defense I can muster. I don't have a choice."

There was a flicker in the woman's eyes. Like most experienced social workers, she was familiar with many of the laws governing her work, but it had been some years since she'd left the agency. And then, there was the fact that Johnnie had been arrested in Florida. She wasn't sure. She wanted no more trouble. This lawyer seemed kinder than most. Perhaps . . .

She kneaded her hands. "This has already been in the papers, you know. Johnnie was born and raised here in Buffalo. If they find out I was the social worker when this all started, the reporters will want to ask me questions. They'll show up here and my boss won't stand for it. I'll lose my job."

Then, puzzled, she asked, "How did you find out about me, anyway?"

Chris answered the question. "We had the records unsealed, Mizz Brown. We've read your reports."

Her face went white. "You had the records unsealed?"

"We had to," Chris said. "If you've been reading the papers, you know that John Slocum is possibly a serial killer."

The air seemed to go out of her lungs. "Then it's only a matter of time before the reporters will find me, isn't it?" Her eyes began to mist.

"There's no reason you have to talk to any reporters," Chris said.

"Really? And what do I tell my boss when they start hanging around the store?"

"Why don't you issue a statement to the effect that you have nothing to say to the press? Once they realize you're serious, they'll leave you alone. They have no right to bother you at work. I'll give you the name of an assistant district attorney who should be able to help if they pester you."

It was a patently idle promise, one she immediately saw through. "Oh, I'm sure some DA is going to worry about my problems," she said.

"I'll keep our conversation confidential," Laura added.

"Please," she said. "I'm not a fool. I know what this is about. I want no part of it."

Despite her words, Laura could see she was vacillating. An experienced social worker knows that lawyers can make their lives a living hell. They're often drawn into cases involving their clients. Her desire to be left out of this was strong, but she knew the reality of her position. By cooperating now, she might stave off future problems.

"Look," Laura said, "I really don't want to make trouble for you, but you must understand that I'm defending a man accused of murder. Unlike New York, we have the death penalty in Florida and John Slocum is staring it right in the face. I'll be candid with you. I don't think whatever you tell me will make much of a difference other than to help me understand what happened to him when he was a kid, but I just can't let it go. The sooner you and I talk, the sooner I'm out of your life. Why don't we go across the street, have a coffee, and get this out of the way?"

Constance let out a deep sigh, then walked to the back of the store where her partner was tagging inventory. The two women held a whispered discussion for a moment. Constance returned, reached beneath the counter, and picked up her handbag. "One condition," she said, facing Laura.

"Yes?"

"This has to be off the record. If you want to talk to me officially, you'll have to get a court order."

Both Laura and Chris nodded. Without a word, Constance moved toward the front door, looking as if she were on her way to the electric chair.

They went to a small soup-and-sandwich shop less than a block away. Over coffee, she told them what she knew, most of which had been included in the reports Chris and Laura had read the previous night. It had been ten years ago, but the woman displayed a remarkable memory.

"I first got the case when Johnnie was eight," she said. "One of the doctors at the hospital finally made an official charge."

"Dr. Conners?" Chris asked.

She nodded. "By that time, most of Johnnie's bones had been broken at least once." She sighed. "Johnnie's mother had never worked a day in her life. Her husband was killed in an industrial accident before Johnnie was even born, and I guess there was a pretty good insurance settlement, because she was never on welfare or anything like that. If she had been, we would have had the case sooner."

She took a deep breath. "Anyway, she gave birth to Johnnie three weeks after her husband was killed. Two months later, Johnnie was in the hospital with a fractured skull. His mother said he'd fallen off a bed. Then, six months after that, he was back with a fractured arm. His mother said he'd fallen again.

"The case was referred to social services. Someone from the agency checked out the home and talked to the neighbors, but no one had a bad word to say about Johnnie's mother. Not then. Nobody even knew about her drinking. So nothing was done.

"Then, when Johnnie was eight, he was rushed to the hospital with a fractured skull. Dr. Conners treated him and swore out a complaint. I was assigned the case until the court hearing. That was the first time I met Johnnie. He was terrified. Absolutely terrified. Not of her, though. Even though she treated him something awful, she was all he had. He was more terrified of losing her than of being beaten. He was used to being beaten, but he wasn't used to not having his mother around, you understand?"

"He told you that?"

She shook her head. "Of course not. He wouldn't open up at all. He denied he'd ever been hit. I got a psychiatrist involved and he tried to get Johnnie to talk about it, but he just wouldn't, insisting that he was accident-prone. He kept saying his mother never laid a hand on him, so they had to drop the case. Without Johnnie, they had no case."

Her gaze flicked from Chris to Laura, then back again. "You're both lawyers. You know how hard it is to make a jury believe something when it's just circumstantial evidence. Without Johnnie's testimony, we had no chance."

Laura nodded. "Go on."

"Well, about a year later, Johnnie was in the hospital again. This time he almost died from internal bleeding, and when he was going under he told the doctor that his mother tried to kill him. Later, when he was recovering, he denied she ever hurt him, but at another hearing, the judge allowed the doctor to testify about what Johnnie had said under the anesthetic."

That was unusual, Laura thought. Normally inadmissible, this evidence had been allowed in by a judge who cared.

"This was a trial?" she asked.

"No. It was a hearing. I was trying to get Johnnie out of that terrible home and into a foster home. The agency was concerned that if Johnnie stayed, he would eventually be killed, so we got an emergency hearing."

Laura smiled at her. "You mean *you* got an emergency hearing."

"I guess. Did Johnnie really kill those girls? The papers here make it appear all but certain. You've talked to him. What do you think?"

Laura was impressed by the concern and caring written all over this woman's too-old-too-soon face. The case had been years ago, yet it was clear Constance Brown still harbored a brave hope that John Slocum might have turned out all right. The caring ones always held out hope, she thought. That's what eventually burned them out.

"As John's attorney," Laura said, "I'm unable to give you an answer to that question. However, based on the evidence I've seen, I'd say the police have enough probable cause to lay a charge. Does that give you some indication?"

Constance looked as if she wanted to cry. "But you're up here asking questions," she said. "You must have some thoughts on a defense."

"I do. I hope to convince a jury that John is insane."

Constance flinched, then looked at Chris. "And you? What's your plan?"

"My job is simple, Mizz Brown. I present the evidence to a jury, that's all. They make the judgment, not me."

"He never had a chance," she said quietly.

"Perhaps," Chris said softly. "Neither did Wanda

Brooks. Tell us what happened at the hearing."

She stared at Chris for a moment, then said, "The judge ruled in our favor. Johnnie was taken away from his mother and placed in a foster home. His mother was sentenced to a year in jail.

"Johnny went into a shell after that," she continued. "He was uncommunicative, uncooperative, and pretty hard to deal with. He was in three foster homes in the space of two months. Most of the time, he was kept in the center, waiting. He failed his year at school and had to repeat. Then when his mother got out of jail, she got herself a new lawyer and applied to get him back. We had to go to court all over again.

"The lawyer brought a psychiatrist to the stand who said she was undergoing therapy, wasn't drinking anymore, and was a changed woman. He also said he'd examined Johnnie and felt the kid was doomed unless he was placed back with his mother. The court gave her temporary custody for a year. I was assigned the job of regular visits to ensure that Johnnie was safe.

"I went over there at least once a month. She was always sober, polite, and nice. Johnnie was doing better in school and for a while there, I really thought things would work out. Then, after a year, the court ruled that she could have him back for good. I was taken off the case. A month after that, he was in the hospital with a broken jaw. They both said he fell down the stairs again. We all knew better, but what could we do? Six months later, he killed her."

"How did that happen?" Laura asked. She already knew what was in the report, but she wanted to hear it from Constance.

"Johnnie said she was drunk and out of her mind. She came at him with a kitchen knife and he tried to take it away from her. During the struggle, she fell on top of it and died. The autopsy backed up the fact that she was drunk and the evidence supported Johnnie's story. Even the policeman investigating the case testified and said it looked like self-defense to him."

"Lieutenant Trickle?"

"Yes."

"This was a family court case?"

"Yes. There was a lot of discussion back and forth and Johnnie was to be examined by another psychiatrist. The one he'd seen before had died. This new one finally got through to him. I guess Johnnie realized that he needed to tell the truth. At the next hearing, Johnnie admitted he'd been abused from the start. Not only did she beat him, but she sexually abused him as well, according to the doctor. Of course, we couldn't develop any evidence to support that, so I don't know if she did or she didn't. In any case, the district attorney decided not to prosecute and once again, we tried to place Johnnie in a foster home, but none of them would take him. We had to put him in a children's home."

"How did he take that?" Laura asked.

"He seemed okay," she said. "He was very quiet and got average marks. There was never any trouble, really. Then, two years after that, I left the agency. I saw him a couple of times after that, just on the street or something, and he seemed okay. I lost track of him after that."

Laura signaled the waitress for the check. "Mizz Brown, you've been a big help. I appreciate the time and the information. Would you be willing to . . ."

Constance cut her off with a wave of the hand. "You're a lawyer. I guess you can force me to do whatever you want, but I won't be involved willingly."

"Why not?"

"Because," she said, "it doesn't matter whether Johnnie is crazy or not. You said yourself he killed that girl. He's a killer now. He has to be taken off the streets, and I understand that. Just another failure. It doesn't really matter whether he dies in the electric chair or spends the rest of his life in prison. He's no good to anyone anymore. He's already been destroyed. What happens now is irrelevant, isn't it?"

"Not really," Laura said. "If John is truly insane, then he isn't responsible for his actions."

"What difference does it make?" she said. "He'd be better off dead now." There was a new note of harshness in her voice. "Once they're gone, they're gone. Johnnie Slocum started dying twenty-one years ago, the first time his mother beat him. He was halfway there when he killed her in self-defense. Now he's killed others. He's really dead this time." She stared at Chris. "You might as well complete the job."

Chris and Laura walked her back to the store and then said good-bye to a shaken ex-social worker. Standing by the rented car, Chris handed Laura the keys. "The shrink is next. I'll let you handle that one yourself."

"Where are you going?"

"I think I'd better take my old friend Donnelly to lunch. I'll meet you at Dr. Conners's office at three, if that's all right."

"Sure," she said, "but why don't you want to see the shrink with me?"

"It's redundant," he said. "Whatever Slocum's state of mind was years ago, it has no bearing on the Brooks case."

"If you believe that, you must also believe that everything we're doing here is redundant. If that's so, why did you bother to come?"

He grinned. "I'll explain that over dinner."

"Can I drop you?"

"I'll take a cab," he said, then walked quickly down the street.

Dr. Wayne Frezell's eyes appraised Laura through steel-rimmed glasses as he greeted her in his waiting room. He was a tall man, and like many tall men, he hunched over slightly as if trying to avoid banging his head on the tops of door frames. His full, pure gray hair was combed to one side in no particular order. His sixtyish, pleasant face was unsmiling.

"I don't have much time," he said as he shook her hand. "Why don't we talk in my office."

His office, a cramped, stark room with little warmth, was adjacent to his interview room and exemplified the personality of the man. "I was given to understand there were two of you," he said.

"Mr. Marshall had to see someone else," she said.

"And you're the one representing John Slocum?"

"Yes."

"What do you want from me? I told Mr. Marshall on the telephone I'm unable to discuss John's case with anyone. As an attorney, you should know that." His eyes were turning hostile.

"Dr. Frezell," she said, "I'm aware of the law. I'm also aware that we, as a society, have a tendency to point fingers when something terrible happens. I've read the local papers. Because Slocum was born and raised here, he's getting a lot of press. Naturally, his early life will be of great interest and it won't be long before you'll be mentioned. I can understand your reticence. There are those who will eventually say that you, as his doctor, are responsible for the fact that he was turned loose. I don't happen to share that view."

Some of the hostility left his eyes. "Why not?"

"Because I realize that psychiatry is an inexact science for one. For another, I've read your report."

He was stunned. "That was sealed," he snapped.

"We were able to arrange for the records to be unsealed and released," she said. "Since this is a capital case, the court saw fit to give us access."

"I see," the doctor said, rubbing his chin.

Laura opened her attaché case and removed the report Frezell had written three years ago. "This is all I wish to discuss with you," she said. "Under Florida law, I cannot compel you to submit to a deposition, nor can I subpoena you. My only interest is in providing the best defense possible for my client. Will you at least comment on your report?"

He stared at her for a moment, then shook his head. "I'm sorry, but I can't do that."

"Why not?"

"For several reasons," he answered. "The doctor-client privilege still exists. Until John Slocum personally releases me, I am bound by that privilege, but that's really beside the point. Your presence here would indicate that you're looking into a possible insanity defense. If John Slocum is insane, his illness manifested itself during the three years he was on his own. He was not in any way insane while I was treating him. If he was, I would have said so in my report."

"How can you be so sure?"

"Because I am trained to make such determinations. Prior to his release, I gave John a battery of tests, including an MMPI profile. There was no indication of severe emotional distress."

Laura looked at her notes. "You stated that you had prepared an MMPI profile on Slocum prior to his final hearing, and that you felt the profile was inconclusive, yet you recommended his release on the basis of other data. Please don't misunderstand. I'm not being critical here. I'm just trying to understand. What exactly is an MMPI profile?"

She thought he was going to refuse to answer, but he didn't. "The Minnesota Multiphasic Personality Inventory, MMPI for short, consists of 566 statements that are addressed by the person taking the test. Statements like 'I love my mother,' or 'I have never stolen anything in my life.' The statements can be answered three ways; true, false, or not applicable. In the hands of a skilled clinician, the answers can provide an insight into the basic personality of the person taking the test. It's very hard to beat."

"But you said the report was inconclusive."

"It was. John Slocum clearly lied in answering most of the questions. The MMPI cannot be conclusive if the person taking the test is untruthful. The fact is, John Slocum was a pathological liar. Given his background, I considered his condition reasonable in that he'd been trained to lie since he was old enough to understand what a lie was. His lying was almost involuntary, like breathing in and breathing out. Nevertheless, his general behavior was otherwise acceptable sociologically. He was never violent or abusive, his school marks were good, and he got along well with the teachers and other students. Aside from his lying, he exhibited no other sociopathic tendencies."

"None?"

The hostility returned. "Mrs. Scott, I've already told you that I'm unable to discuss this case with you. The last time I saw your client was over three years ago. At that time, he was not considered a threat to himself or anyone else. If everyone with a paranormal personality was kept locked up, there would be fewer than fifty thousand people walking the streets of this country." He stood up. "We all have our neuroses."

Laura remained seated. "I would call murder something more than a neurosis," she said.

"I have patients waiting, Mrs. Scott."

"Let me ask you something. You say that Slocum lied when he took the test. You say he's a pathological liar, in fact. How do you know he was telling you the truth about the killing of his mother? Could he have been lying about the details?"

The doctor moved away from her. "I'm a doctor, not a detective. The evidence supported his statements," he said. "That convinced me he was telling the truth."

"But . . ."

"Look, Mrs. Scott, I have no more time for you.

When I treated John Slocum, he was not a violent person and I shall so testify if I'm required to do so. If something happened in the intervening years to cause him to crack, it has nothing to do with me. You'll have to have someone down there do an evaluation to determine his present mental condition. Now, please leave. I have patients waiting."

Beneath the calm facade, he was smoldering, and Laura knew why. He'd been fooled by an eighteen-year-old boy three years ago. It wasn't the first time a well-qualified doctor had been fooled and it wouldn't be the last.

CHAPTER

19

CHRIS WAS WAITING FOR LAURA AT DR. CONNERS'S office. Unlike Dr. Frezell, Dr. Conners was a young man, vital and animated, totally open and quite warm. After Laura explained her reason for being there, the doctor said, "I dug out the charts after Mr. Marshall called yesterday," he said. "I've examined the X rays carefully. I see no evidence of physical brain damage. You realize, of course, that these X rays are quite old."

"Yes."

He handed Laura the files. "These should have been discarded some time ago. I can't imagine why I kept them. You can take them with you. Under the circumstances, I suggest a full CAT scan. X rays just don't give the full story. A CAT scan would be much more revealing. I've made some notes for you. There's a list of experts I'm personally acquainted with who've done studies on physical abuse of children and its effects in later years. I'm sure they can be of assistance to you. I've also given you a list of pertinent medical papers published on the subject in recent years. Some of the authors might be willing to assist you."

Chris seemed upset. "Doctor, you've gone to much trouble. Why the intense interest?"

Dr. Conners fixed a crystal-clear gaze on Chris. "There have been enough studies done on violence in this country to fill the Library of Congress, yet it just gets worse. John Slocum may or may not be brain-damaged physiologically, but there's no question in my mind that he's a killer because of his environment. If Mrs. Scott is prepared to make some effort to link his murderous acts to his abuse, I'm more than willing to help her in any way I can."

Marshall's face reddened. "So, as far as you're concerned, no human being is responsible for his or her actions. It's all in how he's been brought up. That certainly makes it simple."

"That's not what I said," the doctor retorted.

Laura cut them both off by standing up and extending her hand. "I appreciate your interest, Doctor."

There were still two people on the list of appointments. One was the director of the children's home where Slocum had spent seven years of his life, and the other was one of Slocum's former teachers, who had given testimony at the family court hearing. As Chris drove silently, Laura reconsidered the value of seeing them, the words of Dr. Frezell ringing in her ears. He'd said that John Slocum's mental state three years ago was irrelevant. He was speaking as a doctor, but in legal terms, he was right on target as well. Laura had thought that Slocum was reliving the killing of his mother every time he killed. She was even more convinced of it now, but she knew the only way insanity could be used as an effective defense was to have Slocum appraised by an expert who was prepared to testify that John Slocum was legally insane when he murdered Wanda Brooks. No one in Buffalo could possibly do that, but still she'd come. Why? Was it in the hope that someone would provide a magic bullet? Or was it simple curiosity? Perhaps, she thought, she was trying to understand what drove someone to commit a series of murders, needing to be empathetic to properly defend her client. How was one empathetic to a man who'd brutally murdered over a score of women?

Her mind flashed ahead to the expected trial. She'd need more than one expert to make any kind of impression on a Seminole Springs jury, and such experts, often called hired guns in the business, were extremely expensive. The state of Florida certainly wasn't about to pay for it and neither was Laura. That was only one of several problems with this case she would have to address. It was clear to Laura she was wasting her time in Buffalo.

"Chris," she said, "I think I'd like to go back

tonight instead of tomorrow."

"How come?"

"I don't think this is very worthwhile."

He seemed disappointed. "Are you sure? Dr. Conners seems anxious to help you."

"Chris, please don't patronize me. Would you allow me to put him on the stand?"

"I'd have to think about it," he admitted.

She snorted. "I'll bet. Even if you did, I doubt Judge Fry would allow it. Which brings me back to something I asked you earlier. Just why did you come here with me anyway? You know I'd have a devil of a time getting any of this testimony in. You weren't even taking notes and why should you? All you have to do is cite precedent and I'm probably dead in the water."

"Look," he said. "Why don't we see the next one on the list, go back to the hotel, relax, then have a nice dinner? It's already past checkout time. We'll have to pay for the hotel in any event. We can discuss it over dinner."

"I'd rather discuss it now," she said. "Please, let's go to the hotel. I'll phone the children's home from there and explain why we're not coming."

Chris pulled the car over to the side of the street and parked. He shut off the ignition and turned to face her. "You asked why I came on this trip. I'd like to tell you."

"I'm listening," she said.

"In the first place, I'm worried about you. Not about your legal talents, but about your own state of mind. I'm not sure you realize it, but I think you're suffering terribly. You've had to deal with more emotional trauma in the last few days than most people face in a lifetime—Dan running off, your daughter's death, Ferris taking potshots at you in that rag of his, the heat you're taking for defending this guy. It's a big load, Laura."

Laura was touched. "So you wanted to watch over me?"

"In a way. I know you're capable, but you're human, too, Laura, and all human beings have their limits. I just wanted to be there for you, providing some support, letting you know a friend is near, that's all. I know we're on opposite sides of the fence when it comes to your client, but that isn't important. What's important is your getting through a very difficult time."

"I'm impressed," she said. "I really am. You're very sweet, Chris."

"Thanks. I should also tell you I'm thinking of the future."

"The future?"

"Yes."

For a moment, she didn't understand. "I like you, Laura," he said. "I like you a lot. If I had to make a guess, I'd say your marriage is over. You said yourself you didn't love Dan anymore and you're much too smart to throw away the rest of your life on someone you don't love. You're also not the kind of woman to want to spend the rest of your life alone. Someday, you're going to be looking for someone to fill that void in your life. I just want to be close by when that happens."

Laura held up a hand. "Chris, this isn't the time . . ."

"Hear me out," he said, cutting her off. "You're a beautiful, sensual woman, Laura. I'm very attracted to you. I realize that this is not the time for serious romance. There'll be a time for that down the road, but there's something else besides romance, Laura. There's that good old-fashioned lift that comes from some honest, straightforward sex."

Laura found it hard to believe what she was hearing.

"God knows, you haven't had a good roll in the hay for much too long," he continued. "I'm good, Laura. I mean it. I know it sounds arrogant, but I can't help that. I've heard the rumors around town. Hell, I'm not gay. I'm just very, very discreet." He laughed. "You know, I never get involved with women in town because it's just not smart, but for you, I'm prepared to make an exception. You need this, Laura, and I think you can be as discreet as me. No one will ever know."

His approach was so obviously predatory, so stunningly selfish, Laura could barely catch her breath.

"I've shocked you, haven't I?" he said.

"A little," she mumbled.

"Don't be alarmed. I'm not a phony, Laura. I say what's on my mind. I don't fill your ears with bull-shit. If you really think about it, you'll realize I'm right. You need this."

She fought the rising anger as if it were a living thing. In a few months she expected to be facing Chris Marshall in a courtroom. She'd already learned that a man with a wounded ego could be as vicious as any animal, and here was a man with an ego more prodigious than any she'd ever encountered. She wanted to slap him, to scream at him, to tell him to his face how unspeakably rapacious he was, but in a small corner of her mind, the cool breeze of reason chilled the hot fires of outrage.

"You're very sweet," she said, struggling to bring a smile to her lips. "I like you too, Chris, but right now, I'm a poor candidate for romance."

"I wasn't talking about romance."

"I know, but I must," she said. "One of my hang-ups is that I equate sex with love. I know how immature that is, but I can't help it. Perhaps, after I see what happens with Dan, and the pain of losing Victoria fades a little, I can approach things with a different attitude. Right now, you'd find me a very big disappointment."

She closed her eyes as she touched his hand, not wanting the image to be etched in her memory. It was like touching the skin of a snake. "When we . . . get together, I want it to be special." She almost choked on the words. "You know what they say about first impressions being lasting. I want your first impression of me to be a good one. I'm afraid it would be anything but right now." She squeezed the snake's hand and opened her eyes. "Can you be patient with me?"

He glowed, despite the obvious disappointment. "Sure, Laura. I understand. I hope you're not offended."

"Not at all," she said. "I appreciate your honesty and I'm flattered by your . . . thoughts. Let's go back to the hotel and talk to the manager. Maybe we can make some arrangement for late checkout. And I really appreciate your help. I really do. You're a very kind and thoughtful person, Chris."

He leaned forward and kissed her on the cheek. She wanted to vomit.

CHAPTER

20

THREE DAYS AFTER RETURNING FROM BUFFALO, LAURA was finally allowed to see her client again, but it wasn't easy. The little town of Seminole Springs was now an international focal point for news. The story of John Slocum and his incredible string of suspected victims—a story now distorted and twisted with the death toll rumored to be over fifty—was being instantly beamed all over the world by state-of-the-art communications equipment. Reporters from at least twelve countries were already here, and more were on their way. Almost every major American city was represented by at least one crew of media types, both print and electronic.

With the competition raging, one major television network sent their two-million-dollar-a-year anchorman to report on the story. A specially constructed platform had been erected in the park across from the civic center, from which this famous journalist was to telecast his evening report. Even at this early hour, almost a hundred people were milling about, vying for the best place to view the celebrity in their midst.

With motel space limited, many reporters were staying as far away as Orlando. Others, not wishing to be absent when some new story element broke, were sleeping in rented cars. Some had waved hundred-dollar bills in the faces of retired residents, who'd taken them in as boarders.

Both the civic center and Memorial Hospital looked like buildings under siege. At the hospital, state troopers had set up yellow wooden barricades that had to be manned twenty-four hours a day. Additional, private security people guarded each entrance to ward off an increasingly obstreperous press corps. On side streets adjacent to the hospital, vans of varying sizes were parked, their large parabolic up-link dishes aimed at unseen satellites thousands of miles away in space. Black cables snaking from van to van littered roads and sidewalks. Power generators growled, their acrid fumes fouling the air.

Reporters had resorted to every ruse known to man in their attempts to get a look at Slocum. The photographers were worse. At least three had posed as heart attack victims, calling ambulances in an effort to get inside the emergency room. The paramedics had realized two were faking it as soon as they performed some routine tests prior to taking the "victim" to the hospital, but one reporter/photographer had resorted to an old draft-beating trick, eating a bar of soap before calling the ambulance. His EKG was erratic and he was dutifully carted off. As soon as he was wheeled into the emergency room, he leapt from the gurney and started running up the stairs to the top floor, small camera in hand. He fainted before he got there. Jim Pickett arrested him for malicious mischief, slapped him in jail for half a day, then let him go with a fine. A stern letter was sent to his employers suggesting that if this man returned, he'd be clapped in jail forever. Seminole Springs had become a zoo, and Laura Scott was caught right in the middle, totally exposed to the animals.

Laura parked her car two blocks from the hospital, then strode purposefully toward it, her attaché case held tightly in her hand, her handbag slung over her shoulder. About a hundred feet from the front entrance, the horde saw her and rushed forward en masse. Her ears were assailed by the shouted questions of thirty or forty people at once, a babble of undecipherable noise. Three times, she'd released a statement that she would not, under any circumstances, speak to the press. To no avail. They were everywhere—in front, behind, and on either side of her. One microphone struck her nose. Another man holding a small minirecorder accidentally thrust it into her eye. Instinctively, she crouched down, and brought up an arm to protect herself. The handbag swung out and clipped someone on the mouth.

The crush of humanity was pushing her from all directions, making it impossible to move. She was starting to panic, feeling like a person being dragged to the bottom of a swimming pool.

Then she heard a familiar voice, bellowing at the top of his lungs, using language more suited to a sewer, but the effect was almost instantaneous. The crush of humanity receded and she could breathe again. With her one good eye, she looked into the concerned face of Jim Pickett. "Come on, Laura," he said as he held out a hand to her.

Once inside the hospital, she sat on a bench to catch her breath, pulling out her makeup mirror to examine her eye. There was a small, swelling cut at the corner of the eyelid, but it would be fine. She snapped the compact shut. "Thanks, Jim," she said.

"Next time you want to come over here, you let me know first," he said. "Save us all a lot of trouble."

"I will," she said. "I had no idea it was like this."

"It's all happened in the last twenty-four hours," he said. "Don't ask me why. It's crazy. All of a sudden, it's like there's nothing else going on in the world. Seems your client is the only bad guy left worth doing a story on. God only knows what makes these people tick. I sure as hell don't. You gonna be okay?"

"I'll be fine," she said. "A little touch-up on the makeup, comb my hair, and I'll be fine."

"You'd better get a nurse to put something on that eye."

"I will."

"All right. When you're done with Slocum, you

tell the trooper upstairs. He'll get me on the radio and I'll come and help you out of here. We'll take you out through the service entrance."

"Thanks, Jim. Isn't there something we can do about those people?"

"Not much," he said. "This is supposed to be a free country. I talked to the mayor about limiting the number of reporters, but he said no way. Can't really blame him. That doesn't mean you need to be assaulted. Anybody lays a hand on you, you let me know. Okay?"

"Okay."

"We caught a couple of them heading for your house again, but we gave them the word. I don't think it'll happen again, but if they bother you, just call. There's a limit, dammit."

"I appreciate it, Jim. I really do."

He patted her on the shoulder and left.

Rick was in his office. He smiled at Laura, then poured coffee for them both. "I didn't have time to ask when I called. How was Buffalo?"

"Great," she said. "It was wonderful breathing air with a temperature of less than ninety-five degrees."

"Find anything out about your client?"

"Yes. You were right. He was abused from the time he was a child."

"I knew it."

"How's he doing?"

"Well, as I told you, the operation went well. He's completely out of danger now. I don't think there'll be any other complications. He should be out of here in about five days. I won't miss him."

"You said I could see him."

"Yes, but I'm going to limit his visitors to yourself for a couple of days. I don't want any more cops interrogating him."

"That's fine with me," Laura said.

"Try to keep it under an hour, if you can."

"I will," she said.

He turned his attention to some files. "Rick?"

"Yes?"

"I'd like you to do something for me."

"What?"

"I'd like a CAT scan of Slocum's skull."

He placed the pen on his desk, and leaned back in his chair. "Why?"

"I may want to bring an expert in to look at it, but before I think about that, I'd like your opinion. There's no use pursuing this if you don't see any evidence of brain damage."

Rick gave her a funny look. "Laura, if you're thinking what I think you're thinking, you're going at this backward. As Slocum's doctor, I can tell you that brain damage is not indicated. If you want to bring in a consultant, and he orders a CAT scan, I'll do it, but I can't do it on your say-so. The hospital won't stand for unnecessary tests."

"All right," she said. "I'll bring someone in. You have any recommendations?"

He looked as if he'd just eaten something unpleasant. "Not for this," he said. "I know some specialists in the field, but what you're after is a hired gun. None of the people I know fit that description."

"I'm not trying to play with the truth, Rick."

His eyes narrowed. "Sure you are," he said. "I

just told you brain damage is not indicated. Slocum's murderous actions do not qualify as a symptom. When there's actual physical brain damage, there are a host of other symptoms that give an indication. Slocum lacks them all, and I don't think any legitimate neurosurgeon is going to find anything I haven't found. However, I'm well aware of the fact that there are doctors in every field who will say whatever you want them to say for the right price. I'm sure you'll find one if you look hard enough." There was an undercurrent of anger in his voice.

"Rick," Laura said, "I wish you wouldn't put words in my mouth. I'm just exploring the possibilities, that's all."

He stood up. "I don't mean to be a tough guy, Laura, but in my opinion, your client does not suffer from brain damage. If you want to go over my head, you're free to do so. I know you're just doing the best for your client and I don't have a real problem with that, but I'm not ordering any CAT scans. Sorry."

"I understand, Rick. Do you have any objection to me bringing in someone?"

"Not at all." Then he laughed. "I think you may get an objection from your client, though."

If anything, Slocum looked thinner than the last time she'd seen him, less than a week ago. The rat-like eyes appeared to have grown even smaller, sunk in their sockets like those of small animals hiding from a predator. A stump of a leg was covered in gauze, the other leg and one arm still manacled to the heavy steel bed frame.

"How've you been?" Laura asked.

"You really wanna know?"

"I do," she said.

He stared at the ceiling for a moment, then said, "Every day's the same. The bring me my food, then let it fall on the floor. Then they tell me to eat it. They unlock the chains and put me on the floor. I gotta eat off the fuckin' floor. I'm so hungry, that's what I do. Then they hit me in the stomach until I puke it all up, and then they make me clean the floor."

"Let me see your stomach," Laura said.

He laughed. "Won't do no good. These boys know what they're doin'. Ain't no bruises. Nuthin' shows. I know all about beatin's, lady."

"I'll have a doctor examine you," she said.

Again he laughed. "Won't do no good. You're wastin' your time with this. They gonna kill me is all, and there ain't a damn thing you can do about it. Nuthin'."

His lies were pathetic. "John," she said, "have you considered the reality of your position?"

"Reality?" he said, sneering. "You're the one who says I'm crazy. What's a crazy person supposed to know about reality?"

"I didn't say you were crazy, John. I said that insanity is the only defense we have. The evidence the police have against you is so strong, no lawyer in the world could counter it. You keep insisting you didn't kill her, but we both know that's not true. The only chance I have of preventing your execution is to prove you didn't know what you were doing. That's the *only* chance."

"Well, you're wasting your time," he said. "I ain't sayin' I'm crazy, and I ain't lettin' anybody else say it either. Besides, you shouldn't be talkin' about no trial. I'll be long dead before any trial ever starts."

"Stop it," she snapped.

His eyes became slits. "You still think I'm lying to you?"

"Of course you're lying to me," she said. "God! Do you think I'm stupid? They don't have to play around, John. All they have to do is present the facts to a jury. You'll be convicted and sentenced to die soon enough. Can't you see that?"

He stared at her for a moment, then looked away.

Laura walked to the window and looked out. The sky was clear and blue. Serene. A fat bluejay flew lazily by the window, then took off like a jet plane, heading straight up. Laura was jealous of its freedom.

"You ever kill anybody?" she heard him say.

"No," she answered, not looking at him. She was tired of him, fed up with his lies, his constant denials, his foul mouth, his stupid stubbornness.

"Too chicken, eh?"

She felt her heart begin to pound. The Baltimore cop Petrillo's words started echoing in her mind. "He has to tell you," he'd said. Passages from the books he'd given her flashed in her mind like some images from a picture slide show. She tried to remember the techniques that had been recommended for drawing Slocum out, but her mind was a blank. It was happening too soon, and she was totally unprepared. She felt as though her feet were nailed to the floor. She continued to stare out the window. "Is that what it is?" she asked. "A matter of being chicken?"

"You bet your ass, lady."

She waited.

"You're my lawyer, right?"

"Yes, I am."

"And you said that means you can't say anything I tell you unless I give the okay, right?"

"That's right, John." She could hardly breathe.

He laughed. "You could be in deep shit?"

"Very."

"Very don't get it done. How much trouble?"

She took a breath, then said, "Under the law, if I reveal anything you tell me without your permission, I would be kicked out of the profession. I could even go to jail."

"You could always be a hooker," he said. "You're a little over the hill, but you'd still turn some of them old farts on, I bet."

She turned. "So you've killed someone? Big deal. Lots of people have killed someone. It doesn't take that much courage."

"How the fuck would you know? You never did. It's easy to talk about things you ain't never done. Fuckin' women! Women ain't no good at killin'. My mother tried to kill me and she fucked it up. I was just an eleven-year-old kid and she still fucked it up. Just another stupid bitch. You're all bitches. Stupid, fuckin' bitches."

Laura waited, not saying a word.

"She came at me with the knife up over her head," he said. "Everybody knows that ain't the way you do it. You wanna kill somebody, you keep the knife down low and bring it up, not down. I was only eleven and I already knew that."

"How did you know that?" Laura asked.

"I seen it on TV. You ever watch those guys on TV, you see they never hold the knife above their heads, 'cause that's the wrong way. They always hold it down low, in a crouch. Nobody can stop you when you're down low, but when you hold it high, they can deflect it by bangin' on the arm."

She feigned disinterest and turned back to the window. A slight breeze stirred some trash that had failed to make it to a dumpster, the trash whirling in small circles, going nowhere. Her mind was racing. She tried to concentrate, but everything seemed a jumble. She heard him say, "That's what I did. Banged her arm. The knife fell on the floor and she was too drunk to pick it up. So I did. I held it the way you're supposed to, down low, and then I stuck her with it. Real hard."

He laughed again. "God! You shudda seen the look on her face. It was weird. She wasn't in any pain, 'cause she was too drunk, but she sure was surprised. Her eyes were as big as Cadillac wheels. And then she fell down. Never said a fuckin' word.

"I thought she'd just passed out, but when I leaned down to see if she was breathin', there wasn't no sound at all. I couldn't believe it! One stick. Musta hit under the ribs right into the heart, just like you're supposed to, and I was only eleven. Pissed me off though. I wanted to hear her scream. Yeah. Long and hard. I wanted her to scream until her fuckin' mouth wouldn't work no more. But she beat me on that. She died without a goddamn peep."

"I don't believe you," Laura said, turning to face him.

"Why not?"

"Because all you do is tell lies. You've never

uttered a truthful word to me since I first laid eyes on you. Why should I believe you now?"

He was incensed. "It's all in the records," he said. "You can check it out with the cops."

"I already did," she said. "The police report says your mother fell down while you two were fighting for the knife. They say it was an accident, that your mother fell on top of the knife. You didn't have much to do with it. They also have the statement you made at the time, which confirms the autopsy report. You didn't mean to kill your mother, John. You were just trying to protect yourself. Why are you trying to pretend you killed her deliberately? You think I'll be impressed with that?"

He laughed again. "The cops are just as dumb as my stupid fuckin' mother. They wrote down what I told them. I made it look that way, 'cause after she was dead, I rolled her over on top of the knife. Pretty smart, eh? They bought it. If you talked to the cops, you musta read the report. One through the heart, right? Isn't that what it says?"

"Yes."

"So? Am I lyin'?"

"Yes," she said.

"Fuck you."

Reluctantly, she moved toward the bed. "If you want me to believe you, why don't you tell me something I can check."

"Like what?

"Like where some of those other women are buried."

His head went back and he laughed until the laughs turned into a spasm of coughing. When the coughing stopped, he used the sheet to wipe his mouth, then sneered at her. "Right. Whaddaya gonna do then? Dig 'em up?" He started laughing again. "You're so fuckin' stupid."

"I guess I am, John."

"Yeah, you are. Real stupid."

"So you're the smart one. How do I prevent you from being executed? Tell me that. You refuse to cooperate in any way. You won't let me pursue an insanity plea, and you won't cooperate with the police. What am I supposed to do?"

He looked at her intently. "What are you talkin' about? You said I didn't have to tell them nothin'."

"You don't, but it's possible we could make some sort of deal."

"What kinda deal?"

"You tell the police what happened with those other women in return for a life sentence instead of the electric chair."

He laughed again. "What the fuck good is that? I ain't about to spend my life in no jail. They wanna kill me, they can kill me. I don't give a fuck and I ain't confessing to things I never done. 'Course, you don't believe a word I say anyway, so when I say I didn't kill them women, it don't mean nothing to you."

Her racing heart began to find its normal rhythm. If John Slocum had had an inclination to tell her everything, the inclination had passed. He was back to the old mode now. Her approach had failed. She would have to do more research if she wanted Slocum to talk.

"I'll see you tomorrow," she told him.

"Yeah, right."

*   *   *

Laura walked down the hall to the elevator, then headed for Rick's office. He wasn't there. She inquired with one of the nurses, who told her he'd be back in a few minutes. She waited.

When he arrived, she handed him the autopsy report she'd picked up in Buffalo. "I'd like you to read this over carefully, and tell me what you think," she said.

He glanced at it, then said, "I'm not a forensics expert, Laura."

"I know. I just want your opinion."

He sighed, then sat down and read the report. When he finished, he handed it back to her and said, "I'd say the medical examiner was reaching."

"Why?"

"The angle of the knife." He took a piece of paper from his desk and started to sketch. "According to the report, the woman fell on the knife during a struggle."

"Yes?"

"Well, as you can see from the sketch included in the medical examiner's report, the angle of incision is almost parallel to the woman's body. If she fell on the knife while it was at that angle, there wouldn't be enough force to drive it *into* the body. The weight of her body would have knocked the knife to the floor. She would have been cut, but it would have been an external wound.

"In this case, the incision starts just below the rib cage and goes upward into the heart. That takes force. If the force was caused by her falling on the knife, the blade would have entered perpendicular to the body, not parallel. The blade would have pierced the midsection organs, not the heart."

Laura looked carefully at his sketch. "Should you be discussing this with me?" he asked.

"It's all right," she said. "This is public record now, which means anyone can read it."

"What are you trying to prove?"

"I'm just curious," she said. "So, you think the medical examiner blew it. Why?"

"Who knows? Maybe he'd already talked to the police and they gave him their version and just wanted confirmation. Maybe there was some sympathy there. Maybe the cops knew Slocum was an abused child and thought the mother had it coming. Maybe the ME was just incompetent or overworked. There are lots of both around. I don't know."

"But you're sure it couldn't have happened the way it's depicted in this report?"

"No, I'm not sure. I told you, I'm not a forensics expert. I guess it's possible, but I just don't think it happened the way the report says it did. However, if you ask me to testify to that point, you can forget it. I'm not a qualified expert, and even a rookie prosecutor would eat me alive. Chris Marshall's not exactly a rookie."

"So what do you think happened?"

He groaned. "Why is this so important?"

"I can't tell you."

He sighed, then said, "I'd say that the knife was deliberately thrust. It was an overt act, not an accident. Why are you smiling?"

She patted him on the cheek. "I can't tell you," she said, "but I do thank you."

As she walked down the hall, she felt a tremor of excitement run through her body. John Slocum has just uttered his first truthful words to her. That was progress. He might eventually tell her everything, and when he did, she would have something—as Petrillo had put it—to deal with.

Maybe.

CHAPTER

21

It had been ten days since Dan had entered the clinic. Laura had been making inquiries almost every day and had been told she'd be contacted, nothing more. Now, a woman on the telephone was telling her that the doctor treating Dan, a man named Benton, wanted to see her.

"How is he?" Laura asked. "My husband, I mean."

The unctuous female voice on the other end of the telephone line said, "You'll have to discuss that with the doctor. I'm just to set up a time for your meeting with him. Would tomorrow afternoon be convenient?"

"Yes," Laura told her.

"Three o'clock?"

"That would be fine. Will I be able to see Mr. Scott?"

"You'll have to discuss that with the doctor."

Laura felt as though she were dealing with a prison warden. "I'll be there," she said.

At three o'clock the next afternoon, she arrived at the clinic. The lobby looked more like that of a fine hotel than a hospital for substance abusers. Thick carpets on the floor, modern art on the walls, and not a white coat in sight. The receptionist greeted Laura warmly and talked to Dr. Benton on the telephone. Laura assumed the woman who'd telephoned the day before worked for Dr. Benton personally.

In less than a minute, Dr. Benton arrived in the lobby, smiling warmly and extending his well-manicured hand. He was in his mid-forties, tall and thin, with thick, jet-black hair topping a pleasant face. His eyes sparkled, and his handshake was firm. "It was good of you to come," he said as he placed an arm on Laura's back and gently aimed her in the direction of his office. He wore a fine quality Italian silk suit and his gleaming black shoes were imports as well. A thin gold watch was the only jewelry visible.

His office was larger than she expected and featured several works of art that looked expensive. She resented it, since she was the one paying the cost of Dan's treatment, a cost clearly heightened by such ostentatiousness.

The doctor waved to a leather couch and sat in a chair that faced it. "Could I get you something?"

"No thanks," she said. "How is my husband?"

"Your husband is doing quite well, Mrs. Scott. He's come through the detox phase with flying colors, and we've managed to have some frank discussions. It's too soon to give you an official prognosis, but I think he's going to be fine."

Laura felt a wave of relief wash over her. "When can I see him?" she asked.

"Well, that's one of the things I wanted to talk to you about." He slapped his hands together, peered at her for a moment, then broke into a deep smile. "Your husband told me you were a beautiful woman. He was right."

"Thank you," she said, "but you're evading the question. What's the problem? Doesn't Dan want to see me? Is that it?"

He leaned forward. "I'm a psychologist, Mrs. Scott. I specialize in various types of substance abuse, though my real forte is in the treatment of alcoholism. I've spent fifteen years in this field and I've learned that the truth, as brutal as it sometimes is, is the essential core of good treatment.

"When we talk to our patients, we ask them to be honest in their self-evaluations. In the early stages of treatment, most of our patients find it difficult to verbalize their feelings, and often they aren't even aware of them. Denial is the first barrier to be breached. Dan was an outstanding exception."

Laura felt her jaw drop. "He was?"

"He was indeed."

"I'm astonished," she said. "At home, he spent most of his time denying he even had a drinking problem. The last time I saw him, he was filled with hatred."

"And that hatred is quite real," Dr. Benton said quickly.

"Pardon me?"

He smiled. It was an expression she was beginning to find offensive. "I realize how harsh this must sound," he went on, "but as I said earlier, I'm a firm advocate of dealing with the truth."

"He hates me? You're saying that's the truth?"

Dr. Benton nodded. "In my opinion, the root cause of your husband's illness lies in his inability to deal with the guilt he feels for hating you. Once he understands that his feelings are normal, we'll be able to effectively deal with them. We've made some remarkable progress in a very short time. I'm very excited."

She was beginning to doubt her hearing, but before she could respond, Dr. Benton said, "I'm sure you find what I've said shocking, and that's quite understandable. Let me attempt to explain."

"Please."

"Your husband has some very deeply entrenched ideas of what men and women are all about, ideas that were instilled in him at an early age. Fairly stereotypical views, in fact—antiquated, nonsensical views to most people, but they are *his* views, and we have but two choices in dealing with them. We can attempt to undo forty years of perception, or we can accept the actuality of his views."

"I'm afraid you've lost me, Doctor," she said.

"Please forgive me," he said, flashing his insidious smile. "It's been my experience that long-held perceptions are very difficult to change. A tremendous amount of time and energy can be expended in trying to erase long-held preconceptions, then attempting to reeducate. In the end, it usually doesn't work, other than temporarily. To accept what *is*, is often the more prudent treatment. Rather than waste our time explaining to Dan the reasons he shouldn't hate you, it's much more important to accept the fact that he does, then help him deal with the guilt he feels because of it."

Laura simply stared at him.

"Dan's relationship with you is beyond the scope of his experience or ability to comprehend. You don't fit the mental image he has of what a woman should be. At first, he found this confusing, but as the years passed, that confusion turned to dislike and finally hatred. That's where he is today.

"You are in no way to blame for this. You are what you are, just as he is what he is. There are no wrongs and rights, here, Mrs. Scott, just realities. In simple terms, you two are as wrong for each other as two people could ever be, and until you are out of his life forever, his chances of making a full recovery are remote. He seems to think you'd be amenable to a divorce. Are you?"

She was too shocked to answer.

"Please don't misunderstand, Mrs. Scott. I repeat, I'm not suggesting that you are in any way responsible for your husband's alcoholism. You aren't. But the fact is, your husband simply cannot relate to you in a meaningful way, nor could he ever. If you two were to stay married, I fear your husband's self-destructive behavior would increase markedly. Frankly, I feel it would be dangerous for him to continue in this relationship. For that reason, I have wholeheartedly supported him in his desire to seek a divorce."

"I see," she said softly.

"I don't think I've ever had a more clear-cut example," he continued. "Dan cannot survive with you in his life. Again, that is not a reflection on you, but a statement of fact."

"Opinion," she said, correcting him.

"Perhaps, but an opinion presented by someone highly skilled in these matters. You must admit that your personal bias precludes the possibility of you having an objective view. I realize that sounds very harsh, but we are simply doing the best we can to help your husband. He is, after all, the patient.

"You see, Dan is a weak man. You, on the other hand, are perceived as being a very strong woman. Since I don't know you, I can only deal with Dan's perception of you, and that presents a dichotomy that cannot be resolved. Dan recognizes this, and his hatred of himself is almost as strong as his hatred of you. Once we remove you from the scene, he can focus his energies and talents on his self-hatred and guilt. I understand you're an attorney."

"Yes."

"Well, it would probably be best if you prepared whatever documents are necessary and presented them to our legal department, which will act on Dan's behalf. Since both of you are amenable to the divorce, I see few problems." He handed her a business card. "This is the name of the attorney handling Dan's interests. If you'll deal with him directly, I think we can have the legal necessities resolved quickly."

Laura stood up. "Doctor, nothing will be resolved until I see my husband."

"Of course," he said. "But after you've talked to him, I'd appreciate it if you didn't see him again. Naturally, there'll be contact during visitation periods, but the less you see of Mr. Scott, the better it will be for him. You understand our interest lies with *his* welfare."

Laura was fuming. "Now, Dr. Benton. I want to see him now!"

"Of course." He stood up, walked to his desk and pressed a button. In seconds, a giant of a man dressed in white rapped lightly on the door, then entered.

"Take Mrs. Scott to see her husband," Dr. Benton commanded.

"Very well."

It was a small conference room, with bookshelves lining the walls and soft elevator music piped through two speakers hidden somewhere. Dan was wearing blue jeans and a T-shirt, was clean-shaven, and looked five years younger. He'd even put on a couple of pounds. His eyes gleamed.

"Hi, Laura. How've you been?"

"Fine," she said.

"How's Ted?"

"He's doing fine."

They sat down at the table across from each other, having neither shaken hands nor embraced.

"Did Dr. Benton fill you in?" Dan asked.

"He said you wanted a divorce. Do you?"

"Did he explain why?"

"Yes," she said. "He says I'm the wrong woman for you."

Dan beamed. "Isn't he something? You know what he did? He contacted Lou at the air base and had a long talk with him. Lou's gonna take me back, Laura, soon as I'm out of here. Can you imagine? How many doctors would go to bat for a guy like that?"

"So, you really like him?"

"You bet! The guy is terrific. He zeroed in on the whole thing within a few hours. He knows me better than I know myself. Jesus! He's a genius. I'm really feeling strong, Laura. I know this is tough on you, but you can handle it. Hell, you can handle anything. You're the toughest person I've ever met. You're terrific, and someday, when you meet the right guy, you'll have a great time, but you know we can't make it together. I want us to be friends, though. Really."

Laura took in a deep breath. "Is that how you really feel, Dan?"

He waited a moment, then said, "Yeah. I know. You probably think the doctor's talking me into this, but he isn't. I think it's the first time I ever told a stranger how I really feel about things. You know, real heavy stuff. He understands exactly how I feel and doesn't criticize me for it. He says it's perfectly normal. You know why I was drinking so much?"

She shook her head.

"I thought I was crazy. I really did. I thought I had to be nuts to feel the things I was feeling. I mean, you're beautiful and smart and a good mother and all. You make good money, more than me, in fact. I figured most guys would be thankful to have a woman like you as a wife and I couldn't understand why I wasn't. Benton set me straight and it all makes sense. You have no idea how great it is to find out you're not crazy when you think you are. I feel like the world has been lifted off my shoulders."

"You look good," she said.

"I feel good, too. You look great. A little tired maybe. You been working hard?"

"A little."

"So, you gonna make trouble, or can we settle this thing?"

Laura thought it over for a moment, then said, "Is this what you really want?"

"Yes," he said without hesitation.

"All right," she said. "They gave me the name of your lawyer. Have you told him what you want?"

He nodded.

"I guess there isn't much else to say, then."

Dan stood up and awkwardly extended his hand. "I really appreciate this, Laura. I really do. I'm sorry about all those things I said. You're really a wonderful woman. It's just that you're the wrong woman for me. Dr. Benton has made me see that. I didn't want to admit it to myself before, but I guess it was always wrong for us. I wish you the best of luck in the future."

"And I you," she said, shaking his hand.

"I hope you don't stay mad at me. I know you're pissed right now, and I don't blame you, but once you have a chance to think about it, you'll see that this is best for us both. I know you will. You were always the smart one, Laura."

"I'm not angry, Dan."

He grinned. "Good. That's real good, Laura."

He left quickly, and for that Laura was thankful. She didn't want him to see her cry.

The next morning Dan's lawyer, a man named Henry Lyons, telephoned and outlined the terms of a proposed property settlement. It was quite fair, and Laura agreed. Then he said, "As for visitation, Mr. Scott wants to have his son one weekend a month as long as Mr. Scott remains in Florida. If he moves out of state, he wants him for the months of July and August, and one weekend every three months. Quite reasonable, I think."

"I have a problem with that," Laura said.

"Which is?"

"Mr. Scott will be on probation once he leaves the clinic. Should he break the terms of his probation, he loses all visitation rights until he's been free of alcohol for a period of six months."

"I don't think that's reasonable," the lawyer said.

"Then we'll have to let a judge decide," she said. "I don't want my son spending time with Dan if he's drinking."

"You can't deny a father visitation rights, Mrs. Scott. You know that."

"I can if he's a danger to his son. You're aware, of course, that he's a convicted felon. The conviction was for reckless endangerment of a minor child. I won't allow that to happen again."

"So you want this to go to a judge?"

"Not necessarily. I have no problem with reasonable visitation as long as Dan remains sober. If he moves out of state, two weeks in the summer is enough. In state, one weekend a month is fine, but he'll have to be sober. I suggest you talk to your client and see if he's agreeable."

"You're being unfair," he said. "You know as well as I do that the recidivism rate is fairly high for the first go-around."

"I'm aware of that," Laura said. "It's exactly my point. This will provide further incentive for Mr. Scott to stay sober."

Lyons paused for a moment, then said, "I don't

think it's fair to present this to Mr. Scott at this point in time. He's very enthusiastic about his progress, and he may well agree in the flush of sobriety. I would advise him to reject such an arrangement."

"That's up to you," she said, "but I'm not prepared to let our son be exposed to any more drunken escapades. That's the deal, Mr. Lyons."

"I'll get back to you on that."

"Very well."

Laura hung up the phone and leaned back in her chair, thinking. Was she being unreasonable? she wondered. No, not in the least. She was just trying to protect the only thing left in life important to her, her son.

Kim stuck her head in the door. "Jim's on the phone for you," she said. "You want to take it or call him back later?"

"I'll talk to him," Laura said, picking up the phone. "Good morning, Jim."

"Morning, Laura. Just thought you should know we moved your client."

That was a surprise. "When?"

"Middle of the night. Rick figured he was ready to leave the hospital. He's in the civic center, county side. Listen to this. They had me move him, can you believe it? They said it was for security reasons, figuring since I'm outside the loop, nobody'd be keeping an eye on me. I think different."

"Like?"

"Well, if something went wrong, they could always blame it on the local yokel."

Laura laughed. "You know, Jim, I think you're getting as paranoid as I am."

"Maybe, but you know what they say. Doesn't mean they aren't out to get us, Laura."

"Very clever."

"So, Chris is pretty confident the grand jury will go his way. You figured out what you're gonna do?"

"Not yet. I'll need to talk to Slocum first."

"Well, I hope you don't make this tougher on yourself than needs be. Take care, Laura."

"Thanks, Jim."

It was almost noon when Laura visited her client in the county jail, a place with but twelve cells, and one small conference room. It was a strange place, burrowed within the civic center, that colossal monument to shortsighted budgetary thinking. Eight of the cells were maintained by the county, and the remaining four were the responsibility of the city of Seminole Springs, yet all twelve cells were located in one common area, eight cells on one side, four on the other. The remaining space was used for a guard's room and a small visiting room for lawyers and relatives.

In theory, the idea made sense. What was the point, the planners argued, of having two jails in such a small town? In practice, while it was true some actual savings were realized, the setup was ludicrous. A kitchen used to prepare meals for prisoners required two cooks, one employed by the county, another by the city. Instead of one set of jailers, the law required two; one for the county and one for the city. Within the cell area, people like John Slocum were housed across an eight-foot hallway from people jailed for something as minor as shoplifting. It wouldn't be long before some enterprising lawyer with ties to the local construction industry brought a suit claiming the setup was a violation of a minor offender's civil rights, a suit he'd probably win.

But the most ludicrous aspect of the arrangement was the fact that the county employed no police officers. County law enforcement was handled by the state for a fee. Which meant that all of the normal county functions were handled by state employees, and the bill presented to the county each month was staggering. Still, the county commissioners wanted no part of building their own police department, and probably wouldn't anytime soon.

For security reasons, Slocum was not allowed to use the crutches given him, and was instead chained to a wheelchair when allowed out of his cell. Inside his cell, the chains were removed. The jailers were afraid he'd use the crutches to bash someone's head in.

Laura said a silent prayer of thanks for that insightful decision as she looked at her client now. As usual, his expression was one of sullenness as he slouched in the wheelchair.

"What are they worried about?" he said as he displayed the chains that bound his arms to the wheelchair. "They afraid I'm gonna hurt somebody?"

"I have some news," she said, ignoring his question.

"What news?"

"The grand jury hears your case today. Your arraignment is set for tomorrow morning."

"What does that mean?"

"It means that the charges against you will be formally entered. The prosecutor has no doubt the indictment will be issued and he's ready to go. It means that we have to determine how we intend to answer the charges."

He snorted. "I already told you. I ain't guilty. I didn't kill that girl. I didn't kill nobody."

Laura took a deep breath, then exhaled it slowly. "John," she said slowly, "I don't know how much you understand of this, but I'm duty bound to explain it anyway."

"Explain what?"

"There are three ways we can go," she said. "I can plead you not guilty, not guilty by reason of insanity, or guilty. That's it. There are no other options. Now, I want to explain to you what each entails."

He shook his head. "Don't bother. I ain't guilty, so that's how I plead it. You understand?"

"Not so fast," she said. "If I plead you not guilty, there is absolutely no question in my mind that I will lose. You will be convicted and sentenced to death. Based on the evidence the prosecution has and summaries of previous murder trials in this state, it's an absolute certainty."

He laughed. "Really? Then what the fuck is the trial for? I thought you was supposed to defend me. It sounds like a fixed horse race. Big trial, but the verdict is already guilty."

With someone else, she might have conceded the point. With Slocum, she said, "I have to tell you the truth, John. The evidence against you is impossible to beat. It proves beyond a reasonable doubt that you killed Wanda Brooks. There's just no way on this earth any lawyer is going to convince a jury that you didn't. You can sit there and pretend all you want, but it doesn't change the facts. You killed her, and you'll be found guilty."

He stared at the ceiling.

"That's why I want you to consider the other two options very carefully," she said. "They hold your only chance for survival."

He snorted again. "You said one of them was pleadin' guilty. How the fuck does that help me?"

"Before I entered such a plea, I would talk to the prosecutor and try to come to an understanding."

"A what?"

"I'd make a deal."

"What kinda deal?"

"You would give him details on the whereabouts of all of the other women you've murdered. In return, he would ask the judge for a sentence of life instead of the death penalty."

His rat eyes flickered for just a moment. "You're my lawyer, and you sit there and tell these lies. What the fuck good are you? Why the hell can't I get a lawyer who believes in me?"

Laura leaned against the wall. "For a million reasons, John. You play the fool, but you're far from being stupid. You must know by now that you're wasting my time and everyone else's. No one believes you because you don't speak the truth. The only honest words you've uttered in my presence are those relating to the death of your mother."

"How come you believe that?"

"Because the evidence *supports* what you told me."

"What evidence?"

"Never mind."

"That ain't what the Buffalo cops thought."

"I know. They were wrong. It happened just as you said it did. Your mother was drunk and came at you with a knife. You knocked it from her hand and stabbed her with it. There wasn't much of a struggle. You knew exactly what to do, and you did it. I think the cops felt sorry for you."

"They what? Cops? You're the one who's crazy."

"I don't think so," she said. "Cops are human beings. You were eleven years old, and they were aware of what your mother did to you. I think they genuinely felt you acted in self-defense, and ignored evidence to the contrary."

"You don't think it was self-defense?"

She shook her head. "Not really. Once you had possession of the knife, you could have held your mother at bay and called the police. There was no need to kill her."

He laughed that sick laugh of his. "Easy for you to say. If I hadn't a killed her, you know what woulda happened? The cops woulda come and they woulda believed every fuckin' lie she said. They woulda left me with her so she could finish the job. It was only a matter of time before she was gonna kill me, the drunken bitch."

Quickly Laura asked, "Is that why you killed those other women, so you could get back at your mother?"

His eyes widened. "What is it with you? You working for the police?"

She shook my head. "You know I can't reveal anything you tell me. Tell me! Is that why you killed them?"

His expression was almost one of coyness. "Why do you want to know?"

"So I can properly defend you," she said.

Again the laugh. "Maybe it's because you're curious. Maybe you want the details 'cause it turns you on. Maybe your pussy gets all slippery just thinkin' about it. You gettin' off now, lady?"

She stared at him silently. He was right about one thing. She was curious, all right. Not about the details, but about something else. She was certain he'd killed at least thirty-two women in the last three years. Here was one of the most unattractive human beings she'd ever encountered. How had he enticed these women to go with him? Perhaps one or two had picked him up on the highway, thinking, in a misplaced moment of charity, they were helping a hitchhiker, but not all, surely. Any woman with a shred of common sense would give this man a wide berth. How had he done it?

The shovel he'd carried with him was an indication that he'd buried them, but until his encounter with Billy Haines, not a single witness had come forward to claim seeing anything suspicious. No hikers had stumbled across shallow graves in the woods. No police patrols searching areas close to where the missing women had last been seen, in thirteen different states, had found a single clue. Truly incredible. It would take extreme brilliance to plan and execute the murders of thirty-two women without leaving any clues aside from the innocuous ones already revealed. Was John Slocum this brilliant? If so, why was he hiding such brilliance in his relationship with the only person in the world attempting to save his life?

"So?" he prodded, his mouth twisted in a leer. "You still gettin' off?"

"I was explaining your options," she said. "I told you that a full confession regarding the other women might save you from the death penalty. The operative word is 'might.' Even if we make a deal with the prosecutor, the judge doesn't have to honor it. He can still require the jury to determine the penalty phase, which means they decide what happens to you without regard to any deals made."

As usual, he was disappointed she hadn't risen to his taunts. "So, what good is it?" he said.

Laura chewed her lower lip for a moment, then said, "There are higher powers than judges. There's a possibility I could make the deal with someone very high up. We could arrange for your case to be handled without a jury. The judge could be directed to give you a life sentence."

"By who?"

"By someone with more power than the judge."

"Like who?"

"I can't say just yet."

"Is that really possible?"

"Yes," she said. "It would be very unpopular with the public, but it's possible, and I can't do it without some solid evidence, which only you can provide."

"Forget that," he said.

"Why?" she asked.

He glared at her. "You just don't fuckin' listen, do ya? What in the hell is the matter with you, woman? I didn't kill those women, so why should I say I did?"

"Okay," she said. "Then we're left with option three."

"Insanity? No fuckin' way, lady."

"Why?"

"Because I ain't insane, that's why. I know what they do to you in those places. You really think I'm crazy or just stupid? The people run those places are the crazy ones. I ain't gonna be locked up in no insane asylum and be used for some weird experiments. I'd rather take my chances in jail."

Laura sighed. "John, in jail, you'll be locked up on death row for anywhere from two to ten years, then you'll be executed. Is that what you really want?"

He grinned. "They ain't gonna kill me."

"Why not?"

"Because I have you on my side. You're all wrapped up in this, aren't ya? You got this attitude, like it ain't right for the state to kill somebody. You're a bleeding heart bitch at heart. You'll spend the rest of your fuckin' life savin me from the electric chair, that's what you'll do. There ain't no way it's gonna happen."

"You're wrong," she said. "I'm just a lawyer. Lawyers work with facts, and the facts in this case are so solid, there isn't a single thing I can do, other than what I've described."

"Either make a deal or be crazy?"

"That's all there is, John. I want you to think about it. We have a little less than twenty-four hours."

"I don't have to think about it," he said. "I didn't kill nobody. I want to plead not guilty. If you don't want to do that, then you get me some lawyer who will."

"You're sure?"

"I'm sure."

Laura pushed the bell on the wall that would

summon the guard. "Then you leave me no alternative, John."

"What do you mean?"

"At your arraignment tomorrow, I'm going to make a motion. I'm going to require the court to have you examined by a psychiatrist."

"You can't do that 'less I say so," he screamed.

"Yes, I can."

Two guards arrived, one to escort Slocum back to his cell, and another to escort Laura out of the jail. "Wait a minute!" he yelled. "I'm not finished yet."

She ignored him. He was still screaming when they wheeled him away.

CHAPTER

22

As usual, it had been a full day for Laura Scott. When she finally arrived home, it was almost six. She parked the car in the driveway, turned off the ignition, and felt her body sag. She was exhausted, both mentally and physically. For a moment she considered taking Ted out for dinner instead of cooking. Quickly, she discarded the idea. They'd have to drive to Orlando if they wanted to eat in peace, and even Orlando was no sure thing. Laura didn't want to face any more hostility than was necessary.

Ever since she'd become involved in the defense of John Slocum, it had been impossible to eat in a local restaurant. Not even the club, once a haven, was safe anymore.

Twice, she'd tried to take Ted out for dinner and

both times, they'd been forced to leave. The first time had been at the club, and Laura had been immediately confronted by two people she hardly knew who stood by the table and insulted her. Ted, quickly assuming the role of the man of the household, had stood up and threatened bodily violence. Laura had pulled him away and they left hurriedly. As horrified as Laura was by both the scene and the thought of Ted involved in some awful brawl, she was secretly proud of her son, so anxious to leap to her defense.

They'd tried again at a small restaurant on the highway. They'd barely taken a seat when the owner of the place, a man Laura knew only slightly, had hustled over and pointed a finger at her. "You," he'd bellowed. "You don't eat in my place. I don't want you stinking up the place. Get out, now!"

This time, Ted hardly moved a muscle. He was beginning to accept the hostility as a normal thing, and that troubled Laura more than the incident itself.

Even the fast food joints provided no respite. Once, they'd ordered pizza in. When Laura opened the box, she discovered an extra topping she'd never ordered, a layer of baked-in cockroaches that immediately turned her stomach. Enraged, she'd called Jim. Charges were quickly laid.

The regular Saturday issue of the *Clarion* told the story. No one at the store would confess to having anything to do with this sickening stunt. Nor would the delivery boy. Tom Ferris speculated that Laura Scott had done it herself, possibly because she was in the midst of a complete nervous breakdown. An angry Jim Pickett had sworn to get to the bottom of it, but so far, nothing.

Tonight, Laura would cook, like every night. She left the car, went inside, and called out to Ted. There was no answer. She assumed he was in his room, either studying or listening to his music. She went upstairs.

He was lying on his bed, his face to the wall, the earphones plugged in. Laura leaned over, gently removed the earphones, and noticed that he was holding a wet towel to his face. "Are you okay?" she asked.

"I'm fine," he said, his voice muffled by the towel.

"Why the towel?" she asked.

"Headache. Nothing serious."

"Want something special for dinner?"

"Not hungry," he mumbled, his back still to her.

Laura shook his shoulder. "Come on, you're always hungry. Give me a clue. You've got a choice of chicken, pasta, or leftovers. What'll it be?"

"I'm really not hungry," he said. "Honest." This time she detected a strange lisp to his voice.

"Are you sure you're okay?"

"Yeah."

She took his shoulder and pulled him away from the wall. The towel he was holding was filled with ice cubes. Slowly, Laura eased it away from his face and gasped.

His upper lip was so swollen it was three times normal size. Crusted blood was caked on a nose that was obviously broken. One eye was closed shut, and the other was almost as bad. One cheek was badly swollen.

"Oh, my God!" she exclaimed. "Who did this to you?"

"It was just a thing at school," he lisped.

"We'll discuss that later. Right now, I have to get you to the hospital."

He grabbed her arm. "No, Mom. I'm okay. Nothing's broken. I'll be fine." His lips could hardly form the words.

Laura was insistent. "I want you examined, Ted. Please don't argue with me on this." She picked up the phone and called the hospital. Rick had left. Laura called him at home. Gerry answered the phone.

"Is Rick there?" Laura asked.

"He's at the club, Laura. Tonight's his night with the boys, you know? They pig out on junk food and play a little poker. Anything wrong?"

Laura started to cry. "Ted's been badly beaten," she said. "Could you ..."

"I'll pick Rick up myself," Gerry said quickly. "We'll meet you in emergency."

"Oh, Gerry ..."

Rick and Gerry arrived three minutes after Ted and Laura. Gerry stayed with Laura while Ted was being X-rayed and examined. "What in God's name happened?" she asked, her face reflecting her concern.

"The most I can get out of him is that some boys from school started giving him a hard time on his way home. Obviously, they got into it. He hasn't told me who they were."

"Oh, Laura," Gerry said, "I'm so sorry. This is awful. What is it with these kids? You know where they get it? From their parents."

Laura leaned back in the waiting-room chair. "This

has got to stop, Gerry. I've had enough. I don't care what they do to me, but I'm not exposing my son to any more of this mindless animosity."

"What can you do?"

"I can get off this case and leave this stupid town, that's what."

"You're upset, Laura. I don't blame you, but this isn't the time to be making those kinds of decisions."

"It's exactly the time," Laura said, "before it's too late. Who knows what will happen tomorrow? I'm not going to wait and find out." She turned and faced her friend. "Do you know how many new clients I've picked up since this started? Zero. And I've had three clients drop me. For what? Why should I destroy my life? Why should I expose Ted to this . . . idiocy?"

Gerry patted her arm. "Laura, I don't blame you for being upset. I know how you feel. You know what I think? Ever since this started, you've been avoiding everyone from the press. You've let Ferris take potshots at you while you've remained silent. Maybe it's time you spoke your piece. Why don't you call a press conference and explain exactly why you're defending John Slocum? You probably could get on the national programs. You could have Ted there, too. You could show them what you've been putting up with. You could tell them you were appointed and that . . ."

"No. I won't become one of those who use the media to advance their own ends. I've always despised that. Besides, the people in this town already know I was appointed to defend that man. Judge Fry made that clear the day he appointed me. He went to great pains in a very long statement designed to prevent this very thing from happening. It's just that everyone chooses to ignore the facts. They're angry, Gerry. They're angry that some stranger has come into their midst and murdered one of their own. They can't take it out on Slocum, not now, anyway, so they attack me, and now Ted. It's human nature. If I hold a press conference, I'll be in effect apologizing for being part of the system. If I have to apologize, I shouldn't be part of it in the first place."

"But if you quit, will it really make that much of a difference? Won't people . . .?"

"I don't care about these people. I'll move. Maybe back to Montana. Someplace where . . ." Laura stopped when she saw Rick coming out of the emergency room.

"Well," he said, sitting down beside her, "the nurse is finishing up with him now, but I can tell you he has a broken nose, a very badly lacerated cornea, a lacerated lip, and two missing teeth. He has one cracked rib and some bad bruises on his chest. I don't see any evidence of internal bleeding, thank God, but somebody kicked him pretty good. He also has a mild concussion, and that prevents me from giving him anything for the pain."

Laura's hands covered her mouth.

"He's going to suffer some serious discomfort for a few hours," Rick went on. "I want to admit him overnight for observation. Tomorrow, I'll talk to Dr. Snell in Orlando. He's an orthodontist. Lots of experience with dental implants. I'd like him to have a look." He took a deep breath. "What the hell happened? I can't get a word out of Ted."

"Some kids from school beat him up," Laura said. "On his way home."

Rick's face reddened. "Terrific. Over the Slocum thing?"

"He didn't tell me, but I imagine it is," she said. "This has been building the last few weeks. I should have seen it coming. Damn! Will he be all right? You said the cornea . . ."

Rick took her hand and held it. "Not to worry. He'll be fine. The eye will have to be carefully monitored, but it was confined to the cornea, and they usually heal well. The rib will cause him pain for a few weeks, but he's young and in good shape. The teeth are gone and he doesn't know where they are, so Dr. Snell will have to make new implants unless Ted wants a bridge." he smiled. "Somehow, I doubt that."

Laura started crying in earnest. Gerry held her close while she fought to gain control over her emotions.

Rick squeezed her shoulder. "Laura, he'll be fine. Really. Have you talked to Jim?"

She used Gerry's hankie to blow her nose. "No, but I intend to. I won't stand for this."

"You shouldn't have to," he said.

"Can I see him now?"

"Sure," Rick said as he took her elbow.

Ted looked a mess, with his chest all taped up and bandages covering most of his face. Laura took his hand in hers and noticed, for the first time, that his knuckles were badly scraped. The wounds had been treated but not bandaged. Some boy in town was probably wearing a shiner, if she knew her son. "How're you feeling?" she asked. Then she laughed. "Stupid question." The tears returned with a vengeance.

Ted patted the top of her head. "I'm okay, Mom. Don't cry. Dr. Taylor says he wants to keep me overnight. I'd rather go home."

"I know you would, but you've got a concussion, Ted. Dr. Taylor just wants to keep an eye on you for the next few hours. You'll be home tomorrow."

He rubbed his forehead. "I've got a killer headache."

"I can imagine," she said. "I want you to tell me the names of those boys."

He grimaced. "Mom, I don't need you to fight my battles."

"This wasn't a battle, Ted. This was a brutal attack. How many were there?"

"I don't remember."

"Ted, come on. You've been seriously hurt. I can't just forget about it."

"Mom, please. If you bring the police in on this, it'll just get worse at school. I'm trying the best I can. You'll just make it worse."

Laura sat beside the bed and rested her head on the mattress. "It must be awful for you if it's come to this."

"I can handle it," he said.

She lifted her head and looked into the one eye that hadn't been bandaged. "Just how bad is it, Ted? I want you to be honest with me. Remember we said we'd be honest with each other?"

He turned away.

She felt her heart breaking. "Remember," she

said, "I made you a promise. I told you that if this got too rough, I'd drop this case. Remember?"

"I remember."

"I think it's reached that point."

For a fleeting instant, it seemed as though the weight of the world was being lifted from his shoulders; a quick, involuntary glimpse of his true emotions instead of the brave front he was projecting purely for her benefit. "No," he said. "It isn't that bad. I can handle it."

So courageous, so loving. Confused, frightened, all of fourteen, but trying to step in, a pillar of strength replacing the weakness that was his father, attempting to shield his mother from additional pain. Laura had never loved anyone—not even Victoria—as much as she loved her son at that magic moment. Her heart was bursting with pride.

She stood up. "I want you to rest, now," she said. "Dr. Taylor's going to stay for a couple of hours until you finally fall asleep. I'll be back in the morning."

"Okay, Mom," he said. He gripped her wrist. "Promise me you won't get the police involved in this."

She leaned forward and kissed him on the forehead. "I can't do that, Ted. You were assaulted."

"If you involve the cops in this, I'll never be able to show my face in that school again." He was pleading now, begging. Laura considered it for a few moments, then nodded. "All right, Ted. We'll handle it your way. But if it happens again . . ."

Laura begged off having dinner at Gerry's. She wanted to be alone with her thoughts, isolated from humanity while she contemplated her choices and her future. She left a worried-looking Gerry at the hospital, drove home, poured herself some wine, and sat at the kitchen table.

She took stock. Her marriage was over. Her career, at least in Seminole Springs, was at an end. Nothing would repair the damage already done. She'd have to move. She was sure Ted wouldn't mind. She'd seen the look on his face when she'd suggested the possibility. There was Shirley, of course, but Ted was young. At fourteen, a first infatuation was not much of a consideration. He'd find other girls. His whole life was ahead of him.

Where to go? She'd mentioned Montana to Gerry. Why? She'd rather die than go back to Havre. Was it some weird Freudian slip? She pushed the thought from her mind. This was no time for self-analysis. This was a time for decision-making. Havre was out. Where, then? She didn't know. Move to the next question.

What to do? Resign from the case? She had sufficient grounds, albeit cowardly ones. Judge Fry would be angry, but he'd go for it, knowing what she'd been though these last few weeks. What then? A new attorney would be assigned to the case and the result would be the same. John Slocum would be found guilty of the murder of Wanda Brooks and sentenced to die. So what? He *was* guilty. Why should she care?

Money. She had enough money, thanks to the Gilbert settlement. What should she do once she got to wherever she was going? Continue in the legal profession? If she did, she'd be a private practitioner—again. Because this case was news throughout the country, she'd always be branded as someone unable to take the heat after a few short weeks in the Big Time. A fatal curse, for Americans loved winners but hated losers with a passion. That would be her trademark, as good as emblazoned on her forehead. Loser. Taking this case had been the biggest mistake of her life. She'd have gained respect if she'd refused to take it in the first place.

And what of the practice of law? She was beginning to loathe it, being projected into other people's problems, many of which could hardly be resolved by the application of legalities. The Gilbert triumphs were few and far between. Most of the time, she was left with a bitter taste in her mouth. She was tired of it. If she practiced at all, it would have to be innocuous paperwork. No criminals, no large suits. Just wills and leases and mind-numbing paperwork. She wanted no more tugging of her emotional strings.

Her thoughts turned to Slocum. What if she didn't quit? Unless she spent her own money on a succession of experts who'd swear he wasn't responsible for his actions, he'd be convicted, and even if she did expend the money, the odds were that the jury would reject the experts anyway. They almost always did, unless the accused was foaming at the mouth. No. A thousand experts wouldn't save Slocum. The exhaustion of her funds would be the ultimate exercise in futility. A completely stupid waste of money. Even if Slocum agreed to a deal, which was doubtful, no one from the other side would. Neither Chris nor Judge Fry was about to toss his career in the ash can for the sake of easing the pain of some very bewildered parents. Petrillo had been the first to suggest a deal. At the same time, he'd suggested she'd have to go over Chris's head. To whom? She couldn't think of anyone who'd entertain the thought.

A deal was out of the question, and Petrillo probably knew it, hoping, personally involved as he was, for some miracle. There'd be no miracle. John Slocum was a serial killer. No one with political ambitions would ever make a deal with a serial killer. Not if they wanted to stay in office. The path leading to the electric chair was inexorable. Even at this early point, everything Laura had done was a waste.

Once, she'd actually pitied him, at least part of her had, that part of her still hurting from the cruelty imparted by her own parents. While their meanness was the fruit of their own upbringing cloaked in the always respectable blanket of parental manipulation, the hurt for Laura was there nonetheless. But Slocum's pain—both mental and physical—had warped him, and understandably so. He'd been subjected to every kind of abuse meted out by a very sick woman consumed by a thousand unseen devils. Her abuse had created a monstrosity.

What good was pity? Empathy served no purpose. To understand John Slocum was to comprehend nothing. He was beyond help, his tortured soul a hideous mass of scar tissue. A killing thing, capable only of inflicting pain and suffering and death, lashing out at his long-dead mother by substituting innocents whose only failing was that they resembled her in some vague way.

In her heart, Laura knew she would lose this case. The state was not yet ready to accept the full scope of insanity, choosing instead to limit the perimeters to the narrowest of terms. Though Slocum was the paradigm of true insanity, he was regarded as simply a killer, the reasons he'd become one of no importance.

Her thoughts turned to people she'd never met, the parents of the missing children. How were they being served by this idiotic ritual? Unserved was more like it. Living victims, whose interests were being abandoned by an unfeeling society devoted to form rather than substance. Bewildered, terribly hurt, powerless in their quest to have the questions tormenting their minds answered. Who spoke for them? No one.

So what would be accomplished by the exercise? A waste of time and money. A futile, quixotic effort to expand the rules of law. For nothing. Unless . . .

Laura focused on a thought so initially foreign it frightened her. An idea diametrically opposed to everything she believed in—or thought she did, for the more she considered it, the more sense it made. A way of dealing with the recalcitrant Slocum and provide a modicum of solace to the parents of the missing girls. A trade-off. Laura would be forced to give up something, but in return, she'd gain something much more valuable—her self-respect.

She walked to the living room and sat on the sofa. The harsh words exchanged with her parents echoed in her mind. And then, in her mind's eye, she saw Dan sitting beside her, his eyes half-closed, his mouth open, his utter contempt for her leaching from every pore of his skin. He'd almost succeeded in making her hate herself. So had her parents, and Ferris, and Slocum—and the cruel, unthinking people in this rotten town.

There was a way to change that.

C H A P T E R

23

IN THE MORNING, LAURA'S RESOLVE WAS FIRM, COCOONED in concrete. It was so strange. A few short weeks ago, she would never have allowed such thoughts to enter her mind, but now she felt like a completely different person. She was seized with a purpose that bordered on obsession, and yet, for the first time in years, she felt very, very good about herself.

She showered and dressed in a hurry, then dashed to the hospital. Rick had not yet arrived, but one of the nurses escorted her to Ted's room. His bruises had turned much darker and he seemed to be in considerable pain.

"Dr. Taylor will be here in a few minutes," the nurse said. "The effects of the concussion have dissipated overnight and the doctor will be able to administer some painkillers. I'm sure that will help. Your son has had a comfortable night, all things considered."

"Can he go home?"

"The doctor will have to release him, but I think he will." She smiled at Ted. "This guy is one tough kid." She left them alone.

"How are you?" Laura asked, kissing Ted on the cheek, afraid to hug him because of the cracked rib.

"I'll be okay," he said through still-thick lips. "You didn't call the police, did you?"

"No. I promised you I wouldn't, Ted. I think you're wrong, but I'm letting you call the shots on this one."

He expelled a painful breath of air. "Thanks, Mom. I know you think it's crazy."

"True."

"But you understand?"

"I think so. When I was your age, I wasn't that concerned about the attitude of my peers, but I realize you're not me. It's important to you, which makes it important to me. Everything you think and feel is important to me. If you want to handle it this way, that's how it will be handled. We have a deal, remember?"

"I remember."

The door opened and a smiling Rick entered the room. "Well," he said, "if it isn't the human punching bag. They say you managed to live through the night. Did you?"

Ted grinned weakly. "I guess so."

"So, how do you feel this morning, Ted?"

"I'm okay," Ted answered.

Rick examined the chart, then checked Ted's eyes, his heart, pulse, and responses. He seemed satisfied. "Still have the headache?"

"Yeah. Not so bad now, though."

"How about the rib?"

Ted touched his chest and winced. "Hurts pretty bad. Hard to breathe, you know?"

"I know. I'll give you something for the pain. We couldn't do it before because painkillers can mask certain symptoms when a concussion is present. Sorry about that."

"I understand," Ted said.

Rick turned to Laura. "Dr. Snell will be here in fifteen minutes. He'll give Ted a look-see, then give you some options on the missing teeth."

"When can I go home?" Ted asked.

"As soon as Dr. Snell sees you. You can get dressed now if you like."

True to his word, Dr. Snell arrived within fifteen minutes, examined Ted, then suggested several options, none of which could be immediately performed because of the swelling inside the mouth. They agreed on implants. Then it was home.

"I want you to stay in bed today," Laura told Ted as she tucked him in bed. "Tomorrow, you can get up, but no school for a couple of days."

Once again, he looked relieved.

"I have to be in court in fifteen minutes," she continued. "I really hate to leave you like this, but this is the day Slocum is arraigned. When I get back, we'll talk about the future. Okay?"

"Okay. You go. And, Mom?"

"Yes?"

"I know this is real hard on you. I know you want to do something about it and I really appreciate your seeing it my way. I'm sorry I've caused you more problems."

She kissed his forehead. "You've given me joy, not problems. Whatever problems we have are not of your doing. I love you very much, Ted."

"I love you too, Mom."

She resisted the impulse to squeeze him tight.

The grand jury having handed down an indictment the previous afternoon after ten minutes of deliberation, the formal arraignment of John Slocum was to move apace. At ten in the morning, a bailiff called the room to order and Judge Fry scurried in to take his position at the bench.

Over outraged protests, Judge Fry had limited the media inside the courtroom to a mere half dozen, to be chosen by the most senior accredited journalists or by lot. It was up to them how the news was covered. There were to be no cameras allowed, either TV or still, anywhere inside the building. Tape recorders were also excluded. Anyone attempting to break the rules would be held in contempt, and searches would be made of everyone entering the courtroom. The judge did allow a single artist, dubbed by the media as "Salvador," to make sketches, but that was all.

Slocum had been brought in earlier, chained to his wheelchair, which was positioned behind the defense table. His eyes scanned Laura's face with hostile intensity. He was allowed to remain seated as everyone else rose. With little fanfare, Judge Fry turned to Laura. "Does the defense wish to waive reading of the information?"

"Yes, Your Honor."

"Very well. John Slocum, you have been charged with one count of first-degree murder. How do you plead?"

"Not guilty, Your Honor," he replied in a strong voice.

Judge Fry looked at Laura and nodded.

"Your Honor," she said, "it is my belief that the defendant is incapable of assisting in his own defense. I move that the Court arrange for an independent psychiatric examination. Pending the results of such examination, it is my intention to plead the defendant not guilty by reason of insanity."

Slocum started thrashing around in his wheelchair, screaming epithets at the top of his lungs. "Be quiet!" Judge Fry thundered.

Slocum took no heed. The stream of invective continued, his words a torrent of disjointed gutter language. His small eyes almost bugged out of his head as he struggled futilely to break free of the steel shackles that bound him to the wheelchair.

"If you're not quiet, you'll be gagged," Judge Fry bellowed.

After one more unheeded admonition, the judge motioned to the bailiff and Slocum was gagged, amid a buzz of conversation from the small number of spectators crammed into three rows of seats. The pool artist's hands seemed to fly over the sketch pad in his hands.

Chris Marshall shot Laura a quick, hard look,

then said, "Your Honor, the State opposes the motion. The defendant is not insane."

"That remains to be seen," Judge Fry said, banging his gavel to quiet the room. "Mrs. Scott, your motion is granted. The court orders a thirty-day psychiatric evaluation of the defendant. Accordingly, this arraignment is postponed until such time as the report is forthcoming. The defendant will remain in pretrial custody without bail. Court is adjourned." Then he leaned forward and said, "I'll see counsel in chambers."

The six media types were already out the door before Chris and Laura started to move.

Inside Judge Fry's chambers, they took seats across from the judge's cluttered desk. Chris, red-faced, said, "Your Honor, can we go off the record here?"

Judge Fry hung up his black robe, then glanced at Laura. "Sure," she said.

Chris banged his fist on the arm of the chair. "What the hell are you pulling here?" he snarled, glaring at her. "It's obvious you never discussed this with your client. You did that deliberately, just to make him look like the lunatic you're trying to get him to portray. You pandered to the press. It's outrageous."

Laura looked at the judge, who seemed to be hiding a smile. Then she faced Chris. "In the first place," she said calmly, "I did discuss the insanity plea with my client. He refuses to hear of it and that refusal is, in itself, an indication of his total inability to understand the reality of his position. I've carefully explained to him the import of the evidence arrayed against him. I have told him countless times that he has no chance to a fair trial unless he cooperates with me, yet he refuses to either discuss the case or consider the options I've presented to him, clear evidence that he cannot assist in his own defense. I'm firm on this, Chris."

Chris was growing angrier by the second. "Your client wants to plead not guilty? Fine. You have no right to stand in his way. If that's what he wants, you should plead him not guilty and let us get on with this."

"That is not in the best interests of my client," Laura said. "Besides, the issue is moot. Unless I misunderstood him, Judge Fry has already made a ruling."

Chris was on his feet. "What the hell is this? We've got a man who brutally murdered one of this town's most accomplished children. Have you forgotten that? You know damn well that we can handle this with a minimum of procedural folderol if you'll just listen to reason."

The judge, who had been silently taking all of this in, finally decided to speak. "Chris," he said, "back off. Laura's doing exactly the right thing. Anything less would be grounds for appeal and you know it. This trial is being covered by at least three reporters who are former members of the legal profession. If you think we can pull the wool over their eyes, you're sadly mistaken. We have to conduct this entire proceeding with the utmost care.

"If Laura had not moved for an independent examination, I would have ordered one myself. That's one issue I want cleared up immediately."

Chris glared at the judge for a moment, then stared at a plaque on the wall. "I fail to see why we're so damn worried about the rights of one multiple killer," he said. "Nobody seems to give a damn about Wanda Brooks."

Judge Fry's hands turned into fists, then slowly, he opened his hands. "I'm going to forget you said that," he said, "but don't ever say anything remotely similar again. Understand?"

Chris glared at the judge, then Laura. "I apologize, Your Honor."

Laura waited for tempers to cool, then said, "There are some other things I need to discuss with both of you. On the record."

They both looked at her.

"I've prepared motions that I now present to the Court." She removed some documents from her attaché case and laid them on the judge's disordered desk. "I'm asking for a change of venue. There's no way my client can receive a fair trial here. I've included two affidavits plus some other corroborating material. Not only has my client been depicted as guilty by local media, but I have been subjected to personal vilification, depicted as incompetent and mentally deficient. I'm convinced, as are the signers of the affidavits, that the people of this town—people who will ultimately serve on this jury—are biased. There's just no question of it."

Judge Fry looked at the affidavits. "Jim Pickett and Dr. Taylor. You play real hardball, Laura."

"Not really," she said. "Facts are facts."

Judge Fry sighed. "I'll take it under advisement. I'll have an answer for you within a week."

Chris was livid. "Your Honor . . ."

Judge Fry cut him off with a wave of the hand.

"Chris. We'll do this by the book. Laura has presented her motions. You can present yours. I'll review them and make a ruling. That's it."

The judge turned to Laura. "Anything else?"

"Yes," she said. "Until you make your ruling, I'll proceed as though we're still going to have the trial here. As of today, I have talked to a total of thirty-two jurisdictions who claim to have evidence that my client may be involved in the disappearance of one of their citizens. All of them have interviewed my client, who has disclaimed any knowledge in each case. In addition, there are another forty-three jurisdictions that want to talk to my client and I've refused to allow that because they can present no evidence that he was ever in their area."

"So?" Chris said.

"So, the possibility exists that my client is responsible for a number of other deaths. Actually, it's much more than a possibility and you both know it. I want to know if you'd be amenable to a deal if my client decides to cooperate at some future date."

"A deal? What did you have in mind?"

"If, and it's a very big if, I can get Slocum to tell me what happened to these other women, you both agree to a sentence of life instead of the death penalty."

"Not in a million years," Chris snapped. "I'm responsible to the people of Florida, and the people of Florida have made it very clear they expect those who wantonly kill their citizens to be executed. I'd be derelict in my duty if I even *considered* a deal of any kind."

Laura sighed. "Chris, there are three of us in this

room, that's all. Just us three. Let's consider what's really happening here, and let's go off the record for a moment, all right?"

Judge Fry nodded.

"Chris?"

"Yes. Off the record."

"All right," Laura said. "If John Slocum is responsible for the deaths of others, and I'm not saying he is, doesn't it seem reasonable that we try to find out what happened? If there are thirty-two women buried somewhere in this country, and if John Slocum is responsible, he's the only one who knows where the burial sites are. If he refuses to reveal those sites because there is no incentive to do so and is eventually executed, the parents of those poor, unfortunate victims will never know what happened to their children."

She took a deep breath, then said, "As you know, I recently lost a daughter myself. As terrible as that was, I knew what was happening every step of the way. Victoria's buried now and I can get on with my life, but if those missing women are never found, there will be thirty-two sets of parents, not to mention other loved ones, who will spend the rest of their lives wondering what happened. Was this man responsible or wasn't he? I believe not knowing is worse than the truth. The truth may be a terrible thing to accept, but at least it's something a person can deal with. How do you deal with not knowing? Why is it so important that John Slocum be executed? Doesn't it make more sense to keep him alive? He may someday decide to tell us what happened to those other women. He can't talk if he's dead."

Chris was shaking his head. "You want truth? I'll give you truth. If I were to accept such a deal, I'd be run out of town on a rail. My career would be finished. The people of this town don't really give a damn about the problems of some strangers they don't know. All they know is that John Slocum killed Wanda Brooks and they want him to pay the price. Anything else is unacceptable to them, and they are the ones I represent. I won't betray their trust."

Laura turned to Judge Fry. In a very soft voice, he said, "Laura, as much as I sympathize with your motives, there's no way I could ever consider taking this case away from a jury. It's up to the jury to make the decision on guilt or innocence and it's up to the jury to recommend the punishment."

"But you can refuse to follow those recommendations."

"True, but if you expect me to give you some indication pretrial, I can't. You know that. If I did, I would have to excuse myself. Look, you're talking to the wrong people. In the event your client is found guilty and sentenced to death, the person you need to talk to is the governor. He's the one with the power to commute a death sentence."

Laura stood up. "You both know where he stands on this issue. With an election coming up next year, he's not about to stick his neck out. Besides, he can't make a deal before the trial, but you two can. You're trying to shift things here, and I resent it."

"Well, you can resent it all you want," Chris said, "but there's no way on this earth I'll consider any deal with John Slocum. None. So forget it."

"So, the parents of those children can whistle. Is that what you're telling me?"

"Not necessarily," Chris said. "If your client is responsible for those deaths, you have an obligation to try to get him to cooperate. If he does, every person on that jury will know that he cooperated. You can make your appeal directly to the jury at the sentencing phase. If the jury comes back with a sentence of life, I'll live with it. Besides, if you succeed in getting a change of venue, this whole thing is redundant."

"I'll withdraw my motion if we can strike a deal," Laura said.

"No way. No deal. Maybe someone else will deal with you, but I sure as hell won't."

"Because of your career? That's more important than the mental well-being of thirty-two sets of parents? Are you really that selfish?"

His eyes were blazing. "It's got nothing to do with me! It's the goddamn law! Stop trying to lay some sophomoric guilt trip on me." Chris looked at the judge, then back at Laura. "You have my answer, Laura. No deal. And now, I want to go back on the record."

"So noted," Judge Fry intoned.

It was their way of telling Laura the conversation regarding a deal was over. In a matter of seconds, the one option she'd hoped might have some potential had been shot down, just as she'd known it would be. Perhaps she'd harbored a small hope that she'd been wrong, but from the looks on the two faces confronting her, she knew she wasn't.

"The court-appointed doctor. Who's he to be?" Chris asked the judge.

"There are three doctors in Orlando who've been accepted in other cases," Judge Fry answered quickly, eager to move away from the previous subject. "No one in town." He frowned. "Having given this some thought, anticipating Laura's motion, I'd rather see Slocum committed to a hospital while this evaluation takes place. I'd like him the hell out of town for a month. It'll get the media off our backs and allow things to cool down a bit. I want you both to agree to it."

"I have no objection," Laura said, "providing the examination is done by one of those three and not the state doctors."

Judge Fry nodded, then looked at Chris. "What about you?"

"I don't like it," he said. "I think it's a waste of time and money. Just because the defendant is a killer is no reason to assume he's in any way insane. I've watched him during hours of questioning. John Slocum knows exactly what he's about."

Judge Fry cleared his throat, then said, "Chris, I've already made a ruling on that, so don't test my patience. I'll give you both a chance to agree on one of the three doctors on the list. If you fail to agree, you'll have to leave it with me. I'll have my clerk deliver their credentials to you before the close of business today. You'll have forty-eight hours, that's all. I want to set a trial date as soon as possible if the doctor deems your client sane, Laura. Pending, of course, my ruling on your motion for a change of venue."

"I understand," she said.

"And understand this also," the judge said. "If the doctor finds that your client is capable of assisting in his own defense, you may still enter an insanity plea, but I can tell you that there are no funds available for the hiring of experts. As a court-appointed attorney, you're entitled to be compensated for your legitimate expenses, but once that doctor declares your client sane enough to assist in his own defense, I'm prohibited from authorizing additional expenses. I want you to understand that."

"I do understand it," she said.

It didn't take a genius to figure out that Judge Fry was assuming a shrink would find John Slocum sane enough to stand trial. For good reason. Slocum was insane all right, but not in Florida legal terms. If Laura wanted to explore it further, it was going to cost tens of thousands of dollars of her own money. She couldn't think of a single organization that would want to foot the bill for that. There are principles worth fighting for, some of them very esoteric in the minds of a lot of people, but Slocum was on his own, and so, she knew, was she. She'd already decided she wasn't going to waste her own money.

"One other thing," Chris said, glaring at Laura.

"What?"

"I've arranged for a press conference as soon as we're through here. I know you've stayed away from them, Laura, but I think you owe the people of this town some explanation for your actions. Right now, they see you as a woman trying to play tricks to get your client off. I don't think that's in your best interests. I'm inviting you to join me."

"I think I'd rather pass," she said. "I don't really care what people think."

"Really? You know they see the insanity defense as nothing but a trick. You're willing to leave them with that impression?"

Laura groaned. "You're a competent prosecutor,

Chris, and *you* think it's nothing but a trick. How can I be expected to explain the law to laymen?"

He smiled for the first time. "I'm just doing my job, Laura. You know I understand what you're doing and why. You mustn't confuse my public persona with the real me."

Judge Fry stood up. "You two can work this out on your own time. I have things to do. Let me know on that doctor."

They both thanked the judge and left his chambers. In the hallway, Chris prodded Laura again. "So, what about it? You want me to have the media all to myself, or do you want to defend your actions?"

"I don't need to defend my actions, Chris."

"Suit yourself," he said harshly.

Laura watched from a third-floor window as Chris Marshall faced the press in the park across the street, on the same platform used by the two-million-dollar anchorman just days ago.

He did what she expected he would, said what she expected he'd say, the reason she'd failed to rise to his bait.

She saw him take a position in front of a forest of microphones, an army of all-seeing television cameras, scores of still cameras and hundreds of reporters. Behind them stood almost five hundred citizens of Seminole Springs who had gathered in the park.

"It seems to me," Chris began, "that something is terribly wrong with the criminal justice system in this country when the rights of the accused are considered more important than the rights of the victims."

He went on in the same vein for fifteen minutes, castigating the criminal justice system, bleeding-heart liberals in general and Laura Scott in particular. Interrupted by shouts and applause at the end of every sentence, he ended by standing with his hand over his heart, imploring the crowd to join him in the singing of the national anthem.

Laura smiled to herself. Chris had suggested she not confuse the public persona with the real Chris Marshall. She'd seen both. They were one and the same.

CHAPTER

24

THE NEXT TWO WEEKS PASSED QUIETLY FOR LAURA, except for one small flurry of activity when Judge Fry made his ruling on her request for a change of venue. To Laura's astonishment, he rejected it, clearly setting the stage for an appeal should Slocum be convicted.

The judge opined that the pending trial had received ardent attention statewide and nationally. Seminole Springs, though the hometown of the murder victim, was no more biased than any other town. "I have faith that a fair and impartial jury can be impaneled," he wrote. "In the event it cannot, I will grant a new motion for a change of venue."

He was leaving it to Laura to prove through the jury selection process that her motion had merit. A canny and politically wise handling of the motion. Obviously, Judge Fry had ambitions that went far beyond the courtroom. His decision served to further Laura's resolve. The concrete cocoon had evolved to one of high-carbon steel.

Ted returned to school and surprisingly, there were no more incidents, but each morning as he bicycled off to school, Laura worried.

With Slocum confined to a mental hospital for thirty days, Laura could give her attention to other matters. There were the property settlement and other papers to be prepared for her pending divorce and pretrial depositions to be taken on two civil suits.One of the suits was proceeding normally, but the other was interrupted when Laura's client asked for a new attorney. She didn't argue, just tendered a bill for her services that was immediately paid. It was in keeping with what was happening to her practice, a practice fast becoming nonexistent.

Then, just days before Dan's sojourn at the clinic was to end, she received a visit from Henry Lyons, the attorney representing him. He'd called for an appointment, and arrived promptly at eleven o'clock. Kim ushered him into Laura's office and Laura extended her hand. He shook it firmly.

"Can I offer you something?" she asked as he took a seat.

"No thanks. I'd really like to get down to business, if you don't mind."

"Fine."

"I've discussed the proposed settlement agreement with Mr. Scott, and he's in complete accord."

That was a surprise. Lyons opened his attaché

case, extracted a file, and laid two copies of the agreement on Laura's desk. She looked them over, and noticed both had already been signed by Dan.

"Well, that's it then," she said. "I'll have Kim round up a witness and an uninvolved notary. Shouldn't take a minute."

Lyons smiled. "Fine. Mr. Scott will be leaving the clinic in two days. I've located an apartment for him, and we'd like to move his personal property as soon as possible. Tomorrow, if that can be arranged."

"It's fine with me," Laura said. "He's not going to come home at all?"

"No. Dr. Benton feels it would be best if Mr. Scott starts his new life immediately. I'm sure he's explained it all to you."

"He has," Laura said. "However, Dan has a son he hasn't seen in some time. I would think they should spend some time together as soon as possible."

"Mr. Scott's first visitation will be in three weeks, as per the agreement," he said.

"Not until then?"

"That's right."

Laura's face reddened. "Are you telling me that Dan is going to move to an apartment in the city and not see Ted for three weeks?"

"Exactly."

"Why, for God's sake?"

Lyons looked uncomfortable. "I believe," he said, "that Mr. Scott feels you were unduly harsh regarding the terms of visitation. He's of the opinion that seeing his son at times not specified in the agreement might create a problem."

"That's easy to fix," Laura said sharply. "I'm prepared to amend the agreement right now. Dan can see Ted as soon as he's released from the clinic. I have no objection. In fact, I insist on it."

Lyons shook his head. "Mrs. Scott, it's too late for that. Mr. Scott has already signed an agreement prepared by yourself. I think it best that things are left as they are."

Laura visualized a trip before a judge to amend an agreement she'd prepared personally. She'd be laughed out of court. "Why is he doing this?" she asked. "To punish me?"

"Well, you did have him arrested. He is now a convicted felon, Mrs. Scott. The terms of his probation are quite clear. Mr. Scott has expressed his desire to give you no cause for complaint whatsoever. Accordingly, he'll abide strictly by the terms of the agreement. He wants to see Ted only when specifically called for and at those times, he'd like to have Ted come over on his own. If you don't mind, that is."

"I don't mind," Laura said. "But this is carrying things a little far. I realize Dan's feelings toward me are hostile, but he shouldn't take it out on his son."

"Mrs. Scott," Lyons said, a pained expression on his face, "could we just get on with this?"

"Is this your idea, Dan's, or the doctor's?" she asked.

"I'm a lawyer, Mrs. Scott. I counsel Mr. Scott on legal matters. I leave the other decisions to the doctors. My main concern at this time is keeping Mr. Scott out of jail. Obviously, Dr. Benton has an agenda for Mr. Scott that's based on careful evaluation."

"He really thinks I'm that vindictive?"

"I have no idea, Mrs. Scott."

Laura sighed. "How is he?"

"Mr. Scott?"

"Yes."

"He's done remarkably well, I understand. I think part of that is due to the understanding and compassion of his former employers. By giving Mr. Scott a second chance, they've given him a tremendous incentive. My understanding is that Mr. Scott will be transferred to another location after he serves a three-month probationary period. I guess they want to be assured he's sober before they go to the expense of a transfer."

"I see."

"It was Mr. Scott's idea, I believe. He feels it would be better. Many people like to start their new lives in a new environment after an experience like this."

His words struck a chord. There was no point in further discussion. Kim rounded up the necessary people and the documents were signed, witnessed, and notarized. "Good," Lyons said, tucking a copy in his attaché case. "The agreement will be filed along with the divorce papers today. I'll represent Mr. Scott at the final hearing, but since everything has been agreed to, I don't see a problem."

With that, Laura's marriage was over, pending a final stamp of approval from the state.

Two days later Laura placed a phone call to Omaha and talked with a former client. After a satisfactory discussion, she made arrangements to fly to Omaha the next morning with a return flight the very same afternoon.

Omaha was enjoying an Indian summer. Temperatures in the low eighties, bright sunshine, and gentle breezes. As Laura sat in the cab taking her to the south end of the city, the familiarity of the city brought back a rush of pleasant memories.

She and Dan had been young and full of hope in those days. She'd given birth to both her children at the hospital the cab was passing now. It seemed like yesterday in one sense, and a century ago in another.

She still had friends here, friends she would dearly love to see, friends with whom she'd maintained a steady correspondence over the years, friends who would have lent a sympathetic ear to her torment. But she couldn't take the chance. She was here for a purpose, one that could end her career. It was not a time for memories.

His name was Willy Towne, and as Laura shook his wizened hand, she was shocked at how much he'd changed over the years. He looked much older than his sixty years, small and frail, but the boyish grin was still there.

"You're looking great, Counselor. Damn, you look good."

It was a hovel, this small apartment of his. Cluttered and messy, dusty and dank. A one-room walk-up, with a small kitchen and bathroom and a small combination living room/bedroom. Willy pointed to a worn chair. "I never expected to see you again. You could have knocked me over with a feather when you phoned yesterday. I'd offer you a drink or something, but if I remember right, you don't drink. My coffee I wouldn't give my worst enemy."

"I'm fine, Willy," Laura said, looking around. The kitchen counter was covered with empty cans and bottles. "Why don't we have lunch somewhere. I've got four hours before my return flight."

He grinned again. "That would be great. I apologize for the mess, but I don't usually have visitors. I guess I'm a slob at heart."

"You never used to be," Laura said. "You were always very fastidious. I always saw you as a perfectionist. I thought it went with the territory. Are you all right?"

He held a thin finger to his chest. "Big C, Counselor. Lungs. All those cigarettes, I guess. Matter of months, they say. Don't hurt, though. Not so far, anyway. Guess it will at the end. I ain't afraid, though. I'm ready. I had a hell of a time, you know? Wouldn't change a thing."

She leaned forward and squeezed his hand. "I'm sorry, Willy. I really am."

"I know you are," he said. "You was always good to me, Laura. You treated me with more respect than I deserved. I don't know what you want from me, but it's yours if I can do it." He frowned. "You in some kinda trouble?"

"No," she said. "Not yet. Let's have that lunch."

It was a small cafe less than a block away, frequented by an assortment of ragtag-looking people, most of whom seemed to be on their last legs. They all stared at Laura, nodded at Willy, then left the pair alone. It wasn't the kind of place Laura would have come by herself. Willy ordered a hot beef sandwich, and she stuck to coffee.

"So what's the deal?" he asked, his voice just above a whisper.

"I want you to forge a document for me," she said.

His eyebrows rose and his mouth dropped open. "You? I don't believe it."

"It's true."

"What, a will or something?"

"No," she said. "I haven't sunk that low. Not yet."

"What, then?"

"I brought several items with me, Willy. One is a letter from the governor of the state of Florida. It's nothing special, just a note of thanks for some charitable thing I was involved in a couple of years ago. I want you to change the text. I want it to appear as though the governor has written something else. For you, it should be a snap. I'll pay whatever you think is fair."

She handed him the letter and the text she wanted inserted. He looked them over carefully, and then stared at her. "You gotta be kidding me. This is the guy I saw on TV with you. I was in a bar one night and they were doing this big story about you and this Slocum guy. When your picture came on, I told all the guys I knew you." He shrugged. "They said I was fulla shit. They always say I'm fulla shit."

He looked at the letter again, then shook his head. "What the hell are you doing this for? This ever gets out, you're cooked."

"There are at least thirty-two sets of parents scattered all over the East who have no idea what happened to their daughters. I know in my heart what happened. They were murdered and buried by the animal I'm representing. The only way I'll ever pry the information loose from him is to make him think the letter is real."

He shook his head. "You do this, you're through, right?"

"Possibly. If so, it's no big loss. I'm ready to leave the legal profession if it comes to that."

"But you'll be in deep shit. They'll tear you apart. Lawyers aren't supposed to do this kinda stuff. You could end up in the slammer, couldn't you?"

She smiled. "No. They don't put lawyers in jail for things like this. I could be disbarred, but the odds on that are fifty-fifty. I'll be suspended for sure, but it's worth it if this works. I have to do this, Willy. If I don't, I can never look at myself in the mirror again."

A waitress brought his food. He picked up his knife and fork and wolfed it down. Laura sat in silence as he demolished the hot beef, two rolls, and a heaping mound of vegetables. When he was finished, he put down the cutlery and leaned back in his chair. "You want it, you got it, Laura. But you're making a big mistake."

"Maybe."

"When do you need this?"

"As soon as possible."

"I'll have it for you in a day. This it?"

"No," she said, removing a copy of the *Clarion* from her attaché case. "This newspaper has a lot of stories about the murders. I want you to make a copy that has a different story." She handed him a large manila envelope. "The date will have to be changed and so will the headline, and one of the front page stories. Everything's inside this envelope."

Willy quickly scanned the newspaper, then folded it and placed it on top of the envelope. "This will take a little longer," he said. "Maybe three, four days."

"That's all right," Laura told him. "There's no rush."

"You're going back right now?"

"Yes."

"You want to risk the mail for this stuff?"

"It'll be all right," she said. "Just don't put your return address on it. I don't want you in trouble."

He laughed. "What trouble? There's nothing they can do to me anymore."

Laura winced. "I'm sorry, Willy."

"I know."

"I'll pay you now."

He shook his head. "This one's on me, Laura."

"No."

He grinned again. "I know I look poor, but I ain't as poor as I seem. I got money, enough to last me to the end. The government takes care of the medical stuff. I just got no incentive, you know? Knowing you're gonna be dead in a few weeks kinda takes the snap out of a guy's step."

"I'm really sorry, Willy."

"I know you are, Laura. That's the kind of person you are. You know, when you were defending me on that check rap, I fell in love with you. 'Course, I never said nothin'. You was married and I'm long over the hill, but if I hadda been younger, I mighta really took a run at you."

"Willy . . ."

"Naw. Don't you worry."

"Tell you what," she said. "I'll give you five hundred dollars. If you don't want it, then give it to the Salvation Army or some other charity. I'll leave it up to you."

He rubbed his chin for a moment. "Well, when you put it that way . . ."

Laura gave him the money in an envelope. "My address is inside. I appreciate the help, Willy."

"I owe you, Laura. Wasn't for you, I'd be in the slammer yet. You pulled out all the stops that last time."

"You don't owe me, Willy. I was just doing my job." She smiled at him. "Besides, you were kind of fun to work with. Probably the most interesting crook I've ever met." The smile faded. "I wish there were something . . ."

He patted her hand. "Not to worry. Like I said, I had a hell of a time."

CHAPTER

25

IN THE EARLY MORNING OF A MID-OCTOBER DAY, THE debilitating summer heat that had baked Seminole Springs for five interminable months was finally broken by a monster storm preceding a fast-moving cold front sweeping down from—of all places—Montana.

The morning air was fresh, dry, and cool, and Laura Scott reveled in it. After breakfast, with Ted off to school, she took her first brisk morning walk in almost half a year. In the summer, she confined herself to indoor exercise.

John Slocum was back in town, ensconced at the civic center. This time, the media interest was considerably less than the frenzied attention of a month earlier. They were back in town, of course, but not in the numbers of before. Instead of armies, there were platoons.

As Judge Fry had anticipated, the town had regained much of its collective composure during the month Slocum had been held for evaluation. In general, people had tired of hearing about Slocum and his string of victims—for the moment. Everything that could be said had been said. All that remained was to see if the trial would proceed. Most thought it would. A hearing to receive the doctor's report was scheduled for ten. If the doctor determined Slocum was sane, the hearing was to be immediately followed by the once-delayed formal arraignment.

At nine, Laura met with her client and explained what was about to take place. In the month he'd been away, Slocum had learned to walk using his new prosthesis, and the crutches had been discarded. The plastic leg was a new security worry, however, and to prevent Slocum from using it as a weapon, it was padlocked to an elaborate locking harness that ran from his waist to his stump. The keys to both the harness and the leg were passed from guard to guard. Slocum, as usual, was aggravated by such a lack of trust.

"They treat me like a fuckin' animal," he complained. "When I sleep, they unlock the thing and take the leg away. Then in the morning, the put it on and lock it up. Every time they touch it, they handcuff my arms behind me. Assholes! Can't you do something about that?"

"No," Laura said. "I guess they're afraid you'll club somebody over the head with it. Considering everything, they have a right to be careful."

"They really think I'm crazy, huh?"

"No," she said. "They think you're sane."

His face lit up. "You got the results?"

"Yes. The doctor's report claims you're quite able to assist in your defense. He says you're legally sane. The hearing is just a formality."

"See!" he exclaimed. "I told you!"

"You did," she said. "So, I assume you want to plead not guilty."

"Fuckin' true."

Laura sighed. "I've explained to you before that you haven't a chance."

He grinned that stupid grin of his. "They had books in the nuthouse, you know? I looked it up, lady. Less than one in a hundred people sentenced to die actually gets executed, and most of them are niggers. They ain't gonna kill me. No fuckin' way."

"Most of those cases are simple murder cases, John. Your case is different. If you're convicted, the state will claim that your crime comes under the heading of 'special circumstances' which is a term applied to particularly heinous crimes. If you did the research you claim, you must have checked on the people who were executed. Usually, they fall into that category."

"They ain't gonna fry me," he insisted.

"Have you ever heard of a man named Ted Bundy?" she asked.

Some of the joy left his face. The rat eyes narrowed. "Yeah, I heard of him."

"He was executed, John. He was white, good-looking and charming, and he was convicted on a lot less evidence than they have in this case." She threw her hands in the air. "But, if that's what you want, that's what we'll do."

Again, he brightened. "You're not gonna say I'm crazy anymore?"

"No. I'm going to do as you ask. I'm going to plead you not guilty and let the chips fall where they may."

"Good," he said. "We're finally starting to get somewhere."

The hearing took less than ten minutes. The doctor was sworn and declared that he had examined John Slocum carefully over a period of thirty days. After exhaustive tests, he was prepared to say Slocum was fully capable of assisting in his defense. If he chose not to, it was a voluntary act, not the act of an insane person.

Chris took it one step further. "In your opinion, Doctor, is the defendant able to distinguish right from wrong?"

"Yes."

"And, in your opinion, does the defendant exhibit any signs that would support an insanity plea should one be presented?"

Laura could have objected, but didn't. It no longer mattered.

"No, he does not," the doctor intoned.

The arraignment followed immediately. Slocum pleaded not guilty. Both Chris and Judge Fry were clearly astounded. The plea was entered, a trial date was set for January fourteenth, Slocum was ordered held without bail, and court was adjourned. Judge Fry asked Chris and Laura to see him in chambers again.

Slocum was beaming as he limped away on his new leg.

In chambers, Judge Fry looked puzzled. "I thought you were going to use the insanity defense," he said to Laura.

"I was," she told him. "But I've changed my mind."

"Why?"

"I think it's a waste of time. It's rarely proved successful in cases like this. For another, my client refuses to cooperate if I do plead him insane. Finally, there's the money thing. I can't afford to spend the money on experts. It's hopeless."

"But . . ."

"If you're worried about an appeal," she said, "don't. This will be handled by the book. There won't be an appeal. Now that the doctors have certified him as sane, we're all off the hook. If some anticapital punishment organizations decide to pick this up after the trial, which I doubt, you're on solid ground. The only possible grounds I see for appeal rests with your decision to limit my funds, but since the state supreme court has already ruled on similar cases, you're in the clear on that one as well. It's up to the legislature to change the laws, and they aren't about to concern themselves with the welfare of someone like Slocum."

"I think you've made a wise decision, Laura," Chris said.

She repressed the desire to spit in his face. "Does that mean I can stop worrying about where and when you'll stick the next knife in my back?"

His face reddened slightly. "You're still steamed about that press conference? Come on, we'll all grown-ups here. That was just for show. You know that."

"I guess you're right," she said.

Judge Fry held up his hands. "You two can bicker on your own time. All right, it's set then. I want this to go smoothly. I expect the media will be back in force in January. I don't want any more surprises from either of you. If anything changes, you're both to let me know immediately."

Laura tapped her fingers on his desk. "The only change I anticipate would be a change to a guilty plea, and that will happen only if my client has some motivation to do so."

Judge Fry gave her a sharp look. "We've already discussed that, Laura."

"I know we have, Your Honor. I just want to be sure you haven't had a change of heart."

"I haven't," he said.

"When do you want to get together?" Chris asked.

"For what?"

He seemed puzzled. "Depositions, motions, stuff like that. We'll need to discuss witness lists with the judge so he can plan time."

Laura nodded. "I'll let you know," she said.

Outside, Laura noticed a man leaning against her car. Since his back was to her, she didn't recognize him. Wary, she walked across the street to get a better look. Then he turned his head and she recognized him as Vince Petrillo. The detective smiled and gave her a little wave.

She walked over, stood in front of him, and said,

"What are you doing here?"

"Well, I hope you have a nice day, too," he said, his blue bow tie bobbing and glimmering in the bright sunlight.

"Okay, I'm a little crusty," she said. "I'm sorry."

He looked at his feet for a moment, then said, "I came down for the hearing."

"Oh."

"But that wasn't the real reason."

"The real reason?"

"Actually, I wanted to apologize. The first time we talked, I dropped some personal stuff on you, and that wasn't fair. I'm sorry."

"No need," she said. "You were just doing your job, just like me. As strange as this may sound, I'm glad you're here. I still have your books. The last two times you talked to my client, I forgot to bring them. I've been meaning to mail them back to you. You'll save me the trouble."

"How about lunch?" he asked.

Laura laughed bitterly. "Impossible. I'm persona non grata in this town. I'm afraid someone would drop hot soup in your lap if you were seen with me."

"So I've heard," he said. Then, crooking a finger, he said, "Come. I want to show you something." His car was parked two slots away. He pointed to a picnic basket in the rear seat. "I brought it down on the plane this morning. Genuine pastrami on rye, the best you ever tasted, made fresh this morning. I picked it up on the way to the airport."

Laura was astonished. "Why?"

"I've been talking to some people. I understand you spent three years in New York when you were in law school. A fella I know says you developed a passion for good pastrami even before that. You ever tasted Baltimore pastrami? Puts New York to shame."

"No," she said, her brow wrinkled in curiosity. "Who told you I liked pastrami?"

Petrillo grinned. "Fella named Gibson. He used to work with you in New York. You were both working summers and nights as clerks in some investment firm. Redheaded guy, tall, kinda quiet."

"Tommy Gibson?"

"Yeah, that's the one."

She remembered. It was a wonderful job, one that had helped pay her way through law school. Even then, she'd never have been able to make ends meet without the scholarship. "How'd you meet him?" she asked.

"He's one of Baltimore's bigger shakers and movers these days," he said. "There was some press in the local papers about me being down here working on this case. There was a picture of you in the *Sun* and some background stuff. Gibson read the piece and contacted me. Asked me to pass on a big hello. We got to talking and he told me some things."

She frowned. "What things?"

"Just what you were like back then. He was telling me how hard you worked and how dedicated you were. I told him you hadn't changed much."

"Really."

"Yeah. Gibson says he was madly in love with you but too shy to ask for a date." He grinned again. "Too late now. The guy has eight kids, but I guess he never forgot you. I thought you'd like to know that."

"Thanks."

"Did you know he was in love with you?"

"No. I didn't date at all." Then, with a touch of bitterness in her voice, she said, "I was saving myself for Dan."

"I'm sorry."

She changed the subject. "You really brought this down from Baltimore?"

"Yeah. We can drive out in the country. I saw some picnic tables by the highway. I've got a blanket and pickles and a couple cans of tonic." He pulled a wax-paper-wrapped sandwich from the basket and held it in front of her nose. "Tell me this doesn't smell great."

Laura sniffed the still-warm sandwich. "You're quite a character, Petrillo."

"Call me Vince."

His smile was so warm and the smell of the food so mouth-watering, Laura was helpless. "All right," she said. "You win."

He beamed, then ushered her to the passenger seat like a high-school senior taking a date to the prom. They drove to the picnic area Petrillo had seen, some three miles outside the city. It was a marvelous spread. The sandwiches had been carefully wrapped, then packed in a thermal container to keep them warm. Thin-sliced and lean, over an inch thick. She hadn't had one this good in almost twenty years. When she'd finished, she wiped her mouth on a linen napkin. "Delicious," she said.

"Glad you enjoyed it," he said, looking around. "I couldn't live in Florida. There isn't a good Jewish deli in the entire state."

"Obviously, you've never been to Miami or

Lauderdale," she said. "So, what's going on here, Vince? Why the attention?"

He smiled sheepishly. "You really want the truth?"

"Uh-huh."

He took a deep breath, then said, "I felt something the first time I met you. I can't explain it, because I don't know how. I don't know what it means, because I've never experienced it before. All I know is I like being near you. Crazy, huh?"

She blushed. "I'm flattered."

His face grew serious. "I'm no prize, Laura. I was married once. Lasted three years. Typical cop deal. We have the highest divorce rate in the world, you know. No kids, thank God. I'm old before my time thanks to a slug that took out most of my knee. I'm not hell to look at and I'm not too bright, but I'd sure like to get to know you a little better. The right way, I mean. I mean . . . well, you know what I mean."

The blush deepened.

"This feeling of yours," she said, "would it have anything to do with John Slocum?"

His eyes narrowed for just a moment, then softened. "It has nothing to do with your client."

"I'm sorry," Laura said quickly. "That was cruel. I must be getting a bit paranoid."

Petrillo held up a hand. "No. I understand. A natural assumption. You think I'm trying to manipulate you and I can't blame you. Fact is, there's no reason for me to try anymore, assuming you were subject to manipulation."

"What do you mean?" she asked.

"I talked about a deal, remember? Well, you can

forget it. I hear things. There have been six or seven approaches made already. Marshall's boss, the attorney general, even the governor. They've all been approached by people trying to work a deal. The governor won't hear of it."

"You?"

He nodded. "I got as far as one of his junior aides. He wouldn't even talk to me. From what I hear, a direct appeal from God wouldn't make a difference. Your governor is a real law-and-order freak. Let me put that another way. Your governor wants to be perceived as a law-and-order freak. Anyway, I know you'll do what you can to get your client to open up. I still think he will someday, but that isn't why I'm here. So, am I making an ass of myself, or what?"

She laughed. "No. I told you I'm flattered, and I am. Right now, my mind is on other things. I'm not a candidate for romance."

"I understand," he said, "but I don't give up easy. How about dinner tonight?"

"No," Laura said. "I'm just not . . ."

"Look, if I called you sometime, would you get upset?"

"No, but don't do it soon." She grimaced. "I don't mean to sound so negative and I'm sorry about what I said. It's just a bad time for me, Vince."

"I know. You've been stuck with a particularly nasty client at a particularly nasty time. Who knew this guy was a serial killer when you took the case? No one. Now that they know, they aren't rushing to let you off the hook. But what's this Ferris guy's beef? You turn down a pass or something?"

"Something," she said. "He wanted me to cooperate on some book deal he has going. I turned him down. Funny thing, though. Chris Marshall turned him down, too, but Ferris has been treating him like a prince. Maybe it wasn't the book. Maybe Ferris just doesn't like me."

"And maybe he never actually talked to Chris about the book. Did you ever think of that?"

"No," she said. "But, now that you mention it . . ."

"I think that's one of the things I like about you, Laura. You're a real throwback, you know? Refreshing. These days, when everybody plays the angles, you hang in there and play it straight. And besides the class, you've got guts. If you were halfways good-looking, you'd be a real find."

She burst out laughing. "Thanks, Petrillo. Thanks a lot."

"You're welcome," he said. "You have a nice laugh."

"Will you stop?" she said. "Now, you *are* starting to make an ass of yourself."

He held his hands in the air again. "Okay. Time to get back. I'll give you a call sometime. Maybe after the trial."

"You're not coming back until then?"

"Oh, I'll be here for a while, along with the rest of the gang. We'll keep after your client. It seems hopeless, but you never know. After the trial, it won't be quite so easy. I just meant that I won't pursue the issue with you until the trial is over. Maybe then, you'll feel a little more comfortable."

"I hope so," she said.

"You said something about my books?"

"Oh, yes. I have them at my office."

"Well, let's drop by and pick them up."

"Fine. The lunch was wonderful."

"I'm glad you enjoyed it."

As he ushered her back to the car, she turned and looked into his eyes. "I'd like it if you did call me after the trial, Vince. I'd like it a lot."

"You can count on it," he said softly.

CHAPTER
26

DURING THE NEXT WEEK, JOHN SLOCUM WAS AGAIN QUES-
tioned by most of those representing jurisdictions
convinced he was the man responsible for the disappearance of their missing women. For some
interrogators, it was the second or third time
they'd tried to pry information from Slocum. In the
case of Vince Petrillo, his latest meeting with
Slocum was his eighth. During each interview,
Laura was present as Slocum blandly fended off
every question, and even the once-confident
Petrillo was beginning to doubt his previously held
conviction that Slocum would eventually tell Laura
everything.

As he and Laura shared a sandwich in the civic
center cafeteria, he said, "I guess I was wrong about

Slocum. Just goes to show you, as much as we think we know how the human mind functions, we really don't, especially wackos. God, it's frustrating."

Laura sipped some coffee, then leaned back in her chair. "You're a paradox, Vince."

He seemed surprised. "What makes you say that?"

"Well, you've been a cop for over twenty years, you've been shot and wounded, you're involved in a case with highly personal overtones, you've probably been through as many private tragedies as the rest of us, yet you exhibit more equanimity than I've ever observed in anyone, not just cops. You're usually cheerful, and you appear unaffected by the horror you must have witnessed in your career. What stops you from becoming as cynical as the rest of us? What's your secret, Vince? Drugs? Religion? What?"

He laughed. "Good genes."

"That's it?"

"Yeah. Afraid so. Pretty boring, eh?"

She grinned. "Not really. If you're telling me the truth, that is. I'm afraid I'm fast becoming a person who believes no one anymore."

Petrillo's soft eyes held hers. "Don't get discouraged, Laura. Not everyone lies, not everyone is a killer, and not everyone is filled with hate. Remember, when you deal with the criminal element, you're dealing with a very small portion of the general population. Most people are decent folks, hard-working, law-abiding, concerned about their kids and the future. They just get lousy press, you know? Maybe they need a lobbyist or something. Or start an organization called United Nice Folks of America."

Laura rolled the words over her tongue. "I come up with the acronym UNFOA. Not real punchy. How about Americans Sincerely Seeking Happiness Or Love Everywhere Society."

"Cute," he said. "Now there's an acronym with punch. You're just down because of everything that's happened the past few weeks. You'll get your head on straight when this is over."

"Do you really think so?"

"I'm sure of it," he said. "You remind me of my brother Aldo. He was a corporate lawyer for a couple of years, got bored and became a prosecutor in the criminal division. In five years, it literally drove him nuts. He said the hell with it, quit, and opened up a storefront in one of the crummier sections of the city. He has three or four part-time volunteer attorneys, a couple of paralegals, and the rest he does himself. Over the past ten years, he's probably saved two hundred kids from screwing up their lives. More than a few adults as well. He used to be a cynic, but now he's the happiest guy I know in the world."

"That's wonderful," Laura said. "But how does he eat?"

"That's the hard part," Petrillo said. "But it's getting easier. We've managed to get some local corporations to chip in, one or two churches, and some private citizens who feel like putting their money where their mouths are. It's starting to work out."

"You said 'we.' Does that mean you're involved in this?"

Petrillo grinned. "Yeah. I'm one of his paralegals."

Laura leaned forward. "Isn't that a conflict of interest? I mean, you're arresting them and at the same time trying to defend them?"

"It doesn't work like that," he said. "I stick with the slum landlords who turn off the heat in mid-March to save a few bucks, or turn the water off, or refuse to fix broken stuff. Aldo deals with the gang kids, the dopers, the smash-and-grabbers. He's a saint, Aldo, but he's not stupid. He knows when a kid is open to something and when he's too far gone. He doesn't waste much time."

"You must be very proud of him," Laura said.

"Seriously?"

She nodded.

"I am proud of him. He's two years older than me. We're kinda proud of each other."

Laura sipped her coffee for a moment, then, on impulse, she said, "How would you like to come over for dinner tonight? I have someone I'd like you to meet. Someone I'm very proud of too."

"I'd like that very much," he said, his face glowing like a neon lamp.

At dinner, Vince told jokes. He had a hundred of them, some old, some new, all told in grand style complete with dialects and facial animation. Halfway through dinner, Laura and Ted were laughing so hard they could hardly eat.

After dinner, Ted went up to his room to study and Vince helped Laura with the dishes. He complimented her on her cooking and her son. "That's one of the things I regret most about this life," he said. "I always wanted to have a son. Many sons, and daughters, too. Hell, I'm Italian. It's a tradition."

"Why didn't you?"

"I told you the first marriage only lasted three years. It wasn't her fault. I was never home, and when I was, she was out working. We could never get our act together as a team. She was determined not to have kids until our life had some normality. I don't blame her. We knew it was wrong early on."

"But you never remarried," Laura said softly. "Why not?"

"Fear, I guess. I was afraid I'd just repeat myself. Being a cop was something I couldn't give up. Don't ask me why. It's the only job I've ever wanted. I had some relationships, but every time I got close to falling in love, I'd get nervous and take a walk. Now, I'm forty-three and I see the light at the end of the tunnel. I see it clearly. A big white candle lit for me."

Laura laughed. "Midlife crisis, they call it."

"Maybe. All I know is the time has come."

"So, you're looking?"

"Yeah. She has to be special, though. It'll take a special kind of woman to live with me. I'm still afraid of failure, but I'm even more afraid of being alone the rest of my life."

"Again, that's a paradox. Most people who've been on their own as long as you have like that independence. They're accustomed to doing what they want when they want, and never having to account to someone else. They aren't rushing into a relationship that requires a lot of giving and sharing. Are you sure that's what you really want?"

"Yeah. I'm sure. If you'd asked me that question a month ago, I'd have been just as sure the opposite was true."

Laura blushed. "You hardly know me."

"I know. I also know I'm being a jerk. I apologize,

Laura. Like I said, dinner was wonderful. It was good of you to ask me over."

"You're leaving?"

"Yes. I think I'd better before I wear out my welcome."

CHAPTER

27

"SO, WHERE'VE YOU BEEN FOR THE LAST TWO DAYS?"

They were sitting in the conference room within the confines of the jail. John Slocum had his false leg locked to the harness and was wearing his usual arrogant expression. Laura, sitting across from him, looked unusually distraught.

"I've been up in Tallahassee," she said.

"What'd you go there for?"

"I had to talk to some people."

"About me?"

"Yes."

"What about me?"

"Do you remember that first day we met?" she asked.

"What about it?"

"You said you wanted a male lawyer."

He grinned. "Yeah. Well, you may be a bitch, but I'm gettin' used to you."

"I'm sorry to hear that," Laura said.

His eyes widened slightly. "Whaddaya mean?"

Laura stood up and paced as she explained. "John," she said, "ever since the first day we talked, I've been convinced that the case against you is too strong to be successfully defended. That's a bad attitude for a lawyer to have. Negative attitudes create bad strategies. The problem is, nothing that's happened in the past few weeks has changed that attitude. I'm still convinced the only way I can save you from the electric chair is to make a deal."

He threw his hands in the air. "That again?"

"Yes," she said. "That again."

"That's all you ever talk about. Make a deal. Make a fuckin' deal! That's all you assholes are good for, isn't it? Makin' fuckin' deals. You don't defend people anymore, you just take their money and then make a deal. Shit! Anybody can make a deal."

She placed her hands on the table and leaned forward, smiling at him. "You're right, of course. I guess my problem is that I keep thinking you're guilty and you keep telling me you're not. That makes me the wrong lawyer for you. I've decided to ask the judge to let me off this case. I'll tell him you want a male lawyer. Maybe he'll find you one and maybe he won't, but whoever he finds will be better for you than I am."

Slocum's eyes narrowed. "You're quittin' me?"

"Not just you, John. I'm quitting the profession. I don't belong in this business anymore. I'm just no good at it. Hell, I can't convince the most important client I've ever had to accept a word I say. Once a lawyer reaches that point, it's time to get out of the business."

"So go," he snapped. "Who the fuck needs you?"

"Not you, obviously. Too bad, too. I got you a pretty good deal in Tallahassee."

"I ain't interested in no fuckin' deal! I told you that a thousand times!"

"I know," Laura said. She extended her hand. "Well, I wish you luck, John. I really do."

He ignored her hand. Laura shrugged, walked to the door, and rang the buzzer that would bring the guard. As she waited, she could feel her heart pounding unmercifully. If she lost her gamble and Slocum let her walk out that door, she was in trouble. On the other hand, if he didn't, she was in even worse trouble. Laura stiffened her spine as she shook off the negative thoughts. She'd made her decision and would stick with it.

The guard opened the door. Laura turned and waved good-bye. Only then did Slocum say, "Wait!"

Laura turned slowly and faced him. "Yes?"

"What kind of deal?"

Laura dismissed the guard, the door slammed shut behind her, and she took a seat. "A simple one," she said. "You tell me where the bodies of those missing women are buried. In return, you serve a minimum of fourteen years in prison. You'll only be thirty-five when you get out, still young enough to have a good life."

He laughed. "You must think I'm really stupid. They ain't gonna stick to that. Once I open my mouth, they'll forget they ever made a deal. Fuckin' liars, all of 'em. And you went for this bullshit?"

Slowly Laura extracted an envelope from her attaché case and slid it across the table. "This is a letter from the governor. He's put the deal in writing."

Slocum stared at her for a moment, then picked up the envelope. He opened it and slowly removed the letter, handling it as if it were something contaminated. As he read it, his eyebrows rose slightly. When he'd finished, he looked up at Laura, rubbed his chin for a moment, then leaned back in his chair. "Suppose I do give you some information? What's to stop one of the guards coming in here and takin' this letter away from me and sayin' no deal was ever made?"

Laura opened her attaché case and removed a newspaper. She threw it on the table. It was a copy of the *Clarion*. In three-inch-high bold type, the headline read, GOVERNOR OFFERS DEAL TO SUSPECTED SERIAL KILLER. Underneath the headline, the story, with pictures of the governor, Slocum, and Laura. On the inside pages, pictures of ten of the missing girls, with related stories on their disappearances.

After quickly reading the three first pages, Slocum slowly placed the newspaper back on the table, then picked up the letter again. For a moment he smiled, then his eyebrows pinched into a frown. "It says here that the offer expires tonight. What's the big rush?"

"There are several reasons," Laura said. "For one, the governor is running for reelection next year. He wants this over and done with immediately because he knows he's going to be severely criticized for making such a deal. Both the press and the opposition will tear him apart. He can handle that for a little while, but not if this thing drags on.

So, you either make a deal now or you don't.

"Also, the governor has been under a lot of pressure from the parents of the women you're suspected of killing. If you fail to act immediately, the governor can say he gave you every opportunity, present himself as a fair-minded person, and get those people off his back. He figures you'll turn this deal down. In fact, he's gambling that you will, because he really doesn't want to do it. He's smart enough to know that, come election time, this will come back to haunt him. So, he's trying to kill two birds with one stone. He can say he tried and failed. That's all he really wants."

"Cocksucker!"

"He's giving you a break. The biggest break of your life, John."

Slocum looked at the letter again, then said, "So, what you're really saying is that if I turn down this deal, you're through bein' my lawyer."

"I'm through with the practice of law no matter what you do," she said. "That's not what's important. If you turn down this deal, no one will ever again lift a finger to help you. Oh sure, you'll have a lawyer, but that's just a formality. Knowing you've turned down a deal like this, no lawyer will try very hard, and why should they? The case against you is too strong anyway. You'll be convicted and eventually executed and that will be that. But . . . if you agree to this deal, I'll find someone who'll be there in fourteen years to make sure you get out when you're supposed to."

Laura stood up and turned her back to him. "If I had the choice," she said softly, "between dying and being free at the age of thirty-five, I know what I'd do."

She turned and stared at him. He seemed to be vacillating. Laura tried to will her heart to stop pounding as Slocum read the newspaper again. She fought to keep the expression in her eyes impassive, struggled to keep her knees from knocking and her hands from shaking.

Slocum put down the newspaper, picked up the letter again, smiled, and said, "Can you keep this in a safe place for me?"

She smiled. "I was going to talk to you about that. Even though it's been quoted in the newspapers, you know how that goes. The governor could always say he was misquoted. They do that a lot."

"Fuckin' true." He grinned. "How'd you work this? You give the governor a blow job or something?"

Laura ignored the remark as she put the letter back in the envelope and the envelope back in her attaché case. "What's it going to be, John?"

The grin widened into a big smile. "I ain't no fool. Which one you wanna talk about first?"

Laura felt her heart stop beating. She opened her attaché case and removed a folder filled with photographs of young women. The one on top was Betty Lou Krache. Laura placed it on the table. At the same time, she turned on a small tape recorder inside her open case, not trusting her trembling hands to properly transcribe notes.

"Yeah," Slocum said, looking at the picture. "This was the one that asshole from Baltimore kept after me on. I remember her. It was a year ago." He laughed. "I had these cards sayin' I was workin' for a Christian ministry. Learned that little trick in school. People always think if you carry a Bible and say you're a Christian, you'll never hurt a hair on their heads. Stupid fuckers.

"I was going around the restaurant passin' out the cards and askin' for money. Most times, I work in supermarkets until they catch me and throw me out. Then I work the parking lots. Every once in a while, I see a bitch that reminds me . . . That's how I used to get money, that and steal it off the dead ones. This one never gave me any money, but when I asked her if she'd give me a lift outta town since I was on the move, she said sure. Stupid fuckin' bitch.

"She drove me about three miles out on I-95 and then told me that was as far as she wanted to go. She was startin' to get nervous." He laughed again. "She had reason. I took out the knife and stuck it up her nose. She fuckin' near crashed the goddamn car right there. I made her drive out to Patapsco Valley State Park, waited till dark, then did my thing. You know what my thing is?" He was grinning like the maniac he was.

"Not yet," she said, "but I need to know everything."

"Think you can take it?"

"I have no choice."

"Yeah." He laughed. "Guess that's right."

Laura felt a wave of nausea sweep over her. The tape recorder was running, so there was no need for her to listen to this now. If she did, she knew she'd be sick to her stomach.

As Slocum explained, in excruciating detail, what he had done to Betty Lou, Laura forced herself to concentrate on Vince Petrillo. She imagined Vince holding her hand as they walked along a quiet beach in Hawaii. Sand and surf and sea and sun. She could visualize her hair blowing in the wind, feel Vince's hand squeezing hers, hear his voice as he mumbled sweet words in her ears.

She heard the sea gulls, the pounding of the waves, and felt the sun strong on her face. The words of John Slocum started receding, as if he were being dragged away. Vince was there now, pulling her close to him, telling her that she was the perfect woman for him, that he wanted to spend the rest of his life with her, just loving her and Ted, the son he'd always wanted. They'd be a family, sharing, helping one another, loving one another . . .

"I love to hear them scream, you know. I guess that's 'cause my mother never screamed. She went down without a fuckin' word. So I wait until I'm tired of fuckin' around and it's showtime. Shit-or-get-off-the-pot-time. When I know I'm gonna stick 'em for real that first time. I take the tape off their mouths just before I stick 'em. Most of them scream real good." He laughed. "Funny how some of 'em can't. They shit themselves and piss all over themselves and they open their mouths and nuthin' comes out. It's freaky. Fuckin' eyes as wide as Cadillac wheels and they can't scream. I always tell 'em that if they don't, I'll hurt 'em. By then, they know what I can do, so they scream. So fuckin' surprised when the knife goes in hard.

"God! I get off on those screams. I can fuck 'em all night and some times nuthin' happens, but when I hear that scream, it's pop-off city, man. Jesus! It's the greatest fuckin' high in the world, knowin' that seconds after they scream like that, they're as dead as my fuckin' mother. Man, it's a trip."

Vince was holding her tighter now, almost yelling into her ear. "Laura, I love you. I'll always love you. Maybe it's not too late. I'm only forty-three and you're forty. I'd like to have a child with you. I want to marry you. I want to live the rest of my life with you. I want . . ."

"What's the matter? This making you sick?"

She stared into Slocum's eyes. "No."

"Well, you sure look like shit. Come on, who's the next one. I ain't got all fuckin' day."

At four that afternoon, Laura found Vince Petrillo in the bar of the Seminole Springs Motel, the largest in town. He was nursing a beer, his body hunched over the bar as he squinted at the TV set. He jumped when Laura tapped him on the shoulder.

"Nervous?" she said, smiling.

"What are you doing here?" he asked, surprise in his eyes. "I was just about to get myself ready. I was invited for dinner, right?"

"You were, and you are," she said. "I just need to talk to you first. I didn't want to do it in front of Ted."

"You look upset," he said. "Is something wrong?"

"Yes and no. Can we talk in your room?"

Concerned, Vince took her arm and guided her out of the bar, down the hall and into his room. Closing the door behind him, he said, "You look like you've seen a ghost. Has something happened to Ted?"

"Ted's fine," Laura said. She opened her attaché

case and removed two small audio cassettes. Vince picked them up and stared at them. "What gives?"

Laura sat on the edge of the bed. "This morning," she said haltingly, "I spent almost three hours with John Slocum. Those cassettes are copies of the originals I have just placed in my safe deposit box at the bank. I want you to have them."

Petrillo looked puzzled. "I don't think I understand."

"You will when you listen to them," she said. "You'll hear Slocum describing how he killed thirty-two young women. He reveals where sixteen of them are buried. He has only vague recollections of the burial sites of the rest, but what he does remember may prove helpful. As for the sixteen he remembers clearly, I don't think you'll have any trouble finding the bodies."

She grabbed his arm. "One of them is your niece, Vince."

Petrillo looked as if he'd been slapped. "He told you this willingly?"

"No," she said. "This is privileged information. I tricked Slocum into telling me. I told him I'd made a deal with the governor, a ridiculous deal, but I was trying to give him an incentive. In exchange for the information, he'd receive a fourteen-year sentence for the murder of Wanda Brooks."

"And he bought that?"

"I made it look good. I forged a letter from the governor and a phony newspaper as well. I was sure he wouldn't take my word for it."

Petrillo gasped. "You . . . Laura! You can't!"

"I already have," she said. "Don't worry. I got the letter and the newspaper back. I've destroyed them both. He was afraid the guards would take them."

"But . . ."

"Don't. I know what you're going to say. It's wrong. I agree, but it's too late. I made this decision when I realized no one would consider any kind of deal. I can't really blame them, but I was afraid Slocum would take the information to the grave with him. I didn't want that to happen."

"This is *so* wrong," he said.

"I know," she said, cutting him off. "I've broken the rules quite badly. I don't really care. I'm leaving the practice of law. If they disbar me, so what? As for possible criminal charges, no chance." She took a deep breath. "There's not a word on this tape relating to the Wanda Brooks murder, so there's no way the tape can be used to help Slocum beat that. Since he is charged *only* with that crime, this tape cannot affect the case in any way. I made sure of that. All I've done is screw up possible additional charges for the murders of the other women, and that doesn't matter. The case against him on the Brooks murder is so strong, he's certain to be convicted. As you said, Vince, they can only kill John Slocum once."

Vince looked stricken. "Oh, Laura. This is so wrong. I know your heart's in the right place, but this isn't the way to go about it."

"I don't care," she said. "I'm tired of it, Vince. Tired of the game, tired of the system . . . all of it."

He sat beside her and put his arm around her. "Laura, they'll tear you apart. Maybe there's a way to undo this."

"Too late," she said. "Besides, I don't want to undo it. I couldn't live with two lies. I can live with the one I told Slocum, but not a second one. From here, I'm on my way to see Judge Fry."

"Laura. I'm so sorry. I feel I've pushed you into this."

"I didn't do this for you. I did it for your sister and all those other mothers who are wondering what the hell happened to their daughters. Mostly, I did it for myself. I feel good about that. I know there'll be those who will say Slocum would have told what he knew at some later date, and maybe that's true. I made the judgment that he would never talk unless there was something in it for him. Even if I'm wrong, I can be sure of one thing. He wouldn't have talked until the electric chair was staring him in the face, and that's years away. Much too long for worried parents. I couldn't live with that, so I had to take a chance I could pry the information loose now."

Petrillo fingered the tape. "Betty Lou? He talked about Betty Lou?"

"Yes. He told me where she's buried. He also explained . . . Vince . . . it will make you ill, but I think you need to hear it."

Petrillo put the tapes in his pocket. "Later. I'll listen to it later. Right now, I want to go with you to see the judge."

"No," Laura said. "I have to do this myself."

"The hell you do," he said firmly.

There were four of them in chambers. Judge Fry, Laura, Vince, and Chris. Judge Fry listened intently as Laura started to explain what she'd done. Vince quickly interrupted her, saying, "Your Honor, I accept full responsibility for this. I kept pushing Mrs. Scott, who was fully aware that one of the missing girls is my niece. I'm sure that had Mrs. Scott not lost her own daughter at this particular time, she would never . . ."

Laura jabbed him in the ribs, then smiled at him. She felt relaxed, confident, even serene. "Your Honor, Sir Galahad here had nothing whatsoever to do with this. It was completely my idea. If I have to, I can prove it, as silly as that sounds."

"You've been under a terrible strain," the judge said softly.

Laura stood up and placed her hands on the desk. "Stop it! I have not lost my mind. I'm thinking more clearly now than I ever have. I made a decision and I'm sticking with it. To be sure, it's wrong in the eyes of the law and I'll accept whatever punishment is due me, but I do not for a moment regret what I've done."

Judge Fry looked at her for a moment, then said, "Exactly what have you done?"

Laura told him everything.

CHAPTER

28

LAURA SCOTT WALKED SLOWLY DOWN THE BEACH, WATCHING the sea gulls dive and swoop, then gather as some bathing suit-clad tourist threw bread on the sand.

Daytona Beach seemed a strange place for tourists to spend Christmas, with its wide beaches, near-perpetual summer, and automobile-racing background. The Birthplace of Speed, they called it. The assortment of Christmas decorations festooned on the hotels and motels crowding the beach looked odd, as though left over from a season long since past. Forgotten and abandoned. But it wasn't so, for this was the morning before the night before Christmas. In an hour, Laura was to drive back to Seminole Springs and spend the holiday with the Wilsons.

For two weeks now, she'd been alone, having left Ted with Gerry while she retreated from life and contemplated her future. The incredible turmoil within her had dimmed and for the first time in three months, she was sleeping through the night, a sleep uninterrupted by horrific nightmares.

She was pleased with the way it had all turned out. They'd found many of the bodies, though it hadn't been easy. Weeks of searching, then digging, sometimes in frozen ground. But they'd managed and found a total of nineteen so far, and they weren't giving up. The first discoveries had helped, giving the investigators an insight into the pattern used by John Slocum, allowing some very vague descriptions to aid them in other searches. That, and some remarkable machines that looked into the earth and detected shapes that shouldn't be there.

There'd been an initial outpouring of sympathy for Laura in the national press, then a backlash of criticism from many in the legal community that soon blotted out whatever understanding had pre-existed. She'd not only betrayed her client, they'd said, but the entire profession. If an accused was unable to trust his attorney, who could he trust? Those who felt that the ends justified the means were an anathema to everything America stood for.

She'd expected nothing less. They still hadn't seen the point, and Laura had refused each request for an interview that would have given her an opportunity to express it. She'd been besieged by those wanting her story, offered large sums of money for articles and books, but she'd turned them all away. No interviews of any kind, she'd said. Their constant badgering had finally driven her out of town.

Now she was here, in Daytona Beach, wearing a blond wig and large glasses, registered under a false name, reveling in her anonymity and her solitude, wrestling with the question of what to do with the rest of her life. Petrillo had begged her to consider working with his brother in Baltimore and she'd told him she'd consider it. It was, after all, work similar to the kind she'd started out to do, helping people with nowhere else to turn. At first, she'd be a paralegal instead of an attorney, but there was nothing to prevent her from applying to the Maryland Bar.

The idea had a certain appeal. She'd always missed the changing of the seasons. It would be wonderful to feel the crunch of snow beneath her boots. Then again, it meant having Petrillo nearby and that worried her. He was a wonderful man and she liked him, but the feeling she harbored for him frightened her. She wasn't ready for romance just yet. Perhaps never.

Two weeks, and she still hadn't made up her mind.

She sat on her towel, closed her eyes, and felt the breeze on her face. She pulled off the blond wig, pulled out the pins, and let her hair fall to her shoulders. The wind blew it away from her face. She felt free, both mentally and physically, for the first time in her entire life. Free to decide where to go, what to do, and when. Perhaps it was the joy of knowing such freedom that caused her to procrastinate.

"Good morning," she heard a voice say. A familiar voice.

She turned and looked into the eyes of Vince Petrillo. "How did you find me?"

"I'm a cop," he said, smiling, as if that said it all.

She had to laugh. He was wearing the most outrageous Day-Glo green bathing trunks she'd ever seen, something more appropriate for a college student on spring break than a forty-three-year-old policeman. He'd parted his hair in the middle again, and his eyes were covered by oversize sunglasses of a color that matched his trunks. On his feet, he wore a pair of rubber flip-flops in neon pink.

"You look atrocious," she said. "Is there some contest for the nerdiest outfit on the beach?"

He put his hand to his heart. "You've wounded me deeply."

"Sure I have. What *are* you doing here?"

"Looking for you."

She groaned. "I can see that. You're just in time to see me leave. I told you I'd be back in two weeks."

"You did," he said. "I thought perhaps I could go back with you. I understand you're spending Christmas with Dr. Taylor and his family. I've been invited."

Laura grinned. "You conned Gerry into that?"

"Conned? Again, you wound me. Christmas is a time to be with people, and I'm people. I think Gerry figures I'll be fun to have around."

"What about your family and friends in Baltimore?"

"I'm with them every year. They can live without me for one Christmas." He sat beside her. "I brought two presents with me."

"More pastrami, I suppose. And what else?"

He laughed. "No. Both of these are a little more lasting."

"Vince, I told you how I feel about you. I like you a lot, but I'm still not ready for romance. I can't accept a gift from you. Not yet."

"Tell you what," he said, "one I have with me, and the other is up in my room. Let me tell you the first one."

"Tell me?"

"Yeah. It's information."

"About what?"

"Your hearing. I've been sniffing around. The word I get is that you won't be disbarred after all. They're talking a six-month suspension, that's all."

She was astonished. "How can that be? They haven't held the hearing yet. I'll be crucified in there."

He shook his head. "You've been out of touch for two weeks. Public opinion is swinging very hard back toward you. Finding those bodies made all the difference."

"Well, I'll admit, that's a very fine present and I thank you for bringing it. As for the one up in your room . . ."

He laughed. "Again, it's not what you think. Come and take a look. If you don't want it, I'll take it back. Just look before you decide."

She winced. "Vince, I really can't."

He looked heartbroken. "Laura, just this once. I've never asked you for a favor. I never will again. Just take a look. I really need you to take a look. Please?"

She stood up and shook her towel. "All right. I'll

look, but that's all. You *are* persistent, you know?"

Vince grinned. "Yeah. They say that about me. May I make a suggestion?"

"What?"

"Change first. If I take you into my room and you're wearing that suit, people will get the wrong idea."

Laura looked down at her suit. It was rather skimpy, showing off a figure that looked just fine for forty—and two children. Real fine.

"You have to change soon anyway," Vince continued. "Better yet, I'll go change too. I guess this outfit is a little too much. I just wanted to fit in, you know? Soon as you're ready, you come over, take a look at what I brought you, decide if you want to keep it, then give me a ride to Seminole Springs. Okay?"

"Okay. Where are you staying?"

He pointed to the motel. "The Americano. Room 714. See you there in about thirty minutes?"

"All right," she said.

She was there in forty, her packed bags in the trunk, ready for the three-hour drive home. She was looking forward to seeing Ted, and she was touched that Vince wanted to share Christmas with them, but Petrillo made her nervous. She hoped the gift was something small, something silly, something she could accept.

She knocked lightly on the door of his room. Vince, dressed in casual attire, opened it and ushered her inside. Two men and a woman were standing on the balcony, waving to three teenagers romping on the beach. As soon as they saw Laura, they hurried inside.

"Laura," Vince said, "I want you to meet my sister Vera and her husband Joe. And that ugly creature is my brother Aldo."

For a moment Vera Krache simply smiled, then she held out her arms and drew Laura to her. They embraced as two long-time friends would embrace, though they'd never met. Then Joe put his fireman's thick arms around both women and hugged them both.

Laura pulled away and wiped her eyes. She looked at Vince. "This is the present?"

"Part of it," he said.

"We wanted to tell you personally how much we appreciate what you did," Vera said. "I'm sure it must have been very difficult for you, but you've saved our lives, Laura. Without knowing what happened to Betty Lou . . ." She started to weep.

"We've formed a support group," Joe continued, "with the parents of the other missing girls. We had our initial meeting last night. One of the first things we decided as a group was, well..." He picked up an envelope from the dresser and handed it to Laura. "It's just a Christmas card, Laura, but it's signed by all of the parents. They just wanted you to know how grateful they felt."

"Merry Christmas," Vince said softly.

HARRISON ARNSTON'S success as founder, chairman, and CEO of an automotive accessory manufacturing company enabled him to retire in 1984 to pursue his dream of a writing career. He has had six novels published. He enjoys playing jazz piano, reading, and traveling in the United States. He lives in Florida with his attorney wife, Theresa.

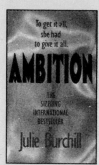